FAERIE HUNTED

FAE ACADEMY FOR HALFLINGS BOOK 6

USAT BESTSELLING AUTHOR

BREA VIRAGH

Cover Artist: Heather Marie Adkins, CyberWitch Press & Graphic Design
www.cyberwitchpress.com

Editor: Deborah Anderson

She'll break every magical rule to survive

Half fae and half wolf-shifter, Tavi Alderidge is still reeling from the last attempt to kill her. On the bright side, she used her powers of cognitive manipulation against her enemy—and now she has a new direwolf to protect her.

But now the truth of her bloodline is out in the open, and in Faerie, shifters like her are bound for the executioner's ax. Surviving attacks from both Unseelie and Seelie fae will take all her skill and determination...especially when there's nowhere to go where magic can't find her.

Soon, Tavi finds herself on the run, hunted, with the son of her enemy at her side. Onyx Grimaldi might be related by blood to her violent fated mate, and a murderer, but he's also dying. And it's her fault.

Her own secrets aren't the only ones that come to light, just like her heart isn't the only one in the balance. Crown Prince Michael Thornwood believes in her innocence and he's determined to find her. Unless they reunite and stop both sides from killing each other, there's no hope for a future. For anyone.

Fans of Sarah J. Maas, Bella Forest, and K.F. Breene will find themselves enthralled with this dark paranormal romance full of magic and betrayal.

Coral Ferenze somehow managed to look haughty despite being covered in blood, sweat, and dire-wolf spit.

The redhead stood with her hands on her hips and groaned at me, beleaguered and put-out.

"Are we almost done, Tavi? I swear, I spend more time standing around watching you or flat on my ass than I do actually learning."

She flipped her hair over her shoulder, eyes piercing me.

I struggled to tune out her voice, although it's much less annoying now than the first time I'd heard her in the halls of the Elite Academy. Instead, I focused on my enemy.

Or rather, my pet.

"I know you're holding back," I told the direwolf.

He cocked his head to the side but his eyes were intelligent enough that I knew he understood every word. His dark fur bristled and he huffed a breath out from his long snout.

"Stop holding back and attack me the way you did in the forest. It's the only way the three of us are going to get stronger. Okay?" I adjusted my stance and gestured for him to *bring it.*

"Tavi!"

Coral was perilously close to throwing a temper tantrum, which was one of her favorite pastimes. I'd seen her in action more times than I wanted to count and she always blew me away.

Sometimes literally.

Often, when we were at the Academy together, she'd toss a burst of invisible yet potent magic at me just to put me on my ass and have her minions laughing at my misery.

"Just do it," I whispered to the direwolf.

"If you're ready to stop talking to your pet, then—" Coral never finished the statement.

The direwolf, whom I'd named Noren whether he agreed with me or not, let out a roar that shook the leaves of the trees and set them trembling.

He lifted onto his back legs to his full, terrifying height, and finally launched himself at Coral.

The sight of his red open mouth packed with teeth longer than some of my fingers made my insides tremble. Yet my bully, my cousin, stood her ground and adjusted her stance the way I'd taught her.

In the next breath, she'd called on her own change and the strawberry-blonde hair on her forearms, too light to see normally, darkened and grew until fur covered her arms entirely.

She completed the partial change in time to meet Noren's attack and swipe her claws low across his belly. She never made contact, but then again neither did he.

I held my breath, tensed and ready to step in if necessary, but Coral pivoted on her back foot and lashed out with the other leg.

She held the change through it all.

Noren leaped over the kick, launching himself over her head and landing on the balls of all four feet. Coral barely had time to rear her arm back before he pounced. A low growl split the air.

"Girls! Who's thirsty? I made tea with lavender and pea flowers. I think it gives the tea a beautiful color."

Coral's Mom, Nexa, didn't blink when she strode across the overgrown backyard toward the garden clearing where we practiced.

Didn't blink at the way her daughter rolled on her back and slashed at Noren's underside with curved claws.

Even I swallowed over a gasp at the snap of his teeth inches away from Coral's pretty, snarling face. She was really getting the hang of things, though, especially with her mom's unwavering support.

"Sorry, I didn't realize I was interrupting."

Nexa set the tray of drinks down on the ground inches away from my feet. We were far enough from the sparring for the glasses to be safe, but if I looked away now...I might miss something.

"It's fine, we're almost finished," I told her. "Have you, ah, had any luck? Tracking down your sister?"

Her sister, my missing mother.

A familiar clenching sensation began in my heart and traveled down my torso before it settled, low and hard, in my gut. My mom was alive. I'd found my family here in Faerie, and accidentally gotten my pure-blooded fae cousin turned into a shifter.

My fault.

Nexa shook her head and strands of shiny reddish-brown hair slipped from the intricate curled updo she sported today. "I'm sorry to say, Tavi, but I haven't had any luck yet. I won't stop trying for you."

I nodded and swallowed down my disappointment. I should be familiar with *that*, too.

"Just because I haven't had any luck yet doesn't mean I'm going to give up." Nexa's tone took on a happier, upbeat quality. Was she trying to convince me, or herself? "She's out there somewhere. The last word I received from my people said she was in Yelaine."

The name clanged through me.

I tilted my head to the side, only half paying attention to the way Coral and Noren attacked each other, Coral going on the defensive more often than not.

"What's Yelaine?"

"It's a large metropolitan area. I know, it's hard to imagine a faerie city out there but it's nearly eight hundred miles away. The topography of the land changes the closer you get to the coast. Most fae have chosen to test their mettle in a more progressive setting rather than the forests." Nexa sighed, reached a hand behind her neck to work out a kink. "Things aren't what they used to be."

I wasn't sure if she missed the old ways or not.

"Why would my mom want to go to a city?" I pressed.

"I'm only guessing here, mind you, having not spoken to my sister since your birth..." Nexa cleared her throat, slightly embarrassed. "I'd imagine she'd want to get as far away as possible from the king. She escaped his death sentence, which makes her a wanted fugitive. But stop worrying!"

She broke off to grab me in a hug. It took me precious seconds to return the gesture, my muscles twitching as if I wasn't used to it.

And on some level, I wasn't. Physical touch still felt all kinds of awkward for me.

"I promise I won't give up looking," Nexa finished.

"I appreciate it."

We called it a day five minutes later. Coral wasn't much on goodbyes, however, and skulked off to the house with her pretty painted nails in the air.

It was about the best I'd get from her—not like it mattered—because although my own wounds had healed, I still had a long way to go before I felt right again.

Which made long practices like these ultra-hard.

The second she and Nexa disappeared, I hunched over and sucked overheated air through my burning nostrils.

Squeezing my eyes shut against a swell of pain, I counted to ten, then another ten, until I managed to get things under control.

At last I clicked my tongue and Noren fell into step beside me.

We made our way carefully out of the backyard through a side gate hidden almost entirely by roses. He knocked me with his massive shoulder and I rubbed my hand through his fur, gliding my fingers through the thick strands.

"Sorry, buddy," I whispered. "I'm not feeling the best. Today took a lot out of me." Nexa's tea had settled my stomach at the moment but not for long.

It was only days since my fight with Claribel, the rogue Bureau agent working for Dorian Jade. Days since I mentally manipulated Noren from a raging mindless beast into the docile pet he was now, and although my physical wounds were gone...the rest of me remained fragile.

Hot, nauseated, you name it.

My joints ached, and there were times when I listed sideways under a random attack of dizziness.

I'd had a flu that felt the same. Which meant this had to be some kind of reaction to using up too much magic.

I'd gotten sick a couple of years ago at the Fae Academy for Halflings, in the human realm. That had been abnormal enough.

Getting sick again? In the freaking Fae realm where I was supposed to be my strongest?

Ugh. No.

The walk back to the palace was a long one though, and before I reached the massive courtyard gates, I leaned even more heavily on Noren. I'd held out long enough to keep Coral from seeing me this weakened, but playing pretend cost me in the long run.

It would give her teasing rights for the rest of our lives and fae were notoriously long-lived. Plus, she trusted me to teach her and show her the ropes.

Staying strong counted for extra now.

With Noren keeping me upright, we made our way through the palace gates. Guards stood at strict attention on either side and stared at me as I passed.

Did they still suspect me of being a mass murderer? What a joke.

They probably did. They refused to meet my eyes.

I glared back at them in response. How much longer would I have to keep defending myself against that stupid accusation? Everyone seemed too willing to think the worst of me.

Noren let out a low rumble of warning from the back of his throat. The guards shifted, lifting their attention forward as we walked through without incident.

The castle loomed ahead of us with its spires reaching up in the rich sapphire sky, and although dark clouds remained on the periphery of the forest at the castle's back, magic seeped through the stone.

Flowers remained unfurled under the prismatic sunlight.

I drew in a deep breath and willed my emotions to calm.

"Just a little bit longer." I spoke more for my benefit than for Noren's, although he had the uncanny ability to look as though he actually heard and understood every word I said. "A little bit longer and we'll be back."

I refused to think of the castle as home no matter how long I'd lived there.

A smooth male voice cut through my inner chatter. "Tavi? There you are."

I glanced up and blinked, a familiar golden head of hair swimming into view.

Prince Michael Thornwood cut an imposing figure. He strode across the courtyard with his elbow bent at a ninety degree angle and his mother gliding on air beside him.

Queen Laina.

I suddenly felt as if the ground dropped away underneath me.

Mike waved, a smile spreading across his features, and my heart flipped over in a rough tumble inside my rib cage. Had there ever been a more handsome male created? He was so attractive. And his smile...for *me*.

I picked up my pace as much as I could, and with only ten feet separating us I felt my skin go hot as a wave of dizziness crashed over me. *Oh, god. Please don't throw up.*

I gripped Noren's fur, locking my knees and greeting them both with an easy and totally faked smile. "Hi."

Queen Laina was radiant. Her expression remained a picture of grace and beauty, and today she wore her long hair twisted behind her head in an assembly of braids that left small, tight curls fanning her ageless face.

"You look well today," I told her.

"Thank you, Tavi," she replied easily. "You as well."

Mike stared at me and a question formed on his face but the grin remained in place.

I used to be terrified of discovery by the royal family of Faerie. After all, a person like me is not supposed to exist. Fae and shifters were sworn enemies of each other, and to have an offspring produced from the match basically amounted to heresy in the eyes of the monarchy.

Yet Queen Laina knew my secrets. She kept secrets of her own hidden from her husband and the other pure-blooded fae, and I knew if there were anyone out there who would protect me, it was her.

We'd come to an understanding.

"Will you walk with us?" Laina extended her other elbow to me and I swallowed an exhausted groan.

The last thing I wanted to do was walk. What choice did I have? It wasn't like I was in a position to say no to the queen herself.

I bowed my head in deference before I moved to her side and slid my arm through hers.

The moment we lurched into motion, Mike shifted to stand on my other side, and Laina bent her head to mine and spoke in an undertone too low for anyone passing to catch.

"There have been a few updates, mostly concerning my recent conversation with King Tywin," she whispered.

I jerked at the name. "What did he say?"

"I went to bat for you." She scrunched her pretty face, her mouth a hard line and her desire for me to shut my damn mouth evident. "And in the course of our discussion, I managed to get you reinstated in the kitchens. Your job is safe."

I inwardly cringed at the mention of my old job working for Raelynn, the busty fae in desperate need of an attitude adjustment. Not so exciting news.

"I'm also convinced that the king has a completely warped view of you, Tavi. As far as I know, in speaking to Mike regarding everything happening over the course of the last year, this has all been a misunderstanding or a mere coincidence," Laina continued.

"It's true," Mike insisted hotly.

His trust meant the world to me. And under different circumstances I'd have a lot more to say and a better outlook for the future.

But the tight skin and hot flashes made thinking almost impossible.

For whatever miracle I'd received that earned me Mike's trust, I'd be forever grateful. There was a point in our near past where I thought we'd never be on the same page again. Sometimes I wait to wake up from this nightmare and be right back at square one.

Plus the queen appeared to have genuine affection for me, which certainly helped. Laina was the reason I'd been cleared of all suspicion regarding the pure-blood fae murders and the tarot reader Madam Muerte's untimely death.

"Darlings, compose yourselves. We're being watched." Laina straightened, her gaze fixed on something in the distance that grew larger with each passing breath.

I tried to focus on the figures and failed miserably when everything went blurry.

"What is it, Mom?" Mike's voice hardened.

"We've been expecting a delegation of several leaders

from distant regions. We were unsure of their arrival but it seems to me they have recently crested the borders of our city."

I glanced up in time to see her face twist into a beatific smile, the apples of her cheeks pink and her eyes kind.

A mask. A different kind of magic.

"You two be careful and watch out for each other. I need to take my leave. Michael, my love, I'll see you in a few days."

Laina raised on the tips of her toes to kiss her much taller son on his cheek before gliding away from us back toward the castle. Faster than I'd seen her move in the past with her feet hardly touching the ground.

The moment the queen was out of earshot, I cast a concerned look at Mike. "Distant leaders? Why are they coming here?"

And why was his mother practically running back to the safety of the castle, *away* from them?

A hard pit in my stomach grew into a chasm, and sensing the change in my mood, Noren whined and pressed against my leg.

Mike hardly spared a glance for the direwolf now. He'd gotten used to the addition and, I halfway suspected, was curious how this would play out.

"When other diplomats come to visit, Mom…"

Mike dropped his voice and at the same time lifted a wall of silence around us. A full one would be much too noticeable, but this spell dampened our conversation enough to avoid suspicion or eavesdropping.

"Mom remains in seclusion so no one can discover her status as a half-blood witch. It would cause a huge scandal, and some of the more bigoted leaders of the realm might use it as a ploy to try and unseat my father. It's always been this way."

My gut flipped in disgust. "That's awful."

There were parts of Faerie so backward it made me sick. I'd always thought of this place as an escape from the harshness and cruelty of the real world. Instead, it had more problems than I ever imagined.

Noren whined louder and threw the bulk of his massive weight into my legs until they buckled.

"Stop it," I corrected without any heat in my voice. "What are you doing?"

"He's protecting you," Mike replied with a little laugh. "He takes his job very seriously."

"Protecting me from what?" I batted the direwolf away, just as the edges of my vision suddenly went black and blurry.

The wave of dizziness crashed down over me with such force I toppled into Noren, heat scalding my veins like acid.

The darkness overtook everything else and I went down into unconsciousness, with the approaching delegation of distant leaders watching me fall.

2

The agonizing swim back up to consciousness wasn't for the faint of heart.

Reality intruded on me more slowly than it should have, returning in spits and spats and hazy images until I finally pried my eyes open.

The room swam into view, first in triple, then double. Then at last the world solidified into a familiar space where I'd spent way too much time already.

I groaned and shook my head, or tried to shake my head but found myself unable to move.

How many times had I woken up in the Claw & Fang Hospital?

At least Mike knew to bring me here, for which I'd be forever grateful. As a half shifter, a regular fae hospital was too dangerous for me because they'd likely figure out my genetics and possibly eject me from this realm.

Shifters weren't welcome here.

We were tainted or something.

It was a huge risk being in this land in the first place but it sure beat the alternative.

I tuned in to the weight at the bottom of the hospital bed and found Noren curled up asleep at my feet. His enormous body took up most of the damn bed, actually, and heat rolled off of him.

What a giant.

At least he kept my feet warm.

His concern was sweet. Noren understood more than any normal wolf I'd ever met, and despite his massive size and his ferocious claws and teeth made for disemboweling, he'd started to act like a giant puppy around me.

He'd jumped in front of me, as well, right before I passed out, almost like he'd known something was wrong before I did.

I'd have cracked my skull open on the ground if not for his quick reflexes to break my fall.

"Thanks, big guy." It took me a hot minute to haul myself up to a seated position and reach out to run my hand through his fur, ruffling the dark strands. "You're always looking out for me. I appreciate it. You're the best."

Noren cracked open a yellow eye, his gaze meeting mine, and then he snorted and curled up into a tighter ball.

I ran my hand over his shoulder and up to his ear, scratching him lightly.

"You want to talk to the wolf but not to me?" a female voice scoffed, the tenor sweet and airy but also loud enough to pierce the fog in my brain. "Typical Tavi."

Bronwen Minuti set her book down on her lap and grinned at me, the motion bringing her freckles to attention on her pale face. Her relief was evident.

Bronwen knew everything about me and then some. We came from the same kind of background, except her family had gotten her out before I ever realized there was a need to run.

When I initially used my mental manipulation on the direwolf, Bronwen and Melia were the first people I told.

She reached out for my hand, and it took an inordinate amount of effort to lift my arm even just to touch my fingertips to hers.

"I'm glad you're here," I said.

"Where else would I be? I heard about you fainting and I came right away. Like I'd let you stay in this place without someone to keep an eye on you. Well, two someones. Noren does an amazing job." She stood and placed her hand on my forehead. "How are you feeling?"

"I feel like shit. Actually, I haven't been right for a couple of days. It's like the flu on steroids."

I dropped back down against the pillows, blinking away the sudden burning in my eyes.

And my arm, too. It was bandaged at my side and the skin beneath the wrapping felt like I'd held it over a fire and watched my skin crackle and split.

"What's going on?" I asked Bronwen.

Her brows knitted together and she stared at me. Then realization clicked in.

"You mean your arm? It's an infected wound. I've been here long enough to watch them clean and rewrap it three times now. Which the nurse assures me they've been doing for days."

"What do you mean, *for days*?" I bolted upright and jostled Noren in the process.

His expression barely changed—he was a wolf, after all —but I swore he frowned at me for the imposition.

"You've been unconscious for, like, four days now, dude. The hospital staff aren't really sure what's going on or why." Bronwen gnawed on the inside of her cheek. "They also don't have a clue why your shifter abilities aren't healing you the way they should."

Well, that was troubling.

My shifter healing abilities had gotten me out of way too many scrapes in the past for me to be able to operate without them now.

And where the hell had they gone in the first place?

Ice crystalized in my veins and at the same time the palms of both hands were hot and clammy.

Was something wrong with my wolf?

"The infected wound is from where zombie Madam Muerte bit me," I admitted softly.

The grave expression looked out of place on Bronwen's face, and for a moment her eyes darkened and I wondered what the hell she was hiding.

Then she smiled at me and any trace of what I'd seen disappeared.

She settled back down in her chair. "If anyone can figure out what's going on, it's the doctors here. The Claw & Fang aren't fucking around. They know their stuff. Oh, and I told Melia what's going on."

A small measure of relief stole over me.

"Thanks."

"Mike's been in and out to check on you, too. He really is a hunk, and a caring one as well. It's a rare combination." The observation was her attempt to diffuse the tension thickening the air between us. "I know I had some issues with him at first but I think I may actually like him now."

A rush of panic overtook me. "I had another training session with Coral. If I've been here for days, then I must have missed it. Did you tell Coral?"

Bronwen rolled her eyes.

"You have to tell her."

"Ugh. Fine. Okay? *Fine.* I'll go call her now, but you'll owe me."

I owed her so much more than even Bronwen knew.

She and Coral hated each other. It was totally understandable, considering Coral was just about the most offensive person I'd ever met.

At least until I got to know her.

"Add it to the list," I told Bronwen, sighing. "And I'm sorry, again. For leaving you high and dry."

I'd chosen not to go on patrol with Bronwen. And my mentor, Onyx, attacked. He was killing pure-blooded fae, and although he'd been controlled by magic...that didn't make up for what happened.

Or the part I played in how it all went down.

Shame shriveled my insides.

"You almost died because of me," I added when she stayed silent.

Bronwen shrugged, her lips pouted. "Yeah, well, I don't fear death, so don't worry about it. If this life ends then I'll just do my best to enjoy the next one. At least I know there's another chance waiting for me."

I swallowed over a chuckle. "Yeah, sure."

Bronwen leaned forward. "No, I'm serious," she insisted.

"What do you mean, the next one? There's only one life. Don't we have to make the most of this one?"

"It's the old myths, Tavi." She leaned in further and crooked a finger for me to come closer.

Which, as I found out, was pretty much impossible. "What old myths?"

"Come on, don't tell me your uncle never told you about the old reincarnation myths? Every pup right out of the nest knows about the second life of shifters."

"If he did, then I'm drawing a blank," I admitted. "Want

to explain them to a poor invalid laid up in bed?" Yup, that was the card I played.

"So, ancient shifters believed that even an ounce of shifter blood allowed them to reincarnate into another life after death if they wanted to. Which means we get another shot at this whole thing. Another go-around. It's awesome to think about, isn't it?" She sat back in the chair with a shrug. "Either way, I'm putting off this call. Let me go have a little chat with the devil herself."

Bronwen left to call Coral, and at once the burning in my arm ratcheted up a notch, as if acknowledging it somehow made it worse.

Reincarnation, huh?

It sounded like something people made up to excuse their poor decisions and bad judgment in this life. I wasn't sure I believed in it. I'd seen some incredible things, but that?

If we got another shot at life, it meant— A swell of pain cut off that line of thinking.

Sleep wasn't easy but it took me under a few times. I remembered waking up woozy once or twice whenever a nurse came to check my vitals.

Each time, the pain tickled the edges of my awareness before the dizziness got worse and I drifted again.

The sensation left me with no choice. I couldn't have fought sleep even if I wanted to. Eventually I floated back to reality, the din of voices in the room distant and foggy.

I shifted against the pillows at my back.

"None of the treatments are working," someone said. "I'm not sure what other options are left for us to explore."

"There has to be something you can do, Doctor. Please. She's very important."

The second voice was feminine and low, familiar in a way that tugged at the rusty processes in my brain.

Selene Montrosse.

She led the Claw & Fang. So it made sense for her to be here, but how much time had passed since I'd been brought in?

I struggled to sit up straighter to try and catch a glimpse of the two but failed miserably.

"Tavi only seems to be getting worse. We'll keep her here for a few more days to see if there's any improvement, but at this point it makes sense for you to consider taking her somewhere she'll be comfortable. I hate to be the one to tell you this but her outlook isn't great."

I heard what the male doctor didn't say. That I'd need to be brought out of the hospital so that I died somewhere off the premises. Where they wouldn't have to clean up the mess.

My insides constricted and squeezed the air out of my lungs.

"Is there *any* hope for her?" Selene asked.

"We're doing the best we can," the doctor continued.

The next thing I knew, soft fingers stroked across my forehead, and I peeled my eyes open to watch Selene gently brush my hair back.

The wooziness allowed me to watch her lips move but I heard nothing. Sick, dizzy, I existed as if in a wind tunnel. There was nothing outside of the howling in my head.

The doc was definitely right. Whatever was happening, I felt worse, not better.

But her motherly touch broke through my defenses. I wasn't getting well, and the look in her eyes was all steely resolve with a bit of tempered sympathy.

I'd met her as a reporter during the Faerie Trials. Today

her normal sly smile and sharp voice seemed a million miles away and her usually pert chin-length black hair looked messy.

Eyes of a deep silver scoured me.

The next time I woke, Selene wasn't in sight, but her voice lifted in a shout.

"What do you expect us to do, Almighty Prince?" Her tone bit deep but at least I heard her. The knot in my chest released with a small measure of consolation. "We're giving her the best possible treatment. I can't exactly pull a miracle out of my ass simply because you command it. With all due respect," she said, with absolutely no respect whatsoever.

"And yet you're not helping her! None of you. What good is the Claw & Fang if they can't save someone like her? You're spinning your wheels and she'll pay the price."

Mike. Tears pricked my eyes.

He came back for me.

"The castle has the best hospital in the realm. Hand her over to me or I'll send the entirety of the King's Guard here to storm your medical center," he threatened.

"Try to take her and see what happens."

I could practically see Selene's sneering face in my mind.

Oh no, this was going to devolve into something hideous, and fast. I lifted my hand to try and stop the fight but a wave of nausea attacked my insides.

My gut swirled sickeningly and the sudden rise of heat in my throat sent me right back into unconsciousness.

Sunlight warmed the side of my face the next time I woke. For a moment I lay on my back breathing, focusing on the sensation, and slowly I lifted my hand to cup my sun-warmed cheek.

I moved without issue.

That alone had surprise welling up and my eyes popped

open, this time without the accompanying sick feeling I'd gotten used to. I actually felt...decent. Much better than I had any of the other times. And this place—

I reached out for Noren like I usually did when I woke up and felt nothing. He wasn't with me.

Something tugged at my arm with a small prick of pain when I sat up and I glared at the clear IV attached to the crook of my arm.

My current hospital room boasted large mullioned windows letting in a powerful stream of light. Two high-backed chairs upholstered in buttery yellow fabric sat beneath the windows, and the sheets were crisp, clean, and pristine white.

The fresh scent of evergreens and mulberry filled the space. None of the sickening ammonia chemical stench of human hospitals.

I waited for several moments, hoping someone would come.

There had to be a call button somewhere. I rolled onto my side, reaching out with my free hand to search the bedside table. Nope, no call button there.

Okay, think.

Wherever I'd been moved, this place was so very different from the hospital operated by the Claw & Fang. Where was I? Had Mike actually dragged me out of there, or was I dead and trapped in some kind of weird purgatory?

I'd seen stranger sights.

Taking great pains to go slowly, I slid my legs over the side of the bed until my feet hit the cool tile floor. The IV stand moved along with me on well-oiled wheels.

The small private room held my bed, the two chairs, and a small table with a glass of water filled to the brim but nothing else.

A quick twist of the gold knob had the door swinging open silently, and the hallway beyond, although well lit, was as quiet as a tomb.

A chill wracked over me. I didn't recognize the place at all, and although I strained for some sort of magical recognition, nothing outside the low moan of the breeze outside greeted me.

Gripping the IV stand, I shuffled one foot in front of the other, my muscles tensed and a little sore from however long I'd been stuck in bed.

Despite the experience I felt better than I had in a long time. I wasn't even tired. The pain in my arm had all but disappeared and my head wasn't stuck on a Tilt-A-Whirl anymore.

Small miracles.

I turned the corner and the hallway opened up into a lobby. An ornate desk of polished mahogany took up one entire wall but only a single fae in scrubs manned the desk. The strange nurse and—

"Mike."

My voice cracked but his name came out loud enough to draw his attention.

A beautiful smile split his face and he unfolded from where he'd leaned across the desk, talking to the nurse.

"You shouldn't be out of bed yet," he called back to me. "What are you doing, Tavi?"

I shook my head and awkwardly pushed a lock of hair behind my ear at his approach. I probably looked like a hot mess. The hottest of messes, but nothing could have moved me.

Energy crackled between us, the same physical, visceral reaction whenever I saw him.

"I've spent enough time in bed to last a lifetime, thanks."

And there he stood in front of me. Live, in person, and handsome in that odd way of his. "I brought you here for better care. It's good to know things have finally turned in our favor." He dropped his voice. "It took a lot of effort to get you out."

I stared over his shoulder at the nurse. If anyone found out my secret, then it didn't matter if I healed and recovered or not. They'd shoot me where I stood.

Those few fervent glances between Mike and the nurse failed to project my concern to the former.

He placed his hand on the back of my neck, warm and steady, and dropped his forehead to mine. "You're safe, Tavi. You're safe."

He sounded so assuring.

I leaned into his comforting heat and let myself *feel*. To enjoy being in the moment with him when everything felt better than it had for a long time.

"How long?" I managed to ask.

"Have you been here? Only a day. It took a whole lot of posturing to move you but once we did, the doctors worked quickly. You're safe." He repeated the phrase with such surety I almost believed it.

I might have let him sweet talk me into lowering my guard, too, if a high-pitched alarm hadn't sounded in the next heartbeat. The shrill shrieking cut through my skull and I curled in on myself.

"Tavi, let's get you back to your room. *Now*." Mike cradled me against his chest.

"What's going on?"

"It's the emergency alarm. It means the castle is under attack."

3

Mike changed direction abruptly enough to nearly yank me off my feet. Leaving me no choice but to follow him, my IV stand keeping me upright, we hustled down the hallway and turned another corner.

"What are you doing?" I asked breathlessly.

"Just follow me." His hard tone left no room for arguing.

Where the stone met at a ninety degree angle, Mike reached out and tapped the bricks. He drew a complicated ward in the air above them and in the next beat, the mortar and stone dissolved.

The opening was just large enough for a person of his stature to walk through.

"Come on." He urged me forward. "We've got to hurry."

The alarm screeched in my ears and I clenched my jaw against it. "I don't understand what's going on—"

"This is a secret passage from the hospital wing. Baldric, hurry, or else you're going to slow us down," Mike hissed over his shoulder.

It took me a hot minute to realize the nurse from the front desk had followed us.

He stood above Mike, topping close to seven feet tall if I had to guess, his limbs longer than ordinary and his eyes a bit too large.

Baldric had to duck to get into the passageway behind us and cobwebs immediately tangled with the silky strands of his strawberry-blonde hair.

"This corridor connects the fae hospital in Eahsea with the castle." Mike's whisper echoed oddly when the stones closed in behind us. Fae lights immediately burst to life ahead of us and illuminated the way forward. "Stick close to us, Tavi."

"We'll go slow for you," Baldric added. He held his hands out to keep me from bumping against the walls.

We took our time navigating the tunnels and my head spun with the attempt to keep track of the twists. Time meant nothing here.

The tunnels must run deep beneath the castle and although the hospital wasn't far, the building wasn't exactly adjacent. Several times, I tripped on my own feet, my legs struggling to carry me.

Baldric remained close enough to bolster me whenever I needed help and Mike kept hold of my free hand more times than not.

I didn't trust the dude. Baldric, not Mike. But I had no other choice.

Eventually the tunnel turned a final time and ran into a dead end marked by a steel door. My heart clenched at the sight.

Mike blew out a breath. "The safe room," he explained. "Mom and a few others should be waiting inside. The escape tunnels are everywhere in case of emergency, and protected by magic."

I opened my mouth to protest that I'd be able to handle myself, then zipped my lips shut. At least the hospital gown I'd worn in the Claw & Fang ward had been replaced with soft cotton pajama pants and a matching shirt. I wasn't walking around with a gown and open back, my ass on display for the queen and visiting royalty.

"I can't hear the alarm anymore," I whispered.

"It wouldn't be on for no reason. Whatever is happening, we're going to be safe here, Tavi, trust me."

Mike spoke with the utter confidence of a fae of his station, and for half a heartbeat I wondered if this change happened while I was sick.

Because the Mike I'd gone to school with at the Fae Academy for Halflings had to utilize a stolen artifact in order to keep up with the rest of us.

He'd given the world a glimpse of him, a small hint of the reality of his situation, but otherwise he'd worn a mask at all times.

I'd gotten to know the real Mike, and although he was an amazing man and a strong fae in his own right, he'd never come across as self-assured without some sort of hesitation.

Now he knocked on the door and flashed me a tight smile before the latches turned on the other side. The steel swung open with a pulse of magic and my eyes widened in surprise at seeing Raelynn gripping the handle.

Her gaze fell on me, her face as bright red as her hair. "Well, well, good to see you've finally returned to the land of the living," she said sharply in her accented tone. "Get her inside, hurry now. Hurry!"

Raelynn didn't seem to care about speaking informally to the prince.

The moment the three of us made it into the safe room, she closed the door behind us and locked it tightly. There were only a handful of people in the room.

Four guards watched over them, with the queen seated comfortably on a pile of pillows nearby.

"I'm glad to hear you'll be joining us back in the kitchen soon. We've missed your incompetence." Raelynn fell into step beside me, careful not to jostle the IV stand. "Although I'm sorry to say you'll no longer be welcome at the bread-making station. We've found another girl who is rather a whiz with the yeast. Still, I'll be happy to have you back. Despite your troublemaking."

I grinned. "It's good to see you." And much to my surprise, it *was* good to see Raelynn.

Although the reunion wasn't enough to get the bubbling nerves out of my veins.

Mike pressed an assuring hand to the small of my back before he shifted over to check on his mother, their heads bent together and their conversation too low to hear.

Besides them and the guards, there were six others in the room and only one of them was familiar, a courtier I'd seen at several balls in the past.

The visiting dignitaries must either be in a different safe room or they'd left sometime during my sickness.

"Captain Hezarwick?" Mike called out. He hadn't left his mother's side. "What's the status?"

One of the guards straightened his shoulders at being called upon. "We're awaiting updates. My men are in the process of securing the palace from all outside threats." His square chin jutted out. "Once it's safe to return, Your Highness, you will be the first to know."

What size threat had set off the alarms? It had to be big, because I'd never heard them go off before.

Mike's quick thinking had got me to this safe place but how long would we have to stay?

The space was large enough to house double the number of people who were present, and a quick glance around showed all the comforts of the castle overhead.

Two small doors were sunk into the stone walls. One of them probably led to a bathroom, and if I had to guess, the other stored enough supplies to keep the monarchy alive through a siege.

And here I stood with my knees clacking together in a room full of people who wouldn't hesitate to cut off my head. Except for the queen, and Mike.

Baldric stood at my back and pressed me toward a thick pillow several feet away from the queen. "Come on, Tavi, let's get you comfortable," he said in a voice like falling leaves. "It's no good for you to stand this way, not after exerting yourself."

Raelynn drifted away as Baldric helped me seat myself on the pillow.

I glanced up at him, a question in my eyes. "You know me?"

"I've been assisting you through your recovery." Baldric bobbed his head. "You can trust me. I understand the delicacy of your situation."

My chest clenched and I automatically wanted to tell him that I didn't trust anyone. I couldn't.

"Sir? We've just received communication that they're unable to locate the threat." Captain Hezarwick bent his ear to a small garnet-colored stone at the neck of his uniform. He paused, listening, and then said out loud, "They've cordoned off the south wing and are proceeding to the west wing as we speak."

A knot formed in my gut the longer we sat. Several more dispatches came through while we waited, tensed, straining to hear whatever it was the captain heard.

This wasn't how I wanted the day to go, and although Mike remained perched nearby, the room separating us might as well be a chasm.

I wanted to talk to him. I wanted—

Suddenly the captain stiffened and the blood drained from his face.

"What's happening?" Queen Laina asked. "Hezarwick?"

He straightened. "The radios have gone silent."

A moment later, a large boom rocked outside the steel door and the room shook. I froze, Baldric in a similar state of terror at my side, my hand reaching out for a direwolf who wasn't there.

A questioning howl rose from right outside and I gasped.

"It's Noren!" I struggled to my feet in an attempt to get to the door and let the direwolf inside. "He trailed us down here."

"Whoa, whoa." Baldric surged to his feet at the same time two of the guards stepped in front of me to block my access to the door.

"We've got to let him in," I argued. "He found his way for a reason."

Did any of them sense the urgency, the gravity, the same way I did?

My senses tuned in to Noren on the other side of the thick steel, uncaring who got in my way or what they tried to do to me. Several of the guards closed ranks and I felt their glares like a physical rasp against my skin.

"Miss Alderidge? Step away from the door. Immediately."

I barely heard Hezarwick, the magic protecting the room burning the tips of my fingers.

"Miss? You heard him."

I craned my head up to meet the eyes of the guard on the left. My hackles rose and who knows what flashed across my face before Mike interrupted, sliding his body between me and the guards.

His green eyes were shining as he shook his head.

"That direwolf is too smart for his own good if he managed to find you all the way here during an emergency. I'm sorry we left him behind. Open the door."

Mike jerked his head toward the guard, who stared at us for only a moment before he bowed to the prince.

The door was hardly open before Noren pushed his way inside and immediately took up every molecule of air in the room. His massive size made even the cavernous space shrink and several gasps greeted us as I lurched forward and wrapped my arms around his neck.

"Thank you for coming for me," I murmured against his ear. "I'll never leave you behind again."

He huffed out a light growl that felt almost like a wolf-y *you'd better not.*

"Sir, this is highly irregular," the guard re-locking the door commented. "Especially when the current situation upstairs is unknown."

"It might be irregular but that beast would have ripped the door down if we hadn't let him inside," Hezarwick replied with a groan.

The world narrowed to the two of us as I breathed in the familiar scents of forest and fur, dark things and pagan secrets.

There was something infinitely calming about Noren's presence and I wondered if it was the product of the bond I'd forced on us when I used my mental manipulation on him.

Even the sliver of guilt I usually felt when I thought about it refused to surface.

It had come down to a matter of his mind or my life, and at that moment it was a last ditch effort on my part. I'd never expected to be able to penetrate the Unseelie spellwork on the direwolf's mind.

Now that I had, I was forever grateful for his companionship.

I shifted back to look at his familiar snout and dangerous teeth. "Thank you," I repeated.

He blinked at me, which was as much an answer as anything else.

"It's a particular worry to me that your father has yet to show up," Laina spoke from the corner to Mike. "What's the news on the king?"

One of the guards stood near to her with his posture rigid and his face showing none of the worry I'm sure they all shared.

"I'm more worried about the radio silence." Mike lifted his gaze to the ceiling as though he could see right through to the world above. "What kind of threat are we facing, and why have the others stopped responding?"

These were rhetorical questions although I noted that Captain Hezarwick opened and shut his mouth, struggling for an answer.

"If he were able to be here, then he would be," Laina continued staunchly. "Something is wrong. I feel it."

I shuddered at the thought of having to share these confined quarters with King Tywin, who hated me. The feeling wasn't really mutual but I'd rather avoid him at all costs.

Queen Laina caught my attention and subtly gestured toward one of the two wooden doors.

"Tavi, please come with us for a moment." Mike held out a hand for me and I had to break contact with Noren to grab my IV pole. The three of us, wolf included, followed the queen toward the door.

She motioned for the guard to remain on the opposite side as we sidled into a separate chamber. "Michael, if you would be so kind..."

Mike moved into position and closed his eyes. The damping spell started at the floor and rose to encompass the door, keeping whatever we might say inside the private chamber between us.

No one from the outside would be able to hear us until Mike lowered the spell.

The strength of it took me aback. He'd been practicing without me.

This wasn't, as I'd originally thought, a bathroom. Instead, the chamber had been outfitted as a meeting room with a separate door on the opposite side and several couches facing each other.

"Your father should be here," Laina began, working her hands.

"He'll come," Mike said in the dull silence, picking up on the conversation from before. "I know he'll come. He's just... late."

"I'm not content to wait and see." Laina shuffled over to the couch and folded herself down on the cushions with much less than her normal grace. "Thus the need for privacy. Tavi, if you'll keep your...friend...across the room, I'd be grateful. I find he gives me a bit of the creeps."

When the queen tells you to do something, you do it.

"I'll stay over here with him." I found myself reluctant to pry my hand away from Noren's comforting ruff.

"What are you going to do?" Mike asked his mother.

Laina smoothed out the fabric of her skirt and fixed him with a look that told him not to ask stupid questions. "It's a simple spell," she explained regardless. "One of the first they teach young witches. It needs nothing more than my own power and a scrying mirror, which I happen to carry with me at all times."

The queen drew a small circle of black glass from one of the hidden pockets of her skirt. The gilded frame reflected the dull overhead glow of the fae lights and I saw nothing in the darkness, not even her reflection.

Laina gestured for us both to sit and I nestled against Noren, close enough to watch whatever spell she cast while still keeping a respectful distance.

The two of them huddled together, the family resemblance once again startling me even though it shouldn't.

Sometimes it was too hard to reconcile Michael, the same Mike who'd shared my bed, with the crown prince who would one day follow in the footsteps of his father the king.

"The scrying spell will allow me to catch a glimpse of what's happening above us," Laina continued.

She laid the glass out flat on the wooden table between them and held her hands above it, palms faced down.

How quickly had they shepherded her down here? I wondered. My palms went clammy. If anyone caught us—

The hard knot in my stomach grew tighter as I watched Queen Laina start to chant under her breath. The words were obscured, too strange to my ear for me to make out, and all of them done in an undulating monotone.

The fine hairs on the back of my arms stood to attention and Noren leaned hard against my side, just as rattled as I was.

The air became charged, filling the room with some kind of unfamiliar scent. When I glanced back, images floated above the black mirror and the scene unfolded.

At first we saw empty hallways as the spell sought out whatever target Queen Laina had pinpointed, whether it was the king or the intruder.

And when the slender form hidden in the shadows of the throne room finally clarified, my spine snapped to attention and my breath disintegrated one atom of air at a time.

I knew that woman.

The bottom dropped out from under me.

The witch of Everly Lane had infiltrated the castle.

Hoarder, apocalypse prepper, chain smoker, whatever you wanted to call her—Barbara habitually wore baggy overalls and an old red-and-black flannel shirt.

The material hung from her thin frame as she swept her attention across the throne room.

All three carved thrones were empty.

"Who is that?" Mike leaned in closer to the vision like it might give him a hint at her identity. "Mom?"

"I've never seen her before. She's obviously some sort of magic wielder if she managed to get inside the castle," Laina mused. "A witch, perhaps?"

A really fucking powerful witch. And somehow she's managed to rip her way into Faerie. I kept the thought to myself.

"Do you think she put a spell on the guards and that's why communication stopped?" Mike pushed.

"She'd have to have an army with her to be able to make

it past not only the guards but the wards. Wait." Laina sucked in a breath. "What's that in her hands?"

Dumbstruck, I stayed silent, my lips trembling and my teeth chattering together to the point where I clenched my jaw to still the movement.

The three of us watched Barbara exit the throne room, heading into the heart of the castle.

No one stood in her way.

None of the guards.

She practically strolled, as casual as a gray-haired psychopath like her could be, down the corridors, inspecting room after room at her leisure.

"I can't make out what she's got, but she's holding something." Laina leaned even closer.

"Can you zero in on the object?"

Then I heard Mike's audible gulp.

Out of nowhere, a single guard at last ran straight for Barbara, his sword pointed at her chest and his magic building.

She barely slowed before she lifted the object in her hand. And she never looked at him.

The guard jerked to a halt, and his cheeks suddenly caved in, his skin desiccated and stretched thin over bone as the life drained out of him.

His body fell to the floor seconds later but he kept twitching and writhing. He was still alive yet barely clinging on. Worse, I realized, than death.

I knew exactly what she had.

The *Augundae Imperium*, the magical artifact designed to siphon power from anyone and store it for the wielder to use. Roughly the size of a Rubik's cube and made of an amalgam of metals...I never thought I'd see it again.

Not after she'd forced me to steal the object for her and

we'd passed it off in the dead of night, my duty to her fulfilled.

Now she used it on the people of this castle.

My gut dropped straight down through the floor.

In horror, we watched the witch climb toward the royal's chambers. We watched her find the King and the two of them square off against each other.

And we watched Barbara descend like a predator to use the *Augundae Imperium* on King Tywin.

4

The illusion shattered.

Queen Laina picked up the mirror and slammed it down on the rocks, breaking the spell and splitting the glass into two neat pieces. Then she bolted back into the main room, opening the door with such force the wood slammed into the stone wall.

Several pieces splintered off the edge.

"Captain Hezarwick!" she demanded. "Send your guards to the royal bedchamber immediately. King Tywin needs help. Rally the others!"

I heard rather than saw the captain clear his throat. He sounded skeptical when he replied, "Your Majesty, why do you think the king is in danger? And why would you think he's in that particular room? I have eyes on His Majesty and he is in the library."

"The king *is* in danger so I suggest you take action, Captain, rather than wasting your time questioning me." Laina glowered at him and magic crackled off of her.

The room stilled, waiting for the tension between them to explode, and Noren released a low warning growl.

"How do you know?" Hezarwick pleaded. "Your Majesty—"

"I said *move*." Her haughty tone was unmistakable, and I shivered, the stupor that had fallen on me at seeing Barbara again broken.

Mike hadn't moved. He crouched over the now empty table, the pieces of the scrying mirror gone, with his head in his hands and his expression obscured.

I craned my head to peer over Noren's shoulder to watch. The guards stood where they were, standing off against the queen.

Laina seemed to have grown several inches, her chest puffed out and magic crackling around her.

No one else had anything to say and for a long second the room held its breath.

"We can't get through on the comm system," one of the guards murmured to the captain. "The connection appears to be severed."

"Then I suggest you go *yourself*. It is your position. I should not have to repeat myself."

Laina, delicate and pretty, seemed to expand even more and the air in the room contracted in response to her power.

Hezarwick maintained eye contact with the queen longer than propriety would have dictated, and the way she stood, not quite glaring but absolutely regal, had me catching my breath again.

Eventually, as he should have, Captain Hezarwick caved.

Three of his men left to assist the king while Hezarwick remained behind to guard everyone inside the safe room.

I hid my expression behind Noren's massive frame, focusing on drawing in a breath to the count of six, holding it, and releasing it to the same count.

For a time, the room remained engulfed in silence.

Terror took the place of any sort of thin hope I still harbored at this being a false alarm. There was nothing false about it. Barbara had come.

She'd somehow forced her way not only into Faerie itself but inside the castle, demolishing the wards and spells designed to keep us safe.

Her ace in the hole? The weapon in her hands, which she used with wild abandon. The weapon I'd delivered to her.

Guilt mingled with the terror into a new blend of emotion that turned my stomach. I'd given Barbara her tool of destruction and she'd come to harm King Tywin, which would hurt Mike beyond repair.

What would I do if Barbara ended up finding us down here and using the *Imperium* on Mike and Laina? I'd fight her to the death. Or else I'd fight only to have my power drained out of me until I was nothing but a husk on the floor, too.

"Your Majesty?" The captain's voice cut through the heavy quiet and someone sucked in their breath. "It's safe to head back into the castle. The guards have secured the scene. We have our suspect in custody."

My heart skipped a beat and without Noren to hold me up, I'd have lost my balance. Mike frowned.

"Thank you, Captain."

Laina's voice gave no indication of anything except gratitude at a job well done and I wondered how she hid her real emotions so well. I'd seen her walls come down only a handful of times before, less than that, and she had to be feeling some kind of way at the news of her husband being safe.

At least, I thought he was safe. Otherwise they'd have me back in magical cuffs in an instant.

"Tavi? Come on. Take my hand. We'll get you settled upstairs in your room."

I blinked up at Mike, a little surprised to see him holding his palm out for me to take. Baldric was instantly there, and between the two of them and Noren adding his strength, I managed to get upstairs with little fanfare.

It was a testament to how much I'd recovered. I made it without getting winded.

"What happened, exactly?" Queen Laina strode ahead of our group once we rounded the stairs into the throne room. The guards at the door turned at her arrival and one of them stepped ahead, clicking his heels together in acknowledgement of her presence.

"The woman was captured and subdued in the royal bedrooms, Your Majesty. We're unaware of the rest," he answered simply. "A witch, Your Majesty."

Laina's expression remained unchanged. "Michael? We need to check on your father."

He agreed without hesitation. "Yes, absolutely. Baldric, would you mind taking Tavi upstairs to her room? She'll be more comfortable there."

"Actually, Sir, a better idea would be to transport your friend back to the hospital where we will be able to continue her transfusions. She's looking a bit...wan."

Mike waved him away. "Fine, fine. Tavi? Please excuse me. I'll be there to check on you as soon as I'm able."

The conversation swirled around me faster than I was able to understand, and Mike's abrupt departure left me staring after him with my jaw working.

"Tavi? If you don't mind..."

Baldric took my arm to help me out toward the door, muttering the entire way about what we'd expect once we returned to the hospital. There was no question about Noren coming with us.

The surreal and foggy edges of the situation struck me.

The emergency alarm, the attack on the king, Barbara being here...it was straight out of a damn nightmare. Worse than anything my own fucked-up mind might have conjured.

What else was new?

Trouble followed me no matter where I went. If I'd thought the latest drama with Claribel defecting from the Bureau to target me meant the end of my issues, once again life proved me wrong.

I stumbled too many times to count on the way back. Baldric ended up having to lift me into his arms, making sure not to jostle my IV too much, and with Noren protesting with low whining the entire trip.

Baldric used magic to speed our progress but Noren's whines became full-fledged growls the moment we crossed the threshold. If anyone tried to approach besides Baldric, he showed his teeth, his hackles rising to scare them away.

He was my perfect protector.

Nurse Baldric got me settled into the same private room where I'd woken, and Noren clambered onto the edge of the bed. He kept his eyes open and unblinking, and the moment a female fae attempted to enter the room to speak to Baldric, Noren began to growl again.

"Guess he's staying," Baldric said offhandedly.

"You couldn't get him out of here if you tried. Hopefully the hospital doesn't have a policy against companions." I hesitated to call Noren a pet because the direwolf was so much more than that, and having him around soothed my inner wolf too.

I settled back against the pillows as exhaustion swamped me.

"I guess we're going to have to work around any policies, aren't we?" Baldric winked at me. "Make yourself comfortable, Tavi. The transfusion shouldn't take too long but I want to make sure you're lying down before we begin."

He adjusted the IV line attached to the crook of my arm.

"What exactly are you doing?" I asked, a chill settling into my skin.

I'd barely felt the needle through our trip to the safe room but now, with Baldric fiddling, it became an overly large splinter lodged somewhere it didn't belong, prodding me uncomfortably.

"The bite you received triggered an immune reaction in your blood," he explained. "The only way to temper the effects, which don't appear to be going away on their own, is to do a minor transfusion every few hours."

Baldric held up a finger, striding out of the room on those long legs and returning a moment later wearing a glowing pair of green gloves. He pushed a cart ahead of him and gestured toward the assortment of liquids in clear vials in front of him.

"This combination is the best we've found to combat the immune reaction and get your system to relax its defenses, in so many words."

"It sounds confusing and complicated. What kind of transfusion is it?"

"A blood transfusion with the addition of minerals to help replenish your damaged cells."

I started, my jaw dropping. "I can't have blood transfusions every day, multiple times a day. That's ridiculous and insane!"

"It might be just those things, and until we find a way to

combat the way your immune system is reacting and heal the bite, then I'm going to have to keep inconveniencing you. Keep in mind, this is a scientific explanation for something that may be magical. We're simply doing the best we can." He attempted a smile. "Prince Michael tells me you're an excellent student at the Elite Academy."

It was Baldric's attempt at distraction and although I appreciated it, I couldn't stop staring at the way he expertly mixed the blood with the rest of the vials. Within moments, he'd tapped the mixture into the IV line until it mingled with the fluid already in the bag.

"Mike's absolutely lying to you," I admitted. "I'm not the worst student there but I'm certainly not the best."

And it felt like a million years since I'd focused on my classes. Too many other things had happened since the last time I'd walked those halls, or spoken to Juno Ians, my old mentor. Not since she'd been attacked.

"Well, if nothing else, trust me when I tell you I'm going to do the best I can to make sure you're back up to peak performance."

"I'll never be at my peak performance," I muttered.

"Maybe this conversation, if it won't convince you, will distract you from the transfusion. At least the big guy here knows I'm trying to help." Baldric gestured toward where Noren dozed with one eye half opened to watch.

I didn't feel any different once the transfusion started. But the adrenaline rush from the alarm at last began to recede the longer I lay there propped against the pillows.

I offered up a meager grin for Baldric.

It wasn't the easiest thing for me to trust, but he seemed like the kind of guy you could depend on. I wanted to depend on him and believe it when he said he could help me.

Anything was better than the sickening dizziness.

I must have passed out because the next thing I knew, the mattress beneath me sagged and Mike sat there beside Noren, dwarfed by the direwolf's frame.

"Mike?" *Oh god, please let me be sleeping pretty and not drooling or anything like that.* "What are you doing here?" I swept a hand across my mouth to check and pushed the hair away from my face.

He looked haggard, his hair sticking up at all angles and the dark circles beneath his eyes making him appear more human than I'd ever seen him.

"Tavi. I needed to see you." His low tone gave me the shakes.

"What's the matter?"

"It's not good. It's not good at all."

Mike watched the wall and I watched him, neither of us daring to breathe. "You're scaring me."

"It's my father. He's in a coma."

5

"**I**'m not a royal, and I'm not important." I shook my head and dug my proverbial heels in. "I shouldn't be here."

Baldric had come in to detach me from the IV line but I swayed on my feet, staring at Mike where he stood near the door with his arms crossed over his chest.

"You might not be a royal but you belong at my side." He stubbornly met my gaze, his lips pressed into a thin line, his teeth gritted. "This is an emergency, Tavi. I need you with me."

He staunchly refused to budge and we ended up in a staring contest of epic proportions.

It definitely helped distract me from the squirming in my gut. My attention returned again and again to the bite on my arm that refused to heal and the transfusion I had to be given daily just to stay upright.

It would take every ounce of strength to make it through this no matter how optimistic Mike felt.

He'd woken me up in the hospital and demanded that I join him for this meeting. With King Tywin in critical condition, his second in command, Premier Cosmo Foxfall, had called an emergency gathering of the Elder Council and any courtiers in residence.

Mike was required to sit through the meeting. But I wasn't.

I was a nobody.

With all those eyes on me, and my wits stunted from the stupid bite, this was asking for trouble.

"Why me?" Why did hearing him say he needed me only increase the squirming sensation?

He stared at me like I'd grown another head. "You keep me centered. Not to mention you have insight I might not necessarily think about, and right now, with my head spinning, I'm having a hard time focusing on the important things."

I wasn't in a better position but I kept my mouth shut. Because damn, the compliment was nice to hear.

"You're being too sweet to me. Is it because I almost died?" The longer he held my gaze, the harder it was to stay composed.

"I'm being sweet because you deserve it." He moved away from his perch and crossed to where I stood a little wobbly, but every part of me leaning toward him. "But I'm also being selfish. I can't do this alone and I don't trust anyone else."

Something inside of me relaxed in his presence even as he dragged me closer. Electricity pulsed between us when Mike lowered his lips and captured mine in a sweet kiss.

I drew in a sharp breath colored with his scent, and for a heartbeat the rest of the world fell away and there was only the two of us.

I felt that way about him, calm in his presence, and safe.

That was the important part. I'd never felt as safe as I did when Mike and I were alone.

"Come on. You look beautiful, by the way," he murmured, drawing away.

"Lies. You're full of them today."

Baldric had removed the IV but hadn't helped me dress. Some of my things had been brought over from my room in the castle to make me comfortable.

Maybe I should have gone with a dress or something fancy but those kinds of things weren't staples of my wardrobe.

I'd ended up going with something I might have worn when I interned at Uncle Will's law firm: a pair of pressed black pants, and a sapphire-colored silk blouse, tight around the wrists and under the bust, with tiny pearl buttons between my breasts.

For Faerie, I was severely underdressed.

Mike didn't seem to care, although he looked regal in a sharply cut blazer the same color as his eyes, verdant forest green struck through with gold thread.

This was the prince. And he wanted me with him.

The sweetness of the moment faded, as I knew it would, when the intrusive thoughts returned with a vengeance. The king wouldn't be in a coma if it weren't for me.

I'd provided the *Augundae Imperium* to Barbara. And Barbara was in custody. If she told the guards where she'd got the weapon—

I was in trouble.

On so many levels it wasn't even funny.

What else was new?

Mike looped his fingers through mine, tucking me close to his side and keeping his strides short to accommodate me. The walk back to the castle was the only softness we'd experience today.

The sinking sensation in my gut grew worse the closer we got.

Rather than taking a chance on alienating some very important people, drawing more attention to myself, I sent Noren back to his space in the royal menagerie the moment we reached the main courtyard of the castle.

Every part of me stiffened, tensing at the sight of the old place. Especially with the direwolf slinking around the garden and out of sight.

"It's going to be okay," Mike added. He tightened his grip on my hand. "I'll protect you when he's not around."

"Do you have any idea what they're going to discuss?" My voice shook.

He stared grimly ahead, his profile cut from granite. "I've never been in this situation before. Cosmo Foxfall reached the level of Premier for his skills, both with policy and with military. He's ruthless and strong-willed. But whatever he determines is the best course of action in my father's... absence will have to be approved by the Elder Council."

He'd chosen his words with care.

It sounded terrifying.

My footsteps felt bogged down by cement. We made it through the main castle gates and into absolute chaos.

Voices lifted in fear and anger rang out from the space adjacent to the main throne room. Although stone-faced guards manned the door, including Captain Hezarwick, they all looked distinctly ill at ease.

Mike took a moment to compose himself before his grip tightened even further on my hand, hard enough to crack my knuckles, and then he pushed through the door before anyone announced him, his personal retinue behind us.

If I expected a pause in conversation, I was mistaken. No one took a breath to show any sort of reaction to the arrival of the prince. And to my further surprise, Queen Laina wasn't in attendance.

The worry among the attendees thickened the air into something palpable.

I shouldn't be here.

The premier commandeered the head of the long polished table, with the rest of the attendees gathered around him. They stood as Mike approached, and I flinched at the way the temperature in the room dropped to frosty indifference.

"You're sitting in my father's seat," Mike pointed out.

Conversation dropped to a dull roar.

Foxfall visibly bristled at Mike's tone. He stood a hair shorter than the rest of the gathered courtiers, wearing a robe of spun silk the color of spring violets.

A row of black-beetle buttons held the two sides together and he tugged the lapels straighter. His eyes were wide set and too far apart for him to claim any of the fae's normal beauty.

"As I'm sure you are no doubt aware, the king is unable to put in an appearance, thus the reason for our meeting today."

Cosmo flicked his gaze over me, promptly dismissed me, and flashed his sharp teeth at Mike in a smile.

Dead eyes, I realized at once. Cosmo Foxfall might have the power to back up his position as second in command but he had dead eyes and they gave nothing away, which spelled disaster.

Mike wanted my opinion? My senses screamed to get the hell out of here and fast.

"Yes, I am aware of my father's condition." Mike stood to attention. "He's in a coma, fully unmakeable."

The two of them squared off silently against each other before Cosmo bowed his head and ducked to the side, automatically shifting the others down a seat to allow Mike the chair.

Rather than sitting, Mike remained standing with me at his side.

I should not be here!

Several sets of eyes remained fastened on me and I fought against the urge to sink down and disappear under the table. I gave a soft tug against Mike but he refused to let go of my hand.

"While we're on the subject of the king, I will enlighten the rest of the room to the facts." Mike curled his free hand into a fist. He paused until a full lull spread through the space. "We aren't sure what the device did to harm him and we won't likely know until he wakes up on his own and tells us. Our best doctors are unable to rouse him from his coma."

"Oh?" Cosmo's smile sharpened. "Haven't you heard, Prince Michael? We have discovered exactly what sort of device made its way back through the wards of this castle."

Mike went straight, stiff. "Why am I only hearing about this now?"

Cosmo's tone had the small hairs at the back of my neck rising to attention, and without Noren there for protection, my own wolf began to wake.

Her hackles rose, bristling at the energy in the room. Something was going on here beneath the surface.

What did Cosmo really know and how in the world had he figured things out?

Why hadn't he come to Mike straight away with the news?

"The device the witch used is our very own missing artifact, the *Augundae Imperium*." Cosmo paused for dramatic effect. "It disappeared during transport from the Fae Academy for Halflings in the mortal realm."

"I'm not sure what you're implying, Foxfall..." Mike trailed off. He glared at the premier.

"I've made the executive decision to destroy the device. We've seen clearly the sort of devastation it causes in the wrong hands." Cosmo studied his nails, his lips pursed. "Our own monarch was subject to untold horror at the hands of the device. It was too unstable to be left in one piece."

"You destroyed it? Without talking to me first?" The bite in Mike's voice brought me to attention and the rest of the room held its collective breath. "How dare you! That wasn't your decision to make."

In the silence, several low murmurs began, the other courtiers chatting amongst themselves in tones too low for even my sensitive hearing to make out.

The members of the Elder Council, with the lower half of their faces obscured by masks, remained stoic and quiet as a tomb. Taking in the proceedings and cataloging everything.

The premier appeared unbothered.

"My father wanted the *Imperium* because of the Faerie Prophecy," Mike continued in a low growl.

I stepped closer to him automatically.

"The prophecy will come to pass no matter what measures Tywin tried to enact. The fact remains: The device was much too powerful to be in the hands of *any* person. I acted in the best interest of this city and the realm. The *Imperium* has been destroyed."

He held his open palms in front of him in a what's-done-is-done gesture I automatically hated.

He was the type of person who took matters into his own hands and damned anyone else who stepped up to try and challenge him. I knew the type, marking him in a heartbeat as someone to watch.

His history and his skills elevated him to his station for a reason. We'd have to watch him. Who knew what else he'd try?

Mike waited another beat before he inclined his head. "Fine." That was all he said. And then, "What plan does the Council have for the intruder?"

The Elder Council remained quiet.

Once again, Cosmo took up the thread of the conversation. "We will be sending a team down to the dungeons to interrogate the witch and find out exactly how the *Imperium* got into her hands. Rest assured, your Royal Highness. We will get to the bottom of this matter. I've already taken steps to ensure the wards around the castle are bolstered and this sort of thing never happens again."

My mouth went dry, throat constricting painfully until it felt impossible to draw in a breath.

Terror lived in every fiber of my being. *Oh shit, no.*

My entire world stood poised and ready to crash down.

If they got Barbara to talk, then they would inevitably find out about me.

6

The rest of the meeting passed in confusion and terror. I locked my knees to keep standing, and even the final word coming down from the Elder Council couldn't get me to stop shaking.

The momentousness of the occasion did not escape me. This was it. The end of everything. The moment Barbara talked—I was a dead werewolf walking.

And I was still too weak to do anything about it.

Mike did his best to control the meeting, yet despite everything, he lapsed into silence before it ended. Cosmo stole the opportunity to grandstand, commanding the room as though we were all an audience strapped to our seats and forced to add to the laugh track.

Except no one was laughing.

The King's condition was serious, the premier hungry enough to take advantage of the situation, and everyone seemed to recognize that Mike and Laina were practically powerless.

Mike escorted me back to the hospital, quiet during our

walk, and by the time we made it to my room, my knees gave out.

He swooped in to scoop me up before I hit the floor, although my head continued to spiral dizzily.

"Too much excitement for you?" He made it less a question and more of a statement as he deposited me in bed. "I'm sorry. I'm sorry the meeting took so long. I didn't expect the proceedings to be held up like that."

He also hadn't expected Cosmo to destroy the *Augundae Imperium* without discussing it with the royal family first. Things were happening beyond our control, and even the authority of the royal bloodline wasn't working in Mike's favor.

At least that was how it seemed to me.

The premier had taken an ancient artifact and shattered it, just like that.

We'd stopped on our way out of the castle to grab Noren. Mike settled me on the bed, and a string of heartbeats later the direwolf climbed up beside me, the bed creaking ominously under his weight.

"You know, this room is too small for a direwolf," Mike suggested gently.

"He stays." I sucked in a deep breath and settled back against the pillows. "I want to keep my friend with me."

"I'm not going to fight you, not in your delicate condition."

Appreciate it.

I rested my hand on Noren's back. "I might be under the weather but I can still kick a little ass when necessary."

"I have no doubt. Except *under the weather* is an understatement. You didn't see yourself when I came to get you. You really scared me."

I shivered. "There's no reason to be scared. I'll be okay."

As long as the transfusions kept working. And how long I'd have to have them? No idea.

Nurse Baldric rounded the corner and stopped when he saw the three of us together. "Excuse the interruption."

Immediately, Mike's goofy grin fell away into the picture of propriety. "Now there's even less space in here."

Baldric glanced between the prince and the direwolf. "I'm not in a position to deny her, despite policy."

He pushed his cart toward the IV pole to start setting up.

I'd played the pity card too often with Baldric, so he knew I didn't feel good and having Noren here was a bolster. In reality, I needed backup. Just in case the guards came for me.

Not to mention he was more than a pet to me at this point.

"All right, well, I'll let you get settled in. I'm not a fan of needles and there are several things I need to handle."

I reached for him, not wanting him to go. "Thank you for spending time with me. It means a lot."

He bent to press a kiss to my head "You're the one doing me a favor. Remember that."

Despite the dizziness, I went up in flames where he touched me.

Mie nodded to Baldric before leaving the room.

Baldric waited until we were alone to set up the transfusion, sliding the needle back into the crook of my arm with a slight sting. "The prince is smitten with you."

The feeling was mutual. But I kept that thought to myself and only smiled at him. "Have you known him for a long time?" I asked. "You two seem friendly."

"Personally? I'm not sure anyone truly knows the prince or his inner world. I can only say he's been kind, kinder than most of the royals in this place, and he seems to truly care about his people."

"He's a good man."

Better than I deserved.

I turned my face to the window while Baldric finished setting up the transfusion, and when it became clear I wasn't willing to talk anymore, he exited the room.

My hand stilled on Noren and he turned to me once I stopped petting him, a question in his all too intelligent face.

"I'm sorry to say but things might get a little shitty soon. We need to be prepared."

I rested my other hand on my roiling stomach. If the guards succeeded in getting Barbara to talk, they weren't going to bother with a trial for either of us.

We would be headed straight for the executioner's ax.

I should leave, get out of here while I had the chance.

And yeah, I'd make it about a mile before I collapsed, without the transfusions. If I wanted to live, I needed them.

I shifted my head toward the door. Baldric closed it behind him when he left and I waited, on edge, for it to swing open and a swarm of guards to run through. It was only a matter of time.

I kept a close watch and hardly noticed the distinct tapping of something hard against glass. It wasn't until Noren whined that I looked over at the window at the hazy shape of a black crow perched on the ledge.

It rapped its beak against the glass again, insistent, its beady eyes focused on me. *I know that crow.* The leaping in my stomach picked up to an entirely new level.

"Noren, can you please let Bronwen in?" I said in a low voice. "I'm not sure I can move yet."

Not until the transfusion finished.

He shifted off the bed and nosed open the latch.

Bronwen hopped inside, cocking her head left and right to take in the room.

"We're alone," I assured her. "You're safe."

She gave a brief nod before she shifted back into her human form. Magic blanketed her through the transformation and once she finished, she scanned me, with her gaze lingering on the IV connected to the crook of my arm.

"Well, you look less like shit than you did the last time I saw you. So whatever that thing is, it must be working for you."

"It's good to see you too," I drawled, but the sight of her made me smile. "Even if you were skulking around."

"Skulking? It's more like *lurking* and it's done out of care. I worried about you. No one's let me in to see you" Bronwen pressed her hand to her heart. "Now tell me what's going on because this looks complicated and scientific and such."

Noren settled himself on the floor between us.

"It's a blood transfusion," I explained.

"Excuse me?" Bronwen's eyes bugged. "For what?"

"The nurse who takes care of me, Baldric, said there is something wrong with my immune system. The blood transfusions get me upright. Has to be done a couple times a day though."

Her expression went skeptical. "Are you sure?"

My lips pursed. "I mean, I'm not *sure* about anything. It's all a little too crazy to me because with my healing abilities, I should be better by now."

"You know, I spoke to the shifter doctors. Before you left. They, ah, they think something deeper is going on," she admitted. "That it's a magical problem."

Which would only confirm my own suspicions, but I didn't know enough about any of this to form a concrete opinion.

I only knew I was on my ass and nothing helped until now.

Bronwen paced back and forth, her brown hair secured in a ponytail swinging with every step. "I'm happy to see you're finally doing better, Tavi, but it seems like there's a lot more going on. I think it would be best if we talk to a dukun." At my puzzled look, she explained, "A shaman."

My senses tingled. "What do you mean, a shaman?"

"A witch doctor. You need a witch, not a fae or a shifter. A witch will be the only one who can understand the kind of magic we worked that night," Bronwen continued. Her nostrils flared and her eyes went distant and glassy. "These fae doctors are great for their type of magical maladies but we both know what we did with Madam Muerte goes beyond this. She bit you."

At her words, the bite started to throb.

Yeah, the zombie took a nasty chunk out of me. I'd been sick ever since. Baldric's explanation made sense but so did the proposition of this being something different, something no one had seen before.

"Are there even witch doctors in Faerie? Or whatever you called them. A *dukun*?" I asked.

"Oh, yeah," Bronwen agreed. "You just have to know where to find them. I mean, our people aren't supposed to be here either. There are all kinds of creatures hiding beneath the surface who don't want to be found for obvious reasons." She stopped, tapped her fingers to her chin. "Let me dig around and see what I can come up with. If you're okay with it, of course."

"Sure." It couldn't hurt, after all. At least if we got to the bottom of this blood disorder, I'd be back in fighting shape for whatever would come once Barbara spilled the truth.

"Hey, you look worried. I know you didn't just come up here to check on me. Is something else going on?"

Bronwen shifted from foot to foot and the air stilled in my chest, my lungs seized.

"What is it?"

"Okay, well, at least you're sitting down for this," she said at last.

"And I'd feel a little better if you sat, too."

"I'm too nervous to sit. I heard some disturbing rumors during our last meeting of the Claw & Fang, things trickling in from cities outside of our district."

I pushed myself up until I sat cross-legged. "What kind of rumors?"

"Apparently, there are some factions of shifters who have walked away and crossed the wall into Unseelie territory. The enchanted wall that we're not supposed to be able to cross. But they've left, just abandoned the rest of us."

This didn't bode well. Clearing my throat broke the awkward silence that had settled over us. "You mean, they're aligning with Dorian Jade?"

Bronwen frowned. "Yeah, we think so. Why else would they risk going over the wall? There's nothing for them in Unseelie territory except for him and his ridiculous rebels." She scoffed, but she'd gone pale.

"Does Selene know about this?" I asked.

Bronwen shook her head. "Selene left this morning to go on a trip back to her hometown. She won't be back for a few days."

"Hey, instead of getting all in your head about this, it might be best for you to wait until Selene gets back and talk to her, see what she knows. She's the best person to keep everyone else in line."

I was one to talk. I'd delved so far into my own head, I wondered if I'd ever get out.

"Ah, you're right." Bronwen deflated. "Of course you're right. It just seems like things are really boiling over at his point. I mean, why would our people want to join Dorian Jade?"

"Your guess is as good as mine. And I'm no help to anyone in this bed."

"Right, right. I'll go and find the dukun as soon as possible. Melia's been really wanting to find some way to help you. I'd take her with me but it seems like it might put her into more danger," Bronwen continued. "She's going crazy wanting to see you but we all know it's not really safe."

I couldn't risk having her come to visit me. "Tell her I miss her but she needs to stay away. Things are going to boil over, like you said, and sooner than we think."

"It's been hard to keep her back." Bronwen gnawed on her lip. "She's really worried."

Melia had a reason to be worried. "She's a great friend," I whispered, my eyes going teary.

"You know we're here for you, Tavi. We're all here for you. I promise I'll hunt down the witch doctor and—" She stopped short at the sound of heavy footsteps in the hallway.

I waved my hand to get her to be quiet.

"Hey. Hey!" Baldric's voice sounded from the hallway. "You can't just barge in here. Step back, please—don't!"

"Get out. Get out right now," I hissed to Bronwen. "Hurry."

Her face blanched further. Noren leapt up, his hackles raised and a low whining howl erupting from his maw.

Bronwen shifted in an instant and flew out the open

window as I ripped the needle out of my arm. I needed to be able to move, to fight.

To do whatever it took to make sure they didn't follow her.

Within seconds, the guards I'd been expecting burst into the room with their weapons drawn and aimed at me. "Tavi Alderidge? Come with us. You're under arrest for crimes against the royal family."

As the soldier dropped his hold on me, I lost my balance and stumbled, arms windmilling.

Noren attacked beautifully. He made quick work of the soldier and left the fae a mess of blood and armor.

I started to speak but my senses screamed at me to keep moving and my heart jackhammered into my throat.

Noren straightened, shook his head and sent blood spraying everywhere, and with the fever pitch inside of me rising higher, we took off.

He shifted to my side to help me along but my legs were weak and my muscles sore. No matter how hard I pushed, I couldn't go as fast as I normally would.

The ragged pulsing of my heart blotted out every other sound and obliterated my other senses. Fear was fuel. I didn't have the energy to keep going. Or to stop and beg for a break.

Adrenaline leached out of me as fast as my system produced it.

Another corner and two guards stood waiting for me. The soldier on the left broke out in a dazzling smile. They lifted their weapons, and I held out a hand as if it would make an actual difference.

"You see nothing." The command lifted out of me on instinct.

I had no strength left for transfiguration. My cognitive manipulation rose of its own accord. *So much for accomplishing great things.* I used my gifts to survive.

The soldiers stopped in their tracks with identical gazes unfocused.

Without the spell, I had no way to see their energy signatures clearly. I still reached for their minds with a pulse of magic.

"I'm not here. Neither of us are here. You'll leave us alone."

What I saw didn't matter. I had to make sure the soldiers perceived that what I told them was true. And I wasn't going to wait around to see if the command stuck.

In the lull, Noren and I took off again.

The spell wore off when we were halfway down the block and their shouts trailed us.

Adrenaline filtered through me and urged me on faster than my weak body could accommodate. Noren had to slow his strides to stay with me, but turned to gnash his teeth at the soldiers when they inevitably caught up to us.

I kept moving even as Noren attacked the two fae and took them down until their screams cut off abruptly.

Faster, faster.

I had to go faster if I wanted out of here.

Where was I going, though? Where *could* I go? My head spun, and somewhere along the way I lost one of my shoes. The hair on the back of my forearms prickled with awareness, and when I tried to call for the change again, nothing happened.

"Tavi?"

I swiveled automatically at the sound of Mike calling my name. Before I could take a step toward him, a guard swung his fist and slammed his knuckles into my temple.

I saw Mike in the distance, clutching a handful of flowers to his chest, before I dropped, out cold.

THE SLOW DRIP of water on stone came first, before my other senses returned.

I focused on the sound, the sensation of cold unyielding

stone beneath my back. A few more breaths and I found the strength to open my eyes. I regretted it instantly.

The pain returned along with a swell of dizziness and a sickening drop as I realized the truth—without the transfusions, I'd go right back into the sickness that plagued me before.

Noren wasn't with me, either.

Had he gotten away? He wasn't locked down here with me. I'd know.

Dread pressed down heavily and I lost my breath. Worry for the direwolf overrode anxiety about being in the cell. I knew exactly where I'd been brought to.

Darkness pressed closer, but not unconsciousness. Literal darkness. There were no windows, no bars to let in ambient light. *Absolutely nothing.*

I managed to haul myself into a seated position, taking a second to let my head stop spinning like a top.

I shuffled around on my hands and knees, sweeping my arm across the ground in front of me until I felt a wall.

More stone.

I moved until my fingers brushed against the ninety degree juncture of two walls. From what I made out, two of the walls were bars. The space between the metal wasn't large enough for me to reach my hand through, however.

I trailed my fingers along the metal.

"You know, you make an awful racket no matter where you go, Tavi. For someone with your skills, you should know better."

The voice came out of the darkness and I recognized the whiskey-smoke tone.

"You snitched on me," I growled at Barbara, my companion in this prison. My stomach roiled. "I wouldn't be here if you hadn't told them everything."

"Everything?" Barbara said, and her subsequent laugh tapered into a hacking cough. "Do you really think I would have given them *everything*? Shame on you."

"I think I wouldn't be here if you didn't."

But that wasn't entirely true. They came for me no matter how hard I'd fought, and at this point, even the anger petered out underneath the weight of fear.

"You poor, deluded little girl. I didn't snitch on you. The premier himself used magic to force the truth out of me. I had no control over what I said." She paused a beat, and then— "But I'm sorry."

The apology, as surprising as it was to hear, also sounded genuine. I shivered, hugging my arms around my knees and drawing into a tight ball.

"He's a special little freak, the premier, let me tell you. So many delicious things going on in his head. I don't need power to know he's got some major mental issues. He's lucky he's got magic. Painful magic, too."

Barbara groaned as if reliving what she'd gone through.

Well, shit.

"So why the King?" I had to know. "You're not even Fae. What beef do you have with Tywin?"

"I swear, there's no reprieve, even here in this hell hole." The sound of fabric shifting from Barbara's cell, and when she spoke again she seemed closer. "Just more questions."

"I have a lot of them," I told her defiantly.

"And your first one isn't to ask me if I know of a way outta here?" She choked out another raspy, bitter laugh.

It was my turn to scoff. "I've been here before. I know there's no way out until they come to get us and take us..."

"You can say it, girl. It's not like I'm the stupid old witch you always took me for. We're gonna die. Premier Foxfall isn't a kind man and he will never forgive me for what I told him. Under duress, I will stress." Again came her hacking smoker's cough. "So, why the king? You really want to know?"

I nodded before I realized she couldn't see me. "Yeah, I do."

"Are you settled in? Because it's story time."

"I'm not going anywhere."

In addition to the lack of light, something about the stones muted sound here. No one would hear us scream. It also made hearing her a little difficult.

I leaned against the bars, dropping my forehead into the space between them to better hear her.

If she was even going to be honest. My gut told me yes.

"A few hundred years ago, as all the stories begin, a witch married a fae man," Barbara said with all the magnanimity of a seasoned storyteller. "She thought it was a match of love because, let's face it, sometimes good dick can *really* cloud your judgment. At least, it did for the witch."

"You're telling me that you're the witch?" I pressed.

"Shut up or I'm not going to finish."

Her usual acerbic wit helped ground me and I found myself grinning in the darkness.

"As is usually the case, the romance eventually petered out, and his eyes began to wander. Not to other women, because the witch was, naturally, a great beauty." Barbara sounded proud of herself. "But to gambling dens. Anywhere he might go to get his next high. The debts began to rise. They mounted until they were too large for the couple to overcome together. And in order to pay off the debts to the kingdom, the man sold his own child to the royal family. He stole the witch's firstborn, her joy, her heart...her daughter."

A shiver shook me and ice crept down my spine from the base of my neck to my tailbone.

I wouldn't like where this story was going.

I had no choice but to listen and I didn't want to miss a word.

"The king fell in love with the little girl once she matured into a woman, and he bewitched her with fae magic to forget her past. He obliterated her memories of her life outside of him and his vile, corrupt court." Barbara stopped, and her hiccup, if I hadn't known her, might have almost been a sob. "I came here to get my daughter back. She's all I've ever wanted."

"How...old are you, Barbara?"

"Old enough to know you never ask a woman her age, girl. Haven't you learned anything? But to slake your curiosity, I'm nearly 500 years old. And I've spent the last three hundred or so of those years doing whatever it took to hack my way into this cursed fucking palace."

The pieces fit together, finally clicking into place. My mouth rounded in an O and a small groan of distress got past my defenses.

"Queen Laina is your daughter."

No. Way.

A low moan escaped my thinned lips.

Barbara sighed. "I know what you're thinking. Your thoughts are as loud as you are. You're wondering how she can be so beautiful and I look like this? Well, it takes a whole lot of magic to get into this realm. Magic comes at a cost. Didn't I tell you that once?"

So she'd given away most of her beauty to gain the power to get to this point.

I dropped my head to my knees. "I'm so sorry." It was my turn to apologize. "I can't imagine how it must feel to be separated from your kid."

Had *my* mother tried, like Barbara, to get to me even when things felt hopeless? I had to hope.

"I wanted Tywin to pay for taking my child, not only the marriage but for accepting the absolutely ridiculous trade my own husband made, may he rest in eternal fucking misery, in the first place. That's why I did what I did. And I almost succeeded."

Barbara sounded wistful.

"You wanted me to give you the *Imperium* so you'd have enough magic to get to Tywin," I said.

Barbara sighed again. "I'm the Scooby Doo villain in this case, girl. I've lived in the mortal realm for too long."

"Five hundred years old and you still weren't powerful enough to actually kill the king."

Which meant no one would be able to. If she couldn't accomplish it with the *Imperium*—

"Hey, I got through the wards and put that son of a bitch in a coma. Not nearly far enough, as far as I'm concerned, but I'll never stop trying. My daughter is worth more to me than anything else. She's everything."

It made so much sense now. Laina was a half witch and had to hide her truth from everyone. Tywin of course knew exactly who he'd married and all about Laina's past.

He must have constantly been on guard expecting an attack. That Barbara had managed to get into the castle and reach him was nothing short of a miracle.

The *Augundae Imperium* should have been able to do so much more, though. It had been heralded as one of the most powerful weapons in existence. Yet it failed to kill Tywin, and Cosmo Foxfall destroyed it easily.

So what had happened?

"Now we're never getting out of here and I still haven't been able to reach my daughter. That's the rub, isn't it?"

"What about your doomsday prepping?" I wanted to know.

"Wouldn't you prepare for the end if you knew an entire kingdom would be coming after you? I had enough supplies for me and Laina."

But what about her grandson?

The knot in my chest began to twist and writhe as though it was alive. Mike was Barbara's grandson. Holy fuckballs. Oh, god, why did it make me feel so strange to consider?

The lights suddenly flashed on with such intensity that pain shot through my skull from front to back. The world exploded and dark spots danced in front of my eyes until I got control of myself.

Footsteps sounded, and seconds later a familiar form swam into view.

"Mike?" I scrambled up and gripped the bars, using them to haul myself up to my feet. "Mike, what are you doing here?"

He stared at me without sparing a glance at the prisoner in the other cell.

I couldn't look away from him. He was the single source of air in this desolate place.

The fae light behind him turned his hair into glinting gold but none of the warmth extended to his eyes. They were as frigid as glaciers as he stared at me.

"I really thought after everything we've been through we were finally at a point where we could be honest with each other. Didn't you promise me, Tavi? Did you say you wouldn't lie to me anymore?"

"Mike, I'm so sorry—"

He cut me off with a sweep of his hand. "I don't understand why you stole the *Imperium* and teamed up with a witch. At this point, that's not even the real issue for me. You kept it from me. You put me at a disadvantage not only with us but with the premier and the Elder Council. I needed leverage and you knocked my legs out from under me."

"Give me the chance to explain," I urged, then reeled backward from the woozy feeling in my skull. "I-I met Barbara before I entered the Fae Academy, because I needed a potion to suppress my shifter side. I had to steal the *Imperium* for her as payment."

He shook his head. "At this point...I'm not sure what to think or how to feel about you. It seems like every time I think we've turned a corner, there's another secret, another lie. You're not the woman I thought you were."

The kicker of the matter was that he spoke the truth. "If I tell you this is the last one?" I asked meekly.

"Then I'd tell you I'm at a point where I can't believe you about anything." He abruptly turned on his heel and left.

I stared after him long after the lights went out again, and Barbara, in the nicest thing she'd ever done for me, kept her mouth shut.

8

The lights the guards used were extinguished, Barbara and I the only two prisoners this deep in the dungeons, and everyone was content to let us rot.

In the oppressive cells, time became impossible to track. It might have been two hours or it might have been two days.

There were no meals to mark the passage of time and no sunlight to indicate day or night.

Nothing, no one.

Only guilt and terror, which had to be the point. My swimmy-headedness increased, and more often than not I fell asleep and woke up sicker than when I'd dropped off.

Without Baldric to give me transfusions, I'd get worse. And worse. *Not like it matters*. At this point, the clock only counted down toward an inevitable end.

They were not letting us out of here, and by lying to Mike, I'd alienated the only person who might save me.

"That handsome blond boy is my daughter's son, is he not? Why don't you tell me what you've been doing with my grandson?" Barbara asked with an incredulous whisper. "The two of you seem mighty cozy."

"It's none of your business," I snapped, sucking air in through my nostrils. Nothing helped the queasiness.

"Seems as though it's absolutely my business. He's my flesh and blood. I'm well within my rights to worry about him."

"I'm not willing to talk about it, then. Mike and I are friends." We were more than friends but like hell I'd tell Barbara.

"Friends, absolutely. That's a fine word for it. I might not know about your life but I understand people, and that boy is my kin. He's got the same kind of blood I do, hiding behind a thin veil of nobility. Makes sense you'd find each other. Given who *you* are."

"What's that supposed to mean?"

She laughed at me. "You'll find out eventually, girl. They always do."

I tried to answer her, to assure her of Mike's genuinely good heart, and found my throat had closed again. I gasped, desperately trying to suck in enough oxygen.

"You're not feeling well. What's wrong?"

I slammed my palm into my chest, hard enough to dislodge whatever had congested my throat, and coughed until tears pricked the corners of my eyes.

The coughing only exacerbated the nausea until I found myself curled on the floor, dry heaving. There was nothing to puke up. Nothing in my system to come out.

My head spun around in endless circles.

"Tavi? Talk to me."

Hearing my name come out of Barbara's mouth centered me and I clung to it like a raft in an angry ocean. "I was... bitten," I found myself admitting.

And in spits and spats, I managed to get out the entire story of raising Madam Muerte from the dead and having her zombie take a bite out of me.

Barbara waited until the end of my story to huff out a laugh. "You've been busy. Much busier than I gave you credit for, you industrious little wolfie. Now come here."

"What?" I croaked.

"Come to the bars and I'll assess what's going on inside of you. You get bitten by a witch, only a witch can heal you. And your Madam Muerte? Before her untimely passing?" Barbara snorted. "Pure witch."

She made it sound so simple.

I wasn't sure about that, but I was either going to die of this illness in a prison cell or be executed. What was the harm? I might as well let Barbara do whatever it was she wanted to do.

"I thought you didn't have your magic."

"Did I say I ran out of power? Hell no, girl, I've got *some* magic. It just doesn't do me a shit load of good in here. Now get over to the bars and try not to puke on me. I feel disgusting enough as it is."

The last time I'd seen her in the real world, Barbara looked as thin as a rail and highly breakable. Not much had changed, apparently. Her slender wrists fit between the bars, and the moment I crawled over to her, she latched onto me, forcing my hand all the way through as well.

Her palms were dry, callused, her knuckles almost too large for the size of her hand when she took hold. But her witch's magic rushed over me in a soothing wave. I swooned, eyes fluttering back into my head.

It felt oddly familiar.

The same sensation I'd once experienced when I walked through her barriers to reach her house. The heaviness, strange after so long feeling nothing but sickness, fell over me and disappeared in the next inhalation.

I breathed in deep, filling my lungs, and the air itself felt fresher, colored by a hint of her power. My senses tingled and everything smoothed out into a sense of serene calm.

Even my overheated skin began to cool.

I didn't have a drop of witch blood inside of me. Right? Then why did I vibe so well with Barbara and her magic?

It made no sense and my head spun for a completely different reason: confusion.

Barbara finally released my hand and I held onto the bars until my system righted itself.

"It's a kind of blood poisoning, from magic," she said in the gloom. "So yeah, whatever transfusions the nurse gave you, they were helping to keep the poison at bay. But, girl, that's only a temporary fix." She sighed, the sound long and forlorn. "It won't last forever."

"Then what do I need to do?" I was desperate.

"Seriously? You have to get the *antidote*." I practically saw her rolling her eyes at my stupidity. "There is a certain type of flower you will need to mix with dirt from the old broad's grave. Once you mix the two, you ingest it. Yum, yum."

My gorge rose at the thought and I gagged.

The last place I wanted to be was back at the graveyard. After what happened when Bronwen and I tried to raise the old gypsy woman from the dead?

Necromancy got me into this pickle in the first place.

It wasn't as though Barbara was asking me to try to raise Muerte from the dead again, but the idea of going back gave me the creeps. "Isn't there any other way?"

"No." That single word was knife-sharp in the dark. "I can do a small spell to take the edge off but it would be like a Band-aid on a bullet hole. Do you get what I'm saying? You need the *actual* cure. And I'm trying to give it to you if you'd pull the cotton out of your ears and listen to me."

I sighed. "Yeah, well, the *actual* cure isn't going to do me any good if we don't get out of here."

"So glum," she chided acerbically.

"Of course I'm glum. Beyond glum."

Barbara made a low sound of ridicule before saying, "Well, give me your hand back, and I'll work my magic on you."

"What's it going to cost me?" At least this time I understood how it worked.

"How about we say this one is on the house? It's the least I can do...since you're in here with me. Or if it makes you feel better to think I'm doing this for my grandson, since he's moon-eyed over you, then consider it that way."

"As much as I hate it, I'm going to take you up on your offer." I slid my hand back along the bars until I knocked into her palm.

Her magic flowed over me and the dizziness cleared. Everything inside of me went sharp and focused, and for a moment the shock almost overwhelmed me, because I felt like my old self again.

The strong and assured self I'd been before my life took a crazy turn into terror and panic.

"Wow, I do feel better, thank you."

Barbara released me again and I immediately missed the warmth of her callused palm. "Don't thank me yet."

Wind ripping through the passage echoed the ominous tone of her voice.

When would there be time to thank her, then? Because we both knew beyond a shadow of a doubt there was no getting out of this cell until the council and premier demanded our presence.

And then it would only be a matter of time until—

The end.

We'd reached the end of the road, yet the journey felt so far from being finished I could barely put words to the sensation.

More time passed in the damp decay before the echoing thud of footsteps roused me out of half sleep. The lights popped on, blinding and dazzling, but this time I was ready.

I hid my eyes, ducking my head to avoid the flashing sensation of black dots.

Several guards strode around the corner with their shoulders squared and their attention on the bars. One of them stepped away from the others with a set of keys in his hand.

"Come with us," he grunted. "The premier and the Elder Council will see you both now."

Ice frosted over my heart.

Two more guards came into my cell and I didn't need to look to know Barbara experienced the same rough treatment. They slapped a pair of magic-damping cuffs over my wrists and immediately the simmer of power always beneath my skin drained away, cut off without mercy.

I reeled at the loss, and in the adjustment period, they hauled me to my feet and out of the cell.

Barbara was dragged behind me, defenseless. Powerless in a way that neither of us had ever been before.

Except I'd been in the dungeon before, subjected to those cuffs, although the last time I'd been forced in front of a jury it had consisted only of the king. Now, the worry was no less severe and sickening.

There was no escape.

No way I'd be able to overpower any of these guards. None of them were recognizable, either, as they took us both into a separate small chamber down the hall from the massive throne room.

The door thudded closed behind us. The sound jolted me out of my skin but the guards didn't stop pushing us forward until we stood shoulder to shoulder in front of Cosmo Foxfall.

Two members of the Elder Council sat beside him but otherwise we were alone in the room.

Alarm became a wave of fire inside of me but did nothing to thaw my heart.

"I'm sure you were both expecting a much larger crowd." Cosmo flicked at the fabric of his trousers above his knees before he leaned forward and fixed me with a hard stare.

Barbara scoffed, but when I looked over at her, I was shocked to see a stone gag slapped across her mouth and glowing with magic to keep her silent. Regardless, she glared at the others with such ferocity I gulped.

If I were Cosmo Foxfall, no matter what kind of precautions they took I'd be scared of Barbara.

Her hair stood out on end, her wrinkles deeper than the last time I'd seen her, but her eyes were lit with an inner fire that was downright frightening.

"This is no ordinary case, as I'm sure you're both aware. Thus there is no need for a public trial or the presence of the courtiers or the royal family," Cosmo continued.

"This is a sentencing," I said out loud.

They'd already reached their verdict, without us.

Cosmo nodded. "Exactly. The Council and I both agree that it is in the best interest of the royal court, Eahsea, and Faerie in general for the two of you to be eradicated as soon as possible."

Eradicated. Not killed. Wiped from the face of the earth.

"You are both sentenced to execution for your crimes," he finished grandly.

"That's it?" I strained against the guards and they didn't have to work hard to get me back in place. Despair and terror flushed my cheeks. "You're not even going to ask me why? To listen to my side of the story?"

"I'm not interested in your side," Cosmo replied with a sniff. "You stole from the crown. Your thievery resulted in a threat to the life of the king which put him in a coma. You have reached the end of the patience of this court. Above and beyond, Miss Alderidge. You are finished."

He snapped his fingers, and we were taken away.

9

No chance to defend myself, although telling my side of the story would never result in mercy. Cosmo was right: I'd already done too much, skirted a line more often than not, for them to even consider listening to me.

There was nothing left to say. I was beyond redemption and better off dead.

Barbara and I never stood a chance of getting out of this and we'd both known it. She'd made her move. And the second she did, I was doomed to go down with her.

One day after our meeting with Cosmo Foxfall, the guards returned to draw us from the cells. They marched us up out of the dungeon and through the main courtyard outside the castle. The cuffs on my wrist had been amended with a pair of matching chains on my ankles. They dragged against the cobblestone with every shortened step forward.

My stomach dipped, swirling as queasy heat spiraled in my gut. My mouth went dry and stayed that way.

We were long past feeling sick over the situation, though. Long past trying to figure a way out. The only chance I had was from the outside and I clung to my flawed sense of hope.

Maybe, just maybe, someone would step in and help free me. Something had to happen, right? Something had to give.

Surely Mike would never let them kill me.

We loved each other.

I thought we loved each other.

My palms were clammy, my teeth chattering.

I might have lied to him about the *Imperium* but he had to know I never lied about my feelings for him. But if he truly believed I was a part of some plot against his family—

No contest, then. Lover versus kingdom. He'd choose his family and his loyalty to his people over me.

It wasn't like we were mates. That bond, for wolves, trumped anything else. Everything else.

They marched us into the center courtyard toward a small wooden platform the premier had ordered to be built.

Voices grew louder, and once we stepped into the blinding sunlight, I saw a massive crowd gathered. The gates were closed but innumerable fae pressed against the bars, jeering and craning their necks for a look at the execution.

I swallowed hard, my throat closing, my stomach twisting in agony.

Someone already stood on the platform.

Onyx Grimaldi turned his head to watch my approach, his eyes neutral and unfathomable. Those eyes had lost the jaded bitterness they'd sported when I first met him. His aquiline nose now boasted an unhealed hump at its center from being broken, and his platinum-white hair had grown out on the sides though it was still longer at the top. His goatee and mustache were white, his eyebrows dark, and his lips thinned.

He'd hurt people, he'd killed, and the last time I saw him he'd been strapped to a hospital bed trying to heal from injuries *I'd* inflicted. Dark circles drew attention to his turquoise-blue eyes which met mine without blinking. The closer we got, the easier it was to recognize his scent. *Pack.*

I wanted to reach for him and envelop myself in his familiar smell. To squeeze my own eyes shut and pretend this was a dream. Hyperventilating, I held his gaze with a plea in mine.

Save me. Help me save us.

Clearly he'd been sentenced as well, and today was chosen for all of us to meet our end. I missed my next step and stumbled, the chains clinking together.

His resolve, the bravery written across every line of his face...it impressed me. On multiple levels. He chose to meet his end without breaking a sweat or begging for mercy.

Fuck. I wanted half of his courage despite my hope of a last-minute save.

The guards holding me kept back while the others ushered Barbara up the steps and situated her beside Onyx. The old witch's eyes were clear and her jaw set. Her teeth were no doubt clenched together beneath the magical gag.

She cast an acidic glare around to the rest of the crowd that at once belittled and shamed anyone who met her eyes.

Premier Foxfall stood nearby with the others on his Council, watching the proceedings closely. I saw no hint of Mike or Queen Laina anywhere. Had they decided not to attend?

Several loud whoops and hollers came from the crowd outside the gates. They wanted this to hurry up, wanted to see the show, or whatever constituted an execution in Faerie.

It seemed archaic to me. Something private would have

been much better than this terrifying yet humiliating spectacle.

The guards began to push me up the steps of the platform when Captain Hezarwick jogged over and held up a hand, his white gloves spotless.

"Prince Michael has asked for one last word with Tavi Alderidge." He spoke directly to the other men, not to me, his voice hard.

My stomach took a rapid series of flips one right after the other. Mike actually wanted to talk to me. This was it. This was the saving grace I'd been hoping for...he wasn't going to let me die. *Not today.*

It was too soon to tell as the guards reversed my direction.

I felt Barbara and Onyx staring at me, their gazes like daggers through my back, as the others led me away toward a small alcove dug into the outside of the castle. It hadn't been set up as a viewing station, at least.

Mike stood in the shadows with his arms limp at his sides. He stared over my head at my approach and fixed Captain Hezarwick with a dour, disapproving scowl. "We're not to be disturbed. Do you understand?"

"She might be dangerous, Sir," one of the guards commented. "You need someone to—"

"She's weighed down with magic-damping chains. How much danger can she present?" His tone held a warning. "Give us some privacy."

He wasn't asking. This was a side of Mike that I rarely saw, where he made demands and the others jumped to do his bidding.

The guards hesitated only a moment longer before they trailed the captain a few feet away, turning their backs to us. Mike lifted a hand and a silencing bubble fell around us to shut away the noise from the outside world. It was thicker than anything I'd seen him work before.

"Tavi." Immediately, his tone and demeanor changed. His eyes went round, glassy. "Mom and I have been fighting Cosmo all night to get the execution order rescinded. So far nothing we've said has made any kind of difference."

He was frantic, and listening to him, my resolve gave way to every last raw nerve I'd been trying to ignore. I reached for him and stopped at the last moment as my chains clicked together.

"Mike, you have to do something. He refuses to rescind, right? He wants me dead."

"The premier is power hungry," Mike admitted. He bit down on his lower lip. "He's taken over the castle with Dad still in a coma. There's nothing Mom or I can do, especially when he has the might of the Elder Council at his back. They won't stand up to him. This is the opportunity they've been waiting for, to gain more ground, and he's using you and the others to make a statement."

"It's not what you think, Mike, I swear—"

"We don't have time for you to explain," he cut in. "Here. Take this." He reached behind him and drew out a small globe-shaped hunk of metal which he then placed between my palms. "You need it."

Recognition raged through me. "What did you do?" I lost my breath.

"It's the *Augundae Totalis*. It amplifies the magic of the one who uses it. I smuggled it out of Faerie and used it to do better in classes. You're going to need it to get out."

"But the chains. I can't use my magic at all."

"The *Totalis* nullifies magic-blocking attempts. Trust me, Tavi. If you use it with your cognitive manipulation then you should be able to amplify your powers and enchant the entire crowd. You've got to save yourself."

Those green eyes met mine and I found myself wanting to cry.

"Mike, you don't know what this means to me," I managed to get out.

"Look, I admit I don't know what to believe. But I know I can't lose you, Tavi. Okay? Do whatever it takes to get out of this because my hands are tied. This is the only way I can help."

He looked ready to kiss me and despite the sickening dip in my abdomen, I lifted my face to his.

"Sir? We're out of time. We have to take her up now." Captain Hezarwick returned and I hurried to hide the *Totalis* beneath my shirt where no one would see it.

Thank god for stretchy pants.

"I'm sorry."

Mike's last words for me were a death knell and horror filled me. My cheeks paled.

Not that I doubted the *Totalis* would work. I'd seen the way it helped Mike, amplifying his powers to help get him through the last year we spent at the Halfling Academy in the human world. But I was fighting against the cuffs, the chains on my ankles, Cosmo Foxfall, and the rest of his posse.

Was I strong enough to do this?

I kept my hands clasped in front of me and my head down on my way back to the platform. When I finally lifted my face, Barbara was gone already.

They killed her that fast.

My jaw dropped and a pang of regret clanged through me. I hadn't been fast enough to do anything for her. Barbara was just a mother who wanted to get her daughter back. She hadn't been an evil witch trying to take down an empire. Not the way they'd made her out to be.

"Keep moving."

The guards were not unkind but they also weren't about to let me stand and feel my feelings. They hustled me onto the platform in the empty space next to Onyx, where Barbara had stood before I'd been pulled aside.

Onyx gave me the side-eye, and I thought I caught the flash of an encouraging smile. The best I could do was not cry.

If I couldn't work the *Totalis*, I was as good as gone, and Onyx with me.

My gaze scoured the crowd and I found Mike's face among the courtiers. Once again, he pointedly avoided looking at me, his expression carefully pinned in place and giving nothing away.

Cosmo's voice was magically amplified, the way I'd seen during the Faerie Trials. It reached across the courtyard and out over the people outside the castle gates as clearly as though he stood only a foot away.

"Today we have gathered here to eliminate our enemies. To mark the occasion and to show that any future enemies who attempt to stand against the crown will be dealt with accordingly, I've allowed you all the opportunity to bear witness!"

Cheering erupted at his statement.

"We have already seen the demise of one such enemy, the barbaric witch who attacked our beloved King Tywin!" Cosmo paused. "Let no one stand against the monarchy and go unpunished. Let no one attempt to take down our royal family and live."

I gulped hard, the metal of the *Totalis* warming against my skin.

A flash of movement in the distance caught my attention and my senses sharpened. There, in the shadows, crouched the direwolf. Watching. Waiting. Somehow the rest of the crowd had focused too much on the platform to be disturbed by the presence of the massive lupine form.

And somehow I knew that he understood: I had the tool and I was about to make a run for it. Noren was waiting for me to get the hell out of here. Somehow seeing him there made the stakes even higher. I had to escape. I had to take the chance that the tool would work.

Even if I might not be powerful enough to entrance the entire crowd.

I nodded to Noren.

Oh my god.

My god.

One shot to save my own life, and to save Onyx, the way I hadn't been able to save Barbara.

Cosmo Foxfall still addressed the crowd, and after a few more lofty statements of pure posturing, he clapped his hands together. Called for silence. And gestured for the guards to proceed.

The execution was set, and just as a swell of magic rose around us, I reached under my shirt to grab the *Totalis*.

10

"**S**he has something in her hands!"

Captain Hezarwick's voice sounded above the rest of the din, and in the next second he bolted forward, his magic reaching for me.

The *Totalis* warmed further once I had it firmly cradled in my hands, direct contact, and as I tuned into my magic, my hesitation dimmed.

The *Augundae Totalis* was ancient, foreign, almost alien in its depth of power, and my physical body jerked as that power entwined with the essence of who I was.

"Stop right where you are!"

There's no stopping.

My cognitive manipulation rose despite any shredded emotions. A rare gift, I'd been told once. Rare and valuable. And I'd never been so grateful for it as I was now.

"No." My voice rose much louder than it would have been, amplified by the artifact. "You stop. All of you."

The captain did as I commanded, his footsteps slowing until he halted in front of the platform, with the rest of the guards behind him frozen in the act of drawing their weapons.

I paused for a moment to mutter a spell under my breath, something I'd been taught to hone my focus before I reached out for the minds and energies of everyone gathered. I blocked out the future and what might happen if I failed. I blocked out Mike in the crowd and my regret over what happened to Barbara. The bulk of my power needed to focus on escape.

This gift did not manifest often, I reminded myself. I had the magic for a reason. If it wasn't to save my life and the lives of people I cared about, then what good was it?

I took a deep breath. "Stop the execution. Onyx and I are innocent. Cosmo Foxfall has decided to rescind his execution order," I continued.

My magic rose to a fever pitch and I spared a glance at the glowing tool. It really *did* amplify power. I felt everything, roiling inside of me, magnified larger than I'd ever felt it before.

I practically saw it in the air like visible sound waves cresting over everyone. Even the bodies outside the gate went still as my command rippled outward.

"Onyx and I are leaving," I called out. "Captain Hezarwick, remove our chains immediately. We're free."

I reached for the premier and saw his energy signature clearly. It pulsed around him in shades of navy and gold with a thin core of startling red. I grabbed for him, my power clearer and sharper than it had ever been, and sent a powerful pulse of magic his way.

He had to believe *everything* I painted for him. Sights, smells, images—even if I didn't see it in reality, it didn't matter. Foxfall would perceive it all as true.

I held his magic, and distantly the energy signatures of the rest of the crowd, while the captain removed my chains. A huge weight disappeared as they clanked to the ground, Onyx's following right after.

There wasn't time to breathe a sigh of relief. "Nobody moves from their spot for the next fifteen minutes. You stay exactly where you are until we are well out of reach," I added.

"Tavi? What are you doing?" Onyx hissed from the corner of his mouth.

He was the only one immune to my spell.

"Isn't it obvious? I'm getting us out." I spoke in the same hushed near-whisper and gestured for him to come closer, still gripping the tool in my hands.

Sweat broke out along my spine, dripping to my lower back with the effort of holding on to so many energies at once.

Onyx spared a skeptical glance at the statue-still crowd before he stepped over the chains pooled at his feet. He wasn't about to waste any more time but instead of running, I forced my feet to slow. Calm and unhurried, we walked to the steps and out into the crowd.

My heart hammered against my ribs. I clutched the tool tighter yet, afraid of it slipping out of my clammy palms.

What if I missed someone?

What if there was a guard out there, or a civilian, someone on the Council, impervious to my magic?

Miraculously, we managed to weave our way through the courtyard. Onyx kept close enough for the heat of his body to seep beneath my skin, but even so, I shivered.

I glared from one person to another, paying special attention to Cosmo Foxfall. He stared straight ahead, frozen solid, and soon we were past him.

I didn't stop until we met up with Noren.

"How in the world did you manage—" Onyx started.

"Later." I smiled at the direwolf as he bolted toward the side gate. "I'll explain it all later."

We had less than fifteen minutes to get as far away as possible before everyone unfroze. Because at that point, the spellwork might be too thin and my cognitive manipulation unable to remain in place.

Cosmo would remember that we were not innocent. He'd send an entire army after us.

Shit, this had to work, just long enough to let us leave.

My fingers were frozen to the *Totalis*, my pulse thundering in my ears.

Noren wound through the gate, squeezing to get his frame through. Onyx followed, with me going last, sending one last thought toward Mike before we disappeared and broke into a run.

Find me.

The cobblestone streets were eerily silent. Too many citizens of the city had gathered to watch the execution.

Neither of us moved fast. I'd spent too much time in the dungeons for my muscles to respond with my usual strength, and forget about grace. Necessity drove us around the side of the castle and back to the rear greenspace. The field stretched, gently sloping upward toward the forest circling the city. The trees were old, their trunks fat and their branches spreading in a thick canopy overhead.

We'd trained there when Melia first set me up with Onyx, the only other half shifter in her acquaintance.

The paths through those trees were familiar.

Onyx limped but he never complained at the pace.

The climb made talk impossible, both of us too focused on getting as far away from the courtyard as possible. My lungs heaved like bellows and my muscles tensed and strained.

No looking back. There *was* no going back after this.

We moved farther away from the village with each passing breath and into the wilds. The trees grew closer together the farther we went, away from the manicured tending of the palace landscapers.

Only the sound of my name, spoken in a strangled whisper, had me pausing enough to look up. The sky overhead had darkened without me noticing and seconds later a crack of lightning split the sky.

Noren led the way and seemed unbothered when the thunder rolled, the sound like two stones grinding together. The lightning continued to worsen as we scrambled higher and higher.

Soon, hopefully, we'd crest the edges of the mountains around Eahsea, the town cradled in the valley between the ranges. I had no idea what was on the other side or how close we were.

Another bolt of lightning, and the rain poured as though someone split open a seam in the sky.

Faerie was upset.

The same thing had happened the first week I came here, and I knew inherently this weather was my fault.

I'd saved myself but the magic I'd used had caused a stir in the natural elements of this entire land.

My insides were wrecked as surely as if someone had slid their claws across my guts. Everything I'd had to do since coming here had been awful, terrible, for this land.

I really was going to be its destruction. Even though I'd done my best to minimize my impact, the land knew. I knew. Nothing I'd done had been good enough and now the natural elements, the very weather, retaliated.

Noren paused in front of a boulder to glance back at us and huff out a small whine. The rain plastered his fur to his skin.

Chilled to the bone, I scrambled up the rockface, my fingertips numb and the *Totalis* still clutched in the other hand. "I think we're getting close to the top," I called back to Onyx.

Then stopped short when I noticed him several yards away and leaning against a tree trunk for support.

He glanced up at me and nodded, his white hair stuck to his cheeks. He was flagging badly and his limp was noticeably worse as he struggled to close the gap between us.

"Hey, how about we try to find somewhere to rest," I offered. "This rain is going to get worse. Hopefully it will work to our advantage and cover our scents."

He was too out of breath to answer.

I wanted to get farther but the weather and Onyx's condition made the going too slow to be safe. I glanced around, nodding at Noren until he jogged off. A few seconds later he returned and flashed his teeth in a terrifying facsimile of a canid smile.

"This way." I gestured for Onyx to follow and then decided better, heading over and offering him my shoulder to lean on.

He refused and limped ahead as we followed Noren through the trees.

The thin trail wound through several rocky outcroppings, and loose gravel skidded under our feet.

Eventually the trail widened out, taking a sharp turn and ending in a broad flat spot. Noren huffed for us to continue and I lost him around the next bend. The view of the valley was barely visible through the driving rain, and although I didn't see the castle, we were still too close for my peace of mind.

Noren found a cave large enough for the three of us to crouch together. At least we'd have shelter and a chance to talk. I told myself it was a good thing, a great thing, but I refused to let go of the tool on the off chance someone followed us. It worked on a crowd. It would work on a single person, if my magic held.

At this point it was a big *if*—I already felt my strength waning.

I snuggled against Noren, the tightness of the space leaving little room for any of us to move. My shiver deepened as the chill sank deep into my bones.

"This is because of me," I murmured. "The weather. Faerie knows I don't belong."

Onyx scoffed, the bags under his eyes heavy enough to draw his entire face south. "I don't believe that," he assured me.

"It's true, though. Look at how quickly it started to pour. The same thing happened when I arrived. The land knows I'm not supposed to be here." And I'd used enough magic today to put myself back on its radar.

"It's a storm, Tavi, it happens." Onyx breathed deeply, his nostrils flaring. "Now how about we talk about this direwolf of yours."

"I call him Noren. I don't know if that's his name or not but he's my friend. My partner."

Noren groaned and leaned the bulk of his weight into me.

"You do tend to collect outcasts, don't you?"

"I hope you're not talking about yourself."

A small grin flickered across my lips regardless. It was hard to imagine this moment, given the last time I'd seen

Onyx in his hospital bed. Or before, when he'd attacked me in his halfling wolf form. We'd done some damage to each other. I'd fought the way I had to fight to survive.

"Of course I am," Onyx continued. "Still, it's not every day you see a tame direwolf without the help of some sort of spell to keep its mind controlled."

"I broke the spell on him. The same thing you saw me do today, I did with him, on a smaller scale. It's my cognitive manipulation." I palmed the *Augundae Totalis* and opened my fingers to allow Onyx a glimpse of the tool. "Mike got this to me right before...you know. It's the reason we're here and not dead."

Onyx stopped, then groaned, the sound half laugh and half choke. "Then I suppose I'll have to be grateful to good ol' Mike. What's the plan? Do we even have one?"

I opened my mouth to automatically respond and snapped it shut quickly. I hadn't given it a thought. "Honestly, the only thing on my mind was getting us out."

"Thank you," he said eventually. "For saving me. I really thought we were out of time. And luck. Not that I've been able to count on luck for most of my life."

Hell no. Not when your dad was Kendrick Grimaldi.

"Are you okay?" I glanced down at his bent knee, the one he kept cradled to his chest. "You were limping a lot."

He looked like he'd rather swallow his own tongue than answer. Then, finally, "Many of my injuries healed. There are some the doctors who tended me said will never completely heal. I will likely live with debilitating pain for the rest of my life, from those injuries."

"The ones I gave you," I filled in. Permanent damage.

He nudged me with his shoulder, our forearms brushing together. "Chronic pain is a small price to pay for what you did."

"I hurt you!" Shit, was I going to cry again?

"You saved me. I'm grateful. Technically, at this point, you've saved me twice."

I stared sideways at him. "I didn't realize we were keeping track."

In which case, it didn't matter if our fight had broken the spell on him or not. If he lived in constant pain, then I'd be aware of it for the rest of *my* life.

Onyx sagged into the rock at his back, staring out through the rain past the mouth of the small cave. "We need to figure out our next step. It's fine to stop for a while and recuperate but we can't stay long."

Understatement of the year.

"I've actually been trying to find my mom. She's still alive." I realized then how much information I'd learned since Onyx had been in the hospital. How much he didn't know at this point.

There was no turning back now. If we were doing this together, on the run from the crown, then we had to be able to trust each other. I needed to know that he would have my back, and vice versa, and part of that was being utterly transparent.

"Apparently she's been living in Yelaine. From what I've heard, she might be able to help us."

Onyx arched a dark brow. "Do you know how far away Yelaine is? Do I need to remind you?"

"I haven't exactly had a chance to calculate the distance," I said dryly.

"It's nearly eight hundred miles from us."

I refused to let my surprise show. "Then it looks like we need to find transportation. Don't we?"

"I mean...it's worth a shot. At least there will be eight hundred miles between us and the premier."

His eyes fluttered closed. More than anything, I wanted to give him a chance to rest. He'd already pushed himself to get to this point. A few more minutes, I reasoned, and then we'd have to go. It wasn't safe to stay in one place.

If we got caught again, I probably wouldn't have a chance to use my powers.

We'd be killed on sight.

11

The rain refused to stop throughout our trek.

Below us, cradled in the valley, sat Eahsea and the giant castle, now a pinprick in the distance. Both of us were able to see clearly in the dark with a little shift to focus our eyes.

Although the going went slow, we steadily hiked over the ridge of the mountains and cautiously down the other side.

We stopped only when we weren't able to keep going.

I'd flown over this area before, on my way to meetings with the Claw & Fang. And in truth, it would be so much easier to shift and take the next leg of the journey from the air.

But I couldn't leave Onyx behind and he couldn't shift yet. As fast as Noren traveled on four legs, I refused to be separated.

This stretch of forest, as far as I knew, was entirely uninhabited. It would take several days for us to cut through the wilderness. Luckily, we all knew how to survive.

I'd gone on several excursions with my pack in the

human world, as had Onyx. And with Noren adept at catching prey, it was only a matter of time and pushing through the exhaustion to make our way forward.

It took days for us to cross through.

Days of walking through beating rain and eating whatever we could forage or Noren caught, without the benefit of a fire. Any sort of light in the darkness would bring attention to us.

Three days of constant vigilance and hustling as fast as Onyx's ruined body could travel until the trees began to thin. My panic had subsided long enough in the forest for me to recognize when it returned full blast.

Weary, filthy, and ready to drop, I held out a hand to stop Noren and Onyx when the watery outlines of buildings swam into view. I blinked to make sure it wasn't an illusion but the vision held.

Shit, we made it.

"Finally," Onyx muttered under his breath. "Civilization."

"It doesn't mean the inhabitants are friendly." My voice came out as a croak.

"I think it's safe to assume they're not." Onyx flashed his teeth at me. "We stay on our guard, get in, get what we need, and then right the fuck back out again."

I seconded the motion and my stomach gave a pitiful yelp for food.

The road in front of us cut through the town but it was empty.

The transportation system in Faerie had always struck me as wonky. A train had taken us from the portal into the inner city when I first arrived. There were cars, yes, but they didn't run on gasoline or anything like in the modern world. I'd never seen an airplane in the sky.

Most fae biked in the city or took the train when they needed to go a longer distance. If we could somehow find a car, if Onyx managed to operate it, we'd cover more ground.

My exhausted brain latched onto the idea and sank its teeth in. "Do you know how to work a car?" I asked.

We crouched low and watched people on the street making their way through the drizzle. At least the weather wasn't as bad today.

"I can manage," Onyx replied. "I'm used to biking everywhere, but right now it might be nice to rest the legs a little bit." He shifted his stance and winced.

If he looked like the living dead, how terrible did *I* look?

Yeah, we needed something to fit all three of us. Noren was fast but I didn't like the idea of him running behind us if we were to steal a horse or something.

The thought sounded so ridiculous, even inside my head, that I swallowed over a giggle. I imagined myself trying to ride the thing with Noren perched on its backside like some kind of familiar, straight out of a cowboy flick.

Absolutely not.

"This might not be a big town but surely it's so far outside of the city that they have cars. Do you know what it's called?" I didn't remember any of the names of the smaller villages outside of Eahsea, and without a map, I was guessing.

"At this point, I don't even know what I'm called. Let's hurry up and find something, okay? Can you use that thing?"

I lifted the *Totalis* into the light. "Of course. I'm not running at full capacity but this will help amplify my magic."

As long as we made it a fast trip, I reasoned, gesturing

for Noren to stay hidden in the bushes until we gave the signal.

I smoothed my hair down and behind my ears but my clothes were trashed. Nothing I could do about it now.

Onyx was half dead as we traversed through the underbrush and out the other side of the thicket. The pavement beneath my feet felt foreign after so many days in the forest. We moved into step beside each other, both of us keeping a watchful eye out for any kind of suspicious behavior.

We were the crazy ones here. Several fae took one look and discretely crossed to the other side of the road.

Someone had to have a car. The statement repeated like a mantra in my head.

No matter where we looked, the houses neat yet a few of them in need of repairs, we saw no sign of transportation. How would I be able to steal something if there was nothing available?

Panic lifted in my blood and my awareness rose like hackles. Even the fine hairs on the back of my arms stood to attention.

There weren't many people out in the rain. Which worked in our favor.

A fae couple passed with umbrellas lifted high. Another couple bore magical shields of hardened air above their heads to keep the water from touching them. I only saw a handful of others walking open and unbothered in the weather.

This little town had small elements of what made Eahsea charming. There were no flowers in bloom outside of several boxwood shrubs in planters. The houses uniform, more modern than others I'd seen, and the road boasted several potholes.

If I ignored the magic flames burning in sconces lining the road, I could have been anywhere in Virginia.

Once you fell outside of the king's immediate scope, keeping things in repair wasn't quite as important.

We kept our heads down, the rain driving against the back of our necks.

A flash of chrome caught my eye and I held out a hand to stop Onyx, jerking my head to the side. Nestled between two buildings was a vehicle.

I fought the urge to rub my hands together. Finally!

"What do you think?" he asked.

"I think it's a good enough choice, if we can get it to move without a key."

He blew out a breath. "Leave it to me."

The *Totalis* felt like it weighed a thousand pounds in my pocket. "Actually, I think I've got this covered. Watch my back. I'll knock on the front door."

Onyx reached out and grabbed my elbow before I moved. "Tavi, are you sure it's a good idea?"

No. I wasn't sure about anything at this point. I only knew we needed to do something and I had a better chance of stealing the car than he did.

"It's going to be fine," I assured him. "Watch out for me, okay?"

Steeling myself, I drew in a deep breath that almost made me dizzy. I could do this. I *had* to do this because we were tired and hungry and out of options. Which left us with only one option, really.

Thievery.

The door to the small cottage opened at my approach and the fae woman staring at me had three eyes. Two of them were in the normal spots but the third rested on her brow bone, the iris a dazzling shade of amethyst purple.

"Yes?" She sounded skeptical already. She'd probably seen us lurking around outside and eyeing her car.

I flashed her a grin and reached slowly into my pocket for the *Totalis*. Its familiar sensation of ancient magic mingled with my own and the exhaustion fell to the back of my mind. I focused my intent on the woman with three eyes, scanning her energy, isolating it from the magic of this world and latching on.

I can do this.

"I need your car, please," I said with a tight smile. "Hand over the crystal to make it work. It's okay. You can trust me."

The woman stared at me for a long moment, blinking in surprise. A familiar pall fell over her features. "You want my car?"

"Yes." I pushed my magic into her even more.

My powers were waning. I needed food, sleep, and water. I needed too many things to be able to feel like my old self again, and after days of travel the dizziness had started back. My empty stomach flipped queasily.

Barbara's witchy Band-aid wasn't going to last much longer.

"Get me the crystal for the car," I urged. "You can trust me. I need it."

Her eyes clouded over and a flash of guilt took me by surprise. This was a stranger, an innocent person.

"Tavi!"

Hearing my name almost broke my concentration and I tuned Onyx out. Until movement from behind resulted in the sound of footsteps closing in on us.

"Hey. Hey! What are you doing? Who are you?" A couple stood on the sidewalk only feet away from me.

I kept my back to them and cradled the tool tighter

against my chest. "Nothing is going on. This woman is giving me her car."

I tried to push the wave of manipulation out wider to encompass their energies and came up against a wall. Even with the *Totalis*, I didn't have much magic left in me to utilize.

Onyx appeared at my side, his face pale and grim. "It's time for us to go now. Forget the car."

"Get away from the house," the male continued. "We're calling the FIB!"

His concern broke through the spell I'd cast and the three-eyed fae slammed the door in my face. We'd been made.

"Tavi, *now*." Onyx was half a second away from tossing me over his shoulder and running, which we both knew would be impossible for him in his current state. He sagged heavily against the front porch stoop, white-knuckled.

I nodded and we took off in a quick jog, turning around several corners to try and lose the couple.

"Someone saw you," he added breathlessly.

"You were supposed to be keeping a watch and make sure I wasn't interrupted," I said.

And I had failed. Which somehow didn't make me feel any better about using my powers against good people. It was the same kind of shame I'd felt after using it on my friend back at the Halfling Academy, Nora Kwan.

I wasn't sure how long we jogged until Onyx stumbled. "I'm sorry." He ducked his head. "I can't go anymore. I've gotta stop."

His face twisted in an agonized grimace and he gripped the wall like a lifeline.

This wasn't a time for me to give in to the strain, or my own desperation and tears.

I was the only one who could get us out of here. "Okay." I drew in a shaky breath, forcing my mind to head down a dozen avenues of possibilities.

What the hell should we do?

I ushered Onyx into a tight alcove between two buildings, partially hidden from the street by a portico. "Okay, you stay here. I'm going to fix this."

He shook his head. "There's nothing for you to fix, Tavi. We're not going to be able to steal a car."

My brow furrowed. "Watch me."

I just needed a little boost and I'd be able to make my cognitive manipulation work, I knew it.

It was too much of a risk to head back to the last car we saw but there had to be another even in a small town like this one.

Keeping my head low, I trekked down the streets, my magic a thin reed keeping my features blurred if not disguised. It was the best I could manage on my hunt and my heart beat frantically at every dead end. Or in this case, every empty driveway.

Claribel had driven a car so I knew they existed, and not just for Bureau workers.

Finally, between a restaurant and a cobbler's store, I saw one. A little two-door thing painted a vibrant yellow like a buttercup. I suppressed a groan. We'd be super conspicuous in it but Onyx couldn't go any further.

And I highly doubted we'd make it far with him strapped to Noren's back. The direwolf was massive but Onyx was a fully grown adult shifter. Not light by any means.

Before I gave in to my doubts, I went up to the car and tested the door, and found it unlocked. My throat constricted as I slid into the driver's seat.

There was no typical ignition slot to slide in a key but rather a small indentation in the center of the dashboard.

I searched underneath the seat, in the center console, and anywhere I could think of where the owner might have stashed the necessary crystal but I came up empty.

I glanced out the window, nervous sweat beading along my hairline and upper lip.

Too late to turn back now.

I brought the *Totalis* out from my pocket and held it up.

Cognitive manipulation worked on fae and humans.

Could it work on inanimate objects if I had the artifact with me? Time to figure it the hell out.

I pressed my hand to the empty slot and dove deep for my magic until it twined with the artifact. Once I was relatively sure I had a handle on things, I sent the magic out into the car.

"Start," I whispered. Hardly daring to listen in case it didn't work.

It probably wouldn't work and I was wasting my—

The engine roared to life as the *Totalis* warmed in my palm, pulsing with power.

Fuck having someone give me the crystal.

I let out a triumphant whoop and hurriedly pressed my foot to the pedal, throwing the car into reverse and peeling out of the driveway before someone came running.

12

I maneuvered the car around a corner too quickly and the tires skidded over wet pavement.

The roads here were narrower and I wasn't used to the way the vehicle handled.

Still, I managed to get all four tires back where they belonged and somehow found my way to the alley where Onyx rested.

I paused only long enough to roll down the window and call his name. "Onyx! Get in!"

He shuffled up to the side door. "What the hell is this, Tavi?"

"Exactly what we needed," I told him with a rogue smile.

His fingers shook as he peeled open the door and flung himself down on the seat, his skin now ashen gray. I wasn't sure how far the car would take us but if it got us out of this town then I was all for it.

Sirens already sounded in the distance. They were on to us. We'd be lucky to make it out of here without the Bureau on our asses.

My heart thrummed an unhealthy erratic beat against my ribs.

By the time we reached the edge of the forest and I pushed open the door for Noren, I felt lightheaded and only the seatbelt kept me from falling forward against the dash.

He clambered over me to get to the small area in the back, taking up every inch of available space and then some.

Doesn't matter.

The moment the door closed, I peeled down the road with a squeal of tires.

"You okay, buddy?" I asked over my shoulder.

The cab filled with the scent of wet fur.

"I've been better." Onyx blew out a long sigh and rested his head against the window.

"I was talking to the direwolf but it's good to know."

He swallowed over a laugh. "I realize. Maybe I'm trying to fill the silence because my thoughts have gotten a little too loud. Everything hurts."

"I'm sorry." My apologies meant shit. "I'm so sorry."

"No sense apologizing." He closed his eyes.

The road in front of us wasn't empty by any means. We joined a line of traffic, horses and carriages joining lines of cars and bikes. At least we were moving faster. At least when I cracked the window, the sirens were left in the distance and soon I heard nothing but the passing rumble of others and the steady hum of our tires.

"It's bound to happen though," I said at last. "The thoughts. Sometimes I can barely stand myself. My brain is screaming so loudly it's like nothing else exists."

"When you think about everything that's happened to us..." Onyx trailed off.

"What, ah...what did happen to you? If you don't mind me asking." I glanced over at him. "I'm still not sure."

"You mean with the killing?"

He said it with such openness I didn't even have a chance to flinch. "You were attacking pure-blooded fae. Who looked like me."

The terror of that moment returned in full force.

I remembered stepping in when Onyx attacked Professor Juno, my mentor. I remembered our last battle against each other, the one where he'd ended up with his current wounds. The ones no amount of healing could fix.

They'd plague him for the rest of his life. I swallowed over the golf ball-sized lump in my throat.

"I don't remember any of it," he admitted. Something in his tone broke my heart and I found myself reaching over to press my hand against his. "I'm sorry if you're disappointed. I came to in the hospital bed in tremendous pain. Some-times—" He broke off, refused to look at me. "Sometimes I catch flashes of things. Mostly blood. It's hard to get the scent out of my mind especially when it's something I've always enjoyed. You know, running with the pack and shift-ing, hunting. There's always blood when you hunt."

"I know what you mean."

Still, I shuddered thinking about how it would feel to kill another person, especially under the control of some outside influence.

"I know I hurt you, and I know you had no choice but to hurt me." His mouth thinned into a steely line. "I'm the one who should be apologizing, repeatedly."

"Are you trying to call us even in a warped kind of way?" I asked.

"Not at all. I'm trying, in my own twisted way, to tell you I understand and that I'd still like to be friends."

I felt the heat of his eyes on me and when I turned, he was watching me. Onyx hadn't moved his hand away from mine yet. "I wouldn't have saved your ass if we weren't friends, dude."

He blew out a breath. "I know. I felt like I needed to clear the air a little bit. I know it's still a little hard for you to reconcile me with my father."

I jolted at the mention even though logically I knew exactly what he meant. It hit at the oddest times, the realization that the bloodthirsty leader of a rival pack back in the mortal world, the one chosen by the packs to be my fated mate, maintained his youth through magic. And that Onyx was his son who'd had to come to Faerie to escape. The same way I had.

"I've never held your father's identity against you."

Onyx leaned back in his seat with his eyes closed again, like the conversation took a lot out of him. "You might now. After what I did to you."

"We're not going to talk about him." I bit the inside of my lips. "We're pack. We stick together."

At this point, besides Bronwen Onyx was one of the only other halfling shifters I trusted.

"The one thing I've really missed being in Faerie," he admitted.

"What? Being part of a group?" I shook my head. "I used to really hate it sometimes. Everyone was always in your business trying to tell you what to do and how to act."

"The stability, though. The way you always knew there were people who had your back. It was a question of loyalty."

"Yeah, the stability," I agreed. "The camaraderie. Knowing there were always people around, there at a moment's notice whenever you called."

Noren leaned over the seat and rested his muzzle on my shoulder. He huffed against my ear and the tickling sensation had me shivering. I reached back and ran a hand along his face to scratch behind his ears.

"Do you know where we are yet?" I asked Onyx in the silence.

"I don't remember the name of that town we passed through but I know Khoysas is somewhere in this direction."

I'd heard that name before, a neighboring town with its own fae academy.

"We avoid the big towns for as far as this car takes us," I said decisively. "Hopefully it will get us closer to where we need to go."

Onyx waited a moment before he finally drew his hand away and broke the connection. "You know we can't keep driving this. Someone will report it missing whether your spell holds for an hour or days. Eventually we have to ditch it and find another mode of transportation."

He didn't ask how I managed to get the car to start and I didn't offer the information. "Until then, we'll drive."

"And stop for food."

"Yeah, and stop for food." My stomach gave an ominous growl at the thought of a giant pizza or a messy, cheesy burger. Something with lots of meat and salt.

It growled louder still to the point where Onyx turned to me with his face screwed in confusion. "Are you going to eat me if we don't stop soon?"

I shook my head. "Actually I'd like to get a little farther away from that town first."

"You're going to pass out at the wheel if you're not careful." He sat back again with a loud groan. "And honestly, I need something too. Otherwise I won't be in good enough shape to take over driving."

"Who says I'm going to let you take over? From where

I'm sitting, you're looking like dead meat rather than a capable copilot."

His smile was a warm thing that brought an automatic mirror to my own lips. There was something comforting about Onyx, since the moment I met him, if I was being honest. Despite my skepticism when Melia basically forced me to meet with him in a little cafe she'd chosen for the food, we ended up working well together.

Because we knew what it was like to have a pack and be forced to leave, I reminded myself. And he was pack no matter who sired him.

Sure, he was an attractive man, and even better—he was a nice person. When he wasn't being manipulated into murder.

I studied him from the corner of my eye, trying not to be too obvious. Onyx cut a strong side profile with his sharp nose and prominent jaw. If he trimmed his beard, he'd have been handsome, and the draw between his wolf and mine worked. In some way I hadn't looked at before, it worked.

He wasn't mine, not in the way Mike was mine, even though he'd make a much better match for me.

How easily I'd forgiven Onyx for murder.

But he'd always presented himself as different from the other men in the pack I'd known. Kinder and more sensitive. He actually stopped to consider things before he spoke or dove into action. It was a lesson I'd never quite managed to learn.

"Tavi, you're going to have to rest sometime." Onyx reached over and laid his hand over mine this time, giving it a light squeeze and ignoring the way I jumped. "You've been pushing too hard."

The contact felt easier somehow when I initiated it. Why

did it send slivers of awareness through me when Onyx made the first move?

"It seems like these days, all I do is push through," I admitted, gently squeezing back. "There's no time for rest."

"Then make the time. The next village we pass, we're going to stop for food and then I want you to nap. I'm sure your buddy in the backseat will make room for you. I'm sure he'll watch over us, too. No better guardian than an Unseelie direwolf."

Noren huffed out a sound, so much like an agreement I had to laugh.

"I think he's trying to tell you that you're right."

"Of course I'm right." Onyx was self-assured. "One of these days, maybe you'll listen to me instead of playing at being the alpha."

I scoffed. "You know me. I don't play."

"For anyone else, Tavi, I'd make it a joke. But dammit, if you ever end up leading a pack of your own one day, count me in. I'll protect you with my life."

I automatically started to answer, and then stopped, my tongue knotting. My voice was almost a whisper when I replied, "Who knows what the future will hold." *Or if we'll even be alive to see it.*

I wasn't sure if I liked the idea of having my own pack. I hadn't given any thought to it because, all my life, my uncle promised me the wolf council would arrange a match. Would find my fated mate and I'd follow his lead.

My fated mate was certainly *not* Kendrick Grimaldi.

My arm throbbed again and I pushed those thoughts aside.

Two hours passed before we took a side road that opened up into a quiet gathering of homes. The houses here were few and far between, with several of them clustered together in smaller communities, before we hit the town proper.

There were no fast food joints in Faerie, though, as I'd come to find out. It looked like this was the only place the arrogant yellow arches hadn't colonized yet. Although I'd kill for some greasy, sloppy french fries.

Which sucked, in a way, because it meant we had to get out of the car and actually place an order in a small cafe located next to an art gallery.

We had no money between us. Onyx had been brought to the execution from the hospital and I straight from the dungeons. Luckily, and much to my surprise, we found a stack of bills folded over into thirds in the glove compartment.

The Lacrynthos Crown diner in the town of Holsworthy looked more like a pub in some kind of medieval village than it did an actual restaurant serving food, but their menu promised good things and my mouth salivated at the thought of potatoes of any variety.

I added my newest guilt to the ever-growing pile inside of me and shoved the stolen money across the live tree bent and shaped magically into a front counter.

Onyx stared at me and lifted a brow high when I came back with two bags of food. Almost as if he was thinking the same as I was. What was his favorite food order bac in the human world? We'd talked about a number of things we missed when we used to train together but never that.

"You got a lot," he said when I dropped into the driver's seat.

"Of course. It has to last us, doesn't it?"

I'd ordered a separate sandwich for Noren and tossed it to him. He swallowed it down in a single bite without bothering to chew or taste.

My first bite of a panini made with elderflower syrup had me swooning. It dripped onto my fingers and I sucked them clean even with Onyx watching me.

"You eat like you're starving," he said.

I didn't bother with a response, although I watched him in turn. When he took his first bite, grimacing through a wave of pain, I caught every flicker of agonized movement.

"I've never seen anyone get hurt eating mashed potatoes before. Should I not have gotten you a fae version of shepherd's pie?" I said, trying to lighten the mood.

Onyx took his time chewing before he answered. "I'm just not what I used to be."

"If you need me to feed you, let me know. If it hurts to lift a finger."

"Or maybe I just want you to feed me anyway," he teased.

"You're welcome to have anything I ordered, too. If you want to try it."

He grimaced. "I'm not really a fan of those overly sweet syrups some places use. Although you make it look good enough to devour."

"Flatterer." I spoke through another mouthful of food and grinned at him.

Noren whined over my shoulder and nudged me with his nose.

"If you won't try it, he certainly will," I told Onyx as I held a bite out for Noren.

"He's welcome to it, then. I won't take food away from a hungry wolf."

"But you're a hungry wolf too."

Onyx was halfway through his pie when he said, "We both know I'm never going to be the kind of wolf I was again. All those training days of ours are over."

"You might still get better."

Right. We both knew that was a lie.

A small bit of color returned to his face after we'd finished our meals, and, comfortably full for the first time in a week, I let Onyx take the wheel. He kept to the back roads as I lounged in the passenger seat.

The crystal powering the vehicle took us at a steady clip for hours. Somewhere along the line I passed out, and jerked awake when Onyx pulled off to the side of the road and the car fell silent.

"What's going on? Where are we?" My heart lurched into my throat and stayed lodged there in terror.

"Relax, no one is coming for us," Onyx assured me. His voice was soft and his smile matched. "I thought we should stop to do something fun."

"Something *fun*?" I repeated skeptically. "Is this really the time for fun?"

"It's a roadside attraction. Shouldn't be much of a cost to get in, probably take us about fifteen minutes to walk through the fairy glen."

I rolled my eyes and pushed aside the last vestiges of sleep. "You stopped to check out a fairy glen? Come on, Onyx."

"Look..." He paused, drummed his fingers on the steering wheel. "I thought it would be a nice way for us to do something to release a little bit of tension. I know we're both holding it in. We almost died, Tavi. We almost lost our lives a few days ago and we've been running on adrenaline and hope for the last three days. Maybe it's just me but I'm at the end of my rope and I could use a little fairy glen magic."

He made a good point and I felt horrible asking him to keep driving. Especially when my own fear, held inside my muscles for much longer than a few days, twinged in a reminder of its presence.

"Sure, we can totally do that," I agreed. "As long as it doesn't take too long."

"I realize you're anxious to get on the road again. Trust me, I know. And I agree. But we need a break. Come on."

We were slow to pry ourselves out of the car. I opened the door wide for Noren and he automatically hopped out to stretch his legs again, his claws digging into the soft earth where we'd parked. I drew in the scent of night-colored air, moss, verdant greenery.

I lifted my gaze to the sky and drew in a deep breath to steady myself.

This part of Faerie belonged to nothing and no man except for the visitors to the fairy glen.

Even I had to admit the attraction was cute. We used a few bucks left over from our stolen stash to gain entry, only the two of us. Noren went off to prowl in the forest around us. A few trails lit by silvery fae light illuminated the path through the attraction. Here and there, magic arranged to automatically activate when tourists arrived burst to life.

Cute, yes, and a nice distraction for the thirty minutes it took to make it from start to finish.

Onyx kept close and I looped my arm through his as much for my comfort as to support him.

Once we finished and collected Noren, I slid behind the wheel and gunned it, pulling away from the side of the road. The forest became a wall of pure black behind us. The clutching sensation in my chest had eased slightly after our trek through the glen.

He'd been right. It was exactly what we needed despite the way we trudged through it, each of us bogged down by the weight of our respective ills. Me with my zombie disease

—go figure—and Onyx with his chronic pain. We made quite the pair.

"Hey." His voice roused me from my thoughts. "We've got a problem."

"What do you mean?"

"I mean we're being followed. There's a car behind us that doesn't have the headlights on but I see a glint of metal every now and then."

Everything inside of me tightened. "You can't be sure they're following *us*."

"It's the same car I saw back at the Lacrnythos Crown. And the same one that drove *past* us at the glen. Now we're ahead of them, and I guarantee—" Onyx paused. "It's no coincidence."

13

W e were in the middle of absolute nowhere.

What were the odds of someone else being out here, stopping where we stopped?

I trusted Onyx and his observational skills but damn it, we had nowhere to go—there was no one around to help and no other traffic on the road except for the single vehicle following us.

"What does it look like?" I asked him, dropping my voice low and somehow feeling foolish because of it. It wasn't as if our car was bugged. Or had someone gotten in while we were distracted at the glen?

Crap, at this point, anything was possible.

"Look for other roads where we might be able to lose them," Onyx urged, his face gaunt.

This road was about the size of a normal two-lane back in the mortal world but it seemed as though we'd somehow made our way into the heart of the wilderness. The same sprawling forests I'd seen from the air, on my way to meeting with the Claw & Fang, covered this part of the world as well, surrounding isolated pockets of towns.

"There's nothing here," I protested. "Did you see the maps at the glen? This road is the only one cutting through the forest. The best thing we can do is try to make it out of here and once we do, hope we can lose them."

My knuckles went white, my skin broke out in a cold sweat, and Noren whined.

I had a terrible gut feeling that whoever followed us had waited until now to show themselves. On purpose. A calculated move. Whoever it was, they wanted us to see them.

I pressed my foot to the pedal and pushed the car to go faster.

Although their headlights were off, once I tuned in to the vehicle's presence, they were easier to spot. They maintained the same distance behind us and sped up to stay within eyesight.

The cold sweat spread everywhere and my muscles trembled.

"What are we going to do?" Onyx whispered.

No clue. As per usual.

I eased off a bit and slowed down, hoping against hope that trudging along at Grandma Moses speed would entice the other person to pass. To show us that they were a normal person and not a threat.

The other vehicle slowed down as well.

Same distance—no more, no less.

"Well, now we know they are definitely tailing us on purpose." Onyx sounded resigned.

My teeth clattered together and I clenched down on them to stop the movement. It was fine. *We'll make it out of this somehow*. We had to.

With only one road, it wasn't like they had many places to go, either. If I sped up enough then I might be able to swerve off into the trees and have them pass us by. Maybe.

"Whatever you're thinking about, it won't work."

"You don't know that," I murmured. My grip on the wheel tightened despite my now clammy palms.

The sweat pooled under my arms. I caught sight of Noren in the rearview mirror, his hackles lifted and a warning growl rumbling his throat. He was either picking up on my anxiety or something my senses weren't able to quantify yet.

Either way—

"I do know that." Onyx rolled down the window and stuck his face out, drawing in the air. "Shit, Tavi, this is bad. This is *big* bad."

"What is it?" My voice broke.

I took the curve too fast, the tires screeching. The road straightened out and I slammed on the brakes in time to avoid a second vehicle blocking our path. Four brawny bodies leaned against the side and straightened when they saw us coming.

Onyx yelled, slamming his hand against the dash as I hit the brakes harder, trying to keep the car from fishtailing.

We finally skidded to a stop and the only sound was Noren's growl. That sound raised my hackles but the four big men blocking the road in front of us barely blinked.

"Get out of the vehicle," the nearest one called out with a sneer. "*Now.*"

I saw no weapons on them. The speaker was a tall man with a mangy salt-and-pepper beard and only a single functioning eye. Long brown hair fell to his chest. He was dressed in a checkered shirt and stained jeans, with his shoulders slumped menacingly forward. The others slipped in close to him.

"Well?" the man pressed. He tilted his head to the side and one of his associates shifted forward and brought his palms hard against the hood of the car. "What is it going to be, kids?"

Noren's growling grew louder with his sights set unblinkingly on the four men.

When we made no move to obey, the other two slinked forward, their eyes gleaming dully in the darkness.

"Get out of the fucking car!" the leader screamed.

These men were not playing around. We had one shot at getting out of here: We had to shift. It was the only way we'd be able to outrun them.

I glanced over at Onyx and saw a similar gleam of recognition in his eyes. He'd had the same thought. I gave him a tiny nod, hoping none of the others would be able to see it in the gloom.

Then I sent out a wave of magic to open the back door to let Noren out. He headed straight for the closest man, with his maw gaping open and saliva dripping from his fangs.

I turned my attention inward, reaching for my inner wolf.

We're out of options.

The thought played on repeat in my head as familiar magic flooded my system, a power uniquely mine that wasn't dependent on energy. I'd be able to shift exhausted, starving. Even without a full moon.

I gathered my resources and Onyx and I moved in tandem. Our doors blew open, magic erupting out of us and swirling through the interior of the car like a whirlwind. The power lurking beneath his skin shifted his limbs in a blink, and from the periphery of my vision I caught sight of a massive wolf landing on all fours where a man had stood.

The wolf took off in an instant.

My half-shifter warrior form would be bigger, stronger, in case the others caught up to us. But I needed speed.

Shards of panic bit into me as I called the change, a corona of magic swallowing me.

My wolf lifted to the surface and took over. My limbs lengthened, teeth growing sharper and claws digging into the soft rich earth when I landed as well. My senses tripled from my human and fae form, my awareness stretching until I knew two things without a doubt.

Noren was right behind me.

And some of the men at the roadblock were shifters in hot pursuit.

Their musky scents permeated the air around us and I took off without a sense of direction. The change hurt more without the full moon but the first pricks of pain trickled away as my muscles warmed.

This form was more natural. My wolf took control, uncaring about the thundering of my pulse. My tongue lolled out and I kept my head low for speed. Long strides took me far, over scrub, across streams, and through the underbrush.

There was no clear path ahead and I lost sight of Onyx somewhere in the gloom.

I'd find him again.

His scent was unmistakable, like fire on a cold winter night. And there was Noren only a few paces to my side, occasionally nudging me with his shoulder to get me to change direction.

My wolf was sleek, longer and closer to the ground with a pelt of pure black to help me blend into my surroundings. Noren towered over me even in this shape and was unnaturally silent when I tripped and crashed over a downed log.

He refused to leave my side and nosed me, urging me to get up.

Underbrush snapped behind us. The growl of the two

wolves pursuing us grew louder and a howl split the night and raised the hairs on the back of my neck.

I bared my teeth.

Panting, I took off with as much speed as I could. Without warning, the spot on my arm where Madam Muerte's corpse had bitten began to throb. It pulsed with an unnatural heat and I found myself missing my next step and losing my balance.

My snout plowed into the earth and I snapped my teeth and snorted to dislodge the dirt from my nostrils.

Noren huffed and glared at me with narrowed eyes.

My infection may have looked healed in the hospital but with every foot we ran in the forest, it grew hotter, scalding me. I fought against another flare-up of blood magic because Barbara wasn't around to fix me this time.

I had to outrun the other shifters. I had to get somewhere safe, find Onyx, make it out of this mess.

Two massive wolves cut us off and I pulled up short before canines snapped inches from my face.

My heart lurched into my throat, my strength flagging more with every passing second as the two wolves circled me. Noren moved into place with his back arched in a protective stance.

Not now.

I couldn't do this now. Not when I felt this way. Not when I might pass out and shift back into human form. I was as good as dead at that point.

The pain in my arm splintered higher into my shoulder, and when the nearest shifter snapped at me again, I yelped, backing up into Noren. He leaped to attention and stood on his back legs, bellowing out a warning.

The other two attacked him at the same time, coordinating their movements to snap at his sensitive underbelly.

In the next beat, they changed as well. Their forms twisted, warped into halfling wolf form. Powerful warriors designed to stand a chance against something the size of a direwolf. They were as large as fully grown grizzlies and packed with muscle.

They swung at him and forced Noren back a step to avoid the hit. His rear claw stomped down dangerously close to my body and I was too slow to get out of the way.

My small yip of surprise startled him and in the moment he turned to look at me, the warriors moved.

They reached for him, with one moving high and the other low. Somehow they managed to get him between them and they forced him to the ground.

My chest constricted. I ran forward without thinking and the closest one kicked out at me. His hit landed on my shoulder and I buckled, yelping.

Helpless.

Son of a bitch, that hurt!

Black dots danced in front of me, and through the blur I saw them wrestle Noren to the ground, slamming his head down to the dirt repeatedly. His growl cut off unnaturally and he fell still.

The warriors dropped him and turned to me, their eyes glowing red.

The pain took a back seat to the red hot fury coursing through my blood. They'd hurt my partner. Despite my disadvantage, I drew on my power and forced the change as well.

I'd barely escaped against one male in halfling warrior form. Against two, and working with my zombie bite, I stood no chance.

Not a single damn chance.

They snarled out a warning, and without waiting for my

vision to clear, I launched at them. Landing just short and gnashing at the closest warrior's leg. The surprise had him tripping.

I stalked forward, my hackles lifted, muscles contorting as I stepped up beside Noren. My bones gave a twang before they contorted and lengthened. My snout grew longer, teeth sharper, and black hair grew thick along my muscled arms and legs.

They were still much larger than me. Without thought, I pounced, enraged enough to tear them to shreds.

The one on the left saw me coming and opened his mouth to roar out a warning. The ground shook, the trees dropping multiple leaves in a maelstrom around us.

I pivoted to avoid the swipe of his claws and came up swinging with a roar of my own. His eyes grew wide with shock, the whites showing, and I raked my claws across his jaw.

We were motion itself, but to stop would be to damn us both.

Noren needed me.

Noren was hurt and all he'd done was try to protect me.

I went full out, despite not being at my best. Their scents were noxiously strong, a combination of musk and sweat and hormones. I was wild and furious and the smell drove me out of my mind in the worst kind of way.

Without the strength in my limbs, I was as good as meat to these guys.

They worked together seamlessly, partners from way back if I had to guess, and the one on the left brought his paw down toward the top of my skull.

I ducked at the last moment, turning to kick against the nearest tree trunk and gain momentum. I came up swinging with a rock in my paw and let it fly.

It hit the shifter in the side and he yelped, howling, clutching his side.

How do you like some cracked ribs, *fucker*?

I redoubled my efforts and pushed off the ground, grabbing the nearest tree limb and swinging around to land behind the second warrior.

He turned, much too slow with his enormous bulk, and I took him around the midsection and pushed him to the ground.

A bonfire glowed inside of me as I reared back and sliced my claws across the warrior's back. I realized I'd barely grazed his skin as he bucked beneath me.

If I didn't take care of them, they'd take care of me. I just needed them unconscious. Then I could get Noren and find Onyx.

I dug my claws in deeper until I cut through fur and skin and tendon.

The warrior's howl of pain split the forest air, but my triumph was cut short when his cohort grabbed me around the neck and yanked.

I flew off the other one's back, my air supply cut. Choking, I reached for my magic, the deep swirling pool of it. There was more to this than physical might. If I had enough magic to complete the change, then I had enough to work a spell.

I'd call down the sun. I knew how to use the elements to help myself.

I scrambled to get free at the same time, kicking out with my hind legs but finding no purchase. I wrapped lethal claw-tipped fingers around the shifter's bulky forearms to pry him off of me.

Only now, nothing but the smallest scrap of a spark

erupted from my fingertips. Not nearly enough to burn my way out of this chokehold.

Not enough juice left inside of me to call up my power. Okay, so—

I grunted as pain lanced through me and dirt and mud splattered from where I dug furrows in the ground.

My mind scrambled as my body slowed with the lack of oxygen. Panic made it hard to think and I dug my claws down as deep as they would go, puncturing the shifter.

He growled but the sound changed into a pained whine and he loosened his grip. Just a little. Enough for me to twist and jerk away from him.

The second warrior lumbered closer.

My body hurt, every inch of me contracting at the same time until I wanted to curl into a tight ball.

I heard myself breathing, saw the rest of the world through the stars dancing in front of my vision as I drew wave after wave of rage-scented air into my lungs.

The second warrior grabbed me by one of my ears and yanked. He pummeled me with his paws, with his legs, nothing but a mass of muscle forcing me into a defensive position.

I had no time to brace for the attack before he kicked at my knee and I howled in agony.

My tendons throbbed.

I ducked to the side and narrowly avoided the next swing of his claws. The other warrior regained his wits and the two of them stopped to stare down at me. Finally the first one scraped his claws across my ear before releasing me.

I tried to get up, drawing on the last of my reserves, but dropped back down to the ground. Someone had set me on fire. They'd doused me with acid and left me to die but the pressure inside of me refused to ease. Even the pain from the cuts and bruises and slices over my skin were nothing compared to the chorus of agony inside. And with no magic to help me, sending the rest of my power out against them wasn't happening.

I was finished.

Noren...

My head spun in dizzy circles and my eyes squeezed shut on their own. Without having to look, I felt the others loom over me. Staring, deciding what to do to continue this torturous fight.

Through overheated nostrils, I sensed the other shifters as they came into the clearing. Three more werewolves joined the first two and muddied the air with their scents.

I gagged, the magic keeping me in this physical form fading second by second. I lost energy the way some people lost blood, and by the time the clearing filled with bodies, I passed out.

14

I'd gotten used to being unconscious.

It felt like a natural state at this point, much more natural than being awake. Even the slow lift back to reality wasn't nearly as bad as it was the first few times I'd passed out.

This time, I woke up with the hum of moving wheels beneath me and the chill of leather against my cheek.

Both arms and my legs were bound with rope that did little for my magic but certainly cut off circulation. I twitched my fingers to get the blood pumping, and feeling returned with the violent prick of a thousand pins and needles.

I kicked out with my feet, the darkness impenetrable and only a glimmer of sickly sunlight cutting through the horizon enough for me to make out the back of a truck. The entire back of the vehicle appeared to be boxed off from the rest. The windows looked thicker than regular glass and turned the watery light of dawn to shades of blue. Early daylight.

Noren lay with his front and back legs lashed together and his jaws restrained by a horrifying looking iron muzzle.

I didn't see Onyx anywhere.

Relief flooded me with such force that black dots danced across my eyes. He must have gotten away. At least one of us managed to evade the shifters.

Had we been driving all night? My head gave a single, thumping pound before the ache set in and I worked my jaw, trying to relieve the pressure.

Noren whimpered pitifully and I turned to reach for him with my fingertips. "It's gonna be okay, boy."

My mouth tasted like someone ground sand against my gums and I grimaced, running my tongue over my teeth and swallowing. My throat had gone dry. Noren seemed especially anxious and the feeling didn't abate even when my hand made contact with his fur.

He leaned his weight into me like he sensed me getting worse and worse.

My imagination.

"It'll be fine, Noren," I whispered. "We'll make it out of here. Just give me a second to figure out a plan and I'll free you."

He whined again and pushed into me hard enough to strain my wrist.

My arm felt like it was being stung by an entire nest of hornets. The sensation brought a wave of acid to my stomach and my mouth filled with a vile bitter taste.

I wasn't sure how long we drove. I slipped in and out of consciousness until the drone of tires over tarmac changed to the rough crunch of gravel. Eventually, the vehicle pulled to a stop and a ring of large trees obscured any view I had of the sky.

The men came around to the back and a wave of magic had one of the walls sliding open. *The brutes from the roadblock last night.* The dude with the single eye glared at me before he grabbed the rope around my ankles and hauled me out.

I kicked at him, the hit lacking any real strength.

My legs turned to rubber and the rest of me jelly, neither part working in tandem with the other. Not only did my feet not make contact with the brute but I keeled over, losing my balance in the process. I listed to the side and he jerked me up.

"Get up, girl," the man with one eye growled. "You'd think you'd never been tied up before. You can walk."

No, I actually couldn't. My body refused to hold me upright.

Growling in frustration, he threw me over his shoulder as though I weighed nothing at all. He barked out a command to one of the others, who then dragged a howling mad direwolf out of the back.

Every step he took jarred the breath from my lungs and sent my ribs clacking together.

Finally he set me down and grabbed my face, forcing me to stare straight ahead. "*Look.* What do you see?"

In front of us, a giant wall stretched as far as I could see to the right and the left. Made of tightly stacked gray stones, the wall shimmered, vacillating between airy lightness and solid matter.

What was on the other side?

Craning my head high, I looked up, up, the top of the wall nonexistent as it stretched up into the puffy clouds of dawn.

My stomach dipped and swirled in surprise. Vertigo had me tilting dangerously backward. This was crazy.

Almost too crazy to be believed, and I'd seen some insane things over the years.

"Will you stay put like a good girl?" the man whispered in his razor-edged voice, directly next to my ear.

I winced, immediately regretting it. He saw the motion anyway and chuckled.

A second later he wrenched my head back with one hand and slid a thick golden chain over my face with the other. The necklace dropped to my collarbone, and the small stone at the center, adding weight, found the natural hollow at the base of my throat.

The cool metal warmed against my skin.

"What's this?" I croaked.

"It keeps the wall from destroying you on impact, sweetheart. Trust me. You're going to want to keep it on."

"Free my hands and I'll take it off and choke you with it," I snapped back.

He chuckled in mild amusement at my comeback and pushed me forward. There was enough give in the ropes around my ankles for me to be able to shuffle but running away would be impossible. I'd trip and fall flat on my face. A terrible whine sounded and I glanced over to see four other men hauling Noren toward the wall, each one of them the size of a heavyweight champion.

They hadn't put a necklace on the direwolf.

Would he be okay?

I struggled against One Eye.

He knocked me hard enough in the side with his elbow to force the breath from my lungs. "Easy. This will all be over soon."

We walk through the wall, magic cascading over me in a frenzied torrent. It pricked against my skin in an eager, almost hungry inspection before sliding around me, through me. Pure magic, I realize in some distant way.

Pure *fae* magic because I felt it even with the necklace keeping me protected.

The wall connected to the land itself, and although it seemed improbable, it had been built to reach the stars in the sky. It felt old. Primitive and powerful and...sentient.

It knew me, recognized me, wanted to learn more.

All of a sudden we were out the other side and I gasped, inhaling sharply. Had I forgotten to breathe the entire time? I blinked to clear my gaze, my jaw wanting to drop bumpkin-style at the sight on the other side.

A large expanse of tents extended back into the tree line. The canvas structures looked sturdy enough to survive a harsh wind but not out of place in the shadows of the forest.

Several fires had been lit and scattered between the tents of the small village. Camp. Whatever it was.

This felt temporary, like the tents might be easily taken down and reassembled at a moment's notice. Did these people, whoever they were, move around constantly to avoid detection? My stomach dropped further and my heart gave a single threatening thud against my ribs.

"Where are we?" I asked One Eye.

The other men emerged from the wall, the facade of stone melting away with their passing like walking through a waterfall. They threw Noren to the ground and he glared at them, his eyes promising retaliation. I felt an answering need rising up inside of me.

"I asked you a question. What is this place?"

I lifted my voice to make sure they all heard me but there was no forthcoming answer from any of the men. One Eye took my elbow and marched me through the village.

Behind us came the sounds of a scuffle as the others took hold of Noren. Through the camp they paraded us, going slowly I suspected on purpose to give the people here time to come out and enjoy the procession.

They were fae going about their lives but without fail, they stopped to watch me. Us. Curious about the capture, no doubt. They had the vacant stares of the displaced, of refugees, of people on the run. I knew this because I recognized their expressions as the same I'd worn in the past.

Noren growled from my side and although his jaws were still bound, the sound rippled through the crowd and several shocked gasps rang out.

One Eye changed direction abruptly and took me right through the heart of the camp. The tent rising up in front of us stood out from the others with a slightly lighter shade of canvas. It glowed in the dim light from overhead with the gray translucence of fog.

The four men carrying Noren deposited him at the opening flap of the tent and then stepped back to give One Eye the floor. He paraded me inside, snapping to attention once the flap fell closed behind us.

"Sir? We've brought her to you, as requested." His voice carried an alarming tone of deference.

My spine prickled.

A figure rose from behind a quaint little chiminea belching metallic smoke through a hole in the center of the tent. The dimness of the interior cast shadows on his features but his air was unmistakable.

I knew exactly who stood in front of me, without having to ask. The infamous Dorian Jade.

My mouth went dry, my throat constricting dangerously.

Dorian Jade stood a little over six feet tall. Hair so dark it shone almost purple rippled around a rectangular face. Slight stubble decorated a strong chin and his pert lips stood to attention against the pale cream of his skin.

His eyes were a deep rich blue, shining with an inner light and ringed by black lashes and thick brows. His nose was long and straight.

His trousers and shirt were tailored to his slender figure, the cut of his jacket embroidered with silver and gold thread adding to his general debonair civility. He didn't look at all the way I'd always pictured—more like a mad zealot than an attractive thirty-something man.

"Tavi Alderidge. Finally." Dorian took a step closer and his features twisted in an alluring smile. He snapped his fingers and the ropes keeping me bound fell to the floor, undone by invisible hands. "It's a pleasure and an honor to meet you. I've heard much."

I wished I could say the same but anyone I'd asked had been closed lipped about *him*.

He reached for my hand and took it between his thumb and index finger. His lips made a graceful arch across my knuckles.

Charm, I saw in an instant. This was the kind of intensely charming and good-looking combination that established a person as a man a cult would follow.

My guard rose higher than normal.

"Welcome to my village. It's a quaint set-up, don't you think? Morgan, give us a moment alone, if you please. Miss Alderidge, have a seat. Get comfortable."

Morgan, or One Eye, bowed his head and disappeared out through the tent flap. The low tingle of magic burned the inside of my nose as a silencing bubble descended around us. Exhaustion kept me from recognizing its depths but I marked the smell for its uniqueness. Fresh raspberries and sulfur.

What an awful combination.

Dorian continued to watch me, waiting with one hand extended toward a plush loveseat tucked against the side of the tent.

"No one intends to harm you," he continued. "You have my word."

"Will you release my direwolf?" I hiked a thumb over my shoulder.

Dorian arched a brow. "Pardon me?"

"My direwolf, Noren. I won't speak to you until he's free." I made the demand boldly.

These people might not mean any harm to me, *yet*, as long as I cooperated, but I refused to allow my friend to suffer through the iron muzzle.

We both needed to be ready to run.

Just in case.

Irritation flashed across Dorian's face and screwed his features into an ugly grimace. In an instant, however, his smile returned. "I'm not generally in the position of allowing people to make demands of me."

"I'd think as a leader you'd be used to it by now." I took a risk talking back to him, but a moment later, Dorian popped his head out of the tent and motioned for the men to unbind Noren.

An overwhelming sense of the surreal colored the moment.

I'd been kidnapped by Dorian Jade, the man behind the conspiracy against the kingdom. The leader of the Unseelie fae, and he looked nothing like what I'd thought.

Noren slunk into the confines of the tent half a heartbeat later, his head low and his focus entirely on Dorian. The fur on his ruff rose and his eyes were narrow, glowing, his teeth white.

They stared at each other until Dorian made the first move and settled. He dropped down casually into a chair opposite the loveseat and crossed one ankle over the other knee. Utterly unbothered by the menacing growls rumbling from the back of Noren's throat.

"It makes sense for a half-werewolf to have a wolf protector. I enjoy a good bit of irony, and this seems to me the most perfect example. Yes." Dorian nodded decisively.

Finally, I felt like I had no choice but to sit with him. I reached out and kept one hand on top of the direwolf's head before cautiously taking the offered seat.

"As such a half breed, you must have seen how bigoted the Seelie can be. You've had to hide yourself from the moment you were accepted to the Halfling Academy in the normal world. Haven't you?" Dorian asked me.

"You already know my history, it seems, so you tell me," I snapped.

Instantly contrite, I reeled myself back. I'd learn nothing if I antagonized him too much.

I forced myself to relax. Of course he'd have to know all about me as leader of the opposition. One would be ineffective if one knew nothing about the people one was at war against.

Since coming here, I'd made my allegiance to Mike and his father clear to anyone on the outside, even when King Tywin kept his focus on me like a kid with an ant hill. The magnifying glass had inevitably come, and readily, curiously, he'd watched it burn me.

Dorian must have found the answer he searched for somewhere on my face. He tilted his head to the side and studied my expression, taking in every small change before his eyes met mine again. "Their world is unfriendly to anyone who is different," he said at last. "You've experienced it with your own eyes. The terrible burden of being born different, made different, except you are only you. Don't tell me you haven't experienced these things."

"You're not wrong." It seemed safe enough to agree with him.

Dorian leaned in eagerly, shifting again to balance his elbows on his knees now. His gaze took on a fiery light at my admission. "I'm sure you've lived through your fair share of tragedy since you crossed into our world. Beyond what my sources have reported. Being terrorized for a murder you did not commit is only one of them."

It really had been damn hard since I came to Faerie. I'd never fit in anywhere.

I started to agree with him but quickly snapped my mouth shut. *Less is more.* If I wanted to get out of here, then paying attention would work in my favor, rather than spilling my guts.

"I see a future where no one who walks through the portal to Faerie feels unwelcome, Miss Alderidge. A future built on the principles of fairness and equality, where those deemed lesser fae are equal." Unable to contain himself, Dorian rose to his feet, his arms out to his sides in a grand gesture. His manic fervor was contagious. "The king prefers to keep the status quo. I'm sure you've seen his convictions for yourself as well."

Damn, but he was convincing. I saw the image he painted in my head as he tugged on the small thoughts I'd barely given voice to before, thoughts about how nice it would be to finally feel like I was on equal footing with Mike. With the nobility.

Where members of the Claw & Fang no longer had to hide from everyone else.

His ability to express this, I knew, was what must capture the attention of others. And gain him multitudes of followers.

"You would be such an asset to me, Tavi. May I call you by your first name?" He launched ahead without waiting for me to answer. "I'd greatly appreciate us being on a first name basis."

He stepped close enough for me to scent his cologne, something spicy and complex.

"I suggest you join me. Let's see what we can accomplish together. You'd be a rallying point for people just like you, those who have always felt out of place. Which is why I wanted to speak with you today."

I eyed him skeptically and held my tongue again, waiting for him to finish.

"Please, eat dinner with my people tonight while you consider an alliance between us. Relax, warm your hands by the fire, and see who my people are before you automatically answer."

"You kidnapped me to forge an alliance?"

"I brought you here because I knew there was no better time to meet with you face to face. Not to mention you are a wanted person." He let the last part land heavily between us, then flashed a smile. "You are safe with me. Safe to be yourself."

Safe to be myself, I repeated mentally. A pipe dream if I'd ever heard one.

I was a wanted person. And I still needed to track down my mother and find Onyx, who had managed to escape the brutes sent to fetch us.

Dorian stepped aside with a magnanimous half bow. As

though I should be utterly grateful for this short time alone to compose myself. "Here's to the start of a beautiful adventure together."

I had goals to accomplish, my own, not anyone else's. And to be frank...

Joining forces with the great enemy of the man I loved sounded like a really *bad* idea.

15

Dorian Jade left me little choice when it came to dining with his people.

In fact, the harsh edges of his cloying and somewhat choking charm seemed to grow sharper as he led the way through the army of tents toward a larger than normal bonfire at its heart.

He stopped to talk to people when they approached, a motley assortment of fae and other creatures who would have been shunned within the city limits of Eahsea.

There, perfection reigned.

The pure-blooded were welcome, and the halflings, as long as they were half human and half fae, were welcome. But other subsets of fae were not permitted in the king's city.

Here, pixies danced through the air, those who survived the great war. There were nymphs with blush-colored skin like the breast of a dove who lifted their arms in the air and swayed with the wind.

Dryads collected acorns from the trees. There were families and children laughing, though most everyone stopped to stare at me and Noren as we passed. A beautiful picture, yes.

Why did something strike me as wrong?

What was off about the scene and why couldn't I put my finger on it?

I kept one hand firmly on Noren's shoulder, feeling the graceful rippling movement of each step, borrowing his strength as my own.

The fae here didn't appear to be a threat.

They were displaced families who had been driven out of their homes and forced into hiding. Dorian was their savior and he acted every bit the part. He waved magnanimously, he stopped to speak to anyone who approached him and appeared to actively listen to their concerns. He engaged, he took part in the conversations.

And I made sure to reserve my judgment.

After what I'd experienced, it felt much too easy to give in to this idea of a utopia. Too easy because I wanted it badly. The wanting always came easily but the execution fell short. Dreams didn't come true.

Only nightmares.

"Tavi, please follow me." Dorian reached back to me but I avoided his outstretched hand.

Another few minutes and he stopped in front of a circle of flames, with small tables and seats set around the embers. The scent of soft pine smoke drifted through the air and I drew in a deep breath.

The pang of homesickness hit me with the force of a sledgehammer. For a moment, I missed my pack with such an intensity I stopped dead in my tracks. The last time I'd seen them all gathered together had been my eighteenth birthday. Right before Uncle Will—

I shook my head to clear it.

Smoke from the burning wood not only perfumed the air but colored it in shades of navy and violet. And just beyond, with his face partially obscured, sat Onyx with his white hair standing out beacon-bright.

He stood when our eyes made contact and waited for me to round the fire. I stepped into his arms and squeezed him tightly, a hug of homecoming. Absolutely necessary.

"Damn it, I had no idea where you'd gone," he murmured to me.

We clung to each other.

I shifted to press my cheek to his chest. His heartbeat thrummed through me unsteadily. I blew out a breath and said, "I thought you got away. I wasn't sure whether to be worried or ecstatic."

"They must have transported me in a separate vehicle. You and Noren probably took up too much room in yours."

"Your joke is flat," I muttered.

I pulled back from Onyx to search his face for any kind of bruising or fresh cuts. He looked relatively unharmed but that didn't mean they'd taken into account his chronic injuries. I'd have to make sure he was fine. No bullshitting, either.

He was prone to downplaying his hurts.

Who wasn't?

He was pale, thinner, the circles under his eyes darker.

"Where did you go? When they brought you here?" Onyx gripped my face to keep me still but hell, I wasn't going anywhere.

Not when my hands had finally started to shake, as all the adrenaline finally left my body and made me weak.

"They took me straight to Dorian Jade." I gestured subtly toward the dark-haired man.

He'd nabbed a seat near a group of yellow-skinned fae,

their heads all bent together and their voices a hushed distortion too soft for me to make out over the crackling flames.

"I've heard good things about him, but this is the first time I've seen him face to face." Onyx shifted until our backs were to the fire. "Think I should go over and introduce myself? Make a good impression?"

"I think if you give him enough time, he'll come over and give you the same welcome spiel I got," I whispered. "He's trying to sell us a timeshare."

And I hated to admit how much I wanted to buy into the fantasy. Tonight would be a chance to observe, to see if the hype he served up was true.

"You two! Come, please." Dorian's voice cut across the clearing. "Join us for dinner. It would be our pleasure."

One of the yellow-skinned fae vacated their spot and approached us with a smile. A snap of her fingers, and a couple of wooden cups appeared in her hands. She held one out to Onyx and the other to me, waiting until we'd both grabbed hold before she bobbed her head.

"Nectar, harvested from nearby honeysuckles," she told us in a low rumbling voice like a cat's purr. "This drink is a specialty of my people. We're from the west," she continued at my questioning look.

"Your eyes are beautiful." I nodded in thanks for the drink and took a long sip while she watched.

Cold, sweet liquid caressed the inside of my parched throat. But it was the woman's pleased grin that truly made the moment special.

"Thank you." She gestured to her overly large eyes, her pupils multicolored and glittering, more similar to a dragon-fly's wing than anything I'd ever seen. "And the drink?"

Onyx drained his gup before he answered her. "Delicious." His tongue darted out to catch a stray drop of liquid and I chuckled.

"There are only a few hundred of her people that survived one of the king's random purges," Dorian explained when we sidled closer. "The island they inhabit is prime for minerals he uses for weapon production and the transportation system he implemented for the Seelie."

A weight settled in my chest at his words.

We sat on the fallen logs around Dorian with enough space between us for me to be able to watch his expressions. The yellow-skinned fae woman took her seat again but Dorian gestured to someone in the distance, and another fae holding a tray approached. She bowed her head at me and Onyx before crouching, waiting for us to take the food from her.

Both our plates held the same assortment of delicacies. Meat roasted over the fire which would surely compliment the fresh salad, and a fritter made with some kind of faintly sweet cornmeal. Maybe the acorns I'd seen the dryads harvesting earlier?

I thanked the woman and stalled with my gaze lingering on the hammered silver necklace she wore. My hand automatically lifted to my own identical necklace.

She dipped in a curtsy of acknowledgement before disappearing back into the deepening twilight of the woods.

Anyone who approached had nothing but the best things to say about Dorian, how he'd single-handedly saved them, or a friend, or a family member. They damn near worshiped the man.

The only ones who stayed silent were the servants. They were awfully subdued in comparison to everyone else in the camp. The matching uniforms marked them for their station, and if the clothing wasn't enough, the silver necklaces banded them together.

Weird.

Especially since I seemed to be the only other person in camp wearing one. Yet I wasn't a servant.

The honeysuckle nectar went straight to my head and the feast pushed the confines of my belly pleasantly. When was the last time I'd been this warm, or this full? When was the last time I'd had my thirst slaked and listened to conversation without the slender thread of tension pulling certain parts of me tight?

I couldn't remember.

One of the yellow-skinned fae drew Onyx into a conversation and he laughed, his head tilted back on his neck and his knee pressing against mine. My skin tingled where we touched, and even though I hadn't heard the punchline of the joke, I joined in the giggling.

After the feast, those who mingled around the fire broke out into impromptu singing and several others brought instruments out of nowhere.

Soon, the band struck up a lively chord that practically begged me to move my body.

"This is fantastic!" I called out to one of the fae.

She tapped her bare foot along with the tempo. "It's like this every night. We stand together because we want a united Faerie!"

My head spinning, I didn't break away when she placed her hand over mine and linked our fingers together. I felt her pulse inside of me as the music grew louder and brought us together.

"Dorian brought you here for a reason," the fae woman continued.

My heart swelled. This *was* fantastic. This was the way it

should be. The people here really did stand united for a Faerie free of the king's bigotry. Would it be so wrong to stand with them?

To believe the way they did, with utter conviction, that peace was possible?

I couldn't remember the last time I'd had such hope surging up from the depths of my being.

No matter who I spoke to, they were of the same mind. They spoke the same words of heart and hope and all kinds of things. They believed in the picture Dorian painted, and the more the night drew on, the easier it was for me to believe it, too.

Someone pressed another cup of nectar into my hand and I gulped it down greedily. The brew added to the sweet weight in my head, and the heavy blanket around my senses was a comfortable pall.

This time when someone grabbed my hand, I leaned into the contact, a little surprised when it turned out to be Onyx.

"Dance with me, Tavi!"

The music was a loud thrum in my blood. This time when my head spun, it was in the most delightful way, like I somehow spiraled right to the top of the wall dividing the kingdoms. I slapped my hand against Onyx's outstretched palm and allowed him to tug me to my feet.

Both of us swayed, so I knew he felt the way I did.

Tipsy.

Light. Free.

Even the pain lessened until I was hardly aware of the old wounds.

Several of the Unseelie clapped for us as we twisted our bodies in a random dance that forced a giggle bubbling out of me.

"I'm a terrible dancer," I admitted to Onyx loudly.

He shook his head as if it didn't matter, resting his opposite hand on my waist and drawing me closer. Our bodies twined together in the same rhythm as the beating drums around us.

Soon enough sweat dotted my hairline and plastered my shirt to my skin. My mouth hung open slightly, my eyes closed, my body listening to Onyx.

Maybe I could be happy here.

Onyx let out a whoop of pure joy and tightened his hold, jerking me forward harder until my front pressed to his with no room to breathe between us. This could be good. For me, for him. A place for us to really heal around like-minded people.

With him holding me, spinning us in dizzying circles, I let my mind race and my body arch backward. Dancing and flying were one and the same.

As long as Onyx had me, we were happy. For tonight...I could let myself go.

Maybe everyone had it wrong and Dorian Jade *wasn't* the enemy. I liked what he'd done with the camp. And so many people I'd talked to couldn't all be wrong, could they? They had to make a point.

The bigotry of the royal court had to go.

It had no place in this world anymore. Lines should never be drawn separating fae from fae, person from person. Some of the best people I knew were halflings who shouldn't exist, and some of the worst were those considered pure-blood.

Onyx stopped suddenly and jerked me to him. My chest bumped against his and I laughed breathlessly. His eyes echoed the same heat mingling with my blood, overly bright and a little glassy.

My gaze dropped to his lips as his tongue darted out to lick the lower one. I watched as if in slow motion, found myself leaning forward.

Another dancer staggered into us and sent the three of us tripping dangerously toward the fire, which only resulted in another round of giggles.

Afterward, someone led us to our separate tents and only then did I realize the drop in temperature. I shivered and the sweat froze on my skin. It was much colder here than it was in the Seelie court.

But the tent blocked the worst of the wind.

Alone, I snuggled closer to Noren, his warmth providing the perfect opposition to the chill outside. It seeped in through the seams of the tent but the pallet bed was comfortable enough to allow me a little bit of sleep.

More sleep, I had to admit, than I'd gotten recently, so I counted it as a blessing. The dizziness hadn't gotten any better, but being here...it helped. It provided a distraction from my own bullshit and gave me something entirely new to think about.

Another path.

I swallowed a chuckle when Noren groaned and rolled over to half squash me, pushing me into wakefulness. My ribs ached in protest but I scooted out of his way and wrapped my arms around his back.

Another path, and it was for me to decide if I wanted to take it or not. That was how I had to consider things now.

My choice.

It felt better to think of things in those terms. It felt less black and white. Less like I was a victim of fate or a casual observer in my own life, destined to pay the consequences for other people's prejudice.

A soft knock on the exterior bones of the tent had me jolting up in bed.

My hair flopped over my face and I hurried to push it back, noting the slight outline of a shadowy figure outside the flaps. Morning already? I felt like I'd just dropped off.

"Yes?" I called out.

"Beg your pardon, Miss." A slender woman slipped inside, her hair caught somewhere between gold and green in the oddest combination I'd ever seen. She stood and straightened, and the bones of her face gave her away as one of the pure fae. The same silver collar hung heavily around her slender neck. "I've been sent to bathe you and help you dress."

I cleared my throat and pushed at Noren. He yawned right in my face, those curved fangs inches from my nose, before huffing and curling into a tighter ball on the pallet.

"I really don't need help bathing."

"Dorian insists. He doesn't allow anyone to say no to him."

The woman stepped back and held the flap open to make room for two more fae to enter the tent. Unease suddenly crawled along my spine and I forced it aside to watch them. They were here to help, I told myself.

I clamped my lips tightly together as the three women brought in a small basin. One of them dragged over a table while the third set up a short stool with towels and a change of clothes. I definitely wouldn't mind the new clothes. Mine were covered in filth, sweat, and blood. They were practically cement at this point and crusty enough to crack.

Once they were finished, the two left and the first woman straightened. "Come." She wiggled her fingers. "We must start the day."

I shook my head. "This really isn't necessary." Suddenly Noren jerked fully awake, causing me to jolt with surprise.

"Please." She sounded desperate. "Dorian doesn't like to be kept waiting and he especially hates wasting precious daylight hours."

One of the two women returned carrying two urns of steaming water. Outside, I'd gotten a glimpse of a dark sky paling with the deep pinks of dawn.

"There is no need to fear us. We're only here to help you, Miss." She spoke in a soft voice designed to put me at ease.

"Thanks." I awkwardly stood in front of them and let the blanket drop. I'd slept in my bra and underwear last night. My clothing should really be burned. "What's your name?"

She ducked her head and her wealth of hair hid her expression. "My name isn't important."

"I'll need to call you something."

She hesitated a moment before saying shyly, "Elaen, then. Please call me Elaen."

"Then thank you for helping me, Elaen." I stood for a moment longer before I forced my arms to relax to my sides. "How are we doing this?"

"Step into the basin and we'll take care of the rest. Please, there's no reason for you to be embarrassed. We have complete privacy here."

With no other choice and the waiting servant still holding the two steaming urns, I peeled off my bra and undies and stepped over the lip of the bowl, absolutely naked. Noren turned his back to allow us a small bit of privacy but I wouldn't dream of letting him leave me alone.

Feeling awkward, I attempted small talk as a distraction. "How long have you been living at camp, Elaen?"

Elaen started, and when she reached down for a sponge,

her fingers trembled. She drew it across the skin of my arm. "I'm a recent addition. I was brought here six months ago."

"Do you like it so far?" I asked.

Elaen didn't answer. She only poured more water over my skin and alternated between that and the sponge.

The night's chill hadn't reached the inside of the tent yet and it was easier to relax under the heat of the water. The whole bath thing, though...that was new.

"A few people last night wanted to get me and my friend to stay," I told her.

Elaen swallowed. I watched her throat bob." Yes, they would."

The sense of unease grew, knotting inside of me. "Dorian spoke of an alliance between us," I continued. That seemed the best way to put it. "He certainly has big dreams for the future."

"Miss." Elaen stopped and gripped my hand so forcefully my eyes widened under a flash of pain. At once, my arm began to throb. "You have to run."

I went cold all over.

She shook her head and the spell broke as she continued to scrub me down.

"There are others like me," Elaen added, "who have been brought to camp. They've been in service much longer."

"It's the second time you've said it that way. Brought here. You didn't come on your own? Looking for a better future?" I asked, grasping at straws trying to find an answer to why I felt so uneasy.

"You mustn't ask such questions." Now her voice shook too.

It was my turn to stop and reach for her before she lifted my foot to soap my ankles. "Elaen, please. What's going on?"

Her eyes were filled with terror. "Just let me wash you, Miss."

"Why did you tell me to run?"

"You will never be safe as long as you wear the necklace," Elaen whispered. "But you're not one of us. He won't automatically toss you aside."

My mind struggled to make sense of it. Elaen continued her washing and I dropped the subject, mulling it over again and again.

What was I missing?

There was a piece somewhere I'd tossed aside, not making the connection.

But Elaen, the other servers last night, the collar around my own neck—

I stumbled backward and dirty water splashed everywhere. Elaen was pure-blood fae. I knew it, of course. And enslaved. It was clear in her mannerisms. So were the women last night.

Dorian Jade kept pure-bloods in his employ against their will and forced them to take care of him and his people.

The revelation crashed down on me ocean-wave style until it blotted out every other thought. My gaze became unfocused, my heart lurched into my sternum, and the thundering in my ears was louder than the sound of my breathing.

Dorian wasn't interested in equality. He was interested in conquering, and he stepped on the backs of the enslaved pure-bloods to get there.

16

I pushed the heel of my hand into my chest to quell the sudden pain there.

No one saw a problem with this?

I felt foolish that I'd been thinking how Dorian and the Unseelie might be the answer.

"Miss? Are you all right?"

I forced myself to breathe normally and look down at Elaen, with her skin drawn and her eyes dull. "I'm fine," I tried to say but no sound came out. I could only nod.

She rinsed my hair with the last of the fresh water before wrapping a towel around my shoulders. Numb, I stood trembling as she scrubbed me dry, pointedly avoiding making eye contact.

Elaen was a slave, pure and simple, because of circumstances she had no control over. It made Dorian Jade no better than King Tywin and both of them were absolutely certain they were in the right.

As though there was no middle ground where everyone, every single damn fae, had a place to live their lives.

Elaen helped me out of the basin and held out a loose

pair of linen trousers, waiting for me to step into the legs one foot at a time. The material cinched at the waist and flowed loosely around my ankles. She followed the trousers with a loose wrap top that left my arms free, then with a little urging she sat me down onto the stool to braid my wet hair.

"You're upset by what I told you," she said softly.

The first swipe of the brush through the strands had me closing my eyes and swallowing a grimace. Not only because of the sensation but also to avoid staring at her reflection in the small mercury glass mirror and seeing the glint of the metal collar.

I had to be careful what I said. She probably wouldn't report back to Dorian but what if he coerced her? There were ways to get people to talk even without the cognitive manipulation I possessed.

"I just think there should be a world where everyone is equal," I replied slowly, considering every word.

Elaen's hands stilled. "It's a beautiful goal."

Both of us quieted. She finished the braid with deft fingers and patted my shoulder, offering a thin-lipped smile before she ducked her head, disappearing through the tent flap.

She was right, though. I had to run. As fast and as far away as possible.

The sooner I got this over with, the better it would be for everyone involved. My gut told me Dorian Jade wasn't going to let me go easily, but with Noren nearby, I had faith we'd be able to fight our way out of this camp. Most of the people here weren't warriors. If worse came to worst, then I'd shift into my halfling warrior form and raze a path out.

I bent down in front of Noren and scratched his ears

until he turned to face me fully, his attention sharpening on me.

"Find Onyx," I said. I had no doubt he understood every word. "Tell him to meet us at the wall in about fifteen minutes. It shouldn't take too long to reach it. Make sure he understands what's really going on. Can you do that for me?"

Noren blinked, as sure a sign as any that he understood, and I straightened as he jumped off the pallet and headed outside on silent paws.

I drew in a great breath and held it until my lungs ached. Now or never.

I'd memorized the way to Dorian's tent. The maze seemed much less complicated with full morning light piercing through the trees. The same smoke curved from the top of his tent and I paused to knock at the entrance.

"Dorian? It's Tavi." My voice shook.

Crap, no shaking yet. Get a grip.

"You may enter." He sounded as regal as any monarch I'd ever met.

I stifled the urge to roll my eyes at the grandiose tone

Dorian stood staring at a stack of papers when I walked inside and immediately set them aside just out of eyesight. "Tavi, good morning." He offered me an easy smile and a flash of white teeth. "How are you feeling today?"

I swallowed over a knot of nerves and forced my face to mimic his. Actually, my arm barely hurt, although a dull throbbing remained if I tuned into it.

"I'm well, thank you. I wanted to talk to you about the matter we discussed last night."

At this, his grin widened and his eyes took on the manic light I'd glimpsed yesterday, where they seemed to glow. An odd look and a distraction.

"You've given some thought to my proposition, then," he said. "Come, let's chat!"

Now or never. "I have." I puffed my cheeks out and launched ahead. "First, thank you for everything you've done and for sharing your story with me. But no thanks. I'm actually ready to leave the camp and continue on my personal journey."

I'd never even gotten a chance to explain my quest to him. He hadn't allowed me a word in edgewise.

Dorian arched a thick dark brow and waited for me to continue.

This was the quietest I'd seen him.

"I've wanted to find my mother for the longest time and I finally have the opportunity to do so now." *No*, I reminded myself. *No excuses for my choice. Only the facts.* "I have no iron in this fire."

"No iron in this fire," Dorian repeated. He took a step forward, his arms loose and his thumbs looped casually into the pockets of his trousers. "Tavi, I need you to understand. You are a part of this fight simply because of your *existence*. I understand you have personal goals you feel the need to accomplish but at this point, allowing you to leave on a frivolous errand makes no sense."

Allowing me?

"Finding the mother I've never met is frivolous to you?" Immediately my back went up. "I thought you placed a lot of stock on the importance of family."

He shook his head, his gaze sympathetic under his long black lashes. Fingers lifted, he pressed them in a triangle shape to his lips before he lifted his head again.

"It seems as though your priorities are not in alignment."

I blinked at him." Excuse me?"

"There are so many other things requiring your talents and skills. As you can see, it does not behoove me to allow you to leave. Not when I finally have you here."

I started inching closer to the door, preparing to outright run. "What do you mean?"

Dorian simply smiled. His posture remained relaxed, easygoing. "I think you'll find that you won't mind staying once you've had a few days to reconsider."

"You can't keep me here."

"On the contrary. I can. I plan to, until you see reason. Trust me." He still sounded accommodating even as he swung the proverbial ax. "It's for the best."

He lifted one hand out of his pocket and drew out a medallion like the one I was wearing. At once my spine stiffened, heat flooding my entire body. My stomach dropped. What...what was he doing? I turned away...or rather tried. The effort left me wrung out, exhausted, as I fought to move my arm, my leg, a single muscle in my face, and found my body did not belong to me anymore.

"Don't worry, Tavi. No one is going to hurt you while you're here. I simply can't allow you to leave, not yet. Not until you've had time to consider things from my perspective," he continued.

"What have you done to me?" I managed to say through the thin seam of my lips. Terror rose up, screaming, too loud to blot out.

"You and your friend Onyx will stay with us. At least your necklace is not as cumbersome as the collars the servants wear. The same material, however. Magical bindings," Dorian explained. He pursed his mouth. "I find them absolutely necessary. Also, congratulations on your powerful manipulation of my direwolf. I commend you for what you've managed to accomplish. I meant to mention it yesterday but didn't want to startle you."

"No..."

Tears pricked the corners of my eyes. In that single sentence, he'd confirmed everything for me.

Dorian Jade *had* been the one to send the direwolf to kill me, to siphon my powers. When it didn't work...he'd clearly moved on to Plan B.

Now he had me right where he wanted me.

"It's a shame I'm going to have to take him back. You are skilled, Tavi, a powerful halfling who, with the right guidance, could reach staggering heights. There is still time for you. At this point, however, I suggest you take a few days to adjust and make yourself useful at the same time," he added.

"Whatever it is you're doing—"

"*Done*," Dorian interrupted to correct. "It's what I've done, this trap you've fallen into. I don't blame you. For all your power, you're still young. It's hard to consider things from every angle."

He whistled a slow, hissing melody I'd never heard before. My heart thrummed agonizingly against my ribs as Noren stepped into the tent.

"Please, don't. You can't do this," I managed.

"I'm taking him back, my dear. After all, he's my weapon. As you will be as well."

Everything inside of me broke when Dorian lifted his hands. Magic rushed out from him in visible waves. He didn't need a spell. Not when this was his show, and he ran it effortlessly. Flawlessly.

Noren stiffened, a growl building in the back of his throat until all of a sudden it stopped. As quickly as the sound began, it cut off, and the direwolf appeared to grow several inches.

Even his expression shifted, his lips peeled back from his teeth in a snarl, and he trotted back to Dorian's side and sat. Facing me.

Sizing me up the same way he had when we first faced off.

God, no.

My heart cracked at the expression. My friend was gone. Disappeared, as though our experiences never existed. Perhaps they didn't, because the animal who stared at me now only wanted blood. Mine, specifically.

Dorian clapped his hands together and a moment later, Elaen entered the tent with her head bowed.

"Sir?"

"Please escort Tavi to the kitchen. We could use her assistance in lunch preparation for the camp."

I didn't recognize the voice Dorian used, either. Cold did not begin to describe the ice spearing out from every syllable. The disdainful look in his eyes when he spoke to the high fae woman...

Neither of us had a choice. Elaen because she was a slave, and me because the power of the necklace was too much for me to fight. She took my arm and guided me outside with no hesitation. My footsteps were heavy, my stride wooden, and my gaze forced to stare directly ahead.

The farther we got from Dorian, the more control I got back. Unfortunately for me, it was never enough to break his spell.

"Kitchen duty is never fun, Miss. I'm sorry for you," Elaen whispered.

The moment she'd spoken, she zipped her lips tightly

shut again, as if even that small statement would land her in a world of trouble.

Another kitchen. My god, I couldn't get *away* from the kitchen.

I pulled out of Elaen's arm and tugged at the thick chains around my neck, looking for a latch. Two metal studs stood out on one of the chains but I had no way of pulling them apart. They were seamless, perfectly constructed, and although it had first appeared wide enough to make it over my head, it now fit snugly.

Elaen let me struggle, winding through the tents until we reached a massive structure open on one side.

"You won't find a way to get them off," Elaen leaned in close to whisper against my ear. "They'll shock you if you take a step outside of the camp boundaries."

I seethed. "Like a dog with an electric fence."

"I'm sorry."

Elaen scurried off without making any introductions to the people working in the kitchen. None were needed, I found in a moment. A sullen-faced older gentleman with three arms, each of them boasting six gnarled fingers at the end of long hands, pointed me in the direction of a pile of potatoes.

A peeler rested on a butcher block slab beside the pile. His message was clear. Peel. And don't stop until they were done.

It was a world of difference from Raelynn's kitchen. Although my boss had been all business, the walls always rang out with laughter. Conversation flowed and the staff in the castle appeared to have their own language when it came to certain things.

Not a word would be said at times but someone would

let out a snort of laughter that had the rest of them joining along once they understood the reason why.

These people were kicked, kicked, and then kicked again. None of them wanted to be here and I wondered if any of them had family at home missing them.

Those thoughts were too depressing.

I stood staring at the pile of potatoes until the older fae gently cleared his throat, then I moved into position.

How far away were we from the borders of the camp? How bad were the shocks from the collar?

I gnawed on my lower lip as I worked, the brown skin peeling easily away from the tubers to reveal white flesh inside. Shit and double shit. My stomach looped into a labyrinth of stress and with every inch I peeled, the more the acidic throbbing in my arm grew.

If magic made the collars work, then magic might be the key to getting out of them. Unless Dorian Jade specifically bespelled them to turn the user's magic against them if they even made an attempt.

It might be a risk worth taking.

"*Psst.* New girl. Hey!"

A hot whisper ruffled the hair near my temple and I turned to see a small-statured boy with the legs of a goat staring from the workspace beside mine. He stood on a stool, his hooves polished to a sheen like obsidian and his gaze searching.

Maybe he only looked like a boy at first glance.

Because the longer I stared at him, the more his eyes seemed to suggest this faun had seen terrible things.

"I know what you're thinking," he started. "I don't look like a pure-blood fae. But I'm Seelie and that's what got me here. Just my luck to end up running into one of Dorian Jade's minions. I'm going to guess you told him something that pissed him off, because I saw you around the fire with *his majesty* last night. You looked like you were having fun. Right?"

My stomach flipped and took a nosedive. I'd almost banked on the silence to give me more time to calculate a plan to get out of here, despite coming up short.

"He's not my biggest fan right now," I answered honestly.

"I'd like to tell you it's not so bad but I'd be lying. It's really fucking awful."

I jolted at the sound of such a harsh curse coming out of the mouth of someone who looked like a boy of ten. Then I decided I kinda liked his no-bullshit attitude. "Being a slave isn't for the faint of heart, is what you're saying."

The faun shrugged. "In so many words, yeah."

The older gentleman cleared his throat louder this time and both the faun and I turned back to our jobs. For the rest of the time, we worked. My pile of potatoes never grew any smaller and every time I reached for the last one, another pyramid replaced the first.

Lunch came and went, with only a five-minute break to use the restroom and grab some water for the *help*. I gulped down a glass until my throat unclenched.

Dorian Jade was a monster.

A prejudiced, hypocritical monster.

Once our break ended, the older fae, who appeared to be a type of foreman keeping everyone organized, clapped his hands and sent us back to work. Instead of potatoes, this time I exchanged places with the faun and scrubbed the dishes used by the rest of the camp.

The blasting hot water scalded my cramped and aching fingers. Blisters burst open and the soap stung to the point where I bit my lip to stay quiet.

I'd be damned if I let Dorian hear me cry out or complain.

I never saw Onyx through the rest of the day.

Once we completed dinner, cooking and cleaning, I followed the other women across the camp toward a massive tent stretching out between the trees. A sort of female dormitory, one of them explained. I caught a glimpse of Elaen across the clearing along with the other two women who had set up my bath this morning.

It felt like a million years ago.

"Here is your bed, girl." A woman with short pudgy wings that appeared almost clipped pointed to the upper bunk of the nearest bed. "There is a fresh change of clothes on the sheets. Dorian insists on cleanliness at all times. He says it boosts morale for his people to see us so."

Her voice was a murmur in the wind but I heard it clear as a bell, including the emotion behind it she no doubt wanted to hide.

Exhaustion, hopelessness.

I was right back where I'd started.

I said nothing, nodding at her until she returned the gesture and walked off to find her own bed for the evening. Every part of my body hurt, and my hands had gotten so chapped from working in the kitchen that the cracks around my broken fingernails bled.

Several of my nails had broken off below the skin line and I still felt the stinging pulse of the hot water.

The dorms were quieter than any I'd ever been inside. Maybe the raucous laughter of my bunkmates back at the Halfling Academy had given me a false idea, or perhaps things changed when you were locked up by magic and treated as a slave.

The women here had been pushed to the brink. They

went about their duties with a quiet and tense hush, taking turns at the copper basin in the corner with magicked water running in a constant warm stream.

I took my place in line, mechanically washing my face and underneath my arms before I found a dark corner to change. There was no modesty here.

The lights went out automatically and I was already situated in the bed, the bunk rock-hard. I rested my arms underneath my head and stared at the gently wavering top of the tent, the coolness of the night omnipresent.

What the hell was I going to do? There had to be some way out of this even if I couldn't get the collar to release me.

Was there a way to get back to Dorian and somehow use my mental manipulation on him? I had to be stronger than the collar especially with the *Totalis*—

Except I didn't have the *Totalis*.

I'd left it in my change of clothes and those had been taken when they sent me from the tent. I wanted to slap myself.

Stupid. I was so *stupid*.

Tomorrow, I thought with a wide yawn, my jaw cracking. Tomorrow I'd worry about the artifact, and escape, and every other detail pressing on me. Sleep took me whether I wanted it to or not, mid-thought, and thankfully the dreams were not as horrible as they could have been given the circumstances.

I was running, chased by a creature in the dark, a creature with startling eyes and dark hair—

A tongue ran across my face and slurped at the corners of my eyes.

Decidedly not a dream.

A massive paw nudged against my face, pushing with

only a fraction of his strength, and I blinked awake into the familiar wolfy smile of Noren.

"Oh, my god."

He whined low in his throat, my stomach dropping out from under me. Shrugging off the last of my sleep, I crawled toward the ladder and clambered down.

The second my feet touched the cold ground Noren leaped on me and I wrapped him in a big hug. "You came for me." Tears burned, streaking down my cheeks, lost in the sea of his fur.

He chose me. Dorian hadn't broken him. Hadn't erased the kind protective streak of the direwolf I knew. I squeezed him to the point of suffocation.

He didn't move, either.

Glee overrode every emotion as I scratched my hand through the fur at the scruff of his neck toward his jaw. He came back for me. And he brought...something.

My fingertips brushed against a hard piece of metal clenched between his teeth. I reared back, staring at him hard until Noren dropped the item at my feet and let out a low-pitched *woof*.

His eyes bore into mine as I bent to pick up the thing. I turned the device over in my hands, trailing my fingers over two metal studs on one side.

Two studs—

They matched the shapes at the back of my neck collar.

I stood straight up, my gaze traveling between the device to Noren and back again. He bobbed his head slightly in a way-too-human gesture. A loud snore cut through the hush and I almost jumped out of my skin. He'd brought me a way *out*.

If we were going to do this, then I needed to hurry

before someone woke up and saw a big fucking direwolf in the middle of the dorm tent.

Here goes nothing.

My hands refused to obey my unspoken demand to hurry as I placed the device against the collar, struggling to get the right angle so the pieces clicked together. The metal prods did not want to go in the slots. Frustration mounting, I shoved it into a better position, gritting my teeth. My wrist began to cramp.

Hurry!

The two pieces finally clicked together. The collar opened and fell off. I fumbled for it, grabbing it before it hit the floor, and faced Noren.

"You genius boy," I whispered.

Not only had he come for me but he'd come through with a miracle. Whatever connection we had...this situation demolished the piece of guilt I'd carried around about manipulating him mentally. It might have started out that way but he was mine.

My partner and friend.

I glanced around to see if anyone had woken, shoving the device into the pocket of my sleep pants. We ducked out of the tent and I took in the star-lit night with my breath gusting in a white puff.

Several nearby fires had been banked for the evening with the embers glowing orange, crackling as they died.

I had no idea where Dorian had decided to stash Onyx.

I had no idea if he'd even gotten around to *telling* Onyx about the deal or not. To the left I spotted a tent of similar size to the female dorm but through the trees. That must be where he kept the males.

Would Onyx be there with them?

I crouched down in front of Noren. "Are you able to track Onyx?"

The direwolf stared for a moment before he pushed off to the left, his nose against the ground and his hair lifted along his spine. I refused to leave without Onyx. We'd gotten into this situation together and if he had to stay here much longer...they wouldn't know how to help him. His injuries would be exacerbated if he said no to Dorian and they put him to work.

Or worse...what if he said yes?

I clenched my jaw as we kept our footsteps light, trailing around lazy fires and tents filled with sleeping families.

A twig cracked under my foot and I tensed, catching my breath. My awareness sharpened and I realized I felt the magic of the wall this close. Without the collar, its presence was oppressive, not something to ignore.

Why hadn't I noticed it the first time I'd stepped into the camp?

I should have spent more time with Onyx instead of letting Dorian Jade distract me with his idealism. His plans for the future. They'd all felt too good to be true, and they were.

No, he had Onyx stashed somewhere and even Noren seemed to be losing the scent. He turned in a circle around one tent and went in the direction we'd already come from. He stopped in front of one of the tents and a quick peek through the flap showed a sleeping couple with their arms wrapped around each other and their forms surrounded by comfortable blankets. A small pet, a cross between a rabbit and a cat, perked its ears up at my arrival but made no sound.

I quickly headed back outside with my heart thrumming

an irregular beat in my chest. Every breath seemed to tighten my ribs closer and closer to the core of me.

Sneaking around had never been my forte.

I lacked the stealth most wolf shifters had, and even though I tried not to make a sound, I felt like a herd of stampeding elephants. As though every inhalation I took might be my last, I swallowed convulsively.

We approached the edge of the camp and the tents were fewer here, the space between them greater, as though the occupants had opted for more freedom from the community. More isolation.

It suited Onyx but would Dorian have known about that? I highly doubted it. If anything—

A hand wrapped around my elbow and jerked me back, my heart lurching into my throat.

"What the hell is this?" The man tightened his grip on me until his fingers bruised. My stomach sank down to the bottom of my feet. "You're not going anywhere."

17

I reacted without thought, no time to even try my cognitive manipulation.

He yanked me forward and I reared back and loosed my fist at the guy, landing a hit on his chin.

Shit, had I cracked my own bones? I hissed, cradling my hand against my chest.

The element of surprise was on my side though because he hadn't expected me to retaliate. Even if he'd noted I wasn't wearing a collar.

The fae male crumpled into a fetal position on the ground. Down for now, but how long would he stay out? He hadn't sounded the alarm so I'd have to hurry.

Exhaustion rushed at me, too weak from the collar to be of any real good. "We have to find Onyx *now*," I whispered to Noren.

The two of us redoubled our efforts, moving fast and loud. My fingers twitched, the pain in my knuckles fading in comparison to the terror of being found out. We kept to the perimeter of the camp and I followed a few steps beyond Noren.

Finally he stopped and pointed with his snout, his eyes narrowing on a spot ahead.

Adrenaline pushed me forward with such force my stomach dropped. Puking wasn't going to help. Neither would worry or anxiety. But they trailed me on the way to the tent and I lifted the flap to see a single figure with starlight hair sleeping on his side on the pallet.

Onyx.

A breath of relief ripped from my lungs. I hurried inside with Noren. An explosive snore told me he wasn't alone and I turned to glance over my shoulder at two other pallets. Great, roommates.

Or more likely they were spies, sent to watch Onyx and gently persuade him to cooperate with Dorian. He hadn't been put to work, yet.

My numb fingers didn't want to move. They certainly didn't want to get the device into place, and I fumbled too many times crouched beside his pallet. Luckily from the angle of his head, I had unobstructed access. I slid the notches into place and the collar released with a click.

Onyx's eyes popped open at the sound and he sat straight up in bed. I hurried to press my palm to his mouth to keep him quiet.

His eyes went wide and angry until recognition dawned and he relaxed, his chest dropping.

"What are you doing here?" he muttered against my palm.

"Getting you out, clearly," I whispered. "Why weren't you in the bunks with the others?" He was sharing a space, but in the dimness it was impossible to tell if the other two men in the tent were slaves or not.

"I told him I needed to think about things. Guess it put me in a holding pattern. He slapped me with a collar but said he'd give me time." Onyx shifted to his side and rubbed the area around his neck where the chain had rested. His features twisted. "How did you get it off?"

"Noren brought me the key."

Onyx pursed his lips and let out a nearly silent whistle. "Then we're out."

He pushed the blankets away and crept to the other pallets to wake the men. They spoke in hushed voices and Onyx handed the device off to the first one. "Pass it on. Free as many people as possible, men and women."

The fae male stared between us with wide eyes and nodded, pressing the device to the piece at his neck a heartbeat later.

Free as many slaves as possible. Yes, I liked that idea. These people didn't deserve to be prisoners any more than the halflings in the Seelie court deserved their fates.

Onyx stood too quickly and lost his balance, gripping the side of the tent until the wave of dizziness passed. At last he opened his eyes and met mine. "I'm ready."

I cast one last look back at the others before I followed Noren and Onyx out of the tent.

I had to believe those men would do whatever they could to free the others.

With every footstep toward the wall, my focus narrowed, even as my chest tightened. We had to make sure we got there before anyone realized we were missing, and the last few hours until daylight were the only window we had.

"Can you run?" I twisted closer to support Onyx.

"I'll try."

Freedom was close enough for me to taste and that scared me more than anything else. There were hurdles to get over before we made it, huge ones, but the collars were off and that had been the biggest problem.

I prayed he was correct and the device would save many more before it fell back into the wrong hands. No one deserved to live under the thumb of a man who wanted to control them, to force them to work, who took away their choices.

I pumped my arms at my sides and hustled as fast as my legs would allow. Onyx kept up to the best of his abilities, leaning heavily on Noren. The direwolf didn't seem to mind the extra weight.

Every step made the bands constricting my ribs grow tighter and the thud of my heart to pound erratically. If we didn't get away from this camp tonight then we'd never leave. We'd lose our one shot—

I pushed those thoughts out of my head and shook it violently for good measure. We'd make it out. We had to.

Dorian Jade couldn't be allowed to get away with his plan.

We booked it through the trees and into the depths of the forest by the light of the stars overhead, moving as quickly as possible until Onyx started to flag. My own magic had taken such a hit from the collar, I had no power to offer him, only a shoulder.

I fell into step at his side and took some of his weight for him, both of us managing together somehow.

The light in front of us grew brighter and the trees thinned enough for me to make out the shimmering mass of the wall separating the courts. It rose, towering, toward the velvet sky, glowing with its own light.

Oh, shit, it felt...alive, and terrible. It felt heavy and oppressive and drew every ounce of magic out, leaving me hollow.

Onyx and I both stopped dead in our tracks without having to speak out loud to the other.

"The necklaces," Onyx said, his tone seeped in dread.

I'd been too focused on escape to remember.

We had no way to get through the wall. We'd been given the necklaces to protect us from the magic when we first arrived, and without them, we were stuck. Trapped on the Unseelie side.

"What are we going to do?" I asked him through numb lips.

He shifted from foot to foot, Noren moving to my other side and crouching down with a whine.

Finally, Onyx sank, his legs folding beneath him like he just couldn't move anymore. "I heard talk in camp. The city where your mom is supposed to be? It's decently close to the Unseelie wall. If I can figure out a direction, then we'll travel along the wall."

My stomach plummeted. "It's not safe to be on this side."

Onyx turned to me and his eyes radiated an inner power. "We either stay and wait for Dorian Jade to give us two new necklaces or we walk. We're out of options."

My knees gave a twinge of protest at the thought of walking.

"How are you going to figure out what direction we need to go?"

He lifted his face to the sky rather than answer and scented the wind. A small pulse of magic rang out from his hand when he held it aloft and he scrutinized the stars. Then, weirdly, he turned back the way we came.

"West. We go west."

"Isn't it going to take us right back to camp?"

He pushed to his feet again, wavering before he straightened his spine. "Somehow we got turned around, Tavi. Our senses must have been muddled with the proximity to the wall because judging by the constellations, we were heading back to camp already."

Ice grew in my veins at the thought. "Okay." I paused, swallowed, cleared my throat of the pins blocking it. "Okay, let's go."

We'd have to try and find a way through the wall once we got to the right place. We'd—

The thought cut off abruptly as a wave of dizziness crashed down on me, so strong I stopped and held my palm to the side of my head like an anchor.

My arm twinged and the rest of me went up under small pinpricks of flame.

"Hey, are you okay?" Onyx's question sounded at a distance and almost inaudible against the sudden ringing in my ears.

No, not okay. Definitely not okay. I reached out for something to steady myself and came up with empty air instead.

Eventually, the spell passed with a few deep breaths, but the queasiness never left. I pried my eyes open and tried to smile at Onyx.

He took a step in the opposite direction at whatever he saw on my face.

"I'm going to be fine." I sounded waterlogged and sick. "Let's go. As far and as fast as possible."

At least we were together, I consoled myself. Even if we had to push through exhaustion and our own pains and sickness, we were together. I'd found Onyx, and Noren had found me.

The journey would be ten times easier, a hundred times easier, if I felt better. My shirt clung to my sweat slicked back and the ache in my muscles doubled in the next hour. I needed to find a witch, or a doctor or shaman, as soon as possible. We didn't have any more time to waste.

The gloom of pre-dawn slowly melted away into a sunrise of amber and pink. The rising sun chased the last of the clouds from the horizon until overhead, the sky opened up.

Although neither of us spoke, we kept going. My stomach gave a low grumble that somehow translated into pain rather than hunger.

Eventually Noren forced us to stop late in the afternoon. He cut in front of me and sat down, the movement sudden, and I almost tripped over him. He offered a growl before rising to lick my face.

"What's his problem?" Onyx asked, the syllables slurring together slightly.

"If I have to guess, I'd say he's concerned." I glanced around but the forest looked exactly the same here. "Do you think we're safe to set up a camp and rest for a bit?"

"I don't think we're safe anywhere until we get the fuck out of this court." Onyx straightened and purposely wiped the strain away from his face when he felt my attention on him. The change came over his features rapidly but even his best efforts couldn't disguise the lines around his eyes which hadn't been there when I first met him. "We need to find somewhere off the beaten path, with shelter in case the weather turns."

I glanced up at the cloudless sky overhead but sighed, knowing he was right. The land didn't want me here on this side of the wall any more than it did on the Seelie side.

It took several more minutes for us to find two huge pine trees offering shelter, and we made a small makeshift camp between them. The wind bit into my exposed skin with needle-like teeth. Every gust that blew offered no respite from the chill of the evening. It was colder here in Unseelie than in the Seelie court, and the biting nip almost seemed to herald snow, which sounded insane.

The trees were evergreen and moss speckled the ground, but we weren't even close to winter.

It was the same way the weather went crazy when I was unsettled. My fault again? Probably.

Although I'd seen crazier things. The weather always revolted against me when I least expected the change, and right then I was too tired to care.

We couldn't take a chance and light a fire. It would draw our enemies. Instead, Onyx and I huddled together, stealing warmth from the other and passing it between us. Noren was practically a furnace but when he left to hunt, we were alone. Shivering.

Terrified and cold and tired.

I'd never take a blanket for granted again. I always thought I'd rather be too cold than overheated, but these chilly days in the elements had me seriously reconsidering.

Noren returned with a squirrel and Onyx mustered up a burst of magic to roast the thing. Which wasn't necessary, but it helped.

Once again we were back on the run.

Thank goodness for the direwolf. His bulk provided the warmth we needed to keep the chill from sinking deep into our bones.

"It's all going to be okay," Onyx offered.

Something in his voice told me he spoke out loud more for his benefit than for mine but we both knew his words were an empty promise.

"I'd like to believe it but I'm a little old to put my faith in fairy tales."

"It's better than the alternative. Do you want to stay in a constant state of fear, waiting for the worst to happen? That kind of thinking is only going to make you hesitate, make you worry."

Onyx wasn't wrong.

We huddled against Noren and soon the direwolf settled, curling up into a ball and forcing us to adopt the same posture. We were nothing but wolves in our den with our pack, everyone snuggled together until our breathing evened out and sleep crept into our bodies.

Rest did not come easily, but the few hours of shut-eye we got were a blessing. Our stomachs were filled by the squirrel, and with my eyes closed, I might have believed we were safe.

Noren's growl shot me right out of the restless dreaming. I blinked, sitting up fast enough to make myself dizzy. Somewhere in the distance, twigs snapped. The sound stopped abruptly but the rest of the night had gone still.

Someone was out there in the darkness, watching us.

I lurched to my feet in the next breath, magic surging through my blood.

The return of my powers was a warmth in my veins and I found my limbs shifting into the halfway form between human and wolf, my strongest form, without conscious thought. If I had to go down, I'd do it swinging, and I'd take everyone else along with me.

18

"Jeez, hold on! Hold on. Don't attack, it's just me. Tavi, take a chill pill."

The familiar voice came from directly ahead and as my pupils shifted to allow me better vision in the dark, the shadowy form of Bronwen swam into view.

I'd caught her somewhere between crow and human form and as I watched, she completed the shift. She solidified into her usual smile, her face round and her freckles standing out against the paleness of her skin.

Relief was so sudden it made me dizzy.

"I can't believe you got through the wall." In the next beat, I crossed the distance between us and grabbed her in a hug, her slighter form trembling in the cold. "How did you do it?"

And why was she here?

Bronwen glanced behind toward the wall and shrugged. "I came through it as a crow. Nothing happened to me. Why?"

"Tavi, who is it?" Onyx sounded sleepy but Noren stopped growling at least.

"It's Bronwen," I called back as loudly as I dared. I slipped from her hug and hid my stagger by turning, my stomach still flipping wildly and without control. "She found us."

"You wouldn't believe how crazy anxious I've been, searching for you guys. It's been a really bad few days, let me tell you." Bronwen crept over to Noren and rubbed him between the ears before she sat down cross-legged. She flashed Onyx a grin.

"You said you made it through the wall as a crow?" I asked.

She bobbed her head. "Yeah. I mean, being a bird is the fastest way to travel, and my crow form has honestly become like a second skin to me. It's been so long since I changed into a wolf it almost feels like I should just be a bird." Her laughter held no real joy.

"Do you think being in a shifted shape somehow lessens the impact of whatever magic was used to create the wall?" Onyx asked.

I gnawed on my lower lip. I didn't have enough experience with the wall or knowledge of its creation to say for certain, but Bronwen's arrival definitely proved the point on some level.

"You didn't just find a crack in the wall and come through? Or somehow manage to fly over the top..."

I trailed off at the incredulous look on her face.

"I came right through. There was a little bit of pressure, which is totally expected with that much magic, but I'm in one piece." She ran her hands along the front of her body to prove the point. "I caught your scent. Well, actually I caught the direwolf's scent, and followed that."

"You shouldn't have come. You put yourself in danger," I warned.

"Being here puts a pretty big target on your back, too," Onyx added.

"Well...okay, here's the truth. I ran away. Things are not good back home." She caught her breath, looking between us, and somehow withdrew into a tighter ball. "Selene has taken over the Claw & Fang officially."

Dread curdled in my veins. "Why do you sound upset?" Selene was bound to do something with all the unrest.

She was a natural born leader.

Bronwen sucked in a breath, scowled, and said, "Because she's dragged everyone into Unseelie. She's joined forces with Dorian Jade."

I stiffened in surprise, every part of me going taut. *Selene did what*? My eyes went wide and my lower jaw dropped open. "Why?"

"Some things are going down at the castle that have people up in arms. Like, *concerning* stuff, Tavi. The premier has taken over with the King still in a coma. There's a massive change in the guard and it's bad."

I wasn't as shocked to hear that good ol' Cosmo took the reins in hand. And I kept my lips zipped while Bronwen continued with her story, her features growing more animated the longer she talked.

"He's shifting shit around, changing things, and there are a lot of terrified half fae running around not knowing what to do. Selene thought they'd be safer on this side of the wall with someone who was sympathetic to our plight. But —" Bronwen stopped, worried at her inner cheek. "I don't think so. She's said some things, some bad things, but I'm the only one who seems to be concerned."

"Why don't you believe her?" I withheld my opinion for as long as possible because I wanted to hear her reasons.

"The dude is just *off*. I've heard enough stories. I wasn't too happy to find out where Selene wanted to take the others. Before she had a chance to force me across the wall, I ran. Tried to follow your scent and lost it after a couple of days. I was lucky enough to pick up on it again, and that's when I came through."

Bronwen wrapped her arms around herself, her teeth chattering.

"You're right." Onyx shifted into a more comfortable position and hid his wince from her. "Dorian Jade isn't what he appears to be."

I nodded. "He's no better than King Tywin. Instead of wanting equality, he's chosen to enslave pure-bloods." I gave Bronwen a quick recap of what had happened to us and what we'd discovered.

Her moon-pale face took on a distinctive pink quality through the story, with Onyx interjecting occasionally with pertinent information. By the time we finished, Bronwen was flushed and her eyes even darker with rage.

"I knew it," she seethed. "I *knew* there was something wrong with Dorian Jade. No one is *that* good. He's got a hero complex and a villain persona."

Which was usually my favorite thing to read about, but seeing it in real life felt like a different beast.

"I saw a spring a little bit away." Bronwen pushed to her feet and brushed pine needles off the bottom of her pants. "I need to freshen up because I am worked up and it's not a good look for me."

She flashed her teeth in the gloom. Her canines had sharpened. She might not feel like her wolf was close by but I saw it just there beneath the surface.

Rather than waiting, Onyx and I joined her. The sting of fresh water felt horrible against my skin but soothed the ache in my throat from talking. Despite the late hour, none of us were prepared for sleep, too energized to stay still.

"Have you eaten?" Bronwen asked, shaking out her wet hair. "Because I'll go catch something if you haven't. You two look ready to drop. I wouldn't blame you for going hungry."

"Noren brought us a squirrel—" I started to tell her.

But Bronwen was mid-shift, and with a pulse of energy, her form melted and in her place stood a crow with midnight-black wings. Her beady eyes met mine before she took flight.

She returned with a rabbit, dropping it at our feet, before she took off to scavenge more. Another trip and she brought back nuts and berries, the blue sheen of the skin looking fresh even in the night.

She made a good point.

Keeping a full stomach would make this trip much easier for all of us. Except we weren't content to wait to get this journey started. We ate quickly, breaking off pieces of rabbit and eating it raw before tossing the berries down our throats.

Onyx was the first to attempt the shift, mostly because we had no clue how long it would take him or if his failing body could even complete the transformation.

I stood back and watched him struggle through the process, the small bit of food not helping against the constant pain. It took him longer than Bronwen's effortless change to work through the shift but he finally stood in the clearing as a raven, a much larger form than Bronwen and her crow, with a distinctive white feather at the top of his head.

Birds weren't my favorite shape to assume, but in this case they were the easiest form for long periods of travel. They tired less easily than animals with four legs.

I closed my eyes, breathing in slowly through the nose and exhaling through pursed lips.

The magic waited for my use far down within my body. It nestled in a ball at my core and I tapped into it now, willing my limbs to change.

A warm wave of power pulsed out from my core, forcing my muscles and limbs to contract. Smaller and smaller into an unrecognizable form. A twinge of pain accompanied the change but nothing I hadn't felt too many times already.

Countless moments over the years where I let the wolf lurking inside my blood free. Except this time, she and I were something else, in accord with each other and both of us desperate for our freedom.

Onyx and I took flight at the same time. Noren followed beneath us, lifting his head only occasionally to make sure he remained on the same path. But we all headed in the same direction with the wall's magic like a beacon drawing us near.

It loomed ahead, an energy signature of its own, blocking out the rest of the world. It was an oppressive presence and I found myself choking the closer I got.

The bird saw the world differently but one thing remained the same—I didn't want to be anywhere near this thing, and I automatically sensed that flying over it would be next to impossible.

I dropped down to the ground a few feet away from the wall and craned my head up. Up and up. Nerves rippled underneath my wings and my tiny bird body shook. Onyx landed beside me and pressed close enough for me to feel the shudder rippling through him as well.

What happened if it wasn't as easy as Bronwen said?

What if something happened to us and the magic of the wall, without the special collar, tore us to shreds? Or worse.

It might absorb us and use us to power itself for another hundred years.

Animals were able to pass through, but if the wall knew the difference between real ones and shifters, then we were absolutely sunk.

A cold snout pressed underneath my right wing and shuffled me a few inches closer to the wall. Noren, but not to pressure me into moving through. For comfort.

Even his presence wasn't enough to soothe me.

He, definitely, was capable of simply walking through the wall. Dorian's cronies hadn't put a collar on him.

I heard Onyx's voice inside my head, with every bit of panic and anxiety he felt. They colored the words and expressed themselves in shades of orange and red. *Tell me it's all going to be okay.*

I'm not sure, which is why I haven't gone through yet, I answered.

Crows don't sweat, but the woman inside the crow certainly did. Already my psyche splintered in anticipation of all the terrible things that might happen to us. Except we'd wasted too much time already.

I took a small bit of comfort from Noren, as the direwolf took his first step through. Power hummed along his back and illuminated every single one of his hairs in a golden aura.

Finally he disappeared with a flick of his tail.

No time like the present, I tried to tell myself, for confidence. Tried and failed.

Onyx moved first, which prompted me into flight. We lifted off the ground a few feet and hovered in the air for half a heartbeat longer before we darted into the wall.

The pressure increased and the air slowly disappeared as though I waded through water. Things felt lighter than they had when I stepped through originally. Lighter but no less terrifying.

I beat my wings faster, faster, pushing as hard as the little body would go—and then we were out the other side.

I could finally breathe.

Noren waited there, with Bronwen perched on his shoulder. The little crow snapped her beak at our arrival. Onyx was a pace behind me.

The moment we were all together again, we took off, this murder of crows and the direwolf on the ground below. His strides ate up the miles and I had to admit that Bronwen had been right about flying.

It made things much easier.

I'd have tired of running even though I missed the feeling of my claws digging into the dirt, the way the forest looked from the eyes of a predator.

We traveled for most of the night and into the next day, stopping for an hour to rest before we were back in the air. Noren kept guard over us and the direwolf seemed tireless. Once we'd slept, we found a creek offering fresh water and took off again.

We reached Yelaine in the afternoon with the light thinning and the sky going golden.

I squinted against the glare of the sun as Bronwen circled and found a space between buildings for us to shift back.

The moment I returned to my half fae form, exhaustion swamped me.

Onyx drooped and held on to the wall for support. On the outskirts of the town there were few people to pass by and see us. These were the last houses before the town began in earnest and to the left were flat expanses of grassy fields dotted with white flowers and heavy fences of boulders.

"I don't know about you but I can't go much further. We need to rest," he said.

"I'm sure we can find a bed and breakfast or something in the next few miles, if you can make it," answered Bronwen with a small smile.

Where did I even begin to search for Mom?

This place was huge.

We were filthy and travel-worn, and we all knew if we wasted another minute, those precious seconds would count against us. Not to mention my mom was full-blooded Fae. Which meant she wouldn't be associated with the Claw & Fang or any spots they might frequent.

She could be anywhere.

I shook out my head and arms, craning my neck to work out the kinks.

Glimpses of the sea shimmered in the distance. The city, from what we saw overhead, looked like a combination of cottages and chalets close to the water. The further inland you went, the more it grew into an actual city.

"If you want to rest and get something to eat, Onyx, then be careful," I said, finally straightening. I crossed my arms over my chest. "Just stay out of sight while I look."

Bronwen regarded me with overly wide eyes. "You're not going to sleep?"

"No. I'm fine." I flashed her a ghost of a smile. "I want to start my search. The sooner I find her..." I trailed off.

I'd spent too much time imagining what it would be like to finally see the woman who gave birth to me. But to this day I had no idea what to actually expect, and none of my fantasies extended to the conversation we had coming.

I had no clue where to start.

I opened my mouth to say something, the others watching me intently, and my stomach gave a violent and audible rumble.

"I think we should all get something to eat before you head off on your own," Bronwen suggested. "Honestly, I think we're tired and hungry and need support."

"You have an idea?" Onyx wanted to know.

Noren, without prompting, stayed to the wilderness on the outskirts of the green fields. He wouldn't stick out but I wasn't willing to risk his safety. Only mine.

We kept close to each other on the sidewalk, catching glimpses of the ever nearer sea. The view opened up in front of us, composed of individual thatched cottages that reminded me of a television show I'd seen set in England.

The cliffs were not as magnificent as the black rock I'd seen on the show, but there were lichens and flowers leading down to the sea and birds screeching overhead. The expansive sea stretched into eternity with a timeless push–pull.

The sidewalk curved toward the water, the cottages growing closer and more eccentric the nearer we got to the sea wall.

Even this late in the afternoon, there were fae out running along the little beach, with small children splashing and playing.

It was a vastly different scene than anything in Eahsea, or at home in the mortal world. The pale pebbles of the beach were dotted with driftwood and seaweed marking low tide, and a small fleet of white sails bobbed distantly out on the waves, anchored safely.

"This is beautiful," Bronwen muttered, sounding as though she was warming to the area.

"It's definitely something, isn't it?" Onyx added quietly.

His attention had focused on a small group of turquoise-winged fae flitting down the road parallel to the shoreline. They were shorter than the average fae but larger than a toddler's stature. He watched them until the group disappeared among the tall walled buildings and cafes along the walk.

Yelaine looked like the type of place where wealthy couples "got away" from the city for their mental health. All cute, quaint, and safe. The crashing of the waves made a beautiful hum of backdrop noise and my own pulse thrashed and danced to the melody. Partly compulsion and partly nerves.

"There." Bronwen pointed ahead to a black and red flag fluttering in the breeze coming off the water. "That's where we need to go."

"How can you be sure?" Onyx squinted and tried to read the sign in hammered gold beneath the flag. "Trust me, I know what to look for. I've been with the Claw & Fang much longer than you guys. I mean—" Bronwen huffed out a small chuckle and started to walk.

I hesitated behind her, my feet like two anchors and the rest of me unwilling to move.

If Selene had taken the members we knew and brought them under Dorian's wing, then what would make the members in this city any different? What if they took one look at us and decided we'd be better off with him, too?

Then we'd be right back where we started.

Then again, we were out of other options. We had no money and no food, no place to stop for the night. And I knew the chill off the ocean would be worse at night. I forced one foot in front of the other and followed Bronwen and Onyx into the local faction of the Claw & Fang.

Finding it had been much less work than stepping over

the threshold. The fluttering red and black flag above obscured the words of the pub until we were directly in front of it.

Sea's Deep.

I shivered at the words as though there were some sort of deeper meaning hidden in there somewhere. The interior of the pub offered a nice respite from the wind, though. The walls were wooden and stained a rich oak that offset the darker, wider planks of the floor.

A stone fireplace took up much of the wall to my left, and the flickering flames of golden, amber, and crimson heated the place to the perfect temperature with fae magic.

Several pairs of half fae rested at the bar with their elbows balanced on the polished top. They turned our way and I found myself freezing beside Onyx. Even Bronwen had a hitch in her step and her habitual cheerful grin faltered.

The bartender straightened out of a conversation with several others and approached us cautiously. His nostrils flared when he got close enough to draw in our scents and some of the flint from his gaze chipped.

"Members?" he asked in an undertone.

"We're from Eahsea," Bronwen answered for us. "And we, ah, need sanctuary. We've traveled a long way and have nothing to offer."

The bartender's grin widened enough for me to see an empty space where one of his canines should have been. "Sea's Deep welcomes everyone in need," he replied, much louder this time. "Please, come in. Make yourselves comfortable and I'll see about getting you something from the kitchen."

He gestured toward a number of empty tables.

We chose one toward the back of the pub and within a

few minutes, the bartender—Benjamin, as he introduced himself—set several plates of food in front of us. He returned shortly with three glasses and a pitcher of fresh water, lemon slices floating across its top.

Caution would have been advisable, but my hunger got the better of me and I tore into the fresh bread, the steaming plate of roasted vegetables, and the tender slices of cold beef and cheese.

The others did the same and I spared only half a thought for Noren as I gorged myself. He had any number of options in the forest. He'd be fine.

They welcomed us, I thought as I finished gnawing on one of the slices of sharp cheddar. Just like that, with no questions asked. Benjamin somehow knew exactly who we were even when others took one look at us and saw nothing but what they wanted to see.

"You lot look hungry." Another patron of the pub turned his chair around and straddled it, his arms looped over the back rungs and his features lifted pleasantly. He blinked all three eyes at us. "What brought you here?"

I swallowed hard, glancing around at the others before I answered him. "We're looking for someone."

"Seems like your journey has taken you far from home. My wife and I understand." The man glanced up at the arrival of a woman in a sheer seafoam-colored sheath with real flowers holding the straps over her arms together. "We've traveled from the Dasha Plain."

"You're looking for something too," Bronwen noted as the woman seated herself gracefully at her husband's side.

They must be half shifters as well, to be here. I wondered if Benjamin got many people wandering in off the street, with his location, or if those in the city automatically knew something set this place apart.

"A place where we can be accepted," the wife answered for both of them. She wrapped spindly fingers around her fluted glass of liquid and lifted it to her lips. "We're on our way to find Dorian Jade."

"Surely you've heard of him," the husband pressed with a wide smile.

My back stiffened and I hid my reaction in another bite of cheese.

"Why are you searching for Dorian Jade?" Onyx asked, with much more diplomacy than I might have managed.

Even Bronwen hid a cough behind her fist.

"He protects people like us. It's only natural to ally ourselves with him. Most of the half shifters in our acquaintance are joining forces with him because of all the good he's done." The wife offered us a kindly expression colored at the edges with concern.

I wanted to shake the look right off her face.

"How many people do you know who've found him?" Onyx asked.

I applauded his neutrality because just the mention of Dorian Jade had my hands balling on my lap and my cheeks flushing with heat. They were joining the man under false pretenses. Hopefully they saw through him quickly enough. The couple seemed like nice people, if misguided.

They continued to chat with Onyx while the three of us finished the food on the table. Soon there was nothing but empty plates between us and I rubbed a hand over my full stomach. We barely noticed when the door to Sea's Deep opened, bringing with it a gust of salty air.

"Morgan, my friend!" Benjamin called out the greeting. "It's good to see you. Come in."

The hair on the back of my arms stood to attention as my focus narrowed on the newcomer.

I immediately recognized the mangy salt-and-pepper beard, the one eye. The long dark hair falling down to his chest. The half shifter who worked for the enemy. He'd changed his checkered shirt and stained jeans for a black t-shirt and equally dark pants.

He must have felt my gaze on him because the man, Morgan, turned toward us unerringly.

"You!" His voice boomed out across the room and had the three of us on our feet in a surge of motion.

Fast enough to knock against the table and send the empty pitcher crashing.

"Stop them! Stop those three!" Morgan continued to raise the alarm. "They belong to Dorian Jade."

19

I t was unlucky as hell to have the man show up here, now.

And too late for us to hide. He had his sights set on us, and the rest of them were only a half-step behind him. Even the nice couple at the table beside ours had gotten to their feet and were reaching out for us.

The woman's fingers gripped my shirt near the elbow and tugged.

"Don't let them leave," Morgan howled.

Benjamin and the other members of the Claw & Fang collectively lunged for us under his command. They were an angry mob, gone from hospitality to hostile in the blink of an eye.

They'd take us into custody and then—

"No!" The word burned my throat on the way out and I held my hands up in front of me.

Onyx tried to move to protect me and we ended up crashing against one of the tables in our haste.

Benjamin and Morgan blocked off the front entrance.

Dull pain rippled through the hip I'd knocked against the table.

"There's nowhere to run," Morgan growled.

A long roar cut through the melee of voices and Noren crashed through the front door, showering wood splinters. He lost his mind, snarling and snapping in an attempt to get through.

I must have called his name. Must have made some kind of noise to get his attention.

He lunged forward and slammed his skull into the small of Morgan's back.

Someone wrapped their arms around my torso and tugged me back. Only Bronwen's familiar scent stopped me from fighting against her. The others were trying to get behind us, to corral us right into Morgan's waiting arms.

He recovered from Noren's hit soon enough and whirled on the direwolf with his own canines on display.

Torn between Noren and the back door, I paused, stupidly.

A large *bang* rocked the space. In the next breath, the foundations of the bar rumbled, dust shimmering down from the ceiling and visible beams. The lights went out and plunged the world into darkness. In the chaos, a woman screamed. Every inhalation held the familiar taste of smoke and it burned my lungs until I started to cough.

"What's happening?" Bronwen yelled beside my ear.

The lights flickered back on as though someone flipped a switch, and the smoke cleared just as rapidly. The air tasted of ozone. Magic. The scent of magic filled every molecule inside the bar, and standing directly in the center of the room stood two new people who had shown up out of nowhere.

Mike.

Mike.

Queen Laina stood at his side with her golden hair twisted around the top of her head in a braid as regal as any crown. She'd traded her gorgeous gowns for a plain sand-colored tunic and pants combination with leather straps around her waist and over her arms.

Mike looked exactly as he had the first night I met him at school, only more. More than I'd ever seen him. He wore a black t-shirt cut high at the arms and a pair of worn jeans yet he radiated strength and poise and—

My heart leaped out of my chest in an attempt to get to Mike, but before I so much as uttered a word, the two of them jumped into the fight.

Without hesitation. The moment they registered what was going down, they attacked.

Mike moved first and lifted a hand. Wind buffeted out from his outstretched fingers and knocked Benjamin from his feet. The halfling gave a sharp yelp before the unnatural gust knocked him against the bar.

We were more evenly matched with another fae and a witch on our side.

Laina may not fight with her magic but I knew it added heft to any faery spell she cast.

She reached behind her to the space between her straps —a holster, I realized—and withdrew twin whips. The ends were tipped in iron and crackled with a bluish-green magic. Laina cracked the first and the barb landed near the tip of Morgan's boot.

The queen was every bit the warrior I might have looked up to as a kid, spinning with boundless energy and moving her whips like the fae equivalent of Elektra. If ever there was a time for a girl crush, it was now.

She and Mike exploded into action like they were fury given physical form.

I was too mad myself to look for a clever way out of this. With magic pumping through me., I took off toward Mike, toward the door and our exit strategy.

Bronwen gave a *whoop* at my back and her magic supported Onyx. Mike cast a spell around us, and anyone who dared get close enough to him rebounded, their skin scalded wherever they touched.

I expected the magic to dip and fray, the way I'd seen it do before. Only this time, and without the *Totalis*, he saw the spell to completion.

"Take that, you miserable assholes!" Bronwen yelled behind me.

Her battle cry was almost lost in the chaos. With so many members of the Claw & Fang present in one space, it would take a minor miracle to get us out of here without bringing the building down with us.

Noren ran forward and jumped, sailing over the heads of anyone else and landing on the back of another. The man crumpled to his knees under the weight and Noren growled.

The threat rattled around in his throat and I nodded to give him the go-ahead to use whatever it took, whatever horrible means necessary, to break us free.

My own lips peeled back in a snarl and I called my wolf. For half a heartbeat I wondered what Mike would think about my change. *Too late.* She responded to me immediately and my muscles twisted painfully. I kept the same feral expression on my lips through the transformation, my gaze darting back and forth across every enemy in the bar until my human form no longer stood.

I looked out at the world through the eyes of the wolf.

Laina struck again with her whips drawn high. Mike,

propelled by the air magic he commanded, cut a hasty path toward us.

The power of the combined occupants of this room hummed through me as I leaped into the bulk of the fighting. My jaws swung open and I clamped them down on the nearest man's ankle hard enough to shatter bone. He cried out and I threw everything I had into the bite, striking at him with magic in tandem.

Mike boosted me. Not purposely, of course, but by the fierce pride at his arrival.

Bronwen hadn't been the only one looking for me.

Mike came through.

He wouldn't have done it if he didn't feel *something* for me.

A tidal wave broke inside of me and I howled, the noise tightening my skin until my hair stood on end. Onyx took up the cry, followed by Bronwen and Noren, until the room filled with the keening wail.

On we fought, with the battle cry burning my lungs. Every part of me yearned for vengeance. I needed it more than life itself. Vengeance against everyone in this bar who saw three young adults and turned against them.

We'd done nothing wrong.

Another wave of magic poured out of me as I bit and kicked and ripped, using my power to get me toward the door. I came to a halt in front of Mike and Noren landed to my left, his tail swishing and his magic building.

Mike raised his hand in a defensive maneuver and the air around us tightened.

After a startling beat of silence, everything went tight, his magic drawing the air out of the room.

He brought his hand down and the vacuum seal popped. Whoever had been on their feet now fell.

A cruel, wicked, beautiful smile pried his lips open.

I shifted back to human form. "What the hell are you doing here?"

He winked at me. "You're a hard girl to find!"

Laina swung her whips and set her eyes on Morgan, who seemed to grow with the weight of the challenge. He barked out another command but a flash of movement came from the corner of my vision.

I lurched aside in time to make room for Bronwen and Onyx. They moved in tandem, faster than I would have thought possible, and a shower of blades hurtled toward Morgan and his cronies.

Whatever order he'd managed to release didn't matter. We rushed for him, a battle cry uniting us, and the daggers struck home at the same time. Burrowing in a circle around him and his friends.

Onyx snorted and the weight of the power in the room crashed against me as he lit the daggers on fire. Through the flames I saw Morgan glaring at me, his one good eye mirroring the gilded flames.

Bronwen tensed and ducked as someone swung a sword toward her head. The tip nicked her shoulder and she lost her balance, keening forward closer to the flames.

"No!" I cried, and the word echoed from somewhere around me but I couldn't spare Mike another glance as I stepped up to protect Bronwen.

A thought—and weight filled my palm, a replica of the sword the other man carried.

Immediately the use of magic took a toll and I lost my breath, my heart beating wildly. I lifted the sword in time to parry a strike from the man, blocking him at every turn.

They were too close to us, and the fire might keep Morgan and the others blocked off but it also filled the small bar with too much heat. My skin was turning to ash and my forearm burned where I'd been bitten.

Bronwen got to her feet, wincing at the spray of blood across her shoulder. Her magic pulsed and she sliced her own sword at the man.

"Don't tell me you're tired already?"

My head snapped toward her but the pause cost me. The pain in my arm flared and traveled up to my back, hammering every vertebrae of my spine.

Mike brought a solid shield of air around us and stopped the man's next parry dead in the air.

"Tavi?"

I recognized the concern in his voice.

"We have to get out of here." The press of heat, the cost of the shift and conjuring the sword, threatened to weigh me down and I gritted my teeth to remain standing. Several members of the Claw & Fang managed to get themselves together and they threw a blast of water magic at us with such force it nearly sent me flying.

It also doused the magical flames around Morgan.

Laina's whip darted out snake-fast and wrapped around the arm of the nearest attacker, pulling him backward and off his feet. He collided with the back wall and lay still.

"Time to move," she called out.

She was right. We needed to get away from Dorian Jade's followers and get far enough from this place to recover.

Had I thought the Faerie Trials were bad?

If I had half the strength I'd had during those, I'd have blasted every last one of these dudes with magic and gleefully watched them bleed.

But every time I tried to call my power back to me, it receded a little further. Even Mike had gone pale and his spells were losing their potency.

I swung my blade again and my muscles burned from too much force. We were close enough to the door to get out of the building. Laina cast her final spell and it spread out through the interior of the bar, chains of magic the same color as the lethally tipped whips keeping them pinned in place.

I didn't give a crap what happened to them once we left.

Bronwen was the closest and I grabbed hold of her, my body shivering with the effort of trying to continue. She wrapped an arm underneath mine and cried out at the top of her lungs, "We're out!"

Onyx and Noren had been locked in battle with three other halflings. The direwolf turned to me with the promise of fury and violence still in his glowing eyes, but Onyx was like me. He'd pushed himself too far.

Laina recognized it, helping him toward the door.

Black emotions churned inside of me.

We raced off into the city, putting as much distance between ourselves and Sea's Deep as physically possible. Noren outpaced us all and at the end of the group limped me and Onyx, my steps slow to accommodate our injuries. But we couldn't stop.

Not yet.

We had to keep going until we were far away from that cursed building. And hope like hell we were able to control our scents. If Morgan so much as got a hint of us, he'd be able to track us again. We'd never be safe.

In the midst of a cluster of two-story buildings, their cupolas graced in gold, we stopped to catch our breaths. The overlapping rooftops cast shade over the alley, and from this vantage point I no longer saw or heard the ocean.

I slapped my palm against the stone and heaved in a

great gulping breath of air. My lungs seized, unable to accommodate so much at one time.

As the seconds ticked by, breathing became easier.

"Hey, are you okay?" Fingers trailed up the back of my neck and increased their pressure, massaging lightly until I looked up into Mike's concerned green eyes. "You look like you're ready to drop."

Without thought, I wrapped my arms around him and squeezed him tight. His arms banded around me automatically and if he wanted to complain about the way I clung, he kept those thoughts to himself.

"I'm not okay," I answered with a voice muffled by his shirt. "I'm not okay at all."

"Then it's a good thing we found you," Mike replied.

I wanted to ask him how he'd tracked us, and why. I wanted to ask if he'd forgiven me for the part I played in his father's coma. I said nothing.

Finally, Mike cleared his throat, the sound morphing into a dry chuckle. "You're probably not going to like hearing this."

I squeezed him again.

He kept one arm around me and reached into his pocket with the opposite hand, drawing out a handkerchief with a dark spot of dried brown blood on it. "I still had this. Mom used your blood to track your progress but every time we got a lead on you, you vanished again. You never stayed in one spot long enough for us to actually reach you. Until today."

"Until today," I repeated, captivated by the handkerchief.

I had no clue why he still had it but thank goodness for that bit of blood. He'd saved it. Why?

Laina stashed her whips back into the holster and their glow dulled. "We evacuated the castle. Teaming up with like-minded souls seemed the best option for people like us."

"But why? Why leave when the King…" I didn't want to talk about it and chance upsetting Mike.

Either way, if Tywin had managed to come out of his coma or not, it made no sense for the queen and the crown prince to just take off.

"The premier has taken over the palace. In my husband's absence, Cosmo Foxfall has risen to near celebrity status and used his power to reveal his secrets. He's in league with Dorian Jade," Laina said.

Now that was one name I never wanted to hear again. Ever.

Ice slithered into place at the base of my spine and froze me from the inside out. The same ice became a burning sensation in my veins.

"He believes he is doing the right thing by combining his forces with Jade, waxing poetic about reuniting Seelie and Unseelie. And the first thing Cosmo did was deliver the pure-blood fae to the enchanted wall between our kingdoms."

"No, he didn't. How could he—" I cut off, my voice strangled.

The queen dipped her head. "Yes, Tavi. He delivered our people to the Unseelie, where Dorian Jade will decide whether they live or die."

20

D orian Jade was everywhere.

On the lips of people on the street, in the eyes of animals and birds overhead—I had no idea how far his influence spread but I felt him here.

He was in league with Selene and with Cosmo Foxfall. With Claribel and probably an untold number of agents at the Bureau. Was there any place where his toxicity hadn't reached?

Mike and Queen Laina stood out amongst the people of Yelaine as they were meant to stand out.

I pointed that out and a quick burst of the queen's magic had their features subtly shifting in the shade of the alley.

The gleaming sunlit color of their hair slowly shifted into a more innocuous dirty-blonde. Their eyes were less vibrant, their features normal. Average.

A wave of the queen's hand and I felt my own face shift as well, but nothing like when I changed form on my own. A little nip, a little tweak, and I wondered what I would look like to someone who knew me.

"There," Laina murmured. "That will help us. I've

hidden our scents for now but I'll need herbs to work a more complete spell."

"Can you do anything about our clothing?" Bronwen asked.

"Together, yes." Laina held out a palm for her son and Mike slapped his against hers.

A burst of power spread out from the two of them and I wondered if adding my own would help or hinder them.

Within seconds the fabric of our clothing wove itself into different styles and designs. I flinched where the fabric brushed against my skin.

Shit, if I don't eat soon, and sleep...

"Where do we go now?" Onyx leaned heavily on Noren, and even the direwolf appeared changed to a creature similar to a large German Shepherd.

Onyx and Mike eyed each other for the longest time and surprise straightened the curve of my spine. Oh, shit. The last time they'd seen each other had been at the execution and now both of them hovered around me protectively, the stare-down unbreakable over my head.

The pissing contest couldn't last much longer.

I hoped.

Laina lifted her face to the sky. "We regroup for the night somewhere safe. There are several boarding houses in the area. Surely there are a few who cater to people who would prefer to travel with no questions asked. Those, I'm sure, will lie a little farther afield than the financial district. I have money."

"Is that where we are?" I asked.

"Nearest the courthouse, yes. Several members of the Elder Council are in residence here. Farther from the sea, we'll find what we seek. I'm sure of it, although it's been many years since I've been to Yelaine. The city has grown much."

She led the way down the street, navigating easily as the rest of us trailed after her.

I jumped, swallowing over a grimace when something touched my hand. Mike stared straight ahead, his eyes hard and flinty. He said nothing, only squeezed my hand once in acknowledgement as I fell into step beside him, firmly linked.

If we got out of this, I was telling him everything.

Every secret feeling I kept to myself, I wanted out there in the open. Even something as small as how I hate the taste of mustard on a burger.

I'd have nothing left to lose.

Then again, it wasn't like we were getting out of this situation anytime soon.

We finally found a boarding house in the city and Queen Laina paid. One night, she assured the girl behind the counter, who decided it was better to have the cash in hand than to ask us about our travel plans, or the dog we insisted on bringing inside.

We climbed the stairs toward a large room on the third floor outfitted with enough bunk beds for five of us, including Noren, to safely tuck ourselves away. Mike lifted a silencing spell around the room the moment we were inside and his mom bolstered it with a few spells of her own.

The damping hush of their magic cast a safety net around us.

He'd gotten better with his powers somewhere along the line. And at least we were all together.

It counted.

I grabbed one of the bottom bunks and Noren hopped up beside me, once again sensing my exhaustion. We cuddled together as I watched the others move around the room, checking things out before each one of them settled as well. Mike and his mother were together, Onyx and Bronwen on another bunk.

Outside, the sun had already sunk below the horizon and cast the world in shades of night. We were too far away from the ocean to hear the crashing surf any longer and I found myself missing the sound.

I missed a lot of things, I mused, drawing closer to Noren. The direwolf seemed to have the same thought and he voiced no qualms about the closeness. The only thing I'd missed more than the normalcy of the creature's presence, in a safe space like this, was Mike.

I watched him from the other bunk. He was close enough for us to reach out to each other and have our fingertips touch. For some reason, the closeness I needed from him would have to wait while the others were here.

We both seemed to be of the same mind. The look he shot at me was loaded with heat, understanding, and sweet solace. I felt the same.

"Now that we're all here, and the room is secure, tell us what happened," Laina said.

She settled herself on top of the sheets with her loose trousers speckled with blood and her leather holster still firmly in place. Her features eventually shifted back into the familiar beauty I was used to seeing.

Although her face gave nothing away, her fingers twitched, her posture tense. Even here.

There was no way to refuse the queen.

I glanced over at Onyx to find him already watching me, his head tilted to the side. Bronwen bounced her knees, her feet arched to the balls as she moved. No one wanted to speak. Not yet. Not when the silence was tinged and poised to shatter.

"Do you want to go first?" Onyx finally asked. His voice seemed as loud as a gunshot.

No, I actually didn't. I wanted to put it all behind me but that was selfish. Laina put herself at risk to come and find us, and after what happened to Barbara...her mom...

So I took a deep breath and dove in. "As you know, Cosmo threw me in the dungeon." I glanced toward Mike. "You saw me down there."

He maintained the hard set of his shoulders, his lips thin and bloodless, but a hint of confusion remained in his moss-green eyes.

Start to finish and leaving out nothing, I forced myself to talk.

Onyx and I opened up about everything that had happened. Bronwen, when the appropriate moment arose, interjected a few times about her experience within Faerie, and what happened with the Claw & Fang. Things I hadn't heard and stories that made my stomach flip for her experience.

I avoided Mike's gaze at first. Talk about uncomfortable, and it never got easier.

But once it all came out...only my feelings for him remained a secret, as if someone put a physical block at the back of my mind attached to my throat. Everything else poured around the block.

Eventually I couldn't take it anymore and forced myself to look at him fully, trying to judge his reaction to my tale. Surely he'd remember the way Faerie reacted when I first got here. It wasn't like I pulled facts out of the sky.

The land revolted at my presence. All the strange things that happened, all the secrets, were explained to the best of our meager abilities. Mike and Laina listened to the whole story from beginning to end without interruption, although the former had an audible reaction to Onyx's reveal about his father, my fated mate.

Kendrick Grimaldi was a black pit of destruction.

Ultimately, they both looked shaken.

Mike reached out to grip Laina's hand and comfort his mother. "We're in trouble, aren't we?" he asked.

"Rhetorically or literally, my love?" Laina shook her head. "I've felt the energies growing darker over the last few years. It appears things are coming to a head. I don't want to believe this has been in motion for so long. It makes sense, however, what's happening in the castle now."

I hadn't been aware of the tension my body held until she said those words. At once my nervous system crashed and I slumped forward, head bent toward my lap. "Thank you."

Laina offered me a small smile. "For what, sweetheart?"

"For believing me," I whispered.

"Why would I not?" She was so different from her husband, who had been prepared to throw me to the mob on a whim. "It's clear to me that the premier is in league with Dorian Jade, and perhaps placed in a position of power purposely. No one ever suspected him."

"None of what happened to you both should come as a surprise, either," Mike added.

This time I couldn't stop myself. I untangled myself from Noren and walked over to Mike. Took a stand between his legs until he unfolded himself from the bunk and stood over me.

How he'd grown over the last two years. Not just with his magic but physically, emotionally. As a person he was still the same boy with the lopsided smile who helped a stranger on the side of the road. But he was also so much more.

At last he held his arms open for me and I stepped in, stealing every moment of the hug as my own.

"We were trying to track down my missing mother," I said. "That's why we came. It's the last place she was seen, and I thought if we could find her, then maybe—" *Everything would be all right.*

"What do you think will happen?" Mike wanted to know. "If you find her?"

"I don't actually have a plan. We were just kind of moving forward to the next step." I bit my lip. "I lost my place in the human world. I lost my place in Faerie. I thought maybe there was a place for me with her."

Saying it out loud did nothing to stem my sense of worthlessness.

"Hey." Mike's hand fell on my waist and he squeezed to get my attention. "It's okay, Tavi. It's okay."

There was too much pity in his voice for me to feel comfortable being this close anymore. I took a step in the opposite direction, offering him a grimace in place of my body and returned to my own bunk.

Onyx sucked in a breath, shifting his arms overhead and wincing. "If no one minds, I think I'm going to go to bed early. My body has been through what it can take, and I need to sleep."

I agreed wholeheartedly. I'd been holding off the dizziness through our entire talk and now that I'd finally said my piece, it returned in full force. As though acknowledging it somehow made it much more intense.

My stomach gave a sickening dive and my arms pebbled with goosebumps. "I'm not far behind you," I murmured.

Bronwen had already dropped to her side with her head

rested against her pillow, eyes fluttering closed. Listening, as always, but relaxed.

Mike drew in a sharp breath and his jaw dropped as though he had something terribly important to say. But after a beat, all that came out was "Sleep well."

It felt like an apology. The sweetness of it soothed some of the cracks in my heart. Some, but not all.

I nodded to him before turning to the queen. "Before I get comfortable, do you mind if we talk privately? There are a few things I'd like to tell you."

She deserved to know about her mother. And since none of the others knew Barbara the way I did—if anyone could really know a witch like her—then I was the only one who could do this.

No matter how weird I felt when Laina stared at me, through me, and I finally recognized Barbara in some of her features. A *much younger* Barbara, I mentally corrected, before the chain smoking and the excessive use of power turned her into Swamp Hag of the West.

Laina rose and gestured for me to lead the way. We moved to a corner of the room containing a single large wardrobe, and a wave of her hand lifted a second silencing bubble inside the first.

"Only the two of us will be able to hear what's said, Tavi." Her hand slowly drifted back to her side.

"Do you mind hiding our faces as well?" I shifted from foot to foot. "I don't want anyone to read my lips—"

"No need to explain."

The scent of flowers, the smell unique to her magic, filled the small protected space we shared and the bubble around us went opaque.

Her eyes landed on mine kindly, if a little confused, and damn, now I felt lower than low. Because I shouldn't be the one to tell Laina the truth about her past. Barbara deserved to be here instead of me. To hold her daughter's hands and explain what actually happened.

I was only the messenger. And Barbara would never get to have this moment.

"If you don't mind, I want to talk to you not as a subject in front of her queen. Although...I know you *are* a queen." I stumbled over my words and shook my head. A little disgusted with myself.

"Tavi? What's wrong?"

I shook my head again, my mouth going dry. "When I was down in the dungeons with the witch, we talked to each other. It wasn't the first time we'd met, either. Barbara helped me out when I was in a bad way." No need to tell Laina what happened with the artifact, or how Barbara had maneuvered me into a bad position, my back to the wall and her threats at my front.

This heart-to-heart wasn't my responsibility but I was the only one here to do it. I forced myself to take a deep breath and face the queen. To tell her everything that Barbara told me, the story of being her mother and how Laina had been sold to the royal family.

Through the story, she once again waited patiently for me to finish speaking before she offered anything other than facial expressions.

Boy, those were almost too much for me to handle.

Shock and horror I expected. Empathy and sadness, yeah, those I figured on too. But I almost lost it when Laina started crying.

"And you trusted her? This witch?" Laina asked finally as she hiccupped over a sob. "You think she spoke the truth?"

"Yes. I absolutely believed Barbara." Trust? Now that was

a different story. I had to make it very clear to Laina, however, that the story held merit. "The emotion was real and raw, and she loved you fiercely. She just wanted to save you. It was the only reason she did what she did and broke into Faerie. To see her daughter."

A chill took root in my spine and I shivered, wrapping my arms around myself and looking away.

She'd make *me* cry if I wasn't careful. The last thing I wanted was to lose it now. We had too far to go for me to break. I lost my breath when she grabbed me in a rushing hug. Forcing me to her and clinging to me. She pinned her arms around me and a wrenching sob shuddered through her.

"My mother is dead."

Oh, shit, what could I even say to that?

I understood.

I'd gone my entire life thinking my mother had died as well, only to learn later that she lived. Which was almost as bad as hearing she'd passed in the first place. Worse, since I'd had a lot of time to become accustomed to life as an orphan. Laina had had her world rocked, and I'd delivered the bad news.

Slavery. Love. Betrayal.

The makings of a good TV show but a pretty shitty life experience.

"I'm so sorry," I managed to get out.

Laina only hugged me and cried. Cried for what she'd lost, I imagined, for the memories and the mother she didn't remember.

"The life I thought I had, the happy and wonderful loving life—" Laina cut off on a groan. "It's a lie."

No, no. I could not be the one to give the Queen of Faerie a complex. Which automatically had me feeling even worse because this wasn't the time to be selfish and think about myself.

"You have a good life," I tried to say with clumsy backpedaling. "You have a son who loves you and would do anything for you. You have people who care for you and find you to be a kind ruler."

I stiffened when she let me go and stood back, smiling through the tears.

"I never understood why or how I ended up as queen. I'm a half blood. A witch. My makeup has always set me apart and kept me from being a true part of this world." Laina swiped at her eyes. "Now I know why. It explains so much about my life and my circumstances. I know it wasn't supposed to be your duty to tell me these things, but thank you. For being brave enough to do this. For standing up for the mother I never knew."

I understood it, the relief. The horrible sense of being a part of something yet completely separate. My halfling status put me in the same position it did with Laina.

"I'm relieved," Laina continued. "I want you to understand that I'm upset, yes, but not at you. Thank you, Tavi."

"Please don't thank me. This isn't how I thought it would go but you needed to know what Barbara told me." And now I considered it a job well done. My debt to Barbara had been paid on all fronts.

"You're a good woman. And you're lucky as well."

"Why do you say that?"

"Because you have the love of my son, too. And it's priceless. If anything good came out of my situation, it's Michael. I regret nothing if it gave me *him*."

My stomach dropped as heat colored my cheeks, because the last thing on my mind right now was Mike and my feelings for him. Boy, were there feelings.

"I really don't want to talk about Mike right now," I sputtered. Feeling like a total child in front of her.

Laina only continued to smile. A bonding moment, I realized, for the two of us. It put us on much more even ground where I could look at her not as a monarch with absolute power but as a mom. As a daughter. As someone like me who hadn't quite figured out her place in life but continued to do her best.

"Whatever I can do to help you find your own mother, I'll do it. You have my word," she said softly.

"It's a really nice offer."

She gave me a gentle squeeze. "I mean it."

"Well…" *Now or never*. "I actually have an idea."

21

My idea was probably the *literal worst* idea ever.

Especially since I couldn't actually do it alone.

I needed Laina's help, as a witch. Yet the pieces percolated in my mind throughout our conversation, only solidifying with Laina's offer.

She didn't shut me down once I explained, either, which meant there had to be at least a little merit to what I proposed. Even if it was crazy.

But it sure beat going around the city and trying to meet every single citizen in an attempt to find one who looked like her. It wouldn't be so easy as scrolling through social media.

I settled myself on the floor in front of Laina once everyone else fell asleep. Exhaustion rode me hard, the ache in my arm now spreading along my spine and down the back of my legs.

I definitely didn't want an audience for this kind of thing. Not only would we be doing some woo-woo stuff that no one expected, but we were talking blood magic.

We shouldn't be working spells in the room, but with all the wards and protection we each layered together, I wasn't comfortable going anywhere else to attempt this kind of thing.

Big magic, Laina assured me.

Yeah. Much bigger than I *should* be working. It was way beyond my paygrade.

Yet she sat in front of me with the folds of her trousers hiding her legs and rested her palms on her knees, her eyes closed. Drawing energy into herself until her breath evened out.

"This ritual is going to use your blood to search out anyone in the city who shares the same genetics you do," Laina reiterated. "It sounds like a simple concept but it's not going to be as easy as you hope. This sort of magic takes a lot of power behind it to generate, as we're covering a large territory."

"I'm ready," I assured her. Trembling on the inside where she couldn't see me. Sick to my stomach and pale and weak.

Noren was there for me regardless. He'd scooted closer until his body heat pressed through my back and into me, lending me strength.

No way would he let me out of his sight when I needed protection. He was the only one I trusted to be able to have my back no matter what. Okay, that wasn't exactly true, but I couldn't do this without him.

Laina and I sat close enough to touch and our knees form a circle between us. She'd found a map of the city in the lobby of the boarding house, a thoroughly modern thing that kinda left me reeling when she brought it out. She placed it between us.

"Do we need anything else?" I asked, worrying my lower lip. "Like a crystal to guide us where we need to go?"

Laina chuckled softly and tucked a piece of blonde hair behind her pointed ear. "There's no need for a crystal. Our magic is going to do the work for us. Trust me to guide you. Although I may have to borrow a little bit of your power to sustain it if it takes too long."

"You have whatever you need." I hid my tremor from her. I barely had any magic left to donate.

"A little pinprick of your blood will do, to start," she replied.

This was it. I held out my hand for her and Laina drew a decorative pin from her braid, tapping it against my index finger. A quick flash of pain lighter than a bee sting and it disappeared in an instant.

This was the moment I'd actually find my mom.

I'd thought about it too many times to count, dreamed about a reunion, but face to face with reality left me reeling. Nerves gathered in my gut and nibbled on my insides.

Would Mom even want to see me once we found her?

What would happen to me, mentally and emotionally, if she decided not to talk? Or worse, if she outright denied it and made me leave?

Those possibilities were suddenly too real as Laina went through the steps of her ritual.

She held my finger over the map and squeezed until a drop of blood came free. With her eyes closed, Laina chanted under her breath, and the fine hairs on my neck, temples, and forearms lifted to attention.

Magic buzzed and crackled from her in a powerful wave. Much stronger than anything I'd seen her do before but not outward, not showy. It was all on the inside.

The street lines on the map began to glow. They seemed

lit from within, the luminescence radiating from the drop of my blood and weaving, pulsing, until a specific location began to sparkle.

Laina opened her eyes and pointed. "Not nearly as bad as I thought. Your mom is here, Tavi. She's here and your connection is strong. The energy bonds between you..."

I gulped. "What does that mean?"

"It means she's been looking for you, too. Otherwise we wouldn't have found her so quickly." Laina's voice seemed far away.

"She's not looking for me. She's in the city, hiding." Everything else faded and I stared at the spot on the map until dark dots danced in front of my vision.

It was more than I'd dared hope for and easier than I deserved. Another lucky strike, except nothing in my life felt like luck, only a series of missteps that eventually landed me where I needed to be. Or somewhere close.

There were too many scrapes and near-misses in my life to call me lucky. But I felt like it right now. Even when Laina smiled sympathetically at me like she knew something I couldn't possibly understand yet.

She snapped her fingers and the magic dissipated, sparks flying up away from the map. "We'll look for her tomorrow. At least now we have a location to start."

"Are you certain it's really her?" I asked.

"I'm fairly certain, yes. Unless our friends in the Unseelie Court have mastered the art of replicating blood bonds with their spells...but have hope, darling," Laina replied. "Have hope that everything will work out because it's not just you and Onyx anymore against the whole of Faerie."

No, she was right.

I had Bronwen. And Mike and Laina. Melia, wherever she was now. We had an entire team.

I reached behind me and scratched Noren between the ears before getting up. Rather than heading toward my empty bunk, I changed direction and crawled in beside Mike, on top of the sheets.

His chest rose and fell evenly in sleep, his eyes fluttering behind his closed lids in whatever dream he found himself.

He looked innocent sleeping like that. Lightly snoring and twitching slightly.

Our magic hadn't woken him, thanks to his mom's shielding, and I was grateful. Things between us hadn't always been easy. Hell, from the start there were so many obstacles that sometimes it felt like whatever world we were in wanted us to stay apart.

But as I snuggled at his side, curling close as Noren stretched out on the floor, a sense of peace blanketed me.

Tomorrow things would be better. Whether they actually looked better or not remained to be seen. For tonight, we'd accomplished something incredible.

Sleep crept up quickly enough and when I woke in the morning, Mike had wrapped his arms around me, my head on his chest and nothing but safety in his embrace.

There was no stopping anyone once we woke for the day. They all wanted to be part of the search, no one left behind. The argument between Mike and Bronwen, short and easily ended once Laina returned with breakfast, brought a fierce grin to my lips.

Food solved all manner of small irritations. Even I had to admit it felt way too good to have food in my belly.

Those nights of sleeping on the ground and half starving were for the birds.

Bronwen wanted to look for weapons, dividing and

conquering so that we covered more ground. Mike wanted to stick together because we had a definite location in mind. In the end, Onyx was the voice of reason, although Mike bristled whenever my wolf friend spoke.

We'd stay together, and we'd go disguised, just to make sure we were covered in case some Claw & Fang members were out looking for us. Which they most certainly would be.

Covered and disguised from any prying eyes, we ventured out into the city.

Chances were good that Dorian Jade already knew of the boarding house, and the moment the thought birthed in my mind, goosebumps ran up the length of my spine. After what happened yesterday?

I was almost positive he was coming for us.

We had to make sure to watch our backs and fronts and everywhere in between.

Although hands down, this place was on par with other massive cities I'd seen in the mortal realm, places like Boston or Baltimore. Of course, fae cities were filled with magic, the kind entwined in the land and felt with every inhalation. There were flowers growing out of buildings, and houses with no roofs, kept dry during a storm with shields of hardened air.

There were fae with wings and scales and all manner of clothing.

But only fae of a certain class, I realized looking at them.

Nothing on the outside marked them as above their Unseelie counterparts, but they were distinguishable now that I'd keyed into the differences. Their energy signatures were different, which meant they worked their magic in another way from the Seelie.

I kept my mouth shut rather than pointing them out.

People of all walks of life crowded the sidewalks with the return of the sun. The rain from before had dried up and left the landscape bright and verdant. In the distance, the rolling and crashing waves were inaudible but their loamy white caps broke through the rich navy of the ocean.

People went unnoticed.

There were too many bodies crowded together in a single area for anyone to stand out from the crowd. Even us, in our disguises. We huddled together as much for a sense of safety as because the crush of life left no room for us to spread out and maneuver.

No wonder my mom came here to disappear.

We stopped close enough to the sea to see the bobbing of boats on the horizon. Although we were on a different part of the coast, away from Sea's Deep, my skin prickled in discomfort.

I held out my hand to Laina. "Let me see the map." My cheeks flushed, realizing I just gave the damn queen an order. "Please."

My rushed remembrance of manners passed right over their heads. Laina rustled in the pocket of her cloak and held it out to me.

The lines etched in magic were the same crimson-brown as dried blood. Duh, blood magic, I realized with a start.

They converged on a small square at the end of the nearest block, leading out to one of the piers where boats docked.

"Where does the line end?" Mike asked.

He pressed closer and the wind brought a gust of his scent to torture me, I was sure.

The slightly citrusy undertone wound straight through me and stroked claws along my heart. I shuddered. "It looks like we're only a few blocks away."

"Great sense of direction must come with the territory," he joked with a weak grin.

My own smile was genuine when I gave it to him. "People like me have built-in compasses. It's kind of our thing."

Onyx harrumphed his agreement to the statement.

We hurried, checking our surroundings every so often.

I wasn't sure how we'd determine friend from foe unless someone came at us with a knife to the throat. Or wearing one of those medallions to cross through the wall. That might be our only signal.

Worry dogged my steps over uneven cobblestones. Bronwen made some noise of approval in the back of her throat and when I turned around to face her, she stared at the horizon like she wanted to shift and fly toward it.

I ground my back teeth. Focus! We had limited time before—well, before everything turned to shit. I had to find my mom and if the blood magic worked, then we were getting close.

I kept the map in hand and traced my finger along the route, marking every sideroad we passed.

The road curved around following the natural lines of the shore. It reminded me of those places in Scotland, the medieval harbors we learned about in history class.

The shore did have a certain charm, along with the stench of brine and the salty breeze rolling in from the water. I saw how easy it would be to sink into one of those stone buildings facing the water and lose an afternoon. Or two.

A good book and something cool to drink?

Or maybe Bronwen had a point, and the image of floating over the ocean waves bobbed along by an unseen wind held so much appeal my magic began to tingle, heralding the change.

Mike nudged me in the back and I focused on the feeling. "Isn't this it?"

He stared over my shoulder at the map and I glanced down in surprise.

The building at the end of the block boasted salt-worn shutters with peeling paint. No amount of magic would make it look like anything other than a handyman's special. The front stoop sagged under the weight of too many feet to count that had worn the stones smooth from following the same path.

"This isn't what I thought it would be," I muttered.

Onyx heard me. "It's a restaurant."

"He's using the term loosely, of course," Bronwen added.

"I don't understand." The door had been closed over and swollen from the proximity to the water, too out of whack to fully shut. "What would she be doing at a restaurant?"

"We go in and we find out." Laina, determined as ever, adjusted her cowl and stepped up to the door.

One push and it swung open on squeaky hinges, announcing our arrival.

I caught the tail end of Onyx's feral grin before he limped inside after her. "I could always eat."

I shared the sentiment. We did need food. The dingy interior of the tavern invited strangers to claim a corner for their own and hide out among the din and gloom. The windows in front had been covered with inches of brine which filtered the sunlight into cool streams that barely penetrated the haze.

Most of the tables, even at this hour of the day, were lit with stubs of candles affixed to the tables with dried wax.

We grabbed a table near the door and sat ourselves.

From somewhere nearby, a man roared in laughter, the sound followed by the distinctive thud of a fist striking flesh. Someone else yelled in reproach before the first man could follow through on whatever hit had accompanied his laugh.

Three fishermen perched at the table beside ours. One of them had shaved one entire side of his head, and another had an array of fish hooks pressed through his left eyebrow. They stared at us. Knowing instinctively we were not the kind of patrons who frequented a place like this.

Felons. They looked like felons.

Well, we were in the same boat. We might not be rough and tumble but we were certainly on the run from the law of the land.

I scooted over when Noren nudged at my arm, making room for him beside me.

"Hi, welcome to the Black Dog." A chipper young man came over with pad and pen to take our orders. "What can I get you to drink?"

Noren's tongue lolled from his mouth and the poor guy didn't even notice the direwolf until his paws scraped against the floor.

Blood leached from his face and rather than jumping, the way the tightening of his muscles indicated he wanted to do, the fellow took a massive step in the opposite direction.

I rested a hand on top of Noren's head. "I hope you don't mind. There wasn't a sign about no animals allowed."

The two of us watched him gulp over a huge knot in his throat like predators sizing up a tasty, easy treat.

"Waters," he squeaked, the sound like air hissing through a balloon. "I'll get you waters."

"I'm not sure I've ever seen anyone move so fast," Mike commented as he watched the server's hasty escape.

"Coming face to face with a direwolf will do that to a person," Bronwen replied. "Even if he doesn't look like one."

Laina remained silent through the ordeal, her gaze sweeping the restaurant from the smoke-tinted rafters to the scuff marks on the floor. Searching the faces of every patron, every server.

Searching for my mother. So was I, but I didn't see her. Or anyone who might be her. "Do you think the spell failed?"

She tensed at my question. "I'm not sure. I don't see anyone who looks like you in this place."

"You read my mind," I muttered.

Mike scraped his palm against his chin. "It's possible Tavi's mom has disguised herself with a better spell than ours."

"We haven't really searched the place yet." I craned my head to get a glimpse at a door set into the rear wall. "Maybe there's a kitchen here and she's working the stove. The spell might not be wrong."

"I'm casting my power out in a net as we speak," Laina whispered, dropping her tone. "I don't dare risk doing more and drawing attention to us."

Her willingness to do even the smallest magic warmed the splintered pieces of my heart grinding together in my chest. "What do you feel?"

"Nothing yet." She shook her head. "I'm sorry."

I ignored the way my gut plummeted and disappointment followed soon after, filling the empty space. "It's fine."

Mike threaded his fingers through mine and squeezed in a silent show of commiseration.

"I'm sure we'll find her soon." Bronwen, ever helpful, grinned around at the table.

The young male carried a tray of water in two hands and

dumped the plastic cups at the center of the table before darting off again.

"Look, he didn't even bring you a dish, bud." I clucked my tongue for Noren. "Maybe it would have been better for you to wait outside."

Even surrounded by my friends, the people I trusted the most in this world, I still didn't want to let Noren out of my sight.

"I'm sorry about Glenwood. He's new and he spooks easily," a new voice piped up. "I'll be happy to take your order. Have you had a chance to look at the menu?"

The sweet feminine tone stole my breath before I looked up at the newcomer. Slowly, I peeled my gaze from the belt of her trousers up the long line of buttons to the base of her delicate neck. Rich brown hair had been pulled up into a messy bun at the top of her head, leaving tendrils free and curling around her pointed ears.

The eyes, the nose, the lips—they were exactly the same as Nexa, Coral's mother. They had the same wide-legged stance that somehow managed to look feminine and brutal at the same time.

I narrowly resisted lifting my hands to my bust, the same size as the woman in front of us. I knew it. I knew it in my bones and in my blood.

Mom.

22

She's here.

My mom was alive, after believing for two decades she'd been murdered.

The pure adrenaline rush of seeing her in front of me, alive and breathing, tied my tongue into knots.

Her presence stunned me. Absolutely and completely.

She stared at Mike as though trying to place him, her lips pursed and her teeth gnawing on the inside of her cheek. Through it all, she never lost the permanent smile of a public service worker, the one pinned in place even with the roughest clientele.

"I, ah... No. We haven't had—what I mean to say—" I fumbled to speak and mentally beat myself up.

Gone were any perfect first lines I'd practiced. The kind of opening zingers to let the other person know in an instant, and without a shred of doubt, I was special.

I was special enough to be her *daughter*.

The spells we used to disguise ourselves wouldn't matter. All the potions I'd taken or years of hiding would fade away in an instant and she'd drop to her knees with tears in her eyes, apologizing for lying to me. For allowing me to think she'd died.

From the corner of my vision, I noticed Onyx watching with a mixture of confusion and compassion.

"Hi, yeah, we have a few questions for you." Mike, on the other hand, had no such confusion. "Is your name Dae?" he wanted to know.

THE SAME MIKE who knew every inch of my face. Who had recognized my mother in a string of heartbeats based on our similarities.

My heart wrenched up into my throat at hearing the name spoken out loud, and I bobbed my head once at him, to thank him for taking charge.

"You don't have to answer here if you aren't comfortable," he rushed to say. "We'd be happy to speak somewhere privately."

She didn't answer.

Our eyes locked, her gaze penetrating. Unlike Nexa's eyes, Dae's were the color of a blooming lilac, with a rich navy hue near the center. They penetrated past every defense, and I felt the moment the magic rushed out of me. The moment the disguise disappeared and left me raw and aching in front of her.

Something passed between us in her stare. That mother and daughter bond I'd been desperately hoping for.

I felt it too. My soul knew the truth even if this seemed like a real pinch-me moment.

"If you're Dae, then—" I started.

Dae held up a hand and hissed out a low string of sound. "No. Come with me." Her arm darted out and she wrapped her fingers around my elbow to pull me to my feet.

An electric current passed between us.

I slid out of the chair from the force of her touch, with Noren scrambling out of the way just in time to avoid a kick in the snout. The surprise kept me from reacting.

"It's not safe to talk here," she whispered, drawing me away.

The rest of my friends followed. Dae looked over her shoulder at them before she caught my nod and the plea on my face not to leave them behind.

The Queen of Faerie didn't belong in a place like this anyway, and certainly not without a retinue of guards to keep her safe.

My mom held my elbow as she maneuvered us through the slender spaces between rickety tables. She stopped at a small cutout in the right wall leading to the kitchen and rapped her knuckles against the scarred countertop connecting the two.

"Glenwood just completed his training, officially," she called out to the chef. "I'm taking a break."

A rotund fae, eyes like slits, poked his head out from above a range. Sweat trailed down his temples. "Fuck, Livvy, you can't leave that boy alone. He's nowhere near ready yet."

"He's going to be fine," my mom assured the man.

"If by fine you mean he'll scare off the customers, take the wrong orders, and forget who he's served, then absolutely." The cook barked out a laugh. "He's absolutely going to be fine."

"I do enough around this place to warrant a break. If you're worried about him, Xordon, then *you* can come out on the floor," she snapped back to him.

Good naturedly, I noticed.

The two of them clearly had a rapport between them.

But he'd called her Livvy, not her real name.

"Don't think I won't!" Xordon retorted.

Dae—Livvy? —led us to the door I'd seen along the back wall. She pressed her free hand against one of the panels, all the while keeping her hold on me, and we followed her up a narrow staircase.

The gloom lifted on the top step.

One entire wall of the small apartment was nothing but windows. The glass here, unlike downstairs, had been polished to a sheen and afforded a spectacular view of the harbor and ocean beyond.

"It's mine," Dae said. "So is the restaurant below. I own it."

It was a single room with no walls dividing the space outside of a right angle and a doorway I guessed led into a bathroom. The kitchen lay to our right, and ahead was a small bed and a smaller loveseat.

Neither of us wanted to break contact first. We didn't move even as the others spanned out into the apartment.

"Tavi?" she whispered.

"Hi, Mom."

Oh, god. Saying it out loud *to her* finally broke me.

The tears I'd kept in place for so long sprang free and burned trails like acid down my cheeks. I wasn't alone there. Mom cracked too. We moved for each other in unison and her long arms wrapped me up in a hug I'd been dreaming about since I was small.

This was my mother, and she was hugging me.

I wasn't alone in this world.

Uncle Will had done the best job he could but he hadn't been able to replace my mom. I'd never known a life with her, and yet having her here, feeling her softness and her strength, sensing her magic, it was as though she'd never left.

A hole inside of me began to fill.

"That man called you Livvy." Her hair muffled my voice.

She stroked her hand down my back. "That's my name here. I had to change it in order to disappear completely." She stepped back and cupped my face in her hands. "My god. Just let me look at you."

I was a mess and an ugly crier on my best day.

"I see myself here." She pointed to my nose, swallowing over a laugh. "And here. But this is all your father. And the stubborn chin!" She pinched me. "Yes, I know it."

Parts of me finally started to make sense. I leaned into the feeling of her touch. This was so much better than anything I could have asked for. Better than a dream.

Noren bumped his head against her hip and Livvy tore her gaze from me at last. The sight of him brought a smile to her face.

"You've found yourself a handsome protector, haven't you? Look at you!"

Words failed me a second time when Livvy bent down to scratch between Noren's ears. The direwolf, rather than keeping his distance, practically inserted himself between us to be part of the embrace and went so far as to roll his eyes back in his head in pure ecstasy when she moved to his chin.

He'd turned to putty in her hands.

"I've never seen him act this way before," I muttered. "He's strangely affectionate with you."

"I've always had a way with animals. Which it seems you've inherited from me."

Dae straightened, keeping one hand on me and the other on the top of Noren's head to connect us together. He whined but she ignored him, staring at me once again. Her smile stretched from ear to ear, and based on the ache in my cheeks, I knew mine did too.

I trusted Noren's ability to read people implicitly. She must be a pure soul and a good person.

But then again, I'd have said anything nice and good about her. I *wanted* her to be loving and kind. I *wanted* her to love me the way I'd always dreamed about.

I hugged her again and she squeezed me back tightly enough to bruise ribs. All those empty photo frames in my room at home, or the ones I'd left with the store-bought pictures of ready-made families, were a fading memory.

We were together at last.

It mattered. We'd found each other again, and man, it had taken a good bit of work, too. Dae— "Livvy"—had hidden herself pretty well.

But a lingering question still demanded an answer.

"If you were alive, then why did you never come back for me?" I asked, hating that my voice sounded whiny, almost close to tears. "Why weren't you looking for me? We could have been together."

"You were much safer with your Uncle Will." She maintained her grip on me and my body vibrated with the need to pull away from her. To move to cross the room, go where the others stood pointedly allowing us to have this moment of sweet reunion.

A reunion we *never* should have had to have because Dae shouldn't have disappeared and abandoned me with a lie.

She grimaced. "Your uncle has always been a steady man with a good head on his shoulders. He could provide for you and keep you safe."

Despite the good things she said, her expression told a different story.

"It wasn't up to him to do those things."

"I'm a wanted woman, Tavi."

Hearing my name come out of her mouth spun my head in useless circles.

"I've been on the run for over twenty years," she continued. "It wasn't the kind of life one drags a child into. You were better where you were, hidden, and I had to keep my distance even though it killed me. Your uncle knew all this."

"If he's such a great guardian and an upstanding guy, then why the hell did he lie about my fated mate and practically give me away to—" I almost blurted out the name of my enemy before I remembered that his son was in the room. Meaning no insult to Onyx, I dropped my voice and uttered, "Kendrick Grimaldi."

Dae straightened, frozen and expressionless.

I smirked at her reaction. "Okay, so you know who he is. He's been around for ages using dark magic to maintain his youth. Uncle Will said the wolf council foresaw him as my *fated mate*."

Did I even believe in those fairytales anymore? Of mates and destiny and happy endings?

"That's ridiculous and impossible," Dae blustered. Her cheeks went red. "There is no way William would do such a thing."

"But he did. He insisted on it." I wondered how much to tell her and when would be the right time.

The seconds ticked by and my anger gave way to frustration and fatigue. That desperate desire for safety and peace, as always, lingered around the periphery.

I turned to Mike to find him staring at me with his head cocked to the side, as though asking if I needed him.

I shook my own head quickly. "I think Uncle Will prizes the pack over family. He knew Kendrick's pack was strong, and rather than make an enemy out of them, he gave me up."

Dae touched my face and I jumped at the contact. "You didn't allow it to break you."

The current between us grew and pulsed with electric energy. Maybe Laina was right. About the connection between me and my mother.

I lifted my chin. "No, I didn't. And I didn't wait around to let Kendrick use me the way he wanted to."

"You know, Faerie told me that you would come back to me one day. I never actually believed it." The awe in her voice felt misplaced somehow based on the statement.

"Um, what? *Faerie* told you?"

But Mom wasn't looking at me anymore. Her attention was caught on something over my shoulder and she broke away, striding across the small space to a bookshelf I hadn't noticed before.

Instead of answering, she fumbled with the books on the shelf, grabbing titles at random and pushing them aside. Several she let drop to the floor. "I know I have it in here somewhere. Where did I put the damn thing?"

A bit manic, she dug around the books, a pulse of *something* catching my attention. Not just books, I realized when I took a closer look. Spellbooks. There were decks of tarot cards, charged crystals, wands with pointed quartz edges, and ritual candles inscribed with runic sigils.

"It seems like the prophecy was true after all. Even though I prayed it wasn't." Livvy whispered the last part to herself but I was close enough to catch every word. "Now it's time to make sure the prophecy comes to pass."

She would have clawed the shelf empty if Laina hadn't stepped up and took hold of Dae's arm. Mom panted, tensed, before turning to the queen. A ripple of shock erupted the placid set of her lips and her brow furrowed.

Did she recognize Laina?

My insides surged against my ribs and the rest of me went tight and hot. "What are you talking about?'

The two women stared each other for a moment longer before Laina released Dae and let her resume her frantic search of the bookshelf.

She grabbed a book and spared half a heartbeat looking at the spine before she tossed it over her shoulder, forcing Bronwen to step out of the way to avoid being hit.

"It has to be here," she mumbled.

"If I knew what you wanted then maybe I'd be able to help you look," Laina offered.

Noren whined and leaned hard enough against my leg to throw me off balance. I reached out and grabbed the countertop of the tiny kitchen for support.

"No offense, Tavi, but your mom is kinda weird," Bronwen hustled across the room to whisper against my ear. "What is she doing?"

I had no idea but I wanted to find out. Patting Bronwen's hand, I moved into the fray and ducked to avoid another tossed book the size of a dictionary.

"Dae? Mom?" Nope, that felt too weird to say. "Er...Livvy, what are you looking for?"

I yelped and automatically caught another book she tossed but this one was at least closer to a notebook.

She'd moved from the first and second shelves to baskets at the bottom, rifling through stack after stack of what looked like journals.

"Did I send the journal with her? I must have. Right?" Livvy muttered to herself rather than reply. "Yeah, I did. Why didn't I keep it here?"

"Please. Talk to us. What are you doing?" I asked.

Livvy shook her head and more strands of chestnut hair pried loose from her bun. "I have to find it, Tavi. It's time for you to know the truth of your birth."

The way she spoke sent shivers along my spine. There were secrets bubbling up for her to drop such casual words with the force of an exploding bomb.

My instincts roared at me to pay attention.

At last, Livvy straightened.

I wasn't sure what got through to her or whether she'd just given up the search. When she turned, her hands were empty. She held them out to me, palms up, her expression agonized.

"You've survived this long, but if the truth isn't revealed... It's clear I've waited much too long to do this. I just never thought we'd get to this moment." She bit her lip and shifted her weight to the opposite foot.

The movement made her look oddly innocent. Child-like.

She reached for my hands and widened her eyes slightly when I refused to take them. Goosebumps lifted the hairs on the back of my arms at the chill of her flesh.

"There's something special about you, Tavi. More than just being the child of a werewolf and a fae. Halflings are special, of course." She nodded to Bronwen, to Onyx. "But there's more to your story."

I wasn't sure how much more I could take, to be honest. But I held my tongue, even as my stomach did acrobatics.

"You were conceived with a very specific witch magic. I wasn't able to have a baby on my own, and I loved your father desperately. We wanted a family more than anything else. So we contacted a witch. She worked a spell of complicated magic. A magic that sealed your fate with the entire history of Faerie."

"I really don't like where this is going." I took an involuntary step back.

She refused to let me go, and moved with me.

"You're more than what you've been led to believe, sweet girl. A chosen one. Someone who will bring together the realm by annihilating the corruption within it. Not just because you're a halfling, but because you are one third of *each*." Livvy held up her fingers and ticked off on them. "Fae. Shifter. *Witch*. All three magics are combined in you. The spell changed the make-up of my baby before her birth."

Through the ringing in my ears I recognized the sound of Laina inhaling sharply.

"You're crazy," I whispered.

My ribs went tight enough to pierce my heart, which had taken up the beat of a one-legged, one-armed member of a marching band. Livvy's eyes locked with mine and despite a settling in my bones at her expression, I fought.

"You've felt things. I'm sure you have," she insisted.

"One person can't be tied to Faerie. All three magics?" I laughed. "That would make me a freak. I wouldn't be alive. No one is all three. Besides, power doesn't alter someone's blood. A witch spell doesn't make me a witch."

"Don't you ever feel like you're a little *too* good at magic? Have you ever been able to pass through magical barriers without a thought?" Livvy snapped her fingers. "Just because you can?"

My mind immediately ricocheted back to a night I wanted to forget, when I'd walked right through Barbara's wards. I violently forced the thought aside.

"I'm not who you think I am." I threw back my shoulders. "You don't actually know me. Maybe you just want me to be important because the me in front of you wasn't what you expected."

I needed air or I'd suffocate in this room.

Holding up a hand to keep the others from following me, I strode toward the door and skipped a few rickety steps on my way down. I caught myself before I fell flat on my face but none of it mattered. Nothing mattered. This reunion had not gone the way I thought it would, and now it turned out my mother was crazy. I pushed out into the dingy restaurant with Noren behind me and strode for the front door.

Outside, the clawing sensation around my throat remained. I chose a direction at random and took off.

Leaving was a terrible idea but I couldn't stop myself with logic. Not with my gut and my mind swirling in opposite directions.

Noren kept pace and with him at my heels, I broke into a jog, the crash of the surf nothing compared to the tambourine in my head.

When I first went to see Barbara, to bargain for my potions my first year at the Fae Academy for Halflings, I'd walked through the magic barrier around her property. No fucking clue how. Or what it even was.

I just remembered a sensation like a thick wall of water cascading over my head and then it broke apart and I had bigger things to worry about. Like the witch herself, who turned out to be nuts at the time but not so bad in the long run.

I'd even...sensed the witch magic.

Looking back on it, I'd assumed it was normal. My fae side blessed me with certain gifts. But what if it wasn't normal? What if fae couldn't actually sense magic like I could?

I'd never asked any of the fae I knew. It had never come up.

Melia would have been the best person to answer those questions but how do you even begin when you're not sure what questions to ask?

Out of breath and muscles screaming, I stopped at a break in the stone wall separating the road from the beach. Maybe I should have been more aware of those things. There were apparently a lot of missed opportunities in my past.

Did any of them really matter now?

I'd found my not-so-dead mother and she was absolutely loony, talking to me like I was some kind of "chosen one." She'd even used those words!

Chosen One.

I tested them in my head and bile rose, burning the back of my throat. My lips twisted into a disgusted pout. Nope. I wasn't the chosen one. I was Tavi Alderidge.

"Hey!"

I glanced up sharply at the shout. And found a man looking right at me.

My nostrils flared. A half-shifter, obvious from the energy around him and the slightly pointed canines poking out above his lip.

They'd found me.

23

I'm a fool to think I'd be able to outrun another half-shifter.

If my fae side gave me increased magical aware-ness, then my shifter side gave me speed. Which meant the dude who'd found me was also pretty damn fast.

I took off at a run with Noren right behind me and we wound into the crowd. Even the mass of bodies around us wouldn't be enough to keep the shifters from catching up.

They'd follow our trail as surely as they'd followed it here.

My lungs bellowed and my legs ached by the time I raced back to the Black Dog.

Even the dude with half his head shaved jumped back in his seat as I ran by him toward the stairs. Up again, hauling myself along the risers, and into the apartment.

"We're in trouble! They're here!" I somehow managed to screech the words and once they were out, my throat closed and my lungs collapsed.

I'd have fallen to my knees if Noren hadn't been there to catch me, moving faster than a speeding train. Dizziness swarmed me and my vision narrowed slightly with a black outline. When I swallowed, my mouth had gone dry.

The rest of the team jolted into movement.

"We're out of here, then," Mike said. His voice reverberated back to me with a tinny undertone. "Tavi, are you able to move?" he asked. "Let me help you."

I gulped and closed my eyes against the dizziness. I was too weak to push him away or insist on doing it myself. Mike hauled me to my feet and kept a hand on my lower back for support.

"I'm coming with you," Livvy insisted.

She moved to the kitchen, withdrawing a small tote from beneath the sink and looping it around her shoulders. A go bag.

I'd never met anyone with an actual go bag for emergencies.

"You'll be painting a target on your back. After so long in hiding, are you sure you—" Laina began gently.

"It doesn't matter," Livvy interrupted. "The target doesn't matter if my daughter is in trouble. She was brave enough to come find me. It's time for me to take the next step of the journey with her." A pause, a scramble for supplies, and then, "I only stayed hidden because I thought it would keep her safe."

My mind churned. I didn't care if she stayed or not. We just needed to run, immediately, before the Claw & Fang burned the entire building to the ground with us inside. The sense of urgency pushed at me and I drew a deep shuddering breath.

Calm down.

Nope, no calming down.

I held out a hand for Onyx. "Do you need help?"

He shook his head. "I'll be fine. Let's go."

He faltered on his first step, and Bronwen and I stepped up to take the brunt of his weight. She flashed me a look telling me not to say anything.

Together we limped toward the door. Mike held it open, gesturing for us to hurry, and we skipped down the steps as quickly as possible, Laina at our front, Livvy at our back.

The noise from below grew with every riser we traversed and by the time we made it to the last step, I knew.

In my blood and in my bones I knew what we'd find on the other side of the closed door.

Laina opened it. The restaurant was already crawling with our enemies.

Livvy moved faster than I could ever have imagined. She passed us with a sweet breeze gusting in her wake and stepped in front of Laina, her hands lifted in front of her and fae magic pulsing in a golden corona around her wrists.

My heart lurched into my throat and lodged there as a shifter surged forward, knocking a table out of the way. The wood crashed to the floor and he swung a fist at Livvy.

Her magic erupted in a wave and shoved the shifter back. The man flew off his feet and landed heavily on his tailbone.

The crack of the impact was lost in the shouting.

A low growl reverberated through me, and when I turned to Onyx, his eyes had darkened and his lips were peeled back to show overly white, sharp teeth.

My veins lit with terror and bloodlust when a second shifter ran for Laina. Mike stepped up in time to take the brunt of the attack but there was little maneuvering room. They collided, the shifter driving Mike backwards with a yell.

We weren't strong enough to fight. Not now, with our energy stores so low.

Onyx and I were barely able to put one foot in front of the other.

Fear burned through me.

Then Noren rose like a ghost behind me and launched at one of the shifters closing in on us. A blast of magic came from the side and several tables lifted at once before crashing down and taking several members of the Claw & Fang with them.

Livvy yelled an incoherent stream of curses, and out of the corner of my eye I watched the seedy one-eyed dude and his cronies bum-rush her.

Suddenly another voice was heard. "Help Livvy! She needs us." Xordon bellowed out the battle cry and the rest of the room erupted.

The one thing I hadn't counted on was the patrons' love for my mother.

One burly patron wrapped a massive arm around the neck of one of the shifters and yanked, drawing him back and strangling him.

Another blast of magic shot at us from the left.

I ducked, inhaling the stench of ozone and singed wood, lifting my gaze in time to watch the blast hit a shifter square in the chest. My hackles rose, my skin prickling with the urge to change despite my lack of strength.

Noren swept through the crowd, tearing at limbs and yanking people off their feet. He towered over the rest of the fae.

With this many members, not to mention patrons, there was no clear way to the door.

Livvy sent another wave of magic out but it did nothing more than clear the first few feet in front of her.

I helped Onyx forward with Bronwen at our backs now, making sure we weren't taken by surprise. My instincts were screaming at me to do something more than watch. To help the others so Mike and his mom, as well as my own mom, didn't have to handle the brunt of this fight.

This was my fault. They'd found us because of me.

Something clawed at the back of my shirt. I broke out in a cold sweat, lurching forward, unwilling to let go of Onyx. We were getting out of here if I had to put him on Noren's back and send them out the door myself.

The grip abruptly loosened and something hot sprayed my back.

No time to turn around. No time to look behind me and see what kind of death trailed us.

Someone let out a whoop, the sound trailed by a gurgle, and the seedy guy strode by dragging one of the club members by her hair. He winked at me before making a shooing motion with his free hand.

The message was unmistakable.

There was still no clear path to the door but Laina and Mike were halfway across the room at this point. Livvy nearly made it.

"Tavi! Let's go!"

Mike called my name. He'd taken care of his own business beautifully.

Club members mixed with restaurant patrons. Even the sweaty cook from behind the line had joined the fray. He slammed a heavy pan down on the head of one of the half-changed shifters.

I'd gotten too caught up in the pandemonium to think straight, to do anything other than react.

Something hit into the back of my knees and I lost my grip on Onyx and went down. The side of my cheek slammed against the wooden floor, pain ripping through me, before something yanked my hair and dragged me up to my knees.

I screamed, power surging up through my skin and taking the last of my energy with it. The bite on my arm pulsed, throbbed horrifyingly hot, and I ignored it.

My assailant's hold loosened but it wasn't enough to get them to release me entirely.

I kicked out, still on my knees, hoping to land a hit against my unseen enemy.

The burly dude came to my rescue. "People like you don't belong here! Get the fuck out."

He dragged the shifter off me and hurled him against the wall.

Onyx reached out a hand and helped me to my feet. Together we made it to Livvy, who stood at the door motioning wildly for us to follow her.

Onyx limped over the threshold and the door slammed shut behind us.

"Come on!" Livvy's voice echoed strangely against the crash of the waves.

Daylight burned my eyes for some reason. I choked, my lungs filled with smoke from the inside of the restaurant, the salty spray from the waves stinging me. I tightened my grip on Onyx.

Footsteps sounded behind us as shifters poured from the Black Dog, giving chase.

We raced down the street with Livvy in the lead. She knew the city. At this point, I trusted her. We had no choice but to trust her. She slowed her steps enough to reach for me, her fingers brushing my elbow.

With a nod, she turned to the left and cut through a side street. Up a set of stone steps carved out of the cliff face itself. Another left, and then a right.

My attention narrowed on the footfalls behind us, the growls and the yells, like we were actually going to listen to their anxious commands to *stop*.

This was life or death. This wasn't a game.

Not that it ever was.

The maze of alleys and the cramped spaces between houses became an impenetrable labyrinth. After a few moments I lost all sense of direction.

My lungs shrank like balloons without air.

Every tense step had my muscles seizing, and even with the distance from the Black Dog, my attention remained hooked there. Wondering when they would pick up our trail and which shadowy corner they'd pop out of. Dorian Jade was far from the boogeyman of my nightmares but he was real enough for me to worry.

Livvy knew the city, that much was clear. She strode ahead with the purposeful attention of someone confident in their direction. This was her playground.

How long had she lived here and when had she taken it upon herself to explore the backstreets?

It was clear she knew exactly what she was doing.

She led us on a wild goose chase through twists and turns and soon enough, the sounds of the scuffle faded behind us. The Claw & Fang following us were now just as lost in the maze as we were.

When Livvy held up a hand to get us to stop, my legs refused to listen and I stumbled. My muscles were too tense to slow down and the ache traveled up my calves all the way to my hips.

Every part of me shook, whether from adrenaline or the lack of magic.

I'd been emptied out and left to suffer through the effects.

"We're safe here," Livvy said breathlessly.

Bronwen slapped a hand against the brick, sucking in a breath. "How do you know?"

Livvy didn't bother to answer. A bright splatter of blood dotted the side of her face but it wasn't hers. "I must have sent the journal we need with you, Tavi, when you went to live with your uncle."

Her abrupt change of subject took me by surprise.

"You're still going on about the journal?" Onyx snapped. The blood had drained from his face and left his skin as ashen as his hair.

I grimaced. "I never had *anything* of yours. Uncle Will told me I came with nothing when he took me in. Everything I had, he bought."

And my memories of that time in my life were nonexistent. A big black hole in my head and no amount of pretending had ever been able to fill it.

I watched Livvy's face go the exact opposite of Onyx's. The flush began at the base of her neck and crept up to mottle her cheeks until every part of her was a bright crimson in her fury. "That *odious* man. I sent everything with you. Everything I could."

And here I thought she'd had nothing but nice things to say. It seemed that her gentle facade held some secrets buried deep.

"What's in the journals?" I asked. "Why are they so important?"

Maybe if we had an explanation it wouldn't seem weird, a strange focus when it would have been smarter for us to worry about the *actual* monsters chasing us down.

Livvy turned to me and grabbed me by the shoulders to force me to pay attention to her. Her eyes were wide, the whites overtaking everything else. "When Faerie gave me the prophecy that you would return, she said you would be the catalyst for peace. But your witch powers were locked. They always have been, it's safer that way, at least until the time was right. They needed to be unlocked and Faerie gave me the specific spell for doing so."

Witch powers. Yeah, right.

I broke away, my chest heaving. "You're not the one who got the prophecy. Oxana the Sightless did."

"It's the same prophecy, but not the same," Livvy insisted. Her lips twisted in frustration. Like I somehow wasn't paying attention. "She only received a part of the prophecy. Faerie gave me the rest, along with the key needed to unlock your potential."

"I'm not following," Mike muttered. "Explain, please."

Laina gripped his hand and shook her head once to get him to hold his questions.

"Why are you speaking about Faerie like it's a person?" I asked. "It's a place. It's our world. You can't talk to a world and have it talk back to you."

Livvy reared back and rolled her eyes. "Tavi, of course Faerie is a person. Honey...she's a goddess. Haven't you heard the truth?"

Okay, my mom was officially nuts.

She'd lost her mind and that was why she spouted off about goddesses and prophecies and witch powers.

"Don't you see how Faerie is corrupt? Arcane? How things are working against the natural order?" She pointed toward a dark spread of clouds on the horizon. "It's because you're the one destined to stop it."

I couldn't help but agree with her about the weather and the corruption. But the rest of it?

Did she expect me to just let her lead me along, sheep to the slaughter style?

I'd busted Onyx out of prison because he was going to be put to death without a trial for a crime I *knew* he didn't commit under his own volition. Someone had been pulling his strings and using him as an instrument for murder. Because the king—or the premier in this case—was judge, jury, and executioner.

Absolute power corrupted absolutely. Wasn't that a saying?

"I get that Faerie is infected. And maybe something should be done to fix the realm, but I know nothing about it. I'm not the right person."

Oh, god. Was the queen staring at me?

What was Laina thinking through this mania?

"You were born for this," Livvy insisted. "You are not just the right person, you are the *only* person. I was given a spell by Faerie to unlock your powers myself when the time was right. The time is now right."

Something must have gone wrong in her head.

A loose screw but worse.

She was talking about the world like a person, a goddess, talking about me like I'm a savior.

Before I knew it I'd taken an unwitting step back away from her. The space between us turned hot, molten, and made my already overworked lungs shoot into overdrive.

It wasn't me. It could never be me because I wasn't anything special and *Chosen Ones* were for fairytales and television shows.

Livvy, rather than step up to me and make me listen to her, shifted her attention away. Her gaze flickered back and forth and she blinked rapidly. "We're going to have to break into Will's house. We have to get those journals. We need the spell. There's no other choice."

Terror was bright. It scalded my insides and turned every part of me to ash.

"We can't return to the human realm," I blurted out.

The others were there around us, once again pretending none of this conversation was taking place. They were watching our back and our front and our sides for other real enemies and acting like they didn't hear this absolute nonsense.

"What if Kendrick Grimaldi catches me?"

"I'll come with you to protect you." Mike said it as though it was self-evident. "There's no way he's going to get through me. He won't touch you."

I bit down on my lip.

Mike's magic wasn't strong enough to protect me, not against Kendrick, even though it was so sweet to see him willing. To know he'd step up this way for me.

"No, I'll go with them," Laina insisted. "Between the three of us, we'll be safe. And quiet."

"You're serious." I gawked at the queen. "You don't think this is absolutely insane?"

Laina's chin jutted out and from the way she refused to meet my gaze, the answer was clear. She believed it.

So either they were all going mad or I was. Hysterical laughter bubbled up inside of me until I doubled over with it.

Please, let me be insane. Because reality was too fucked-up to be believed.

24

They outvoted me.

No matter what excuses I tossed out, between the two mothers—powerhouses on their own and unstoppable together—there was no way for me to stand against them.

Even when I wanted to.

Even when I wasn't sure why I *had* to.

I looked over to Mike and met his gaze, imploring him to do something. But it seemed even he wasn't immune to the argument or the validity of our next steps. Just as it was clear he didn't really want his mom to go with me.

He wanted to be the one to stand at my side.

All I wanted was to reach for him and find some time and place to be alone, to be in his arms and close my eyes. To pretend like there was nothing and no one else in our world and we were alone somewhere desolate.

Livvy nodded, the decision settled. "We head out as soon as possible, then. The next thing to do is get out of the city. It will be safer than remaining. Those shifters will still be on our trail."

And what would stop them from finding us in the next one, I wondered. There was nowhere safe in this world. Not with Dorian Jade out there determined to see his goals realized.

I leaned heavily on Noren and Bronwen moved up to my side. Her thin smile lacked any real confidence but I appreciated her attempt.

Words failed me and my tongue shrank back to half its size. On leaden feet, I followed Livvy, leaving Mike and Laina to help Onyx on our way out of the city. The countryside wasn't any safer but no one would listen to me if I spoke.

Laina drew on her witch magic to weave protections after us, to erase our tracks as we made them.

What did I expect, really? The thought of going back to the human realm filled me with something similar to repulsion. It had been my home, the place I grew up, back when I didn't know how dangerous the world actually was.

Then my horizons expanded and grew even more dangerous and suddenly here we were.

I tried not to fight against what felt like a tide but there was no stopping my mind from conjuring up the worst-case scenarios and worrying about them like they were already real.

A savior? *Me?* I'd never heard such rubbish.

The sun arched overhead and the space between the buildings grew yet again. From the seaside to the city's heart and out the other side, we traveled in near silence. Watching our every move and scrutinizing the crowd for signs of shifters.

Every set of eyes that turned in our direction was a potential enemy.

Livvy and Laina navigated. As though now that they'd

decided on a direction, it was only natural for them to be the counselors with our group of wayward children. Even Noren fell into line.

None of this had turned out the way I'd thought, the way I'd planned.

Things had twisted from bad to worse.

I thought being accused of Madam Muerte's murder was the worst thing to happen to me. Or being kidnapped by Kendrick in the middle of the Wild Hunt.

None of it compared to the trek out of Yelaine and the nagging worries of what would happen once we made it back to the human realm. It wasn't a question of *if*. The moms would find a way.

It also didn't help not knowing exactly what kind of change would happen inside of me once Livvy unlocked my so-called witch powers.

Or the lingering fears that Livvy was entirely insane.

On one hand, I wanted to believe her. On the other...it would mean accepting that I was special in a way I'd never understand.

"We'll stop here." Livvy drew to a stop outside of a low rising hill. Boulders ringed the base. A pulse of magic maneuvered the stones out of their current positions and left a small black opening visible. "A faerie ring, built around a thin spot between the realms."

"How did you know this was there?" I asked, my lips numb.

"The land speaks to me. I know its secrets and I know where it wants me to go. Our way has been guided." Livvy stepped aside and once again motioned for us to head inside the cave. "Come. It's safe here."

The opening was small enough that I had to get down on my hands and knees to scramble inside.

The granite scraped the top of my head and my knees and for a tense moment I forgot how to breathe. Claustrophobia pressed in close and the walls tightened around me, my heart clawing at the inside of my throat.

Finally the tunnel opened up into a cave large enough for us to move about freely. The ceiling expanded so that even the tallest among us wasn't able to rise on the tips of their toes to touch it.

The constriction in my chest eased somewhat but not enough for me to rest easily.

Noren remained outside and I didn't blame him. If I'd been able to fend for myself, then I might have done the same, but then again there was safety in numbers too. I felt better with my friends and family beside me.

No matter how really fucking weird this was.

Laina nodded decisively. "We'll rest here for a few hours and then we'll leave."

Mike turned to her with his jaw slightly open. "*Mom.* You can't be serious."

She turned to him with her hands on her hips. "Any longer and we are wasting time. You will stay behind with the others."

Mike shook his head. "I'm sorry, but no. I'm coming with you."

The idea of being trapped in this space with Onyx and Bronwen seemed to weigh on him. And to be honest, it didn't sit well with me, either.

"They'll need your protection." Laina glanced at Onyx, her expression softening. "You've been raised with strength and dignity and I expect you to use them to protect those who cannot protect themselves, Michael."

I shifted from foot to foot with my stomach an uneasy mass. "It's not a good idea for you to come, anyway."

"Why?" he pressed. "Why won't it—"

"Enough, Michael," Laina cut in. "This isn't part of your journey."

His eyes narrowed. "Why can't it be? I should be with Tavi."

"Tavi is going to be absolutely fine." Laina's insistence felt misplaced.

All this effort just for me, and I would never in a million years deserve it. I always made it out of these scrapes but what if I didn't this time?

Part of me didn't think Mike would agree. A mottled flush had crept up the base of his neck and turned the tips of his ears pink. His shoulders slumped forward. "Tavi, I hate this," he muttered.

His whispered truth was too vulnerable for me. "I'm not keen on it myself."

"Let's go outside and talk. Take a second for ourselves." His gaze darted to the cave opening.

I twisted with him, sucking in a breath to agree.

"No," Livvy interrupted. "We stay out of sight. Rest." She slid down the wall until she sat cross-legged. Regal despite her surroundings. "My word is final."

There were too many things left unsaid between me and Mike and they were getting closer to the surface with every moment. We'd have our time. *We have to.*

I swallowed hard, my throat constricting, the rest of me tense and aching.

After several hours where no one rested, Onyx, Mike, and Bronwen remained behind in the cave for protection, while Noren prowled around the outside.

The word clanked around inside of my head and lost its meaning along the way. *Protection* felt like a joke.

There was no safe place anywhere.

Especially not when we were going right back into the raging bonfire of shit I'd been desperate to leave behind.

Livvy and Laina crawled back toward the mouth of the cave to travel to the human realm. Livvy paused to greet Noren, who bumped his head against her outstretched palm.

"How do you propose we travel?" My hands went to my hips. "I lost my key." And I doubted, in her mad rush, that Laina would have remembered to grab hers.

Noren whined but a sweet word from Livvy had him falling silent, crouched between us and ready for action.

"I have mine." Livvy reached beneath the collar of her shirt and pulled out a golden chain, linked through the scrollwork of an antique key with its sharp point honed to the same glistening gold. "This will work."

My questions died on the tip of my tongue before I had a chance to ask. Livvy removed the chain from around her neck and sketched the pattern of a door in the air.

The shimmering outline of it pulsed, real and solid, for an instant before she slid the key into the emptiness. The lock glowed like the inside of a forge before she twisted the key and the air split into two distinct pieces.

Here, it was night. The dying twilight showed the first hint of diamond-bright stars in the clear sky overhead.

But the opening in front of us showed daylight.

It was way too weird, and my first instinct was to tell Livvy to close the door.

When I'd come here the first time, the time of day had matched.

Why did it change now?

My first glimpse of the human world I'd grown up in felt wrong. As though some sort of poisonous gas trickled in from this doorway unnaturally.

I took a step back but Laina rested a soft palm on my forearm. Her smile was calming; it assured me we were going to be fine, as they all said.

Livvy was once again the first one to walk toward the door and she stopped before she stepped through it.

"I have to lock it behind us," she said by way of an explanation. "To make sure no one accidentally walks through."

I halfway expected Kenrick Grimaldi's acidic smile to greet me. Laina took the choice out of my hands and stepped over the glistening threshold. Noren gave me a gentle nudge at the back to get me moving, then huffed out a small lupine growl, like *goodbye for now*.

The first thing I noticed was the heft.

The human world didn't feel the same as Faerie. The lightness was missing, the sense of energy in the air. This was a dead place. This was a world where the air hung like anchors and wedged itself into the bottom crevices of my lungs.

Livvy locked the door behind us but the last thing I saw before Faerie disappeared was Mike's head popping out of the entrance of the cave as he came to stand beside Noren. Like he'd somehow find his own way to us.

I swallowed twice but it wasn't enough to combat the dryness in my mouth.

"We—" I broke off and coughed. Everything felt weird, tasted weird. "We have to wait until night. It's Friday, right? Uncle Will always heads out to the bar after work on Friday nights."

Unless the day of the week had also changed on me.

Had time in Faerie somehow gotten ahead of the mortal world, or behind?

Will had his rituals the same way I used to. Even before I began to intern at his law firm, I'd abided by the same routines as the other pack members my age. School and social niceties. After classes, there was work, and then dinner.

Sometimes there were parties when connections needed to be strengthened or milestones celebrated.

Like my eighteenth birthday.

The schedule had to be adhered to. Uncle Will was a stickler for those kinds of things. I didn't know if that would have changed in the time since I'd run away.

I blinked, the landscape coming into clarity although the edges were still a little unfocused.

I'd run away from this place, and the only time I'd come back had been when Kendrick kidnapped me.

What would Uncle Will even say if he saw me now? And we had to break into his house.

My house.

I was gonna be sick.

"We'll scout around for a place to lay low until then." Livvy stared determinedly at the asphalt in front of us.

They were dull too, I realized with a start. Both fae women had taken on the muted tones of this world, like the deadness seeped inside their bodies. I no longer saw the points of their ears, and Laina's hair showed an ordinary sandy shade of blonde rather than dazzling gold.

They'd glamoured themselves on instinct. Of course.

Only there were no passing cars on this stretch of road to worry about. Maybe our luck was holding. The private gated community had always seemed cut off from the rest of the world due to our need to access the forest. The national park backed right up to the place and the gates and high walls kept our pack safe.

Outside of the neighborhood, the tree-lined streets

would slowly become a city, the traffic increased, and the buildings crowded each other.

Not here.

I hadn't appreciated it before.

You're marked for greatness. It is destiny. It is fate. *And therefore, it is out of my control.*

That's what Will said to me once.

Had he known, then, what Livvy knew about Faerie?

I trembled and bent down to re-tie the laces of my old Converse, one of the only things I'd asked Mike to help me magic at the bed and breakfast. The slippers Dorian Jade made me wear were a not so distant nightmare

Now, we had to sidestep the guards patrolling the community.

"We can't use magic here. We'll have to do this the old-fashioned way." Livvy rolled up her sleeves and buttoned them at her elbows. "We'll scale the wall."

"You really think that's the best course of action?" Laina questioned.

"We need to get inside, don't we? This will be the fastest way as long as we do not get caught."

Which was the name of the game.

Our superior strength allowed us to climb the wall and scale the metal points atop it with ease. Those kinds of things were mostly a deterrent for humans, while the guards made sure those like *us* were kept at bay.

There was no stopping us, though. No matter how my knees turned flaccid and my mind wavered, I hopped down on the other side of the fence and braced.

"I know where we can hide."

The community was vast but there was a place I'd always gone to get away from everything. Even when it felt impossible to escape myself, I'd known how to disappear. This time I led the way through the familiar streets.

For the first time, my unease shifted into anticipation.

The community green space had felt like a home away from home even when the mansion should've been large enough to accommodate my uncle's ego and mine. During the day, the pack members and rich moms walked the trails there and complained about the minutiae of their lives. It would probably be packed right now.

I'd always waited for night to go.

Still, we kept to a methodical march up to the black iron fence around the park and slipped through the gate. Up ahead, willow trees marked the entrance to the walking trails and beyond were swing sets and jungle gyms and meadows strategically planted.

Beyond the park, a secondary gate led out to the forest.

My heart skipped a beat.

Would she still be here?

"You're looking for someone," Laina put in.

"You're too perceptive for your own good." I pointed ahead to the sound of wheels over cement. "Will you guys give me a minute, please? There's someone I have to talk to."

And I hoped she would still be around, still willing to talk to me.

Tension kept my shoulders notched up to my ears as I walked further into the park alone. I stepped between large oaks which kept the path shielded during the day, and slipped unnoticed through the shadows.

Elfwaite had been the one person in the world who knew about me and hadn't cared. Well, she cared about my feelings, my well-being, and my safety. No judgment and never any condemnation.

A true friend.

I could be myself around her.

Tears stung the corners of my eyes as I glanced form side to side checking the bay laurel bushes for the familiar flutter of wings.

"Elfwaite?" I called out.

I straightened and stepped out of the way of a frustrated mother pushing a stroller with two squabbling children belted inside. Once they passed, I let out a breath and stepped off the path entirely. Leaves crunched underfoot.

"Elfwaite, are you here?"

Further into the buttery gloam, I saw nothing and heard less, but at least the toddlers' screams faded. I blew out a breath and almost screeched myself when a tiny purple-skinned pixie flew in front of my nose.

"Tavi! Oh my goodness! I never thought I'd see your face again!"

There was no hugging without squashing her. Elfwaite was only four inches tall and her voice as soft as the hint of a breeze through a flower. But I held up my index finger for her to wrap her arms around and the second she made contact, the tears sprang free.

"I've missed you so much," I gulped out. "You have no idea."

"Where have you been? You just disappeared on me! One minute you're here, running away from your own birthday party, and then nothing." Her nostrils flared delicately and her eyes shone with ire. She slapped at my skin but I felt nothing. "Do you have any idea how worried I was?"

"Do you have any idea how rare it is to see a pixie in this land?"

I shouldn't have been surprised that Laina followed me. But it sure shocked me to hear the awe in her tone.

I cupped one hand protectively around Elfwaite's madly fluttering wings and glanced over my shoulder. Unsure what to say.

"Your Majesty." Elfwaite was breathless. She broke away from my finger and sketched a bow in midair, her wings working overtime. "It's my honor to be in your presence."

I cleared my throat. "Her family left Faerie a hundred years ago."

"The great Pixie War," Elfwaite clarified. "I was born in the human lands."

"She helped me learn about Faerie," I added. "We met by accident. A great accident."

"Pixies and wolves, even half-wolves, have never been friends before." Livvy stepped up beside Laina. Her gaze remained shadowed. She stared between the two of us.

I scrambled off my knees to face the two moms. "She was the best friend I had growing up and nicer to me than any of my supposed *kind*." I'd defend her no matter what happened.

Laina held up her hands to show she meant no harm. "It's merely curiosity." She stared at the two of us with her head tilted to the side. "An interesting twist of fate, one might say."

"I'm sorry I ran off." I pried my attention away from them, focusing entirely on Elfwaite. "I shouldn't have left you out in the cold that way. I should have found a way to write."

"What happened?" she whispered, casting furtive glances back at the Queen of Faerie. "Why are you with the queen? And who is that other woman?"

Her little body vibrated against mine as she rested on my palm. As it always did, the magic sizzled and cracked between us, as real as it had ever been, and the constriction in my chest lightened.

"It's a really long story."

"As long as the story of why you're back now? *With the queen?*" She'd repeated it for emphasis.

A laugh got trapped in my throat. "Yeah, exactly. You know I have a habit of keeping strange company."

"But it's *the queen*, Tavi. She's not your run-of-the-mill friend."

"I know. And I promise I'm going to tell you everything. Right now, we could use your help."

Elfwaite blinked. "Anything. You say the word and I'm there."

I'd never been more grateful for another living being in my life. The tears just kept coming and I didn't want to stop them. Not when they fell from gratitude and happiness and absolute pure love for this little pixie. She'd never backed down from a challenge and she'd always been willing to listen to me gripe even on her own hard days.

She knew how rough it was to be away from your family.

"Would you be willing to watch the house for us? Let us know when Uncle Will leaves. I think we're too late for him to still be at the office."

"I'm more than happy to assist. Whatever you need."

"Please let us know when he's gone, then."

She shot me a look that said I was not getting off the hook for disappearing without a trace, then zipped off, leaving a trail like a lightning bug behind her. The after image faded and in the quiet of her departure, I was keenly aware of the moms watching me.

25

I flashed them a toothy grin. "What?" I asked innocently.

Livvy hunkered down beside me, settling her back against the oak's trunk while Laina craned her head as though she could still see Elfwaite.

"You have a pixie friend. Do you know how incredibly rare that is, Tavi?"

Another rarity, when all I wanted was to be normal.

"She's one of the best people I know," I stated.

"It only goes to show the prophecy was right," Livvy said decisively. "You are the one who will unite the races, Tavi. I'm more sure of it now than I was before. There is something about you that draws others to your side, without the use of manipulation."

I cleared my throat, uncomfortable with this line of conversation. My skin prickled. "I've been meaning to ask you more about that, Livvy. About the sentient being that is Faerie."

"The goddess." Livvy was solemn. She inclined her head.

"I've always heard it was a legend, not real. I find it fascinating you were able to speak to it. To her. And to understand her words of wisdom."

Something incomprehensible splintered through my chest. I was holding on to the fragmented pieces of me for all I was worth, but life kept beating me down.

Snuffing them out until I felt lost.

Livvy's presence was a gift but it was also suffocating.

She fixed me with a grave expression. "I don't know much. I'm sure there are scholars out there with better access to records, more complete knowledge than what I've learned from my experiences. I've only received one visit from Faerie. And I was lucky enough to be granted that one."

"But you spoke to her."

My mind twisted up in terrible knots.

Livvy shifted, uncomfortable, and drew her knees up to her chin. She wrapped her arms around her legs and darted a glance in my direction.

"She came to me in a dream after I approached the witches. I knew I was pregnant. Or at least I knew I would be, that things had worked this time." She blew out a sharp breath. "A dream, but not a dream. It was real. I felt her all around me. She spoke to me through a humanoid face. The face of the goddess. And it filled me with such hope and grace..."

Livvy trailed off and I noticed Laina had been hanging on every word. Her eyes seemed filled with pain, although I wasn't sure if it was the mention of the goddess or of the witches.

Her people.

"Tavi." Livvy said my name with the purest love. "It's okay to be scared. It's okay to wish for something else, but you need to know you're strong enough to handle anything."

She held my hand. I was hardly able to believe we were together, talking to each other, as though past and future collided and granted us this one slice of present. A gift.

"What's the matter?" Livvy asked when I stayed quiet for too long.

Her concern dug into my spine, adding to the sense of unease. "Why would Faerie want me? How did I get witch blood?"

I don't want this.

It moved beyond fear. I tried to voice those words out loud but they refused to come.

"The witches used their own blood with the ritual spell to keep you alive in my womb. I've always suspected they knew, as well, just how special you would be. Perhaps the goddess whispered in their ears." Livvy risked a smile and it carved out my insides. "My beautiful baby."

"And the journals?" I asked.

"When I woke from my dream, I wrote everything in those journals," Livvy explained. Her expression darkened. "My thoughts, the words from the dream. The complete prophecy and the spell necessary to unlock your powers when we met again."

"My powers." My voice cracked and fear moved in quickly as she stared at me.

"Tavi, don't you know how strong you are? There is such power in perseverance. It's only one of your gifts. You have survived everything you've come up against."

I nodded and my throat clogged as she scooted closer. Our legs pressed together but the love hurt. I'd spent so much time knowing I'd never experience it...

"You're not alone anymore," Laina added. She continued

to stare into the distance, between worlds, back to her son. "You have us."

"My magic is gone. The bite on my arm... I can't fight."

"You stop that," Livvy scolded. "There's more to you than your magic, which is far from gone. You are not weak, my girl. You never have been."

She seemed desperate for me to believe it.

Heart thundering furiously, I moved away, still within eyesight but far enough to be able to block out their words.

Actually, I didn't want to know.

It made me a coward as surely as running away would have but it was too much. Being here, this reunion, hearing about my birth—

I'm not special.

I just wanted to be me and to do the best I could to make it through school. Maybe find a way to work with Mike and see if things ever developed into something solid between us. My heart stuttered at the memory of the look on his face when we left, part confusion and part devastation.

The moms continued their conversation without me but I blocked them out. Lost in my head, the day passed quickly and we waited until night and Elfwaite's return. No going back now. Not like we'd ever had a choice. We were here, and soon I'd be breaking into my childhood home.

A small zap of electricity popped at the edge of my vision and I turned in time to see her wings fluttering.

"He's gone," Elfwaite said breathlessly in her tiny voice. "Your uncle has left the house. It's all black and empty."

"Thank you for doing this for us," I whispered back.

"Don't leave me again. Okay?"

Her request was simple and it rocked me to my core. I wouldn't. Not if I could help it.

I scrambled to my feet and almost plowed headfirst into a tree as blood flow returned to my legs and ankles.

Livvy and Laina rose as well, both of them swooping up on either side of me.

The quiet disturbed me on multiple levels. The streets should have been louder, people out enjoying the last of the day. But there was nothing and no one and most of the houses we passed were locked up tight. Only a few lights glowed from deep within their four walls.

The streets, familiar from how often I'd walked them, led the way back to my past, and I spared a sideways glance at Livvy, wondering what she thought about this.

What kind of feelings would she have seeing Uncle Will's place? From everything she'd said, she wasn't too fond of him. Would she remember my dad? Miss him?

Did she think about him when she looked at me?

The house looked exactly the same as when I'd left it. A few weeds had grown in place of flowers in the garden, and the cracks in the front brick walkway were more noticeable. My attention drew upward to the corner of the second floor like a magnet.

My old room.

Elfwaite took off from her perch on my shoulder without a word. Within the next heartbeat, or maybe two, the front door swung open and her glow filtered across the path. A flurry of movement, her arm waving, and the three of us joined her inside.

The foyers smelled the same.

I didn't expect tears to burn my eyes again. Part of me really hoped the waterworks from my reunion would have been enough to empty me out, but there they were again.

We were breaking and entering the only home I'd ever known.

I halfway wondered if Uncle Will would have let me search for the journal if I'd just asked him. It was better this way, I assured myself. Better to be in and out before he came home. The only thing he'd come back to was my scent, unless I did a good enough job of blocking it from him.

Something told me I wasn't in full control of my magic tonight.

Livvy's nostrils flared and she moved unerringly toward the office. I was used to seeing the door closed so that was no surprise. But to see the way her pulse of power undid the locking mechanism, to watch it swing open on well-oiled hinges...

Something about the scene struck me as wrong. Of course that's where she would start the search. If she'd sent the journal with me, and I didn't have it, then Will would have kept it somewhere close and hidden.

Like the office I wasn't allowed inside.

"We'll split up," I said harshly, afraid to speak too loudly. "I'll check upstairs."

The place was huge. Will made great money as a defense attorney so we had a lot of ground to cover. I highly doubted the book Livvy wanted was in my room—but it didn't hurt to start there.

The familiar scents of my life assaulted my senses the second I opened the door.

Nothing had changed in here, either.

The empty picture frames graced the top of my desk and the bedside table. The bed was made and my pillows propped in place. Not an inch of dust in the place, so Will must have sent the housekeepers up here to make sure everything remained spotless. Why?

My stomach constricted tightly, my ribs poised to puncture my heart and organs.

The last time I'd been here, I'd packed my bags and told him I had a headache before he left for work. He'd asked me if it was a goodbye. He must have suspected but he'd never tried to stop me.

Please let him stay gone.

I'd break if he saw us now.

There were good memories in this house. Great memories, before Will decided I was old enough to be a pawn. He'd cared about me. As a single male he'd done his best to raise me and make sure I had whatever I needed that money could buy. He was affectionate by nature, as most wolves were, and had helped me through my first shift. He'd been there when no one else was.

I had friends here. I'd come out pretty well-adjusted considering the circumstances.

He'd cared about me and no one could change my mind about it or convince me otherwise. So why had he hidden my mother's journal from me? Did he know the truth about my three magics?

My head spun and I reached out to lean against the wall to my closet to get my bearings.

Elfwaite peeked her head around the doorway in a flutter of movement. "Did you find anything?"

"I haven't even started looking," I admitted. "I'm falling down on the job"

"There's nothing downstairs. Not even a hint of spell-work to show where he might have hired a witch to mask a hiding spot. I did, however, find a lot of alcohol."

"So where would he keep a journal?" I ground my back teeth together. "I don't understand any of this."

"Why is this journal so important?" she asked.

I worked my lower lip. "There's a spell in it that we need.

For me. That's why we're here, risking everything." On edge, I crept further into the room.

"It must be worth the risk."

I shook my head. I wished I had the words to explain it to Elfwaite. Hopefully those would come. Hopefully everything was going to work out and we'd find the journal, but what kind of hope could I really cling to? Nothing beyond Livvy's supposition that it had to be here.

Did I *want* to find the spell? Was that why I wouldn't even look for it?

Elfwaite helped me search the room, and like I assumed, we turned up nothing.

I kept my footsteps as light as possible, so different from my thudding pulse, on the stairs and rounded the banister to find Laina coming out of the living room. Her lips twisted in a pout of disappointment.

None of us found what we needed to find. Livvy emerged from the kitchen this time with her hair disheveled and her normally pale face colored by exertion. With time ticking down, we checked the rest of the house and came up empty.

"It's not here." I stated the obvious. "Where do we go next?"

"I'm not sure. It *has* to be here. I know he has the journal." Livvy crossed her arms over her chest and shivered. "There must be something we're missing."

Something tugged at me. "Look, we don't want to stick around."

"We shouldn't leave until we've found it," she insisted.

Leave? We weren't getting out of here. Not when the door opened and a soft chuckle rang in my ears. I turned, already knowing what I would see, my stomach sinking through the floor.

Uncle Will stood in the doorway, silhouetted by moonlight, with three big pack members flanking him, their fangs and claws ready to strike.

26

Will was ready for battle in his suit, a familiar charcoal-gray double-breasted ensemble I'd seen him wear before.

He rarely changed before heading to the bar with his buddies.

With his familiar expensive scent, I remembered him, and in a flash I remembered my father. The wintergreen and moss and dark forest. The big shoulders.

I remembered both their boisterous laughs, but Will wasn't laughing now.

Not even close.

His gaze skipped between the four of us and landed on me, the lines around his eyes softening slightly. "*Tavi.*"

Oh god, my throat was going to close up. Already, it was hard to breathe. Somehow I forced my tongue into action and my lips to form the words. "Hi, Uncle Will."

The others knew me. I caught the flash of recognition across their faces but they never let on.

I swallowed over the sharp lump in my throat as my eyes took in every familiar line of my uncle's face.

"If I'd known you were going to return for a visit, I would have stayed home." His jaw tightened and on his right, his beta's hand curled into a fist.

"You could have done without the company." I gestured toward the other three. Two betas, one delta.

My fingers twitched, my hands stiff from clenching them at my side. A bead of sweat trailed along my spine and seemed to freeze just above my tailbone.

Uncle Will lifted his chin. "You took off on me. You lied to me, and you bolted. You have no idea what kind of mess you left behind. The Grimaldi pack has done unspeakable things to us in your absence. Now I find you here, unharmed, and surrounded by Faerie pigs."

His delta hissed at the name-calling.

Will's commanding presence filled the foyer in a physical cloud. It was one of the things that made him effective as an alpha and caused the others to fall in line. He was one of the only alphas of the last hundred years who never had any challengers step up. His dominance was so completely established they didn't even try.

A feared opponent in the courtroom, too.

"You shouldn't have forced me into a match with Kendrick Grimaldi." I stiffened, craning to see past him as if saying the name out loud would conjure the devil.

I was scared.

I'd never really felt that way around my uncle, despite our issues in the past.

Panic set in when the betas stepped around Will, their sights set on Laina and Livvy.

Will chuckled. "Dae. I'd love to say it's a pleasure, but then again you did break into my house."

His powerful baritone had goosebumps rising on my skin and my wolf aching to submit to him. Will stepped inside and flicked the switch on the wall. The glow of the massive chandelier overhead cast his tall, muscled frame into relief.

In his late forties, his auburn hair only sported a few streaks of gray. That was where I'd gotten my color from. I'd always thought it, and now that I saw the two of them standing in the same room, the realization hit home.

Livvy's hair had only the slightest reddish hue whereas mine would have gotten me teased if I'd gone to public school.

Will's hazel eyes pierced through me and pinned me in place. "Get out of my house or I will make you leave."

His fury left me cold and dark and hollow.

"Tell me where the journal is, Will," Livvy demanded. She stepped forward and physically blocked the two of us, keeping us apart. Using her body like a shield. "We're not leaving without it."

The fierceness in her voice resounded through me. Tears welled in my eyes but I kept them contained, this moment too surreal to allow myself to weaken now.

"He's not going to hurt me." I reached for her but she ignored me.

He tilted his head to the side in an animalistic gesture. "You come into my house, threaten my niece with your lies, and expect me to speak to you? What have you told her, Dae? Did you spout off about your insane prophecy again? Did you feed her your insane bullshit the moment you met?"

"My lies?" Livvy seemed to grow several inches. "She is my daughter."

"You abandoned her."

The others stepped up behind Will with growls, their hackles raised and their wolves close to the surface. No matter what happened, we had to protect the queen. If anything happened to Laina, Mike would never forgive me, and Faerie would be in more danger.

"I did what I had to do in order to keep her safe. I'm not the one she needs to worry about," Livvy insisted.

The quiet was almost worse than the conversation. My hands froze, my forearm throbbing as it pressed in, and there was no comfort to be found.

My heart was nothing more than a ravaged lump of meat in my chest and a terrible dread sank through me.

I thought I'd been through the worst? No. The worst was yet to come.

The time to talk ended. The room might as well have been slowed like on one of those old-fashioned VCRs. The betas moved first. They flanked Will and stepped forward, their claws lengthening as they swiped the air in front of him, a clear threat to anyone bent on harming him.

Livvy lifted both hands and pressed them together, her magic a shield for all of us.

"I don't think so," she muttered. "You three will stay out of it. This is between me and Will."

Was she speaking to me, Laina, and Elfwaite? Or the others? We were evenly matched body count wise but that was about the only thing matched. My zombie bite burned as I grabbed Livvy's arm, tightening my grip in an attempt to wrench her backwards.

They weren't about to back down, and I waited for Will to give the command but it never came.

Instead he stepped around them and his fist lifted and connected with her outstretched palms. He cut right through her fae magic. I reacted without thought, moving in front of Laina and intercepting the delta stealthily creeping forward while the rest of us were preoccupied.

"I don't think so," he mimicked, crowing in her face.

A growl rocked through the room and before the delta could attack, I forced my leaden legs to carry me forward, intercepting the hit before he reached the queen.

The weight in the air tripled.

Death would come to this place if we weren't careful.

My muscles quaked with the effort of holding back the delta as our strength met. Will's attention fractured when he glanced at me. The opportunity gave Livvy time to retaliate, but rather than use her magic, she met him with fists. Her knuckles plowed into his chin and forced his head to snap back on his neck.

"Baronne would be ashamed of you," she grunted.

She fought with violence and fury, locking her knees and twisting to use all of her weight with each punch. As though she *needed* to use her fists rather than magic.

Veins stood out on the side of Will's neck as he regained his bearings. Pulling no punches, he lifted a knee and slammed it into Livvy's thigh.

"Don't say his name," Will growled. "Don't you dare fucking say his name."

In the distance, I swear I caught the sound of a mournful howl cutting through the tension. Bloodlust filled the air around us as Laina and Elfwaite thundered the betas with their magic attacks.

The foyer beneath our feet rocked and my arms thrust out to the side to keep my balance.

"He was my husband! Your brother," Livvy insisted. Her chest was covered in blood where Will had clawed her.

"He's dead. You got him killed with your bullshit. If it hadn't been for you, he'd still be alive! The best thing you could have done was give up your daughter." Will panted, his suit torn with his half shift.

Their movements were almost too swift for me to follow, and before I had a chance to yell, to tell them to stop, the beta made a move. He dashed for Livvy and shifted mid-jump, the other beta closer to Laina in the same moment.

The delta beneath me squirmed, held in place with a magic that wasn't mine to command.

The wolves were a team. And once, I'd envied them for their ability to work together in such complete trust.

But so were we. I'd formed my own team and I moved to intercept the one on the left.

Livvy and Will were locked together in their own battle but the queen had none of her guards now. Only me. If I didn't get it together, we were done for.

I drove down past the pain, into the piece of my magic growing smaller and farther away with every passing second. Sweat lined my brow and I set my jaw, fighting to channel the magic into the change.

I bared my teeth, my canines lengthening as I allowed the wolf inside of me some breathing space. I was not strong enough to take on the betas if they both chose to attack me together but I'd do whatever it took to protect Laina.

And then...it wasn't necessary. None of it was necessary.

I stalled mid-shift as Laina sent out a wave of magic that forced the wolves, outside of Uncle Will, to their knees and kept them there.

Livvy fought with the vengeance of someone who had nothing to lose and everything to gain and had Will on his back a heartbeat later. Both betas struggled, the one on the left sucking in his breath as he realized what had happened.

He'd failed to protect his alpha.

"Tell me where the journal is," Livvy demanded.

She wrenched Will's arm back and his shoulder dislocated with a pop. Rather than make a sound, he sneered at her.

"You can kick my ass but I'm not talking." He spat at her and she dodged the phlegm, bringing her face in close enough for their noses to touch.

"For the last time. *Where is it?*" she hissed out.

Another wrench and his wrist looked dangerously close to breaking. He stared at her with pure hatred and, torn between them, I didn't move at all. My mother or my alpha. The man who raised me or the woman who birthed me.

Laina's hands fell on both of my shoulders and made the choice for me. She shook her head, a barely perceptible movement. Regal, yes, and powerful beyond reckoning. How had I thought of her as some delicate flower unable to stand up for herself? How had I forgotten what she did for me in the forest?

"I banished the journal and everything of yours to the Abyss," Will bit out.

Behind me, Laina stiffened at the word.

"You'll never see it again. The best thing you can do, Dae, is go there yourself and never come back."

"You *bastard*." Livvy dropped toward Will, going for the throat, and he twisted out of the way so her snapping teeth gnashed against open air.

She wasn't a wolf but she must have been around our kind enough to fight like one. Whatever she could use to gain the advantage she would.

"Get Tavi out of here now!" Even on his back, Will's thought was for me. "Fight these fae assholes for my niece!"

His concern, whether he meant it or not, stoked the flames of Livvy's fury. She roared, her magic blasting out of her and carving a hole in the floor.

Laina's arms banded around my waist and dragged me

toward the door, her spellwork keeping the betas and delta in place. I shook my head, digging my heels in and skidding on the marble. The soles of my sneakers found no purchase.

"We can't leave them like this!"

I lost my balance and dropped hard on my knees, bones creaking and my head dizzy. Black spots danced in front of my eyes as pain shot through my system.

"Come on, Tavi, move!" Elfwaite grabbed hold of my forearm and tugged with disproportionate strength to her small size.

Barbara's Band-aid was disintegrating, piece by piece...

She'd warned me it wouldn't last forever. The attack lasted too long to do me any favors before the dizziness began to subside and Elfwaite hauled me up. Laina was blocked from the door by one of the wolves, his teeth bared in a snarl at her.

He'd somehow managed to break free of her spell.

"You don't want to do anything," she warned.

I found my balance again and thrust myself between them before the beta made a move.

A pain-filled screech sounded and when I looked over, Will had a claw-tipped hand wrapped around Livvy's throat.

"You couldn't just stay dead," he growled in her face.

"You pawned my daughter off on a monster." Livvy fought back with a fury I never would have imagined.

Laina reached for my hand and our fumbling fingers linked together.

"Go for the door," Elfwaite whispered in my ear. "I'll distract them for you."

"I can't leave my mom." I begged her to understand. "She needs me."

"If you don't get out now, they're not going to let you

leave. Her Majesty's spell will only hold for so long before the rest of the pack arrives."

She was right. Elfwaite was *always* right.

My instincts roared for me to do something but when I reached again for my own halfling form, the change refused to come this time. My wolf may be close but initiating the shift was impossible.

Another wave of dizziness rocked through me and I tilted forward, held in place only because of Laina.

"Tavi, hold on," she urged roughly.

I felt eyes on me but I didn't care. None of it mattered when I felt the ending gaining speed, ready to crash down on us and take everyone in this room down.

Laina tightened her grip and hauled me toward the door as my head lightened in the opposite direction. I stumbled over my feet before I regained my composure.

A hasty yell toward Livvy broke through the sounds of growls but I didn't have the strength to look back to see if she followed.

If she could even tear herself away from the fight.

I felt like shit.

Whatever quick fix Barbara had slapped on my malady was almost gone.

My next breath filled with the sweet scents of night and memories of childhood. Something cracked behind us but Laina refused to slow, Elfwaite no more than a flash of pink ahead.

"Keep going, Tavi. My magic will only hold for a short time here," Laina urged. Her cheeks darkened with a blush as she fought to keep the spell in place and help me along as well.

Even Elfwaite's power wasn't enough to shift the tide in our favor.

"What about my mother?" I protested.

"She'll be fine."

Another yelp sounded but Laina made sure we kept pace down the front steps and along the path toward the street.

"They'll catch us. We're going too slow." My snarl fell short and ended on a gargle.

"Trust me when I tell you I have this covered," she insisted.

"Then stop the fight."

Another yelp, followed by a long lupine whine cut off by sudden silence.

My heart thrummed against my ribs. Laina headed straight for the gates to the community at a tempo I had a hard time matching. I held her tight enough for Laina to swallow over a cry of pain yet she never faltered.

My mouth filled with the taste of something bitter. "I've gone downhill fast," I mumbled.

"It's the stress." Laina's voice was sharp. "You'll be fine once we get home."

Home. Faerie was home, not this moral world. Not the house where I grew up with nothing but Uncle Will and his rules to keep me safe. The same house I was now being hustled from.

Footsteps sounded from behind and Laina and I turned to see Livvy booking it, pumping her legs for more speed and blood dripping down the side of her arm. Magic pulsed out from her in a wave, wrapping around me and hurtling us forward at a great clip.

Air magic, tied to the elements themselves.

A fresh chorus of howls sounded from behind and my hackles rose. "I hope your magic can take us far away," I said once Livvy caught up with us. "Because the pack is coming."

"They aren't the only ones," she muttered. She tucked her hair over her shoulder and her next breath rattled in her lungs. "The blockade?"

Laina bobbed her head. "It will hold as long as we need it to."

We got away but if the pack caught up to us, then we were screwed. My head lightened further until the black at the edge of my vision crept inward and left only a tiny tunnel of reality left in front of me.

Somehow we made it to the portal. Somehow we managed to escape, but I wasn't sure how.

Livvy removed her key from her pocket and opened the door, the wolves howling balefully behind us. Then it opened, and Mike stood on the other side gesturing madly for us to hurry.

"Go, go!" Elfwaite added her own magic to Livvy's and carried us further, her tiny voice a bellow of command.

Blinding, needle-like pain drove into me and disintegrated the air in my body. Sweat glistened on my skin and the rest of me shook with fatigue.

"Come with us, Elfwaite. Please." Oh yeah, I was slurring badly.

"Not yet. It isn't the right time. I'll be here when you need me." Her little eyes lit up. "Trust me, Tavi, the time's coming when you'll need me. Now hurry!"

Laina practically threw me onto Noren's back and the direwolf hurtled through the doorway. The moment his feet touched down on land, I sucked air in through my burning nostrils, the lightheaded feeling slowly dissipating and the ache in my bones only a dull roar.

Laina followed with Livvy close behind her.

Mike was about to slam the door shut when another body flew over the threshold. Uncle Will came out of nowhere and reached out with claw-tipped fingers, snagging Livvy's shirt and dragging her backwards.

27

Another werewolf shifter in Faerie that didn't belong here.

I blinked, catching Uncle Will's gaze before he tore his attention from me. He sucked in a breath and stared around him at the open field and the faerie ring beyond.

And suddenly there was Mike swinging his fist. His knuckles connected with the side of Uncle Will's face and the surprise was enough to get the werewolf to release Livvy.

Will recovered in half a heartbeat and moved toward Mike, his mouth open and his growl rumbling through me. Engaging every instinct I possessed as a wolf.

Fear clenched my heart so tightly I lost my breath. I scrambled to get to Mike, to make sure Will didn't shift, to obey the order.

My uncle was the alpha of our pack for a reason.

He had the strength and the savagery to hold the position, although he'd maintained his hold on our people through diplomacy. His instincts made him a good lawyer and a better leader.

They moved at the same time. Mike let out a yell and

slammed both his hands against Will's chest, using the older man's momentum against him. Will staggered a bit but maintained his balance. The hair on his forearms began to grow dark and long.

But he hesitated. Why?

Why didn't he take Mike down?

Suddenly I noticed details in sharp contrast. Will looking around at the surroundings as if memorizing every inch of the landscape. Memorizing the scents and the feeling of the air, the inherent magic of this place.

His eyes went wolfy and Mike managed to shove the older man back through the portal. Livvy reacted in the same instant and drew her key out of the lock, the door disintegrating, locking us on one side and Will on the other.

But it was too late.

Didn't they realize what he'd done?

Will had seen where we were. He was memorizing the landscape to find another way in, with more muscle to back him up. Muscle like Grimaldi, who would stop fighting the Alderidge pack if he knew there was another way to get me back.

"We have to go, *now*." I straightened to my full height.

"There's no way he can get back through," Mike replied breathlessly.

"Yes, he can." If Kendrick Grimaldi could find a way to get to me during the Wild Hunt, then Uncle Will could do the same. I knew it in my gut. "Bronwen! Onyx! Noren! We've got to go."

The longer we hesitated, the more likely it was that Will would find a way to bring the entire pack to Faerie. The boundaries weren't going to hold him off if he was determined enough to break through. And we'd just given him a pretty big reason to rekindle his determination.

Between me and Onyx, our hasty escape was less a run and more a power walk. We navigated the field, the dew-drenched grass soaking through our pants instantly.

"You know, I'm getting really tired of this," Bronwen grumbled.

"You're telling me." I flashed her a smile.

"Yeah, right, I *am* telling you. And I'm in the best shape out of all of us. No offense, Mike."

He glanced sideways at her. "Why am I being dragged into this comparison?"

A layer of nerves underpinned the banter but I appreciated her attempt anyway.

And I liked having Mike close to me. He hadn't hesitated to go head to head with Uncle Will. For me.

Except something Will said tickled my mind. I kept looking over my shoulder to make sure he hadn't somehow found a way to sneak back in through the same door and follow us.

"Hey, what's the Abyss?" I asked Livvy. "Uncle Will said he banished your things there."

Livvy looked shocked. "You heard him?"

"Of course. I was in the same room."

She shook her head before glancing over at Laina. The two mothers shared a long look that sent prickles of cold awareness along every vertebrae.

Even Bronwen and Onyx felt tuned in to the conversation although both of them were doing their best to look disinterested.

"You've never heard about the Abyss before in school?" It was less a question than a statement when Livvy finally spoke again.

"Not before today." But it felt important. "What aren't you telling me?"

I felt her secrets like a change in the wind, a drop in temperature—something real and tangible.

Laina blew out a breath, her lips rounded and her hands trembling. They both looked...upset. Which only made me dig my heels in further. If the topic was off the table of discussion, then most likely I needed to know about it.

These kinds of secrets made for worse problems down the road. I'd seen it before.

My stomach curdled and I clenched down on my back molars in preparation to be a brat and demand they answer me. Luckily, Livvy spoke first.

"The Abyss," she began with clinical detachment, "is a place where magical things—or people—are sent when they are not wanted in *any* realm. It's like a hiding place. A terrible in-between. It belongs to nothing and no one."

"It's an empty corner of the universe to send awful things you want no one to ever find again," Laina filled in. "Which makes it a very dangerous place."

"Any realm? Like the mortal world and Faerie?" I asked.

Livvy marched ahead without looking at me. The blood on her arm had dried and plastered her shirt to her skin. She picked at it and said, "There are more worlds than you think, Tavi. The Abyss is one of those, only we can access it from here."

"No. We do not go to the Abyss," Laina warned.

A chill curdled my gut.

"We have no choice," Livvy tossed back angrily.

The mothers faced off against one another and the rest of us slowed our steps, unconsciously putting distance between us.

"If there were any other way, don't you think I'd take it?" Livvy's hands balled into fists at her sides and she drew in a sharp breath, her nostrils flaring. We need the spell."

An unspoken conversation passed between them and I had no clue who won, but they started to walk again.

"I don't understand. If the journals you want are so important, then we have to retrieve them. How would we even get there?" I asked."

"I know the way," Onyx said softly.

"Wait, what?" Shock rippled through me.

I stopped dead in my tracks and reached for him, forcing him to stop beside me. His eyes were inscrutable and the dark circles beneath them were brought to stark contrast against the paleness of his skin and white hair.

He met my gaze, held it.

I wasn't the only one surprised though. The others had all stopped as well despite our need for haste.

"You never said anything." And there were plenty of opportunities for him to do so.

"Why would you want to know?" Onyx swallowed, his throat visibly working. "It was a time of my life I wanted to forget and it wasn't relevant to our training. There was no reason for you to ask and none for me to bring it up."

I felt like this was the kind of thing that *should* have come up before. If there was really a place in the universe where people, things, were banished into obscurity, then shouldn't it have been mentioned? Especially if Onyx—

"You actually went there?" I clarified.

He grasped for my hand and our fingers brushed, both of us clammy and trembling. The contact steadied us both. "I was banished there by my father. Okay? As a teenager. I was one of those forgotten people. The one nobody wanted. He decided if I wasn't willing to play his games, then I was better off there. Worse than dead, Tavi."

Tears pricked my eyes. All that pain and suffering, all those years in his past where he'd had to survive his father rather than live the life he might have if he'd been born to any other family...

One day, I didn't know when or where or how it would happen, but Kendrick would die. For what he'd done to his son. For what he'd done to any innocent he'd terrorized. I was going to kill Kendrick Grimaldi with my bare hands. I made the silent vow to anyone who might hear me, including Faerie herself–if the goddess existed.

"It was how I managed to get out of his clutches and into Faerie," Onyx finished. "I found my way through the Abyss and out the other side. It wasn't an easy path."

He'd never told me this part of his history. A mix of emotions flooded through me, from concern and rage to terror and gratitude that Onyx trusted me enough to share it now.

"Would you be willing to take us there?" I squeezed his fingers. "To the point where you came out?"

"Tavi." Laina's voice held a world of warning.

"If we really need those journals, then we have to get into the Abyss. And we have a person who has not only been there but made it out. Somehow." I refused to take my attention away from Onyx. This was between me and him. If no one else cared to join us, then it wouldn't matter. I'd go alone.

"Are you sure you need these books?" He asked the question to me, not the others. "Are you really sure? The Abyss...you're right to be afraid. I smell it on you. Your fear is tangible."

Of course he did. The more I learned about the world– the *worlds*, plural—the more it terrified me. It felt like every day I discovered something new, perfectly designed to kill me.

Was I sure? *No.*

"The spell is of the utmost importance," Livvy answered. "It's the only way to unlock your powers, Tavi. And without them..."

She trailed off but I didn't need her to finish the statement. We all knew what had to happen next. A pall fell over our group, a heaviness none of us were able to shake off. We knew where we were headed next, and luckily for us, Onyx knew the way.

Or maybe it was unlucky for us.

Onyx nodded, a decisive movement at whatever he saw on my face. Nothing good.

None of this was good, and every step we took to try to fix our mess led us into deeper and more dangerous terrain. For once, could our escape route head into fluffy unicorn and rainbow territory?

He drew his fingers from mine and limped ahead with a sullen cast to his features. Out of the corner of my eye I saw Mike watching us and silently taking in the display.

"I can lead you to the place where I came out," Onyx said at last. "From there, it might get tricky. But I remember the location."

"Are we close?" Bronwen asked, biting down on her lip.

Onyx huffed out a laugh. "Of course not. I'm not sure how long it will be on foot. Not to mention, time has a different meaning in the Abyss. It may be a year inside, but only a few minutes in Faerie."

Something hard and cold dropped from my chest and burned a hole on its way through me. A future I'd never wanted and never even considered a possibility was now locked into place and a part of me desperately beat against it. One tiny me in the huge face of the D-word.

Destiny.

Do people want to be special this way? Because I sure as shit didn't.

Or are there more of them out there like me who just want to have a life where they feel normal, with a family and friends and school? It's tough enough to navigate those things.

Onyx closed his eyes and lifted his face to the sky, inhaling. "We need to change our course a little bit. We follow the lines of energy. They all lead back."

But Livvy seemed to understand him. I caught a flash of her bobbing her head although the lines of worry surrounding her eyes deepened along with the furrow in her brow.

I halfway expected Laina to argue. She knew more about this land than anyone else. If the Abyss were as dangerous as Livvy made it out to be, then wouldn't Laina put her foot down? Tell us all to forget it?

I desperately wanted us to find another way but it didn't really matter in the end. It wasn't what I wanted but what I needed to do, and once again I swallowed every instinct screaming at me to run.

Onyx set the course for us.

We traveled for a whole day and only stopped intermittently to rest and eat. Or when his legs gave out under a rough spasm of pain.

Laina had been right about my return to Faerie. Whatever had happened to me in the mortal world seemed to have dissipated once we stepped foot into this world, but not entirely.

I still tired out easily and had to rest more often than not. My arm burned, and occasionally the dizziness got so out of control I almost puked.

Another lucky stroke—Onyx set the pace for us and he was no longer able to travel swiftly. Not with the ravages to his body.

We kept the conversation light until even trying to talk took much more energy than any of us were willing to expend. Silence fell easily as we struggled to put one foot in front of the other.

Or maybe it was just me. I had Noren to guide me when I stumbled or got too tired to walk in a straight line.

Bronwen, bless her, stuck close to Onyx and made sure he had what he needed.

The mothers, like they were some hastily grouped together unit, remained close to each other as well and often ducked their heads together and spoke in voices too subdued for any of us to make out. Even with our extra sensitive hearing.

Which left Mike striding on his own. He kept his focus straight ahead, and outside of a few small smiles when he caught me looking at him, we said nothing.

Despite the company, the experience was isolating for me.

Uncle Will knew where we were.

My mother was alive.

And Onyx was leading me toward my doom. Call it melodramatic but we stood on the edge of a change I didn't want.

Finally, we found lodgings for the night at a tavern on the outskirts of one of those farming towns. A large water wheel churned beside it, attached to a mill with a river running through it.

"Are you sure this is safe?" I asked.

Laina drew her cloak over her head and worked a

glamour to disguise her features. "We'll be fine here. I want us to get a good rest in real beds. What we face isn't for the weak."

"How are we going to pay for it?"

The queen shot me a look that told me to shut the hell up and let her handle it. From the pocket of her cloak she drew out a purse.

"We need to be well-rested for what's sure to be a terrible journey ahead of us."

We waited on the front porch of the tavern until Laina came to get us minutes later.

"Here are the room keys." She doled them out. "You'll be bunking two to a room. I wanted us each to have our own space but the availability was limited in a place this size."

Livvy snatched up the key to our room. "Thank you."

"It's the least I can do," Laina answered simply.

Bronwen refused to step away from Onyx, so the two of them would share a room. The height difference would have made me giggle if I'd had the strength for it. He towered over her slight frame, and I wouldn't have been surprised if he rested an arm on the top of her head.

"The kitchen is closed for the evening but the innkeeper assured me we'd be able to get some things from the cook. Money can accomplish many things," Laina continued.

My legs refused to carry me up the stairs without catching my toes on the risers. My own glamour was half-assed at best and probably flickered in and out of existence. Which made it a very good thing we'd arrived so late in the day.

Most everyone was gathered in the tavern, drinking away, and those who weren't were safely tucked in their beds.

I wanted a shower and to sleep for days. I'd take either at this point, and although sleep was more important, I'd kill for the hot water.

Livvy glanced at the room numbers and led the way, with Noren trailing us. No one stopped the direwolf when he was the first through the unlocked odor. Noren checked out the space, sniffing in corners before sitting at the edge of one of the twin beds with his tongue lolling out of his mouth.

"I think the coast is clear," I said unnecessarily.

Livvy offered me a halfhearted grin.

The exterior of the inn had the old-timey Tudor look of a place you might find in rural England. The inside had been updated to more modern accommodations, with our own bathroom, fresh linens, and light-blocking curtains.

"You can shower first if you want," Livvy offered.

I waved her off. "You go ahead. You need it more than I do." I gestured toward her arm.

She slowly shifted her attention to the area as though she hadn't really noticed the healed wound before. God, how long had we been awake for at this point?

Time blurred, and only the increasingly nagging ache in my limbs reminded me of the journey. There were too many blank places in my head for me to feel comfortable.

What would I do without another Band-aid from Barbara?

Livvy finished her shower quickly enough and exited the bathroom with a belch of steam. Her long hair trailed down her spine and she'd wrapped a towel around her midsection. There were still dark circles under her eyes but she looked refreshed.

"Your turn."

"Okay, thanks."

The strangeness of the situation wasn't lost on me. We were alone together after she beat the crap out of Uncle Will.

We passed each other and I made sure to keep a few inches of space between us. Shock rippled through me when Livvy reached out to brush her fingers against my elbow and stop me in place.

"We'll need to talk," she said in a low voice. "Soon. About...everything."

The conversation was a long time coming, but thinking about it brought a sinking sensation to my stomach. I could only nod, holding my breath, waiting for her to drop her hold.

She did and I walked stiff-legged into the bathroom.

The first hits of hot water on my skin were a godsend.

I'd never felt anything this amazing before. The pulsing spray crashed over my shoulders and although the tightness remained, at least the layers of filth from traveling quickly washed down the drain.

Steam filled the tiny bathroom by the time I finished. In the bedroom, Livvy lay underneath the sheets.

"I cleaned your clothes for you," came her soft muttered tone. "A quick spell."

"Thank you. I appreciate it. Will you teach me?"

She let out a breathy laugh. "One of these days, Tavi, I will teach you everything I know. And you will surpass us all."

I quickly clenched down on my teeth to keep from saying anything else. And when she began to snore, I knew I'd made the right choice by not engaging. I brought my clothes into the bathroom, scrubbing the towel over my skin to dry before sliding back into my pants.

The last thing I wanted to do was get dressed but it didn't feel comfortable sleeping in my underwear in front of Livvy. Not yet.

Three quick raps at the door, loud enough to be intentional. I glanced over to Noren but he'd curled up on the end of Livvy's bed with his snout tucked underneath his tail. If he wasn't alarmed…

Mike stood on the other side with one finger pressed to his lips and the other crooked to follow him. Shit, just looking at him took every molecule of air from my lungs.

He'd had the same idea as the rest of us. Wet tendrils of hair curled around his pointed ears and his eyes were shadowed but clear, alert. Watching me as he waited for my answer. I cocked my hip to the side and leaned heavily on the door.

"Why do you want me to be quiet?" I whispered.

He rolled his eyes. "Just come with me," he hissed back. "I'm stealing you away for a talk."

Whatever he wanted to do to me, I'd let him. Heat curled in my lower abdomen at the thought before I glanced behind me at Livvy's sleeping form. There were plenty of other things I considered doing with Mike besides talking but—

I bobbed my head and let the door swing shut behind me.

He reached to take my hand, drawing me down the hallway to his room and pushing open the door. Laina was nowhere to be seen. The double beds rested against the far wall underneath three windows, their curtains already drawn shut.

When he turned to face me, his features twisted in a relaxed half smile, a piece of me swooned and the tension in my chest relaxed inch by inch. His eyes got me every time. Without fail.

Yup, that was the face I remembered from the first night I met him.

On the side of the road with my broken-down car and a stranger offering to help. I liked to believe our paths crossed for a reason but I still wasn't sure what the reason could be besides love.

My heart skipped a beat. "What's going on?" I wrapped my arms around my torso but I wasn't cold.

"Mom went down to the kitchen to grab some food. I think it was her way of giving us the privacy we need to talk."

"I really hate that phrase," I admitted.

"So do I. Especially since..." He trailed off and worked a hand through his golden hair. "We've had some doozies, haven't we? Conversation-wise."

He hadn't turned me in to his father when he learned my secret. My bloodline.

He'd kept my devastating secret to himself, had gone with me and Melia to break into the Bureau office. He and Laina came this far to help with the journey.

I liked to think my heart wouldn't be broken again if we finally decided to trust each other, but the old fear was still there despite my best efforts. I knew no matter where life took us, I'd circle back to him again and again even though I was scared of the hurt.

"We've been pulled apart too many times to count," I finally agreed.

Some people might consider it a warning from whatever

higher powers existed. That Mike and I were too different to ever make this work.

Mike stepped closer. "You still consider us friends. Right?"

"Always," I whispered. "You will always be my friend."

How could I breathe with him this near?

"What about more than friends?"

My heart thumped. "I'm afraid you'll walk away again." There it was, out in the open. Somehow the truth slid out easier than I anticipated.

His moss-colored eyes narrowed. "I do that a lot to you. I know it. Which isn't an excuse, Tavi. I walk away, and you keep secrets."

I moved away from him but the distance wasn't enough to break the spell. Sitting on the edge of the bed, I balanced my elbows on my knees, keenly aware of his presence. My skin prickled and went tight.

"You never made me feel less than average," Mike went on. "Through the Faerie Trials and the tutoring, through murders and lies and bullshit with my dad and your secret society…you always treated me like I was someone worth knowing and not just because I'm a prince." He lifted his gaze and pinned me in place. "You know you mean everything to me. Right?"

Oh, damn. How am I supposed to keep my distance and not kiss him?

My arms dropped from my legs and I stood. Mike closed the distance between us and we were close enough to breathe the same air but not touch. Not kiss the way I wanted to kiss him.

"I've fucked up," he continued.

"So have I." I swallowed hard. "Do you blame me? For your dad? For giving Barbara the *Imperium*?"

Mike took a moment to answer and in the silence, parts of me went numb. "What she chose to do with it...you never could have known. And it's never been the right time to talk and it's never been the right moment for us to clear the table, to consider our issues. But I'm not sure how much longer we can keep doing that when we might not survive."

28

W*elcome to my life.*
Which wasn't fair to say, not in the face of the bullshit Mike had dealt with.

It was easy to think he led a blessed life as a crown prince but it wasn't entirely true. He was under more pressure than I understood.

Too many times, I'd lost sight of that.

He cleared his throat when I stayed quiet. "Can we continue this without you trying to beat the crap out of me?"

His joke lifted my lips. "It was one time, Mike. We were both working out some things." I knew the way I wanted to work them out with him.

Because the exhaustion didn't matter. In this room, it was just us, and if I closed my eyes and focused on him, the rest melted away.

"I don't blame you for what happened," he admitted. "Well, I did at first. Until I realized it was too easy to play the victim. I'm done with the back and forth, Tavi. I'm done with taking one step forward together only for us to take another two massive steps backwards and apart."

We were flawed creatures. Flawed and broken and I wondered if we would ever find a way to be together that actually worked.

Until Mike lifted his hand and brushed his fingers against my cheek and breathing became impossible. "You're everything to me," he whispered.

"I never wanted to be someone else's everything before. But with you...*please*." He knew I was in love with him. I'd told him.

He'd laughed, confused by his own feelings and incredulous over mine. But my feelings for him hadn't changed. They'd only grown, and if I allowed myself, I'd drown in them.

Staring at Mike, I saw emotion shift across his face and I knew he understood. He remembered the moment as well as I did in every lurid detail.

"We said we would give this a shot, right?" He cupped my face in his hands and kissed the tip of my nose, still holding my gaze.

He pressed another kiss to the space between my eyes and my chest constricted. He trailed kisses down the plane of my cheek and my jaw, staying just shy of my lips.

"Yes," I whispered.

"Tavi, I love you. There's only you. There will only ever be you."

Goosebumps lifted on every part of my skin. I lost it entirely, grabbing Mike's shoulders and lifting onto the tips of my toes to kiss him.

Despite the fear churning my stomach, fear of this moment ending, we had another shot to be together. I broke away from the kiss to tell Mike exactly that but he shot out his hand and grabbed the back of my neck to keep me in place.

He pressed his body to mine and I felt every long lean angle of him. Every hard muscle. I felt the way his breath rushed out of his lungs and caressed my lips.

Mike pried his lips away from mine and rested his forehead to mine. Our eyes met as his arms banded around my waist to keep me in place.

"Maybe one day I'll be strong enough to deserve you," he whispered.

"I'll be the judge of what I deserve," I whispered back.

I was on fire, burning from the inside with his touch. No one else did those things to me. No one else impacted me the way he did, and always had, from the first moment I met him on that stretch of deserted road.

He was everything I wanted and more. It didn't matter how his magic needed a boost sometimes.

"Please, Mike."

I wasn't sure what I had to say to him or what I was begging for. The power dynamic between us had shifted and it wasn't about the crown on his head, whether he wore it or not. It was about what lurked in my blood and my bones. I couldn't stand it if Mike began to hate me for the disparity.

We'd already been through so much with the secrets I kept.

Reaching up, Mike took a lock of my hair between his thumb and forefinger and rubbed the strands together. He held my gaze when he brought the hair to his nose, inhaling deeply.

We moved together in desperation and Mike dipped his head to the side to draw the tip of his chin and nose up to my hairline. He kissed down my cheekbone, up across my brow, and the electric current between us sharpened.

I drew my fingers through his hair as my skin tightened.

My eyes closed and I moved by feel alone, finding his lips, kissing him senseless.

He reached out to draw me even closer and my mouth fell open to allow him entry. His teeth scraped against my lip before he pressed himself to me. My breath came harder, my skin tight, nipples pebbled.

"I don't know what I'd do without you," he murmured.

"You never have to find out."

His chuckle flickered through me like the first shadow of a candle in the dark. "Don't make promises you're not able to keep."

"Never," I said. "It's a gift. I never say what I don't mean."

"I thought your gift was finding dead bodies?"

I chuckled. "That, too."

He knew me inside and out. No more secrets between us, not anymore, not after everything we'd been through. His lips were warm and my body tingled where he touched me. The two of us together...it still felt like a pipe dream even with him in my arms.

He broke away to trail more kisses down the line of my throat until heat spiraled down between my legs.

Mike maneuvered us to the bed and I was the first to fall, the way it had been from the first. Need, weakness—they were twined together and made flesh in him. Magic bubbled up from that place inside of me when he joined me, lying on his side and his fingertip pushing my hair aside. His gaze searched my face.

"Are you sure we have time?"

He grinned against me. "I'm sure."

We were intimately aware of each other. There was only the sound of our breath, my heartbeat growing louder with every passing beat, and our magic mingling.

I groaned as his fingers skimmed along my ribcage,

lingering at the base of my breasts. He trailed them lower, between my thighs, and a shudder of electricity had me swallowing a cry.

Mike kissed me again and growled in the back of his throat. He pushed his fingers between my thighs until the dam broke. The light turned green.

Whatever I wanted to call the moment.

There was sweetness, yeah, but there was also need as we collided, kissing each other desperately.

I rocked my hips against his.

"Do you have any idea how crazy I've been for you?" he purred. "How often I've thought about getting you alone?"

He stroked his fingers against my core and my head dropped back. "Yes. I need you."

We exchanged only a brief glance before he pushed me back on the bed and covered me with his body. The contact sent an electric rush through me that made my head spin.

He kissed me hungrily and grabbed a fistful of my hair, kissing me as he settled between my legs.

I whimpered and wrapped my legs around him, arching my back to bring us closer. Too many clothes.

Mike seemed to read my mind. He snapped the fingers of his free hand and everything disappeared. Every last shred of cloth separating us.

Gasping, I gripped his forearms. I trembled against the solid ridge of him, his dick pressing against my hips.

A sense of urgency lit my blood and I stole another kiss as my head spun. Mike bit down on my lower lip before he drew it into his mouth.

"It's always been you, Tavi."

My name on his lips nearly sent me over the edge. Then he reached between us and glided a finger across my core.

Pleasure shot up from his touch. He kept me pinned beneath him, working me until my breath hitched.

His thumb nudged against my clit and his teeth caught my lip again. The small amount of pain coupled with the soft sensation of those circles drove me over the edge and I came.

Fighting the urge to scream my pleasure for the entire tavern to hear.

It was stupid, how easily he got me. How the press of his skin and a little bit of magic turned me inside out. Only for him.

A desperate need grew inside me as he caught my face between both hands and tilted my face up to kiss me deeper yet. I grabbed his shoulders, pulling him close, groaning.

His silky smooth skin against mine, the solid length of him, nudging me, begging for the one thing we both wanted more than anything else...

I reached down to skim my thumb over him and he shuddered. Slowly I took him in my hand, pumping him from tip to base, exploring the feel of him. Loving the way he jerked with the need to control the tempo.

Mike's eyes rolled back in his head.

His hand explored my waist, my breast, his teeth on my nipple and his body moving in time with my hand. I grinned wickedly against his mouth before I pushed him backward, forcing him onto his back and straddling him. I ground my core against him.

Heat spun through me with the caress.

"I'm too impatient to let you control the situation, Tavi." He sounded breathless as he toyed with my nipples and amped up the need until I was wild with it.

In a surprise move, Mike threw me off of him. I had no chance to yelp before he spun me around, my stomach on the bed and my ass in the air. He yanked me backward until I collided with him and he kissed the back of my neck.

Bit me.

Hard.

Oh, god. The dominance in the gesture drove me out of my mind and I was spinning, flying, as he dragged his teeth down my shoulder toward my spine.

"I've been researching," he said softly. I felt every word on my skin. "Werewolves. How shifters show their affection."

He gripped me by the waist and lifted my ass higher into the air before grabbing my neck. Holding me in place and angling his cock against me. My thighs were parted as far as they would go and he stroked himself along my center.

Mike laughed darkly. "I'll remember this forever."

Panting heavily, I shivered as Mike dropped over me, holding me down and grinding the tip of his cock against me without sliding forward.

"You're mine, Tavi. You've always been mine." The possessiveness in his tone struck me before he claimed me with a powerful thrust forward.

The shock of the fullness almost took my breath away. The hard length filled me to the brink and I cried out as he pulled free. Mike surged forward again and I wanted to reach for him, to touch him the way I knew he wanted to be touched, but he kept me in place.

My wolf loved it.

He kept up a punishing pace. I managed to turn my head to take him in, the golden glow of the lamplight on the line of his chest and the length of him moving in and out of me.

My body tightened as I watched him.

"Mine," he growled.

A piece of me broke at that word. I belonged to him. In whatever way he wanted, for whatever time we had left.

"Yours, Mike," I agreed.

He owned my body, my heart, my soul.

He'd never been the one to take the lead before. My cinnamon roll. A sweet man who would one day lead his people, but I'd never pictured him as the one with the crown on his head. No longer in his father's shadow.

Tonight, with him filling me, pounding deeper with every thrust, I saw it. I saw the hunger in his eyes and his barely constrained need. I growled and the air in the room went electric.

I wasn't done with him yet.

His grip on my neck was unyielding and I rocked back to meet his thrusts. But it wasn't in me to submit without a fight. Not even with my blood poisoning.

I reversed our positions again, moaning as I drove forward and he slipped out of me.

"Tavi, what the hell?" He was magnificent, kneeling there, his skin slicked in sweat.

I wanted to be on top. Even as I shivered, as I gasped at the sight and rolled my tongue around my dry mouth, I wanted more. If we only had tonight, then I planned to make the most of it.

My breasts tingled as I maneuvered him onto his back yet again. Hungry, I rose above him, my legs on either side of his hips. I grabbed the base of his cock and angled him before impaling myself.

"*Shit.*"

His hissed curse left me burning with pleasure so intense that for a second I wasn't able to breathe. I gave him no time before I moved, circling my hips around him and using the headboard for leverage. My wolf rose inside of me and for the first time in a long time, we were powerful. We were in control and we were loved.

If I were ever to have a mate, it would be Mike.

The fae prince stared up at me, his hands on my waist as he lifted me and thrust upward. We were merciless with each other.

I absorbed the feeling of his body inside of mine. Emotion flooded me as surely as pleasure and we clung to each other, Mike's fingers biting into my flesh. I tipped my head back, grinding my hips and finding just the right amount of friction to send me spiraling into a second orgasm.

Mike swelled inside of me, his pace going erratic before he emptied himself at the same time.

We stayed there, panting through the waves of satisfaction. The craving that had finally been satiated.

Mike lifted his head and kissed my breasts, my collar bone, my neck.

"You're everything to me," he repeated.

"Good. There's no going back," I replied. The back of my neck pulsed where he'd bitten me.

Mike sighed and dropped back, drawing me down to his side. He faced me, his cheeks flushed and his lips delightfully pink where I must have bitten him too.

Those lips curved upward in a satisfied smile before his eyes fluttered shut. "Stay with me tonight?"

"I'm not going anywhere."

It was everything I could have hoped for.

Every worry I'd worked through, that we weren't meant to be, disappeared. I'd seen how many halflings there were now, how many people of different races had fallen in love despite the danger.

There shouldn't *be* danger.

We were the same where it mattered—our hearts.

Cementing my love with Mike felt like the first step in healing the divided Faerie, especially since I wasn't enough to do it alone.

But I could do it.

With Mike by my side.

29

We woke with the sunrise.

I dragged myself out of bed and hissed when my feet touched down on the cold floor. Maybe it was my imagination but the room felt icy and the lure of falling back under the covers and snuggling in Mike's arms was almost too much to ignore.

He cracked an eye open, sucking in a breath before glancing between me and the empty space beside him.

The moment etched itself in my mind. The Crown Prince of Faerie with his hair mussed, his eyes narrowed with sleep, and his expression peaceful.

Naked, too.

My mouth automatically went dry.

"Come back," he croaked.

"I can't. We have to get going." And I probably had an earful to look forward to for not going back to my room.

Although if Laina had spent the night with Livvy then both of them knew exactly what Mike and I had done.

It almost didn't bear thinking about. Embarrassment warmed me from the inside out.

"You're beautiful."

I caught Mike's whispered compliment and allowed myself a secret smile as I hunted for my clothes.

Within an hour, we were back on the road and continuing our journey to the Abyss.

This time, however, I felt lighter than I had the previous day. With everything going on, I hadn't realized how much tension I carried when it came to me and Mike and our unresolved bullshit. I'd always told myself there would be a time and a place to make peace down the line, whether it meant we'd be together or not.

We'd needed last night.

The moment hadn't been planned, but it was ours.

I forced myself to focus on the journey ahead rather than last night. Otherwise I'd walk with a blush that let everyone know exactly what I'd been doing. As it was, I managed to escape any kind of maternal talk from Livvy.

We were all still too stressed to talk much.

Onyx led the way unerringly forward.

I hadn't expected to feel so awkward around him, but he'd glared when we saw each other that morning. Glared and drawn in a deep breath before his cheeks colored. He knew exactly what I'd done. Could no doubt smell Mike and me on each other's skin. Imprinted.

The bite on the back of my neck still throbbed from the claiming.

I refused to let the moment be ruined. Onyx and I weren't romantic with each other. Even though there had been times where I almost thought—

Where we almost could have—

I shook my head to clear it and offered Onyx a hard smile, urging him not to discuss it. Not to say a word or press the issue.

He'd eventually relented but I struggled with the guilt for the first few hours of our trek. *Why should I feel guilty*? Onyx and I never gave in to the small stirrings of attraction. There was no understanding between us. Friends. A cherished friend.

To his credit, no one stopped to question him on how he seemed to know exactly where to go without the use of a map or compass. The land around us changed and the tension mounted, but otherwise we were content to walk. To be silent.

To worry over whatever fresh hell waited for us.

Slowly, the guilt took a back seat to the worry, one I knew we shared between us.

Even Bronwen, who looked like she had a million questions for me about last night, zipped her lips shut. Although it wasn't as if she and I had ever talked about boys before. There were too many other things, life and death matters, to talk about. Not sex.

I swallowed over a tired giggle then glanced around to make sure no one heard me.

Livvy straightened like she'd stuck her finger in an electrical socket but said nothing.

By the end of the day and after a handful of stops to rest, Onyx halted and lifted his arm to point to something on the horizon. "There it is," he called out.

Bronwen squinted. "There *what* is?"

Noren growled and the hair on the back of his neck lifted.

"You don't see it?" Onyx asked, awed.

The ruins appeared out of the corner of my eye at first, like a half captured flash of something you weren't really sure was there or not. *Real* or not. The longer I focused on them, the more the strange rock formation swam into view and solidified.

After a few minutes I was able to look directly at them.

The ravaged temple was not some majestic site perched on the side of a mountain. The ruins rose out of the ground in the middle of nowhere, halfway between a clearing in the forest and the farmland visible beyond. Faerie seemed made up of more ancient forests than anything else. And what had the temple been before falling to time?

The stones wavered, one moment as solid as the ground and the next as nebulous as smoke.

A tingle of awareness tugged at me and the sensation grew into a tremor of fear. This place wasn't supposed to exist. And we were definitely not supposed to be here.

If Onyx hadn't pointed out the ruins, I would have dismissed the temple as a trick of the light and nothing else.

"I wouldn't have been able to find this on my own," Mike commented. "This is both fantastic and horrible at the same time."

"Agreed," Livvy muttered.

"You're not meant to find it," Laina asserted. She focused on the ruins without blinking an eye and her face was a mask.

Mike's voice remained firm but the tension was evident. "At least we weren't followed."

Foreboding settled over me and my own hair lifted in a cool breeze despite the heat of the day and the sunlight dappled through the limbs overhead.

"How did you know how to get here?" I asked Onyx. "It's not like you had a roadmap."

"When a person is banished to the Abyss," he explained slowly, "they come back—*if* they come back—with a kind of connection that never goes away. The Abyss changes you. On a molecular level."

He stared unblinking at the ruins, his face curiously blank.

"I'm not sure I like the sound of that," I murmured.

"Good. You're not supposed to like the sound of it." Onyx continued to stare unblinking at the ruins. "The Abyss is a special place. It's not meant to be left behind. It's meant to be traveled, survived. Carried with you if you're lucky enough to find a way out like I was. Not all of the banished escape."

I wanted to know more. Before I had a chance to open my mouth, Onyx strode toward the ruins faster than he'd moved since our escape from the castle. His burst of energy surprised me and I found myself hustling forward to try and keep pace with him.

Livvy remained a step behind, quiet when I expected her to start back with the *we need to hurry* stuff.

Noren gave a single whine of protest before he followed me, sticking close to my heels.

The ruins were messing with my brain.

They didn't grow in stature the closer we got. Rather it was like one of those funhouse mirrors or long hallways in a dream where you got closer with every step and yet you never quite made it to your destination.

I gnashed on my cheek, biting down and using the little bit of pain like a tether to the real world. Because this wasn't real.

At once, the ground beneath my Converses changed from soft moss and pine needles to stone. The transition rocked me and I stopped dead, my arms windmilling to keep my balance when the forest disappeared and the temple stood in front of us.

One moment not there, then boom. We were on the doorstep.

"What the hell?"

My voice, rather than echoing out into the forest, landed flat and I realized then that there were no animal sounds here. The birdsong had died somewhere along the way. A pall fell over the land and deadened it to any ambient noise.

Onyx pressed a finger to his lips, his eyes wide and desperate. "You have to watch out. Things aren't what they seem here. Don't speak too loudly and don't yell. You'll draw out unwanted visitors. Follow my lead."

He tilted sickeningly to the side but caught himself before he lost his balance.

At least I wasn't the only one having trouble finding their center. Bronwen had her head bent between her knees and Laina boasted a distinctly greenish cast to her cheeks. Her hands shifted to her shoulders as though she resisted the urge to draw her whips.

I stumbled and my skin scraped the lichen-covered stone. I expected warmth but found nothing. The stones were icy to the touch despite the sunlight.

"Unwanted visitors?" My voice still sounded too loud and it rippled back to me like disturbed water.

My gut churned and I pressed my hands to it.

"Where do we go from here, Onyx?" Laina finally asked.

"We go inside," Onyx said matter-of-factly.

Livvy slid her hands into the pockets of her pants and stared at the entrance. To my right, a gap in the stone provided a way inside the ruins. A kind of strange Stonehenge, although the rocks barely fit together and yet somehow it was impossible to see between them.

Onyx was right. This was a bad place.

My stomach shifted and gurgled and I pressed my hands

tighter to my abdomen. My insides roiled hard enough for me to feel it.

"We should have made weapons before we got here," Mike said.

Onyx sniffed and said, "Weapons aren't going to do much. The creatures we'll see inside are different."

"They can't be cut and bleed like anything else?"

Mike was desperate for an answer but the way Onyx's lips thinned into a harsh line, we all knew what the answer would be.

"No sense wasting time worrying about beasts." Livvy strode forward. "The sooner we get in, the sooner we'll be able to get out."

Maybe she didn't see it but I did—the similarities between us were right out there in the open. We were the same kind of person, only this time I wasn't the one barreling ahead with full steam despite not knowing the situation.

It was Livvy.

She jumped first and asked questions later—if later ever came for us.

My teeth chattered together as I followed her, the others behind me. The shadows quickened around us, swirling masses caught only in glimpses out of the corners of my eyes. Until they weren't.

Suddenly the shadows separated from the darkness and formed incorporeal but very human shapes.

"Watch out!"

Bronwen yelled the warning before one of the shadows moved in a flash to her side, striking the stone beneath her feet. Sparks flew where it touched and a deep crevice formed, the edges smoldering.

She fell, cracking her hip against the stone.

"Guardians of the Abyss!" Onyx explained.

I caught another flash of movement, this time headed toward him, and moved as quickly as my senses allowed. I hurled myself between Onyx and the shadow guardian, throwing up my arms in an X in front of us. A blast of magic rippled out to shield us against the hit.

"What are these things made of?" I yelled.

"Nothing good."

That came from Laina.

A green glow emanated off of her and spread out toward Mike, their magic the same color. A halo of forest-green witch and fae magic spread past them and dissolved the edges of the shadows where they met.

She hadn't drawn her weapons, so she must have somehow known what Onyx meant about the guardians.

Unfortunately for the rest of us, the shadows were not deterred.

If anything, the witch magic made them angrier.

Could a shadow *be* angry?

These guys were. Their limbs became weaponized extensions of their bodies, swords of glittering night.

I used myself as a shield for Onyx. I wasn't the best at forming weapons out of nothing. That wasn't my forte, not in the least. I'd had a terrible time of doing the barest minimum required to get through the Faerie Trials.

Maybe the shadow guardians read my mind.

They came at me with weapons raised and their swords sliced through the air in a unified wave. They were everywhere and nowhere at once, just like the temple ruins.

Livvy cupped her palms in front of her face and blew out a breath. Her air magic became a ball of pure light. The closest guardians moved away from her, hovering at the edge of her light.

Bronwen's yelp came a second later. One of the guardians had maneuvered behind her, slicing its sword across her ankles, just as she made it to her feet. She went down with another cry of pain and the surprise of the attack had Livvy turning and Noren bounding toward my friend.

The guardians knocked the ball of light out of Livvy's hands and the moment it left her physical touch, it guttered and died.

The words were at the tip of my tongue and ready to fall. I blasted them with everything I had. Power rose from the pit in my gut and the moment I let it loose, I went light-headed and dizzy. My knees were like jelly.

Onyx grabbed me by the back of the shirt to keep me upright but we weren't fighting with our full power. Not even *half*. We were exhausted and pushed as far as we could go.

The noise volume inside of the temple went to blasting loud, the dull roar of an invisible wind making rational thought impossible.

"Do you know of a way to make it past them?" I asked, screaming to be overheard.

The terrible howling sound ratcheted higher into a keening wail like a banshee cry. It took everything in me to maintain the shield rather than covering my ears with my hands, the sound spiked into my eardrums and through them to my entire body. I felt it in my toes.

Onyx's eyes rounded, filled with pain. On the other side of the temple were Livvy and Bronwen, their backs pressed together as the two of them supported each other. Blood seeped from the wounds in Bronwen's heels but she gritted her teeth and kept going.

The shadows split apart from each other to surround us. Noren nipped at them and they divided, circling him, striking him hard enough to send tufts of fur flying every-where. He was movement incarnate and yet he wasn't fast enough to outrun them.

"I have no idea!" Onyx yelled back. "Things are different exiting the Abyss than they are trying to enter it."

His father had sent him in. Onyx hadn't gone inside on his own.

My eyes burned with the effort to maintain the shield and I doubled down as the edges constricted and sputtered. Growing smaller and allowing a tiny crack to form around us.

The nearest guardian moved immediately.

It swung its blade through the crack and I wasn't fast enough to avoid the hit. The tip of the blade slid into my skin, splitting it along my calf. Agonizing pain spread from the area and my shield sputtered again before it died.

At once, a calming green glow surrounded us. There was Mike, his arms outstretched and every ounce of his magic poured into us. Into me.

Our eyes met, his narrowed and stubborn and so damn appealing.

It shouldn't be up to him to protect me.

I should be able to handle this myself. Frustration burned my throat.

But he wasn't helpless. Laina was there, spreading her own power over him while cutting down the guardians around her. When one fell, two formed from the pieces. The shadows were relentless.

Their weapons clashed against our shields and only Livvy had the knowledge to form a weapon of light. Laina knew what to do, of course, but with her attention fractured between us, there was no way for her—

The queen fell.

In slow motion, the queen dropped to the ground with the pommel of a shadow sword stuck in her shoulder and piercing out the other side, sent through the single chink in her shield.

30

The sound of Mike's yell colored the air around us, loud enough to cut through the roaring wind. His shield disappeared and left us vulnerable.

In an instant, I reached for Livvy, to grab the weapon from her hands. It split apart and formed two pieces, the weight of it natural in my hand.

I didn't think. I couldn't.

Not with Laina bleeding out on the stone.

The guardians closed in around us and I swung the sword of light, taking out the arms of the one closest to her.

I swore I heard a scream as I charged.

The shadows threw themselves at me but I refused to slow down, calling to Noren as I moved. He was motion itself. The shadows seemed to bounce off of him.

Something about the Unseelie direwolf made it impossible for the guardians to wound him. They may have gouged out chunks of hair but none of their attacks penetrated his skin.

A part of the land itself, Laina had said once, culled from its magic. His strength was mine now.

With him at my side, the two of us deflected the attacks. He was my army, cutting through the shadows.

My lips pried back at the shock on Mike's face when I brought Livvy's weapon down on the nearest guardian and it burst into pieces. I drew it on a second guardian and yelled as it ducked aside to avoid the swing of the blade.

The guardian used its weapon to try and knock the weapon out of my hand but Noren pounced on it and drove it into the stone beneath us with a roar.

My strength flagged. There and gone in an instant. My head lightened under a pulse of dizziness and I was going down. Noren wasn't fast enough to catch me but a blast of air magic somehow managed to knock me into the wall and away from the attacking shadow guardian.

An agonized cry rattled through the ruins and I glanced over to see Mike curling his body over Laina. He'd left the sword in her shoulder, blood pouring from the savage wound.

Alarm paralyzed me.

If someone with the queen's power could be easily taken down, then there was no hope for the rest of us.

The shadows swarmed in the unnatural wind, dark lances of power nipping at my skin and pulling my hair.

Noren leapt on one of the guardians and sent it crashing away. Before it had a chance to recover, he bit down around one of its insubstantial limbs, and the shadows evaporated again.

Bronwen and Livvy sent spears of their magic in a circle around me, around Onyx, around Mike and Laina, the points slamming down through several of the guardians and pinning them in place until Noren could move.

The wind lessened but didn't die down.

I glanced over to Mike and he met my gaze with an

arched brow that required no explanation. We needed to end this quickly.

The guardians were relentless. Several of them wrenched free of the spears of magic and hurled themselves at us. I went to move and my numb fingers dropped the weapon, the light guttering as darkness, like sharp teeth, bit down on anything they reached.

My head spun around and the vertigo bent me in half.

Of call the times for this shitty virus to take me down—

My magic was there—I thought it was there—but I couldn't access it. Like a blockade had formed around me to keep me from the very thing I needed to get us out of this.

Noren, luckily, still had every bit of his magic. And these fuckers couldn't touch him. He towered over me and growled.

I dropped to my knees with my arms over my head and gritted my teeth, summoning whatever strength I had left to form the shield a second time.

I had no way of knowing what would have happened if Mike hadn't erupted when he did. His magic, negligible during our classes, never showing beyond the trickle he used to get by, exploded out of him.

His head fell back on his shoulders and his chest swelled, a green aura pulsing out of him.

The cavernous ruins filled with the green glow of spring growth, of old forests, and the first buds of the year. The quality of the air changed and grew sweeter, like a breeze blowing away stale air.

I stood straighter. Noren quieted, shuddering, before he dropped down to all fours.

I pried my eyes open as the guardians evaporated one after the other. The last one held on longer than the others, howling in agony before the glow split it into two pieces and Noren slammed his massive paw down on it.

The roaring silence disappeared and left my head empty and aching.

For a long moment, no one moved, and the ruins were simply that. Empty, waiting. Nothing but stone.

The spell was broken by the dying glow and Mike's harsh breathing. "*Mom*. Talk to me."

"Is she okay?" At least that was what I wanted to say. Nothing came out. My lips moved but the words were impossibly far away.

Pressing my palm to my temple did nothing to dull the ache. I watched through a narrow tunnel of vision, blackness creeping in around the edges that had nothing to do with the shadow guardians.

Mike shifted onto his rear and dragged his mother up from the ground into his arms.

Her head lolled to the side, with her face already pale and her mouth slightly open.

Her eyes fluttered open. "Michael." She tried to lift her arm to touch his face and failed.

"We need to get her help immediately." Livvy straightened, her expression clinical as she stared down at the wounded queen.

In the next beat she was on the ground as well with her fingertips probing the wound. She hissed when the point of the sword touched her skin.

"We should take the sword out," Bronwen said. She wrung her hands.

Livvy shook her head. "It's the only thing keeping the bleeding to a minimum right now. None of us are strong enough to cauterize the wounds if we pull it out, and I'm willing to bet something in the shadow guardians' magic will prevent us from doing so anyway. Those weapons are meant to kill."

Bronwen limped closer and the motion drew attention to her own wounds. The dark pain in my calf throbbed in response.

"In her dire condition, she needs to be taken to a fae hospital immediately," Livvy added.

Laina tried to speak and coughed up blood. "No fae hospitals," she warned. "They won't know how to care for this. They'll report us to Cosmo."

Mike curled around his mom without touching her. "I know where to take her but it's far." He let out a harsh laugh. "Of course it's too far."

"You have to go with your mother, to get her to safety. We can't leave her here and we're wasting time debating it," I told Mike. "Bronwen can fly ahead and find help, bring them here. The minutes count. She's connected to this place now, right?"

Onyx shrugged, unsure what to say.

Bronwen pursed her lips. "Shifting might be able to help heal my own wounds. It's only a small nick."

I shot her an appreciative look. When the chips were down, she was always willing to step up to the plate to help. "Come back for us when you can. I'm sorry to ask it of you —" I began.

"Stop." Bronwen swiped her hand through the air. "We're all doing what we have to do. We all have a part to play. I'm proud to do mine. For the pack."

Her gaze encompassed everyone, from Onyx to Livvy and Noren, to Mike and Laina. The swell of pride surprised me deeply. *For the pack*.

Before I could say anything, before the tears pooling in my eyes sprang free, Bronwen screwed her eyes shut and shifted. Magic pulsed and in place of her body stood a crow.

Beady black eyes met mine and she squawked before taking off through the break between stones.

"I hate this," Mike admitted. He tried to help Laina up and she screamed, stopping all movement. "I hate that we're splitting up again."

His voice splintered.

It was necessary. Parting ways was the only logical step to take but we were on the same page. Hating every situation that pushed us apart rather than drew us together.

I held his gaze for a beat longer before I bobbed my head. "You'll be okay?"

"I have no choice." He tried to muster up a grin and failed miserably. "Go on. Hurry back to me."

I made no promises but my heart stayed behind with the two of them even as Livvy tugged at my elbow to get me to move. Mike and Laina remained behind while I, Livvy, Onyx, and Noren headed deeper into the temple.

I swallowed hard, my throat dry. Why did it always have to happen this way? I limped along until Noren moved forward to help steady me.

Why did someone always get hurt?

The ruins were deceptive. From the outside, they resembled a henge-type ring with an empty space in the center and no roof. But the further we hiked into the gloom between towering stones, the more the walls constricted and a ceiling formed out of the play of dark on light.

It had woven from nothing into substance before I realized anything changed.

An opening in the floor way up ahead led to a staircase winding deeper into the heart of the temple, whatever was hidden on floors below this one.

I tensed, waiting for another round of shadow guardians to come at us. When nothing happened, I touched my toes to the first stair riser.

"Waiting for the booby traps, Indiana Jones?" Onyx teased breathlessly.

"You never know. You said people don't want to access the Abyss, but it seems to me like someone has gone through an awful lot of trouble to protect the entrance. So who knows. Maybe there are more people trying to get in than we assumed."

But nothing happened on the first step, or the second or the third.

In a lot of ways, descending through the temple reminded me of the Trials, my mind drawn back to them again and again. Except here, there weren't all-seeing orbs and a panel of judges to dog our steps.

Distracted, I tripped on the last stair and stumbled forward. My heart lurched into my throat.

My hand slapped against the wall to stop myself, Livvy and Onyx yelling behind me. A panel slid backward and the floor heaved, stone grinding against stone.

The staircase slid back into the wall and disappeared with a dusty sigh.

Noren made the leap down but Onyx wasn't nearly as fast. He dropped, catching himself on his forearms before his skull hit stone, and he winced in pain. Livvy tried to help him up but he waved her off.

"I'm okay," he insisted with a groan. "It took me by surprise."

His muscles trembled, dark veins standing out to attention as he pushed himself to his feet.

Weary to my own bones, I stood apart and watched him gather himself. The stairs had melded seamlessly into the stone and left us with a view of the open temple above but no way to reach it. Especially not with our powers down to the dregs, and whatever issue I had keeping me weak.

Besides, did we want to retreat? We'd come this far.

"I suppose this proves that there is only one way forward." Livvy pointed ahead toward the winding tunnel. Her voice remained deceptively tranquil.

No escape.

Onyx shouldn't even be here. He should be in a hospital, comfortable in a bed while he received the kind of treatment necessary to manage his pain. Except we both knew there was no end to his ordeal.

I'd broken something inside of him. It was a miracle he'd made it this far. And I couldn't leave him behind because he was the only one who knew where we needed to go.

31

"The Abyss will try to trick you. Or rather, the path to reach it isn't clear. You have to be strong and keep your wits about you. This might not be the only way," Onyx insisted.

His face scrunched as pain wracked through him.

"If this place is as terrible as everyone makes it out to be, then why is it so difficult to get to? No one in their right mind should want to come here."

"The Abyss keeps what it is given. It's less that it wasn't to keep people out, but more that it wants to make sure what it has taken stays with it. Which is probably part of the reason why the connection always stays there."

I glanced back in time to watch Onyx rub his heart.

"It's not a good place, Tavi."

"So why did Uncle Will banish the journals there? Why didn't he just destroy them?" I muttered. "There are less extreme ways to deal with this."

Not like it made a difference. The reason was personal and the act in the past, but curiosity would always get the better of me.

We wound our way through the tunnel of stone with the ceiling growing lower with every step. Small sconces of fire burst to life where we stepped and promptly guttered out once we made it several feet past them.

The tunnel circled around on itself but there were no other options, no side branches to tease us. Only an endlessly dark expanse in front and behind.

"William did it because he hates me." Livvy sounded small and far away. "He has always hated me and my kind, and not much has changed since we first met. I suppose he did it to punish me, not knowing what truth was hidden inside those pages."

I couldn't imagine hating someone so much to go to all this trouble.

Even Persephone and Arlyss, who had both made my life at school a living hell. *Bullies*.

Uncle Will never struck me as a bully but I guessed he possessed the tendencies. Because here we were.

The hallway grew tighter, the stench of must and wetness assaulting my nostrils and burning my lungs with every inhalation. I stooped down until my back ached and panic pressed close.

This was what it must feel like to be buried alive.

The moment I thought about it, hysteria set in and the sweat seeping out of my pores took on an acrid stench I couldn't ignore.

Shit, I definitely shouldn't think about being buried alive. Or what might happen if the tunnel closed in on us, like the staircase disappearing.

Onyx breathed heavily and behind me Noren whined.

Did I make a blanket statement that it was going to be okay? Even if we knew it was a lie?

Someone swallowed loud enough for me to hear.

At once, the tunnel opened up and I heaved a sigh of relief as I straightened, clenching at the walls to steady myself Only to lose the plot when the sconces showed nothing but a firm wall of granite ahead of us.

"What the fuck?" The curse came out before I could stop it. "There has to be something else." We couldn't go back, and forward was a dead end.

The gravity of our situation pushed me down into a pit of shock and pathetic denial. The panicky kind that causes horses to bolt when there is nothing wrong.

Reality swept in, kicking my ass along the way, and then settled.

"I don't remember any of this. I never had to come this way," Onyx said with a frown.

A strange jittery twitch settled in my veins. "You said you knew where we were going."

"I remembered the path to get here, but the insides must change because when I was in the temple, it wasn't a cavern. It was an actual ruin. Like something you'd find in a desert or something."

Onyx pushed his hand against the stone and waited for something to change. When nothing did, he jammed his shoulder to the granite, Livvy moving to help him while the rest of us stood by.

"A real dead end," he offered unnecessarily.

My gut sank, feet rooted to the floor and my knees locked to keep me upright.

"Impossible," I blurted. "You said this is the way in. You couldn't have come out of the Abyss through rock."

His brows screwed together. "It's a little blurry. The details. But you're right. I didn't come out this way."

"Did we take a wrong turn somewhere?" I asked. "I

mean, did we miss something?" I turned too fast in a circle and the dizziness sent me back against the wall.

"We don't have time to waste retracing our steps." Livvy fumed and stalked forward. She swept Onyx back with one arm. "We're going to blast our way through. I refuse to let this stop us. We're close."

I barked out a laugh. "Come on, Livvy. We're not strong enough to bore through granite."

"You are capable of so much more than you think. Both of you. I know you're tired and afflicted. I know you think the pain is never going to stop, and you'll never be normal again." She bit out the words, then shoved a hand through her hair, smearing sweat and blood and dirt across her skin. "We're doing this together. Now give me your hand."

She held out her palm for me to take and I stared at it.

How would it feel to actually work together on this? To do something with my mom that would make a difference? Her resolve was implacable.

I took her hand before I thought of the thousands of reasons why she was asking for the impossible.

"We're getting through this," she repeated for my sake.

Magic sparked where our skin touched. The connection between us, the tether not just with power but with blood, burst to life and dissolved through the wall keeping me separated from my own power.

Finally.

I had my access back. Mom's energy gave me strength to fight against the blood sickness.

The part of me that came from her, the fae side and the inherent magic of my history, twined together with hers and sharpened into focus. Livvy directed the beam at the wall and our fingers slid together. One unit. One force and unstoppable.

Our power collided against the cave wall.

The sensation was there and gone before our beam of light burrowed through the stone. A crack spread from the point of impact and the wall rumbled once in warning before the pieces splintered apart.

The blast brought massive boulders tumbling down, and Noren and Onyx barely managed to step out of the way before the opening widened enough for us to walk through.

But it took the two of us working together to achieve.

"That's one way to do it," Onyx said breathlessly.

Livvy smiled in triumph. "As I said, there's always a way through."

"You never said that."

"I meant to say it," she corrected.

On the other side, a river of black water snaked through the cavern, cut only by the harsh line of a wooden dock. A thick rope tethered a small boat to the side.

An unnatural sight.

We picked our way over debris toward the dock. Sconces of fire glowed the closer we got to the river.

A small divot on the wooden piling gleamed in the unnatural light, rounded at the edges and about the size of a quarter.

"It's a place for a coin. To use the boat," Livvy explained. Her hand went to her hips and she studied the divot. "It's similar to the myth of Charon. Do you know that one? He's the boatman on the river Styx who requires coins to give safe passages to souls."

My heart flipped painfully in my constricted chest. "I have no money for the fare, then."

"I do. One of the perks of owning a restaurant and serving tables. I've always got change."

Livvy dove a hand into her pocket and when she pulled

it out, there were multiple coins shining clean against her dirty skin. Without wasting time, she placed a coin in the divot. The boat vibrated and the rope untied itself from the mooring.

She dropped another coin in place for good measure before gesturing for us to board.

Laina eyed the small boat skeptically. "There isn't room for all of us. You go ahead. We'll wait here for your safe return." The way she emphasized *safe* made me gulp.

I looked to Mike, who appeared to hate the idea of us being separated. But there was nothing for it. The boat simply wouldn't hold all of us. I took his hand. "Take care of Laina and Bronwen."

He gave a curt nod but said nothing. What was there to say?

Bronwen gave me a fierce hug and swiped at her eyes, but she put on a brave face. Laina simply smiled as if this would be a piece of cake and over soon. I wanted to absorb her courage because I was afraid my own wouldn't be enough.

Onyx was the first one in, and we had to help him onto the wooden seat. Then Noren, me, and finally Livvy.

The boat set off without a ripple on the ebony water.

If Charon existed, then hopefully our payment was sufficient to get us to our end destination.

The boat glided through the cave and I saw no break in the walls. Stone fit together seamlessly.

The others were as nervous as I was. Onyx gripped the side of the boat with white knuckles. Noren breathed heavily with his mouth open and his tongue hanging out to the side. Livvy was close enough to touch but seemed a thousand miles away, lost to whatever thoughts occupied the space in her head.

I tried to think of this as a chance to get to know my mom better but we were all too focused on survival to make the most of any given moment.

What would happen once we had the journals?

With my powers unlocked, would the enemies of my past come back not as ghosts but as flesh and blood obstacles? Would I somehow come face to face with Claribel, or Dorian Jade, or even Tywin and Cosmo Foxfall and be able to defeat them?

The boat jolted and I lurched forward in my seat.

"What's happening?"

The moment I spoke, the water churned, the boat moving faster over some rapids. The bow dipped forward and sent us all out of our seats. Noren tumbled, off balance and heading toward the side. I let go of the seat to grab hold of him when he almost flew off.

No amount of magic would stop us now and I halfway wondered if any attempt would increase the rapids.

We slammed against the rock walls, sending loose pieces dropping into the rapids. They hurtled against us like missiles before disappearing into the swirling whirlpools.

Water sprayed, soaking through our clothing, chilling me to bone. Worse than being caught in a rainstorm. Worse than a wild ride because there was no stopping or getting off.

I clung to Noren, my foot locked against the seat in front of us. *Please let us make it.*

Please, please, please.

But who was I praying to?

Who was out there to listen to me and stop this?

We'd made a choice to come this far. The boat careened again into the cavern wall and the wood gave a groan underneath us.

Water sloshed in and around us.

Livvy had said Faerie was a real being, and had called her a goddess. I focused on that concept, conjuring up a clear image of Faerie in my mind. *Help us, please.* If the goddess existed then we needed her. We weren't going to make it off this boat alive.

The front caught in one of the whirlpools and sent us spiraling in a circle. Heading along the river backwards. My stomach flipped and my heart jumped into my throat.

The bitterness of fear filled my mouth.

Noren growled and the sound vibrated through his body and into mine. I lost feeling in my arms and fingers.

Please, goddess, get us out of this.

Something had to give. The ride had to stop so we could get off because we weren't going to get to the other end if the rapids got any worse.

Please!

The boat crashed again and wood splintered as the front end tore off. Behind me, Onyx and Livvy were screaming, their cries suddenly swallowed by the water. Still clinging to Noren, I went into the water, and didn't resurface.

32

I'm drowning.

The water was over my head and I sank fast, my arms and legs flailing and kicking but unable to propel me in the right direction. Or maybe I was swimming down instead of up. The pressure came from every side, and without any light, confusion took over.

Disoriented, I kicked harder.

Everything around me was chaos. I'd lost hold of Noren. Was he out there in the gloom with me, underwater, struggling?

My lungs burned and the muscles in my legs screamed for relief and found none. If I didn't get to the surface soon—

Was Livvy safe?

Had Onyx stayed with the boat?

The pressure increased and my heart thundered in my ears. Everything inside of me pulsed, my lungs constricted, going smaller and tighter. Gods, the pain.

I'm dying.

How could I have made it this far only to have it end here?

I kicked again, desperate to find an indication that I went in the right direction. No matter how far I swam, no matter how hard I pushed, it was impossible to tell the surface from the bottom.

I switched direction but the water was everywhere. I was out of air.

I opened my eyes wider and the water stung, cold seeping into my pores and my blood. This really was the end of the line. Lights sparked in my eyes but they weren't from reaching the surface. My body cried out for air and I couldn't fight the urge to breathe anymore.

I opened my mouth and water jettisoned into the empty cavity, fast, greedy.

Sinking lower and lower.

It's not so bad, actually...

As long as the others were fine, then *I'd* be fine. No matter what happened.

The lights sparked a final time before everything went black.

The pain lancing through me was a huge surprise. But I guessed it shouldn't be. Why was there pain after death?

Could I not escape it even now?

My body seized, my lungs expelling the water out through my ravaged throat. I curled on my side with my eyes squeezed shut and coughed, a puddle forming beneath me.

Sick and still coughing, I huddled into a ball, clenching my stomach through wave after wave of agony.

But I wasn't underwater anymore.

The tips of my fingers scanned over smooth stones.

Once the last coughing fit passed, I forced my eyes open,

squinting against the light. Well, if I had to die, at least I'd gone someplace beautiful. Somewhere *not* underwater.

I took my time pushing up into a sitting position, drawing my knees to my chest until I got the bottom back underneath me. I gasped at what I saw.

The palatial ballroom extended in every direction, with me dead center. A marble mosaic underneath formed a massive star-shaped design. Overhead, the huge domed ceiling was covered in sparkling stars, like the kind I'd seen right before I died.

Those same bright spots of light I'd thought were the last firings of my brain. Had I somehow seen this place before I came here?

I must be dead. I wanted to be shocked but there was nothing left. No feelings, no thoughts clinging any longer than a few seconds before disappearing. Even the scorching, red-hot sensation in my throat and lungs passed into memory.

Where was I?

Standing, I walked toward a wall, each of which was lined by tapestries painted in the most vivid colors. At a distance the individual threads were not visible but up close they were rainbow hues and all of them expertly woven together to form a seamless picture.

With every step that brought me closer, the jagged thrum of my heartbeat grew louder until my head roared and my pulse matched the horrible echoing emptiness. Until it blotted out any ambient sound and the sensation of the rest of the world.

"It's Faerie," I blurted out loud.

The tapestries were all different. The ones on this wall were scenes from history. The Great Pixie War, I realized with a start, that Elfwaite fought in fifty years ago. The one on the opposite wall was the castle, Mike's home. The same castle I'd lived in once I came to Faerie. The turrets of the castle spires were the same, only here the stones gleamed and there were more flowers than I'd ever seen before.

A small grin crept over my features.

Whoever made these tapestries boasted no small amount of talent. A master of their trade. The pictures were detailed, carefully woven, and produced with such distinction I might have been looking at a picture. The closer I got, the more the details stood out.

Not to mention they were huge, covering the entire expanse of wall from floor to ceiling.

The third wall boasted a tapestry of the Fae Academy for Halflings, in the mortal realm.

I ground my teeth against a pang of homesickness.

I'd started my journey within those four walls. The ivy-covered walls were the same and rocked me with such surprise it transported me back to the night I'd arrived.

Everything had been blurry and the world around me shifting under the effects of the potion I'd had to take. But the swirling design on the gates stood out in my mind. The great wide tree trunks lining the drive and my excitement for the fifty acres around the place to roam.

How did it all go to hell from there?

Too much had changed for me to start cataloging in my mind. My life took a completely different path from where I first began and these tapestries felt like snapshots of the pieces along the way.

Except for the Pixie Wars.

I'd only heard about those second-hand through Elfwaite's stories.

Suddenly, a woman's voice sounded from behind me. "You are just as much a part of our history as these images.

I'm not sure you've fully grasped it yet. You will. I have absolute faith in you."

Someone was watching me. I felt eyes on my spine and my hands started to sweat. Only there was no fear as I took my time turning to face her.

"You are a part of the land, the air, the breath of the world."

A woman stood there, willowy and graceful, with her shoulders thrown back and long silver hair trailing past her hips. Her gown, a purple hue in shifting colors of violet and eggplant, flowed down to bare feet. She made no noise as she crossed the massive ballroom toward me. We met in the middle of that star-shaped design.

Still no fear came and I knew exactly who spoke to me.

This was Faerie.

The goddess my mother had spoken to, the one I'd secretly laughed at her for naming and considered her crazy.

Faerie was so bright, beautiful, both young and old in the same instant. I almost couldn't look at her without wanting to avert my gaze. Her features shifted without giving me a full moment to pinpoint her exact age.

It was like looking at the sun. Warm and searing and bright and dangerous.

"Well, I'm dead now," I told her flippantly. "So I don't know how I'm going to be a part of history. Unless someone wants to write a memoir."

The goddess stared at me askance. "You aren't dead, Octavia."

This time I jolted. I'd never heard anyone use my real name. Not even in a serious situation. I've always been *Tavi*. From birth it felt like I'd been Tavi, and never Octavia.

"You are not dead," she repeated kindly. "There are three prices to pay for the Abyss. Innocence. Self. And Life."

If I were dead, then wouldn't it take care of one of those things?

We stood facing each other and life-giving heat rolled off of the goddess in waves. "I'm listening," I whispered.

I swore she smiled. The expression flashed across her face and disappeared in her luminescence before I had a chance to really capture it in my mind. I blinked and black spots danced across my closed lids.

"This is simply the cost of Innocence. Your ordeal taught you the fragility of life. Bad things will always happen to good people. It is outside of your control. And thus, through your experiences, the veil has lifted."

"Why?" It was probably stupid to ask. "Why does it have to happen?"

"There is a balance in the world. It's life. It is the way of existence." The goddess stepped closer and her hair lifted in a halo around her, adding to her glow.

I forced myself to look at her until I couldn't take it anymore and had to close my eyes.

I stood in front of an actual goddess. The force behind Faerie. Did she know how the land erupted when I first stepped foot through the portal? How the thunderstorms and other unnatural weather phenomena had wracked the land?

She had to, right?

Would she tell me why it happened, if I was supposedly a part of Faerie?

"There will be two more prices to pay this night, sweet girl," she continued, "before you reach the Abyss. You will need to make the choice in order to reach the place you seek."

"What the hell do you mean by life, then? Am I going to die anyway?" I thought I had.

Did it make a difference if I died now, or later? No.

"This is not what I wanted for you, Octavia." The goddess ignored my question and considered me sadly. "I am so sorry."

How did I know she was sad without seeing her full expression?

I just felt it. Deep inside of me.

"This wasn't part of the plan. But even the gods are thwarted by the deeds of men. Free will enables them to make decisions outside of the best interests of the few and the many."

I shook my head. "I don't get it. Gods are supposed to be all-powerful and all-knowing. How in the world can mankind—any kind—thwart you?"

"Free will. It is the way of existence as well, as you have found. Directions are not always followed and the future is never set in stone."

At once, the words to the Faerie Prophecy filled my head.

At croaching light of black moon morn
A shifter child shall be born.
An innocent and pure of heart
Born to rip the Fae apart.
Born to rip the Fae apart.
A wicked end, downfall's start.
And falling into endless night
Shall bathe the blood with sweet delight.
And as the light of day is done
The fearsome battle shall be won
For those who claim the heart of Fae
To mend and shape, no more to slay.
The shadows done, the feud descend.

No more to sunder. Done and end.
The shifter child, half and whole,
Tis she unites the factions old.
Tis she unites the factions old,
Tis she who rules.
All hail.
Her soul.

It said nothing of witches or powers or goddesses.

I wasn't going to waste her time or mine asking stupid questions like *why me*? Because sometimes it just was. Like what Faerie said about free will and the deeds of men. Sometimes things just sucked. You adjusted. You rolled with the punches. You did your best with the cards dealt and when things changed, you dealt with those as well.

The goddess took a step forward. The blinding heat of her scalded my skin but I wasn't burning. I was alive.

"You are strong enough to get through this. Trust me, lovely girl. Keep going. Keep being strong and when you get to the end, know it is only the beginning."

Then she touched my forehead and the world spun into darkness again.

33

The sharp rocks of the beach bit into my skin and dug what felt like permanent grooves along my spine.

I came awake with a fierce cough that wracked through me from top to bottom. The pain returned with it. I drowned on land. The sensations were strong; they were inescapable.

Turning on my side, just like in the ballroom, I sucked air into my poor body. Water sifted against the rocks beneath my feet and lapped at my legs. Okay, I was definitely back in my body.

The darkness behind my closed lids was matched by the impenetrable black when I finally pried them open. Pitch-black, oppressive and living. Sheer terror curled my fingers into claws.

I pushed onto my knees and pawed at the ground around me. The water between the rocks was frozen. My hand hit something furry and wet. I grabbed hold of the thick limb, feeling in one direction until I hit paws.

Unmoving.

Adrenaline lit me like an electric zap.

"Noren!" Panic overwhelmed me. I scrambled closer, scooting until my legs pressed against the long length of his back. "No, no, no. Oh god, please, no, don't be dead."

I felt for his face and the lines of his ears. One, the other. His snout. His eyes were closed.

Was he breathing? Did I feel air passing through his nostrils?

The full absence of light made it impossible to know and I was too petrified to find his pulse. There was only mine, racing faster than a rocket through the atmosphere, my lungs working overtime and my head spiraling.

"Please don't leave me. You can't be dead." I moved closer yet and pulled at him until his head and neck fell over my lap, the water freezing both of us together.

Was this the cost of Life?

If so, fuck that. I'd give my own if it meant Noren made it through. He'd only come because of his loyalty to me.

The direwolf woke with a snort, shifting underneath my hands. In the next beat, he lifted his face to mine and a warm, rough tongue dragged across my cheek.

Relief was immediate. I was shaking all over and for a second I thought I was going to throw up.

"Thank you." I wrapped my arms around his bulky neck and shivered. "Okay, so you're with me. That means the others have to be here, too." I dropped my head to his, letting the warmth of his fur sink into my skin. "Livvy? Onyx?"

After a slight delay, two voices rose from somewhere down the beach.

"Over here," Onyx called.

"Tavi? Is that you?"

He and Livvy sounded close to each other.

"Keep talking," I replied. "I'll come to you." I pushed away from Noren and crawled on my hands and knees toward the sound of their voices.

Noren gathered at my side in a comforting presence. The rocks underneath us were both sharp and smooth, small and large. I lost my balance more often than I could count until my head knocked against another body.

A familiar scent reached me first. "Livvy? Is that you?" I asked.

Her arms banded around my torso. "I'm here," she whispered. "I'm here with you. We found each other."

"Come on. We've got to get to Onyx."

"I'm close," he said. "But you have to come to me. I don't think I can move."

The darkness messed with my mind. The space felt both large and small at the same time. There were no strange echoes but the water continued to pulse along the shore without making a sound.

I swore I saw things in the blackness, blacker than everything around us. Finally my hand brushed against Onyx's legs and I used it to get my bearings until our shoulders touched.

The four of us were together.

"Is everyone all right?" I asked.

"I'm unhurt," Livvy answered right away. "A little sore and definitely had better days, but unhurt."

And I hadn't been able to feel anything wrong with Noren.

"Onyx? What about you?"

Another beat of silence, and then... "I can't feel my legs," he said quietly.

Panic hit me, mingled with despair. I couldn't help

crying out before I got control of myself. I fumbled for his hand. His fingers twitched against mine as I grabbed him.

"It's going to be okay."

I regretted the words as soon as I said them. I was in no position to offer up false promises. None whatsoever. Because it definitely didn't feel like things would be okay.

It felt like we were screwed. Royally, fully, however you wanted to call it. We were screwed and lost in the darkness and something had happened to damage Onyx's already fragile body.

"I hit the rocks hard when the boat capsized and I felt something crack in my back." Much to my everlasting shock, he laughed. "This is the first time since the injury that I feel no pain. It's actually kind of relaxing. A marked improvement from suffering through it."

Guilt lived inside of me especially when he continued to laugh.

"It's actually a relief. Chronic pain is no joke."

"You know what? Your dark humor isn't appreciated right now," I snapped.

"It's the only thing I have left, so at least give me this," he retorted.

"Sorry." I forced myself to scoff before the sound turned into a sob. "Not doing it."

I'm the one who hurt him in the first place. I'm the one who damaged his body, who dragged him along on this miserable adventure, who made him come to the Abyss and relive the night-mares of his past.

Whatever happened to his spine was my fault and my responsibility. My interaction with the goddess was all but forgotten at this point.

"Here. Grab onto Noren. He can take you on his back." I

fumbled in the darkness to orient myself with the direction of Onyx's body. "He's strong enough to handle your weight."

"Tavi—" Onyx began.

"I'm not going to leave you behind."

My voice caught somewhere in the back of my throat. How many more people were going to get hurt because of me? How many more friends were going to suffer?

"Livvy, can you help me move him? I'm not strong enough to lift him on my own. And Onyx, if you even think of telling us to leave you behind, I will strangle you."

"I wouldn't dream of it," Onyx said dryly.

Somehow between the two of us, we managed to get Onyx onto Noren's back and we inched along down the shore.

It was slow going. More often than not, I slipped on the rocks, holding onto Noren and Onyx with Livvy on their other side. Keeping in physical contact with each other helped.

"So this is the Abyss, huh?" I asked cheekily.

Onyx chuckled, his bitterness evident. "Is it everything you thought it would be? One of the best vacation spots ever because there's no one else around."

"It's nothing like I thought it would be," I admitted. "Where are all the others who were banished here?"

"What did you think I meant when I said *abyss*? They drift, in their own pockets of emptiness," Onyx explained.

"I'm not sure I actually had a thought. I didn't stop long enough to consider it."

"You know, I've always appreciated that about you," he replied.

"What?"

"How you keep going no matter what happens."

I felt a smile pull at my lips. "I thought the same thing about Livvy."

"I'm sure there were a lot of things you thought about me," Livvy joked.

Speaking to each other helped. Time passed, though, with no destination reached. There was only one foot in front of the other, our movements unseen. Did it even count if we didn't know where we were headed? If we couldn't see the shore beneath us?

I couldn't even see the back of my own hand in the darkness.

Maybe I didn't exist.

Maybe this was the death I thought I'd found when I woke up in the ballroom. My body wasn't here. Only my mind, utterly disconnected from anything physical. Maybe I was nothing but a consciousness floating in a sea of black with nothing around me in any direction.

Faerie told me I'd pay three prices to access the Abyss. Innocence. Self. Life.

Fear trickled in beside the intrusive thoughts and made itself a cozy home.

I did feel like I'd lost myself. I was nothing and no one. No name. No body. Eventually, not even a need to protect the people I cared about. *There is nothing here. And if there is nothing, then I'm nothing.*

"Keep talking." Livvy's voice sounded urgent. "It's too easy to get disoriented otherwise."

"It's too late for that," I said distantly.

I didn't sound like myself anymore. What was left of me when we boiled it down to the raw, base elements? Guilt and fear. Those two emotions were the only sensations remaining when everything else disappeared.

"There's nothing left." Onyx spoke my mind for me. "It's

the power of the Abyss. It shows you exactly what you are when you take everything away, and most people are not able to survive it."

"How did you?" I asked.

"You know, I can't remember," he said with another dark chuckle. "I was too focused on getting away from Kendrick." Even now, he refused to call that monster his father. "He saw it as a banishment. I saw it as an opportunity. He gave me the option of escape. Of survival."

He chuckled again, rather mirthlessly. "You do some pretty crazy things when you're in survival mode."

"You sound tired," Livvy told him.

"I am tired," Onyx admitted.

"Especially for one so young," she clarified.

"You're only as young as you feel. I've heard the expression many times over and I finally get it."

We'd been walking for hours at this point. Or days. But I never grew any more tired than how I felt in the current moment. My legs hurt, my feet were sore, and every part of me was soggy and heavy, but the sensations remained consistent. Soon even the fear took a back seat.

There was nothing left of me.

Onyx had survived this before, but I understood why he wanted to erase the experience from his memories.

Once, I'd wanted the bliss of emptiness and apathy. As though having those things would finally give me peace of mind.

But this was so much worse than anything else. Even the piercing pain of a battle wound was better than this *nothingness*.

Alone in the dark. No way forward and no way out.

The toe of my sneaker collided with one of the rocks and I went floundering forward, losing my grip on Noren and my balance at the same time. But my outstretched hands fell into nothingness. Not even the shore beneath me. There, and suddenly gone.

Screaming and digging in my heels, I somehow managed to jerk back in time. Livvy's overly loud shout came at the same moment.

"Watch out!"

I threw out a hand to stop Noren the second her warning aired. Luckily, Noren and Onyx were a step behind me.

"What's happening?" Onyx asked in panic.

"Hold on a second." I slowly folded myself down to my knees, searching the ground. It ended only inches from me. There and then gone. Nothing but empty air. I jerked back, stunned.

We'd reached a destination of sorts at last. Only it wasn't an actual place but more of a lack of ground. The shoreline ended and even the water failed to drip off the edge.

"What's there? What do you feel?" Livvy wanted to know. "Tavi?"

I have a name.

"Nothing."

I shoved some of the loose stones off the edge and waited for them to hit. They never did. No sound came.

"It's a drop-off," I told the others. "We've reached the end."

What would happen if we headed into the water? Was there a drop there, too? Or what about further inland?

Something told me we would find the same thing no matter where we went.

Life, I realized. This was where Life came in. This was exactly the end of the line where a decision had to be made and a choice executed.

What good did Livvy's journal do if I wasn't around to be

the bearer of the prophecy? It made no sense to me. I couldn't give up my life *and* unite Faerie. I had to be alive in order to do those things.

Ghosts didn't exist for shifters.

Our souls were either reborn into new existence or disappeared back into the fabric of the universe.

I bit down on my tongue but a sob escaped anyway. The ragged muscles in my throat constricted and my eyes flooded. This was my choice to make but there really wasn't one. I was going over the edge. It was that simple.

Onyx spoke up. "It's the sacrifice."

"What?" Livvy sounded sharp.

"The Abyss requires a sacrifice in order to allow us to take the notebook, which has become a piece of the time and space here. I know it innately, because of the place where the Abyss still exists in me."

"Stop it." My words were hardly more than a whisper. I didn't want to hear any more.

"One of us has to die," he finished.

"Me." It was automatic. "It's me."

Onyx laughed, the sound too loud for my raw nerves. "Not necessarily."

Absolutely not. Life may not necessarily mean mine—it meant me giving up someone I loved as well. But I couldn't imagine giving up the mother I'd thought I'd lost just as I got her back.

And Onyx was one of my best friends. We'd been through so much together and literally escaped an executioner's noose. To willingly sacrifice either of them was unthinkable, which meant it had to be me.

"I'm ready to give up and go back home," I said. "We'll find another way."

"No," Livvy replied adamantly. "We're here. I'm getting

you those journals, Tavi. Let me do this for you. Once you have the spell, you'll have everything you need to get you through. Your friends are there to care for you. You're used to living without me anyway."

She didn't sound bitter. Only resigned. Stating facts.

I felt her move, felt her body lurch into motion. Noren and I shifted at the same time to block her. The direwolf threw his body in front of her, then came the sound of someone dropping to the stones. The air exploded out of my lungs.

Livvy let out a yelp of pain. She must have rebounded off of Noren. "You stupid wolf," she spat.

He wasn't going to let her go, that much was clear. And the feeling was mutual.

"What were you thinking?" I yelled. "You were just going to jump?"

My heart lurched into the back of my throat and choked me.

"Of course I was," she snapped back. "I'm not going to let you kill yourself. You're too important to lose. I've already done my part, Tavi. If I can help you get out of here with those journals, then I'll do it."

Onyx had landed beside me when Noren moved, slipping right off the direwolf's back.

"Tavi?" He grabbed at whatever part of me was closer, my knee in this case, and I fumbled for him. "Is that you?"

"Onyx. Let me help you up. Come on. I can take your weight."

His fingers brushed against my thigh, my arm, and finally my shoulders. Then there was fire, my blood going fireworks-bright when he pressed his lips to mine.

What are you doing?

An electric jolt cascaded through my system from the point of contact, his lips soft and the energy startling. *Pack.*

I thought I said the word out loud but the kiss continued, lingering and sweet. His mouth moved against mine but there was no hint of desperation, and rather than shrug him off, I sank into the sensation.

"I love you," Onyx whispered against my lips. Into my heart and my soul. "I believe with every part of me that *you* are the answer to the wrong in our world. It's always been you. I finally understand it."

"What's happening?"

Livvy's voice, but she was far away. Livvy and Noren and the Abyss all far away. There was only me and Onyx in this sea of pure ebony night and his lips became a lifeline through it, keeping me tethered in my body when my mind wanted to fracture apart.

I clutched at him but neither of us were steady. We both shook, rattling the bones of the world.

"You love me?" I whispered back.

"I'm injured beyond repair," he continued. He huffed out a laugh, kissed me again as though he wanted to get in as many touches as possible before I drew a line. "I'm so tired of living in constant pain. I'm at the end. There's no going back for me."

The panic returned and rushed through me as if I'd been dipped in acid.

My fingers looped through the fabric of his shirt.

"I believe in the old legends of reincarnation for those with shifter blood." A hint of mischief echoed in his tone. "Something greater is waiting for me. Who knows? Maybe I'll come back to you someday. I'll try to let you know it's me."

My heart was going ninety-to-nothing. "Stop it." A frozen

numbness swept over me and I tried to swallow but my throat wasn't working. The only warmth left in me came from Onyx and his surprise kisses.

"I'm not going to stop," he insisted. "You risked everything to save me. And I'm still a dead man back home. I can never go back. I've got no future."

"There's always hope. We'll find a way. We'll heal you. I'm not going to let you do this."

He loved me. I couldn't let him go.

HIs lips brushed mine again. He was steady and warm and determined. He was tender and caring and—crying.

Onyx was crying.

"Let me do this for you." He begged me. "I'll see you again. I promise." He pushed me back, with such strength I let go.

Why did I let go?

I said his name. I reached for him and found only open air.

Onyx rolled away from me and even without the use of his legs, he threw himself off the side of the abyss, with only the scrape of stone to mark his sacrifice.

34

I couldn't stop screaming.

Life. Onyx paid the price.

The screams tore out of me, echoing in the nothingness and reverberating back until every cell of my body filled with horror and fear. I scrambled into motion, and only Livvy throwing her arms around me stopped me from following Onyx off the side.

I went with him, though, in spirit. I went with him into the abyss and I stared at the empty blackness until my eyes burned and every inhalation scorched my raw lungs.

Mom held me as my tears finally broke free and trailed fire along my cheeks.

What had he done?

Why? Why, why, *why*?

He's gone.

We'd gotten out of things before this. We'd done the impossible too many times to count, we'd survived, and now he just—he...

We stayed together, with sobs wracking my body for a

long time. Livvy said nothing, only held me in her arms with her breath tickling my hair as I shook.

Noren drifted to my other side, nudging, whimpering. The tip of his tongue flicked at my tears but the absurdity of the sweetness coming from such a monstrous creature wasn't enough to get me to stop.

Onyx was dead, and it was my fault.

He'd sacrificed himself for me, just like that. Gone.

He loved me and he'd decided to jump anyway. What if reincarnation wasn't real? What if he'd sacrificed himself for nothing? What if the Abyss was this horrible, fucked-up place and we were never getting out?

I felt half a second away from exploding. Livvy, for her part, did not budge, and kept me sandwiched between her and Noren...

It was almost enough to get me back into my body instead of the black hole inside my head where nothing made sense. Nothing about the world, about what happened, about me. None of it made any sense, and the harder I tried to get it together, the more I lost it all.

"It's going to be okay, Tavi. It's all going to be okay." Livvy's murmurings were soothing but I did not believe her. "Don't worry. It's all going to be okay. Shh, sweet girl. You feel your feelings. I know."

She refused to move, holding me and whispering those empty words.

Too long passed before I reached a point where the tears ended. My body stopped producing them, as though I'd used up every ounce of available moisture. I licked my lips and peeled back, missing her warmth already.

I blinked, my eyelids swollen and heavy. "Why is there light?"

Livvy shifted to give me an unimpeded view. Right in

front of us, the abyss had disappeared, replaced by a stretch of smooth rock. There was no more darkness, no more beach, no more icy water or cliffside.

After so long in the darkness, I ached in the presence of the light.

Slowly, the fractured pieces of me returned, the loss of Self, but none of them fit together quite the same way anymore. And a large piece, a piece with white hair, remained missing.

A rectangular journal, benign and leather-bound, rested against the gray surface of the rock.

Mom must have been sitting there looking at it this whole time. The spell we'd come for was right there, but she'd been here holding me instead. She'd chosen to hold her crying daughter rather than grabbing the journal.

She'd stayed with me.

My heart turned over in my chest. A healing moment, I realized, being held for the first time I ever remembered by the mother I thought I'd lost forever. My lower lip wobbled. Thankfully, the tears were done, every part of me spent.

"The Abyss has returned what it was given," Livvy murmured. "The cost is fulfilled."

"Is it safe to touch?" I asked, gesturing toward the journal.

"I believe so, yes." Livvy pushed to her feet and reached back for me, holding out a hand to help me up.

Somehow, between Livvy and Noren, I managed to struggle into a standing position. My muscles bunched and had frozen in place after too long curled up into myself.

I stretched them out now with a hiss of pain.

"Let me help." She stepped in front and reached for the journal reverently.

The old book lay dormant in her palms, yet when I

reached out to graze my finger along the spine, the leather warmed to the touch.

Without another word, we turned around, finding an opening in the stone and thin tendrils of gray light reaching toward us. Dust motes danced in the rays.

We moved toward the light.

Noren padded along silently beside me. Halfway leaning against my hip. Nothing and no one stood in our way. There were no more hidden traps waiting to spring and no more surprises looming around the corners, no more boat or solid walls.

Our exit from the Abyss was not the same as our entrance.

It seemed Onyx was right. Once you reached the Abyss, it lived inside of you. I knew exactly where every trap lay on our way back out, as if the tunnels were etched on a map in my head, and navigating them felt effortless. As natural as breathing.

The light was magic, not sunlight, yet the tunnels were open and friendly. No hint of the dark river.

Sorrow sucked me under in a beat. This experience connected me to Onyx in a way I'd never expected. I almost felt him in some cavernous, moonless place where the Abyss also lived inside of me, like he'd become a permanent part of this place.

And therefore a permanent part of me.

No matter where I went after this or what I did, no matter who I met or the things I'd see, I'd feel them both in my psyche. In my blood and my cells and my soul for the rest of my life.

A sob erupted unbidden and my throat constricted around it.

We finally emerged into sunlight, each golden strand

illuminating the tall, thin tree trunks of the woods around the ruined temple. Even the wildlife had fallen silent.

There was no one here. I didn't expect them.

Onyx said time worked differently in the Abyss.

Laina was more than likely getting the help she needed for her injuries, and Mike and Bronwen would be with her.

No one was coming for us.

A hand fell on my shoulder and I turned to see Livvy staring at me.

"The journey to the Abyss is not for the faint of heart," she told me softly, reverently. "Take comfort in how far you've come."

"How can I feel anything when my friend is dead?" I half whispered.

She seemed to consider her next words. "We all make our choices. Some of them are more painful than others, and some of them require a heftier cost."

I wondered if she spoke about what I'd just gone through or her own journey, and if there was any difference between the two. We'd both had to pay a price for our actions. She'd left me. I'd lost Onyx.

Noren bounded off between the trees with a flash of silver, and within a heartbeat I'd lost sight of him. Even so, Livvy and I stood there a moment longer. Staring, watching. Feeling the weight of the air in this sacred, awful place.

Were her thoughts as deep as mine?

Would we ever voice them out loud or were they too personal for us to admit even to the other?

Eventually her hand fell from my shoulder and Mom walked ahead, leaving me no choice but to follow her. I trailed her along a path that wasn't a path, past the ring of stones toward an opening in the trees beyond.

Here, stones decorated with moss rested on either side

of the trail and soon the trees thinned enough to offer a glimpse of intensely blue water in the distance.

Not the farmland I expected to see, but a slight slope in the land rolling down to a massive lake with clear water.

We reached the shore in the next five minutes and I hung back. No way I was going back into water anytime soon. Even the beach brought back too many ghastly sensations for me to get close.

"I hope you don't mind." I turned my back to the water. "It's too soon."

She squinted against the sunlight. "You don't need to explain yourself to me. Not with this. We'll stay here tonight and wait for your friends to return."

I barely heard her talking about resting here while she searched for the ingredients she needed for the spell. Barely saw her disappear back into the forest. One foot in front of the other took me to a spot where the land leveled out and I sat, the grass prickling against my backside.

Even anticipation and excitement for the spell did nothing to clear my head. Trekking out here might have gotten us the journal but I'd lost someone I cared about, someone who loved me.

Was the price really worth it?

I wished Onyx was here. Wished someone would come along and bespell me so that I wouldn't feel a damn thing, or maybe even rip my heart out of my chest.

I wished there was a spell to smother the horrible voice hissing inside my head that Onyx died for me and I did not deserve it.

I failed him despite the victory of navigating the Abyss. And no matter how I tried to quell that part of me, it never quieted.

How did I fix something like this? How did I make it right again?

How did I stop *feeling*?

The clear water of the lake spread out like a sparkling mirror. Tall pines and deciduous trees rose around the rocky shore. My eyes blurred again, stinging, and I curled in a fetal position.

Nothing was going to be the same again.

Livvy returned softly. "Tavi?"

I sprang up, my head visible above the grass. She caught sight of me and came forward.

"Here," she began. "I gathered some of the things we need. Lemonberry, wild rosemary. These small white blooms are greater toadblossom. Then uvelas, night milk-balm. The journal says we need water untouched by human hands, a small flat stone, and you see those reeds over there?" She pointed in the distance. "It is amazing for us to find every ingredient we need to work the spell."

Amazing? No. It wasn't amazing, and it wasn't luck.

She opened her palms and the herbs dropped down to the small spot of crushed grass.

My chest clenched. "Are you sure this is going to work?" I asked in a hoarse voice. "Are you sure this will unlock my powers?"

She bobbed her head. "This is the spell we need. The ingredients will ensure its potency." She cleared her throat. "I read through the journal while I foraged. It's all there. Everything we need."

I should say something to her. I wanted to crush the excitement lighting her eyes and say something foul to squash her smile before it grew.

What if I didn't *want* it to work? What if I wanted to stay exactly the same as I was now, because the person I was now felt normal. The opposite of special, even though I'd never been that way so I had no real comparison.

But it seemed I didn't have a choice and there would be no stopping Livvy. She was determined to see this through and fulfill whatever prophecy Faerie told her.

The lake provided the perfect backdrop for what we planned to do.

I sat and watched her work, setting up the area to work the spell with reverence in every move. Day shifted slowly to night.

Magic, midnight, an epic quest. A reluctant heroine who would rather just spend time with the mother she'd thought had died. None of those things were going to happen now. They'd never been in the cards for me.

Why was it so hard to accept, then?

From somewhere in the distance, a lone howl cut through the taut silence of evening. Noren was close. I let out a breath and finally lifted my chin to face Livvy fully.

She stared at me, eyes the same color as mine boring holes through my skull. "Are you ready?" she asked.

I dipped my head once in a silent acknowledgement.

No going back. I'd come this far, hadn't I?

The magic was always mine, if I chose to believe her. Sealed down in the depths of me and so far I'd never known it existed.

The ruins behind us, the unseen entrance to the Abyss, were an ageless witness to the moment.

"Then sit across from me and get comfortable. I'll say the words." She lifted the journal up, squinting in the moonlight to check the words.

Cross-legged, we faced each other and she left the journal open on her lap.

I sucked in a breath to tell her to wait just as the first syllable of the spell left her mouth.

A sharp, awful breeze split the space between us and settled in my bones. I didn't recognize the words. They were foreign, strange, garbled yet clear at the same time.

Goosebumps lifted the hair on my arms, my legs, my neck. My teeth clenched to keep from chattering, and Livvy kept reading, intoning words of power, precious and sacred, drawn from the land itself. I felt them inside of me and they mingled with the chill and set my veins alight like little fizzes.

I squeezed my eyes shut and braced for the strike I knew was coming. The strike that would split me open and carve out my insides to make room for everything she thought I had in me.

Livvy reached the end of the spell and the last word dropped, detonated in the night like a bomb.

Still I waited. Ready. Unwilling.

Then pried my eyes open when nothing happened.

She stared at me again and this time the fingers holding open her journal were white, her knuckles tense, hands shaking.

Nothing had happened. The spell didn't work. We failed.

35

Invisible chains wrapped around me as she tried again. The same jolt of power was whispered on the wind, a promise all but forgotten, but again nothing happened.

Livvy scrambled to check the herbs and make sure she'd gotten the right items. When she turned back to me, her shoulders slumped forward.

Face to face with her failure, we were both just as lost, and neither of us had the energy to argue. To figure out what had gone wrong.

Livvy sniffed, blew out a harsh breath, then rose with her hands on her hips. "I'm, ah, going to make a fire. A fire will help."

She went through the motions of gathering stones and wood even though none of it was necessary. I sat and watched her. *I should help.*

Why couldn't I move?

Noren returned moments after Livvy snapped her fingers and the flames burst to life.

He approached the fire and dropped his prey at my feet, staring at me with his head tilted to the side.

"You're so resourceful," I said to him in an undertone. I smiled. "Thank you for this. I appreciate it."

He'd caught enough food for us to cook over a makeshift spit, the flames crackling merrily beneath the roasting rabbit. Soon the air filled with the scent and moonlight glinted off the still surface of the lake.

Noren sat on his haunches beside me and leaned until I automatically ran my hand through the fur at the scuff of his neck.

"Someone will return for us soon." Livvy paced on the other side of the fire with her focus a million miles away. Her hand remained at her mouth, her teeth worrying at the skin of her thumb's cuticle. "Until then, the best course of action is to stay here and wait. Then everyone will be back together."

I understood her reasoning even when my instincts screamed at me to go, to run, to keep moving ahead of the people who hunted us. Mike would not be able to track us if we left the lake and the ruins of the Abyss.

Bronwen would, but why make more trouble for her?

After a while, it hurt too much to watch Livvy pace, to wonder at the way her mind worked.

Neither of us had any idea why the spell failed. She knew of no way to contact Faerie to find out. At this point, we'd reached a dead end.

Another one in a long line of them.

I poked at the rabbit with a stick to judge doneness. It needed another little bit of time before being completely cooked but I wasn't willing to wait. My stomach growled and I busied myself with removing the steaming rabbit from the spit.

"Your pacing isn't going to help," I told her. "Why don't you come sit and we'll have something to eat." The heat burned my fingers and quickly dissipated.

"There's nothing else to do besides sleep," she groused.

A sense of the surreal permeated the moment when she settled herself cross-legged and accepted a bit of meat. It almost seemed as though I'd become the more responsible person here. Her nerves refused to settle.

I had them too. I'd have to be out of my damn mind not to be nervous right now but I had to channel them into something else besides movement. Or maybe my body was still reeling from everything that had happened over the last few days. Maybe it would take me the rest of my life to feel like my old self again.

I'd feel much better if Onyx were here.

At least then I'd have someone familiar, a peer, to speak to. Having my mom back was a miracle but I found it more difficult than I'd ever imagined to talk to her.

"This is good." Livvy gestured toward the rabbit. "Your wolf is an asset to you, Tavi. I hope you understand how lucky you are to have him."

"He is," I agreed. "And I literally did nothing to the rabbit except coo it. I can't take any credit."

"You sell yourself short."

I scoffed lightly. "What else is new? Fighting against a tide tends to make you think of yourself as small but compact." I tried to grin at her and found my lips failing me. I took a bite of rabbit and chewed thoughtfully, letting the heat seep into me. Warmth trailed down my throat and into my stomach, settling there.

"I don't like to hear you talk about yourself this way. You've had some incredible experiences, yes, but they have all made you strong," she said, licking the grease off her fingers.

"What if I'm tired of being strong?" I finally asked. "What if there are stronger people out there? Better choices."

"There will always be stronger people out there. Who is on your mind right now?"

She knew. She had to know. "I...just feel like it might be a better situation if Onyx were with me."

"Well, we have some time." Livvy rose and wiped her hands on the front of her pants. "Why don't we scry for him? The lake is placid and the night fresh and full of possibilities. It will give you peace of mind to know he's crossed over. Wouldn't it?"

I arched a brow at her. "I thought you were all about going to sleep."

"We need to pass the time somehow, do we not? It seems the best use of time before we sleep is helping my daughter."

"It's fine, you don't have to." My mind immediately shifted toward the question I'd been pointedly avoiding for much too long.

Who had been controlling Onyx and forcing him to attack those fae? He hadn't known.

"Come on." Livvy gestured for me to follow her. "It will help put you at ease. It's something I can do. I told you I would teach you everything I know."

"You think...you think we can figure out who was controlling him? He's gone."

Her lips set in a thin line. "I think it's worth a try. And besides, it will be a good test to see if my magic is failing. My spell failed. I want to see if this will fail."

I shivered, the drop in temperature having nothing to do

with the beautiful evening and everything to do with my own reservations.

There was no one around to see us work this magic. No one except the night creatures. And once Livvy settled us near the water, once her own magic rose and crackled in the open air, even the crickets fell silent. Bats swung around us in a circle of clear air overhead.

She closed her eyes and when she spoke again, her voice had dropped. "Sit across from me again, Tavi, and open up your energy to me. I'll need to use your connection to your friend to be able to access him. We should see where his spirit has traveled. If he is free, he'll have his answers. And so will we."

I wasn't sure how I felt about this.

We had to do something. *I* had to do something. I couldn't sit and hate myself much longer.

But rather than voicing my reservations, I settled across from her, in awe when a perfectly still pool of water lifted off of the lake itself.

The pool shivered in the air before it shifted between Livvy and I, straightening out into a hammered sheet of pure darkness.

She lifted her hand to me again, inches below the floating water, and I placed my palm in hers. Magic passed between us and my own power lifted and reached for her.

I forced myself to still and focus on Onyx. On the training sessions where he'd taught me more about my shapeshifting. The way he'd looked in the hospital, how he'd stared at me from the executioner's block, everything that happened thereafter.

"Look."

Livvy whispered the word and I peeled open an eye to see the surface of the water rippling.

"Concentrate on the answers you seek. Tune in to his energy. His earthly body may be gone but pack bonds do not disappear with death. I'll be able to scry the rest, and the face of the person in control should become clear."

It was up to me now.

And impossible for me to focus entirely on the things I wanted to know, not when there were a thousand other questions. Why not look to see a way to defeat Dorian Jade? Why not look for a way to reunite the two courts?

Onyx.

The son of my fated mate, who was more than a friend and mentor. A lover who would never be. A solid connection, and someone I cared about. Gone, too far for me to reach, but he needed me to get to the bottom of this.

The surface of the water shifted again and slowly a face filled the confines of the pool. I stifled a gasp as the features became clearer.

"You're sure?" The words burst out of me and dread crawled under my skin. "You're sure this is the person?"

"Who do you see?" Livvy asked.

Black hair, cut in a sharp shag. Pointed ears, dusky skin, a snake's smile.

I saw Selene in the reflection.

Her eyes seemed to penetrate through me.

And I wanted to rip her from navel to neck with my claws and watch her bleed. For the pain she'd caused Onyx while he was alive, the pain he'd live with for the rest of his life, for the shit that happened in her wake.

"How?" The word erupted out of me before I was aware of even asking the question.

"So you know the person you see in the reflection," Livvy said out loud. "Her face is unfamiliar to me. Tavi, who is that?"

My hands had curved into fists and I realized my claws were literally out at the pinprick of pain. When I uncurled my fingers, a half-moon of bloody indentations greeted me.

"She's a friend. Or she *was* a friend," I corrected. "I thought she was there to help me and guide me. Instead she's a monster."

"Sometimes the people who mean the greatest harm to us are often right in front of our face." Livvy stared at me and watched for any changes in me. I was aware of her perusal but felt so little outside of the cold desire for revenge.

I'd pay Selene back for every single misfortune. I made the vow then and there, silently, and added it to my promise of ending Kendrick Grimaldi.

"Thank you." I forced myself to break away from staring at the reflection and meet Livvy's eyes. "For doing that."

She waved her hand and the water dropped back down to the lake, absorbed once again. "Are you okay?"

What could I possibly say? Betrayal cut deep, to the point where my chest tightened as though someone strapped me down with metal bands. Selene had done terrible things...and I needed to figure out why, to what purpose.

I had to get close to her, no matter what happened.

Sleep came eventually but when it did, it refused to stay for long. I tossed and turned on the rocky lakeshore, fitful and uncomfortable.

Bronwen finally returned to us with the daylight. The crow touched down on the boulder next to the dying embers of our fire and I watched through bleary eyes as the bird shifted into my friend's familiar shape. She hunched over, her legs dangling off one side of the rock and her elbows on her knees, her head falling anchor-heavy.

She looked exhausted. More so than I'd ever seen her. Bronwen always appeared perpetually perky, so to see her like this...it was a lot.

She glanced up and her eyes widened. "Tavi. Oh my god. You're back."

I stretched my arms overhead. "Why do you sound surprised to see me?"

"You were gone for seven days."

My jaw fell open. "What do you mean, seven days? It was only hours!"

"I've been checking back for three days and this is the first time you've actually been here," she said, shaking her head. "A couple times a day, actually. I'm ready to drop. It takes a lot out of me to travel."

"Do you want to come sit down here?" I patted the spot beside me. "Might be a little softer than your boulder."

She managed to get herself to my side before she went down. I wrapped my arm automatically around her shoulder, astonished to feel her shaking.

"Queen Laina is still in the hospital," she began, her tone dulled by exhaustion. "Mike is with her. He would have been here to see you otherwise."

"Thank you for the update." My stomach churned. Every part of my body hurt and it seemed like no matter how I moved, nothing helped the aches. Bronwen leaned heavily against me with her head lolling on her neck.

"There's more."

"Tell me," I demanded.

"There's a Faerie-wide manhunt in place," she hissed out.

"Sounds like a normal day, doesn't it?" I tried to smile but my face refused to move. Tendrils of ice constricted my heart at her words. Had Dorian Jade done something? Or the premier?

"It's not what you think, Tavi." Bronwen struggled to push up to see my expression and the ice squeezed, freezing my insides, making my chest tighter yet until I felt like I couldn't breathe.

Nothing was what I thought. Not one single thing.

"Someone in the human realm has infiltrated the Fae Academy for Halflings. He's taken the students captive and that's why…" She trailed off and tears turned her eyes glassy. "I'm so sorry."

"Spit it out, Bronwen." Every word turned to dust on my tongue.

"He's demanding that you be turned over to him if we want any of the students returned to their families alive."

My heart skipped a beat. I knew it could only mean one person, but I needed her to say it.

"Who? Who's doing this?"

Bronwen took a deep breath. "Someone named Kendrick Grimaldi."

THE END

Continue the adventure with Tavi and the others in book 7, *Faerie Fate*.

ABOUT THE AUTHOR

BREA VIRAGH is a USA Today bestselling indie romance author based in a sleepy mountain town with only one stoplight. She loves all things magical and witchy, will never turn down sushi, and spends too many nights reading. When she isn't writing and daydreaming about her newest project, her hobbies include an unhealthy fascination with Rook coffee, hiking and making sure her dog is well exercised (to give her more uninterrupted writing time later), and watching as many scary movies as she can.

Read more at BREA VIRAGH'S <u>WEBSITE</u>.

Please join her FACEBOOK READER GROUP or sign up for exclusive Newsletter content <u>HERE</u>.

ALSO BY BREA VIRAGH

Eternal Chaos

Born of Chaos

The Cavaldi Birthright

Fate Walks

Morning's Light

In the Dark

Twilight Sun

Small-Town Contemporary Romance

Sugar and Gold

Your Hand in Mine

Last Christmas Angel

Stand Alones

Curse of a Feather (A Dark Swan Princess Retelling)

Wake the Dream

Rose and Bane

Shifter by Christmas

Beneath my Skin

Midnight Skies

Myths of the Fae World

As Veronica Shade

Shadow Witch

www.ingramcontent.com/pod-product-compliance
Ingram Content Group UK Ltd.
Pitfield, Milton Keynes, MK11 3LW, UK
UKHW021415160425